5/15

PRINTED IN U.S.A.

W9-AQJ-359

A BARRICADE IN HELL

Also by Jaime Lee Moyer

Delia's Shadow

A BARRICADE IN HELL

Jaime Lee Moyer

TOR®

A Tom Doherty Associates Book
New York

A BARRICADE IN HELL

Grateful acknowledgment is made for permission to reprint excerpts from "Spring Offensive" and "Anthem for Doomed Youth" from *Wilfred Owen: The War Poems,* edited by Jon Stallworthy (London: Chatto & Windus, 1994).

A Tor Book
Published by Tom Doherty Associates, LLC
175 Fifth Avenue
New York, NY 10010

www.tor-forge.com

Tor® is a registered trademark of Tom Doherty Associates, LLC.

The Library of Congress Cataloging-in-Publication Data is available upon request.

ISBN 978-0-7653-3183-0 (hardcover)
ISBN 978-1-4299-4818-0 (e-book)

Tor books may be purchased for educational, business, or promotional use. For information on bulk purchases, please contact Macmillan Corporate and Premium Sales Department at 1-800-221-7945, extension 5442, or write specialmarkets@macmillan.com.

First Edition: June 2014

Printed in the United States of America

0 9 8 7 6 5 4 3 2 1

For Stephanie. I miss you every single day.

ACKNOWLEDGMENTS

There are always people to thank when you finish a book. The trick is not to leave anyone out.

First and foremost, the partner in life and crime, Marshall Payne, for putting up with me being locked away for hours in order to write these books. Thanks have to go to my friends through thick and thin, Jodi Meadows, Rae Carson, Elizabeth Bear, Kat Allen, Amanda Downum, and Charlie Finlay for cheering me on and always being there when I need them, and thanks as well to Jamie Rosen and Celia Marsh for always being ready to suggest character names. I can't forget P. J. Thompson or Marcy Rockwell either, both for being the best beta readers ever and for being my biggest cheerleaders. I need to give huge thanks to Kevin Lovelace for helping me with tarot readings, and Marie Brennan for introducing me to Kevin. Thanks as well to Dr. Jon Stallworthy, trustee of the Wilfred Owen estate, for giving me permission to use pieces of Wilfred Owen's poetry at the beginning and end of this book. I'm immensely grateful for that. Last but not least, my agent, Tamar Rydzinski, for always having my back, and my editor, Claire Eddy, for making me a better writer.

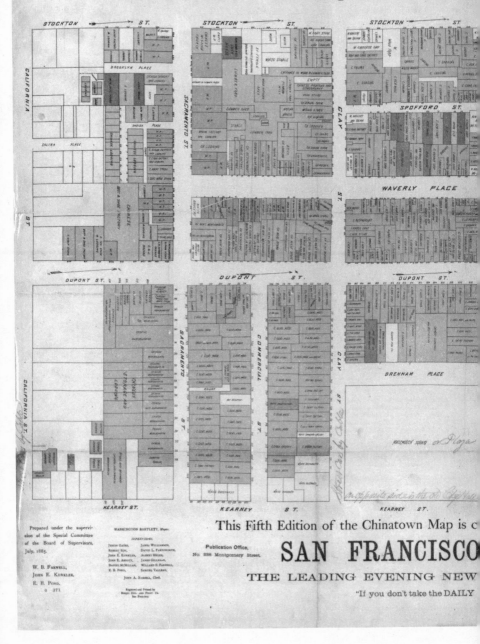

Official Map of "Chinatown"

Prepared under the supervision of the Special Committee of the Board of Supervisors, July, 1885.

W. B. FARWELL,
JOHN E. KUNKLER.
E. B. POND.

WASHINGTON BARTLETT, *Mayor.*

SUPERVISORS:
JESTIN GATES,   JAMES WILLIAMSON,
ROBERT ROY,   DAVID L. FARNSWORTH,
JOHN E. KUNKLER,   ALBERT MILLER,
JOHN E. ABBOTT,   JAMES GILLERAN,
DANIEL McMILLAN,   WILLARD B. FARWELL,
E. B. POND,   SAMUEL VALLEAU,
       JOHN A. RUSSELL, *Clerk.*

Publication Office,
No. 398 Montgomery Street.

This Fifth Edition of the Chinatown Map is c

SAN FRANCISCO

THE LEADING EVENING NEW

"If you don't take the DAILY

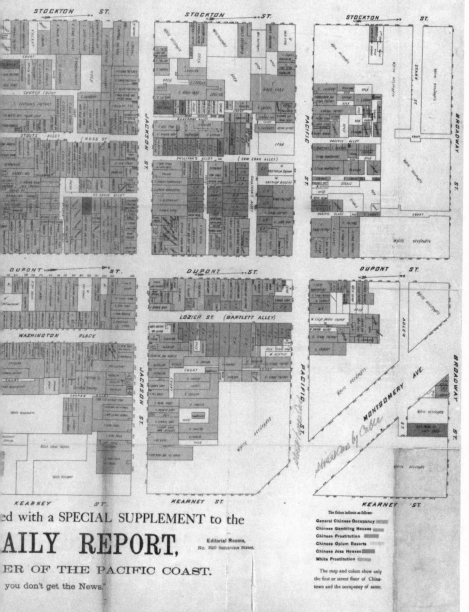

n San Francisco.

Of them who running on that last high place
Breasted the surf of bullets, or went up
On the hot blast and fury of hell's upsurge,
Or plunged and fell away past this world's verge,
Some say God caught them even before they fell.
                      —Wilfred Owen, "Spring Offensive"

CHAPTER 1

Delia

Moonlight filled our bedroom with windblown tree shadows and uncertain light that gathered in pools on the carpet. Gabe still slept peacefully next to me, one hand splayed on his chest and unaware anything was amiss.

I envied him that. Nocturnal visitors seldom summoned my husband from dreams.

A ghost, a tiny girl of no more than four or five, stood in one puddle of light. She clutched a well-loved china doll against her chest, the doll's cotton lawn dress in tatters and painted face near worn away. Her lace-trimmed pinafore was too short to cover her knees, and mud-splattered stockings trailed from a pocket. She was firmly anchored in this world, appearing near as solid as she had in life. Auburn ringlets brushed the small ghost's shoulders, held back from her face by a cornflower blue satin ribbon. Eyes just as blue regarded me solemnly.

I didn't think she was my child. Our daughter had been born too soon, cold and ashen, the cord wrapped tightly around her neck, but I'd often dreamed about her growing older. This little girl looked much as I'd imagined my daughter, healthy and strong, with hair the same color as Gabe's.

Yet I didn't want to believe the child I'd carried under my heart, felt quicken and move inside, might return to haunt me. Uncertainty kept me from sending the ghost away. I needed to be sure.

The sound of weeping filled the room and gave me an answer. She wasn't mine. Someone else had loved this child, mourned her and wept as I'd wept for our daughter.

The moon set, taking away the light, the sounds of grief, and the small ghost. Gabe muttered in his sleep, tossing restlessly. I touched his arm. "Shhh . . . Go back to sleep. Everything's all right."

He settled again and I stared at the dark ceiling, wishing I could comfort myself as easily. More than three years had passed since the morning I first woke to find myself haunted by a strong ghost I named Shadow. I'd seen haunts and phantoms since I was a child, but this ghost opened wide a door into the spirit realm that never closed again. Shadow sent me down a dark path searching for answers. Once I'd started, there was no turning back.

I'd learned too much since then and laid far too many wandering spirits to rest to feel at ease now. Some ghosts were unable to find their way to the other side or had things from life left undone, ties to the living they couldn't sever or wrongs they sought to set right. Others needed help realizing they were dead. Not all of them left willingly.

Our house had been cleansed of lingering spirits before Gabe and I moved in. Now ghosts only came to me for a reason. Awakening painful memories was a cruel purpose, but ghosts were often cruel. If reopening partly healed wounds was the sole reason this lost little girl chose to haunt me, I'd send the ghost on her way with no regrets.

The sound of weeping filled the room again, causing me to wonder if there was more to her visit. A little girl, maybe the tiny ghost I'd seen, sobbed and called out for her mama. Her voice faded and others took its place, men and women, youthful voices and those heavy with years. I couldn't understand all they said, but each voice carried a share of its own misery and terror. Each called on someone to find them.

My newest ghost shimmered into view again; blue eyes bright even in the absence of moonlight, bringing silence and the disquieting knowledge that she wanted more than just to torment me. I whispered, knowing she'd hear. "Tell me what you want, spirit, or leave my house. I can't help you unless I know."

She stared, silent and unreadable, before thinning into a silvery mist that swirled toward the ceiling and vanished. Strong ghosts didn't just disappear never to return. So I listened, waiting to hear the voices crying out again or for her to give me some other sign of why she'd come. None came, but that brought little consolation.

A foghorn on the bay sounded, each note lingering, and our bedroom filled with cold shadows. I turned toward Gabe, breathing in his familiar shaving soap smell and drawn to his warmth.

Gabe kept me from wandering too deep into the world of spirits, lost in someone else's past and unable to find my way back. He was my anchor to the living.

Even so, I lay awake a long time. And when I finally fell asleep, it was to dream of a barefoot little girl wading in a sun-warmed stream, minnows nibbling at her muddy toes.

I'd hoped to wake to a sunny day, not overcast skies that promised rain and chill winds. Winter stripped the sunbeams of warmth, but sunshine might help banish the restlessness I couldn't shake. Strange spirits were common enough in my life, but this little girl's ghost unsettled me. Not understanding why bothered me even more, distracting me from Isadora's lessons on poltergeists. I'd spent far too much of Dora's visit staring out the kitchen window, watching wind herd clouds toward the East Bay hills and brooding.

Madam Isadora Bobet was my teacher, my mentor, and my guide through the confusing world of ghosts and spirits. She was also a friend. Two years before, I hadn't wanted to believe in spirits that haunted the living. I'd seen strange things since I was a child, but I'd always thought stories of ghostly hauntings a clever charlatan's device to bilk money from the gullible. Finding myself haunted gave me no choice but to believe.

Now I swam in ghosts. Without Dora, I'd drown.

"Do you need me to go over the different types of poltergeists again, Delia?" I jumped, jarring the table and sloshing cream from the pitcher, ashamed at being so deep in thought, I'd lost track of the conversation. Dora stirred more sugar into her tea and frowned. "I know this is a lot to take in all at once, but they can be dangerous. Cleansing Mrs. Allen's boardinghouse could prove difficult. It's best if you know what we might face."

"No need to repeat the list. Not now." I flushed, certain her sharp look meant my guilt was plain. Dora was seldom fooled. Still, I felt honor bound to try. "What else do I need to know?"

I made a valiant attempt to focus on Dora's explanation and stop brooding. My efforts met with limited success. I found myself watching our next-door neighbor instead.

Mr. Flynn sat on his back porch, slowly rocking back and forth in a redwood glider. He was dressed in his best dark suit, a starched white shirt and black bow tie, and with his heavy coat lying across his knees. Each time the glider stopped swinging, he nudged it into motion again. He stared out into the yard, still and quiet and much too pale. I wasn't sure he truly saw anything.

His son's ghost stood in the glider's path, each traverse of the swing passing right through him. Aiden still wore his muddy uniform, the tan-canvas rucksack on his back soaked with blood that would never dry, never change from crimson to dull brown. He watched his father, fingers flexing around the rifle strap slung over one shoulder.

Waiting to be noticed. Wanting to be forgiven.

The unit insignia on his sleeve was partly caked with mud, but recognizable as British. He'd volunteered to fight in the Great War against his father's wishes. Aiden was buried on a battlefield in France, an unmarked wooden cross at his head. I'd forgotten the memorial service was today.

Isadora rapped on the tabletop with long, lacquered nails, startling me. She leaned back in her chair and crossed her arms. "Tell me if I'm boring you, Delia. I can call back another time."

"I'm sorry." I poured more tea in her cup and mine, added sugar and lemon, and offered her another cookie. We usually spent Dora's visits sitting at the kitchen table. Even on overcast days, my kitchen was the most cheerful room in the house, a good enough reason to spend time there. But the kitchen had also become my workroom, swaddled in layers of protections to keep spirits at bay. Dora felt more at ease here. So did I. "I'm listening, truly I am."

She smiled brightly and tucked a strand of bobbed blond hair behind her ear. "No, Delia. You're not. I don't think you've heard more than ten words since I arrived. Now, why don't you tell me what's captured your attention so completely. Then I can go back to explaining what we can do for Mrs. Allen. Assuming you're still interested."

"Oh I'm interested. I'm fairly certain all the disruption in Mrs. Allen's kitchen must be a poltergeist. Gabe is very fond of her and I promised I'd see what could be done." Very little slipped past Dora, but the way I babbled was a sure sign something was wrong. She raised one perfect eyebrow and continued to smile, waiting for me to sputter to a halt. I squirmed and decided an honest confession was best. "But I am a bit distracted. I seem to have picked up a new ghost, one I can't easily send on her way."

"Can't or won't?" Dora dug in her handbag, fishing out a tortoiseshell cigarette case and a box of matches. I slid a crumb-dusted saucer toward her for the ashes. She lit the cigarette, taking a long drag and exhaling clouds of blue smoke that wafted toward the kitchen ceiling. "You don't have as much knowledge yet, but in terms of strength and power, you're near my equal, Dee. I expect that one day you'll surpass me. There are very few spirits that you can't banish by yourself if you set your mind to it. Unwilling and unable are two very different things."

"For the moment I'm unwilling to banish her. She wasn't more than four or five when she died. A little girl." I folded my hands on the table and told Dora about my nighttime visitor. "I haven't tried to send this ghost on her way. If not for the voices weeping and calling out for help, I might have, but that didn't feel right. I need to know what she wants before I banish her. I can't take the chance."

Dora reached across the table and took my hand. "Not every ghost wants you to right a wrong. I shouldn't have to tell you that. And there is a possibility that she's—"

"The baby we lost last summer?" I squeezed Dora's fingers. "She's not. I thought of that when I first saw her and I made very, very sure. You don't have to warn me, it's not my own grief haunting me. And I know how dangerous strong spirits are . . . how relentless. I've no illusions about how much trouble this ghost can bring me. But you've told me time and again to trust my instincts, and sending her away until I know what she wants feels wrong. Don't worry, I'll be very careful."

She sighed and sat back again, letting her cigarette rest on the saucer. "Allow me to worry. Concern for your well-being saves me from a life of idleness. I'd feel better if I saw this haunt manifest myself, but that's likely too much to hope for."

"I haven't sensed her presence anywhere in the house. Once the ghost left our bedroom, she was truly gone. But I'm not going to fool myself into thinking she won't return." I toyed with the edge of the old checkered tablecloth, worrying at a frayed spot and no doubt making the damage worse. Annie, the housekeeper who'd helped raise me after my parents died, had given it to me, as she'd given me so many things for our kitchen.

This tablecloth brought back memories of living in the Larkin household and whispering secrets to my best friend Sadie at breakfast. I smoothed the fabric with a fingertip, remembering conversations about our hopes for the future. We'd been closer than most sisters. We still were.

All Sadie's heartfelt dreams, a loving husband and children, came true when she married Jack Fitzgerald. Her happiness brought me a great deal of joy. She was just as thrilled when I married Gabe, and for a time, it looked as if we'd both gotten everything we wanted.

But not all wishes came true, no matter how often you implored the brightest star. Having children was another piece of the life I'd wanted stolen by my connection with the spirit realm. Dora spent a great deal of time explaining why interacting with the restless dead and laying ghosts to rest made it unlikely Gabe and I would ever be parents.

Gabe refused to believe. But in my heart of hearts, I knew everything Dora said was true.

I tucked my hand into my lap, forcing it to lie still. "I've dreamed of this little girl before, Dora. I knew the face I'd see and the color of her hair before I opened my eyes. That must mean something."

Dora rummaged in her handbag again. She pulled out a silver flask and poured a generous dash of whiskey into her teacup. Engraved with swirls of vines and morning glories, the liquor flask had been a going-away gift from Daniel, her paramour of the last six years. He'd gone home to Portugal, hoping to convince his family to flee the war and come live in San Francisco. Daniel had planned to be gone a month after sailing from New York, but that had stretched into six, then ten. Getting his family out of Europe had proven difficult.

I hadn't seen Dora without the flask since the night he handed her the slim package wrapped in burnished gold paper and tied with a pale yellow ribbon. Having a ready supply of whiskey at hand wasn't the sole reason she carried the flask.

She took a long swallow of whisky-laced tea. "I'm impressed, Delia. You have quite the talent for attracting difficult ghosts. How long have you dreamed about this little girl?"

The kitchen was chilly and quickly growing colder. Speaking of ghosts sometimes summoned them, accompanied by all the theatrics strong spirits were capable of displaying. I wrapped both hands around the china teacup, seeking to warm stiff fingers and disguise how they trembled. "The thing is . . . I'm not sure. I didn't remember the dreams until I saw her, but now I remember them clearly. She looked just the same each time, a happy little girl carrying her doll and playing in a stream. It might even be the same dream again and again."

"I wouldn't be surprised if it is the same dream, Delia." Dora set aside the whiskey and watched me, blue eyes narrowed and her expression intent. "I've no doubt that you're dreaming about the day she died. A healthy little girl playing in a stream is unlikely to have died a lingering death. My guess is an accident killed her, or perhaps something more sinister."

"A murder?" I stared at Dora, not wanting to believe and praying I'd misinterpreted her meaning. "Who would kill a child?"

She drummed her fingers on the tabletop and crinkled her nose in distaste. "I didn't say she'd been murdered, but it's not unheard of, Dee. Not all the monsters of the world confine their hunting to adults. In any case, the more details you can gather from that dream, the more likely we are to find out who she was. Once we know her name, discovering what the ghost wants from you will be miles easier."

Spirits who suddenly found themselves torn from a world they weren't prepared to leave were the hardest to deal with. Whether they were old or young when they'd died made little difference. These spirits often haunted those they wanted to stay with, unable to break the tie. Others sought out people such as Dora and me. We could see these lost, woeful souls wandering in search of a way back to life.

Giving them back the life they'd lost was impossible. When luck was on our side, we found a way to stop their wandering.

"And if I can't find clues as to who this small ghost was in life?" I stood and gathered soiled chintz napkins, the sandwich tray and plates, and stacked them on the drain board next to the sink. "What do I do then? I'm sure you must have a thing or two you can teach me."

Dora looked up from brushing crumbs off the tablecloth and into her palm, her expression earnest and not a scrap of amusement in her eyes. "I've not exhausted my bag of witch's tricks yet. Just promise me you won't become attached to this haunt. Remember that no matter what her appearance, she's still a ghost and may have spent a hundred years harboring malice. Manifesting in the body of a child is no guarantee of innocence or that she lacks ill intent. The fact you're still grieving for your baby makes me even more suspicious of her motives."

"I'll remember." I leaned back against the edge of the cast-iron sink. "But I heard her mother weep for her, Dora. I find it hard to think badly of a child mourned that deeply."

"You heard someone weep, Dee. Whether the person crying had any relationship to this ghost or not remains to be seen." She dumped the crumbs in the ash-strewn saucer and brushed her hands briskly. "I know I sound harsh, but you must take this seriously. I'd rather not watch Gabe mourning you. Now, let's get back to poltergeists. I promised I'd visit Sadie tomorrow, but we'll pay a visit to Mrs. Allen's boardinghouse the day after. We should be able to keep the rest of her crockery intact."

I poured more tea and sat down to listen. The wind picked up, rocking the tall cedar tree at the side of the house and lashing the windows with small twigs and cedar cones torn loose. Strong gusts keened around corners and under the eaves. Voices rode the wind, mournful and sad, bringing memories of forgotten conversations to my kitchen.

One heartsick voice wept for a lost child—or so I imagined.

CHAPTER 2

Gabe

A murder investigation was never a good way to start his week.

Gabe perched on the edge of the backseat, peering over Patrolman Henderson's shoulder and out the front windscreen. Even after twelve years on the police force, there were parts of the city he didn't know all that well. He'd probably driven or walked down every street in San Francisco with his partner and best friend, Jack Fitzgerald, but there were still districts they hadn't worked in before or visited often.

The street he traveled now was unfamiliar, a part of the newer neighborhoods built after the 1906 quake and the resulting fire. More than a decade had passed since then, something that still surprised Gabe when he stopped to think about it. The city and people of San Francisco had changed forever that morning, a fact that wasn't altered by patching over the visible scars.

He still thought of the rebuilt areas as patches, poor replacements for what had been lost. Gabe wasn't sure what that meant and tried not to dwell on it.

Instead, he paid careful attention to his new surroundings, adding to the living portrait of the city he carried inside. Little things, like whether people stopped to chat with neighbors and pass the time, or rushed about their business without pausing, or the number of children playing from yard to yard, revealed a lot about the character of a neighborhood. The same things told him what he needed to know about the people who lived in the well-kept, brightly painted houses.

Front-step conversations stopped and heads turned to watch his closed car pass, open curiosity on most faces. People who didn't belong here would be noticed right away. And if he and Jack got a break, remembered.

He settled back in his seat. "One of the neighbors might have noticed strangers or something out of the ordinary late last night. You've spent time with the new rookies on the squad, Marshall. Who would you send out to knock on doors?"

"Randolph Dodd's the best of the new bunch, Captain Ryan. Some of the older men gave him a hard time for being a pretty boy when he first came on, but Dodd's winning them over. Tyler and Erickson's instincts are good. They ask the right questions." Marshall Henderson braked and put the car into a lower gear before he rounded the corner. The engine whined, straining to climb the steep hill. "Those are the men I know best. Lieutenant Fitzgerald might have some ideas about who to send along with those three."

Gabe rubbed the back of his neck and swallowed a yawn. He hadn't slept well last night or any night for the last week. Constantly jerking awake from nightmares left his head stuffed with cotton wool, his thoughts dulled and slow. Not being able to remember any of what he'd dreamed somehow made the fog in his head worse. "The lieutenant's been at the scene for at least an hour. There's a chance he's already sent men to question the neighbors. Find him right away and make sure we aren't covering the same ground twice."

"Yes, sir." Marshall hesitated, stealing glances at Gabe's refection in the driving mirror. "Are you all right, Captain?"

He must look bad if Henderson felt the need to check.

"I'm fine. Just a few too many late nights this week and not enough sleep." Gabe cleared his throat and pointed down the block. "I think we've found our murder scene."

A knot of black patrol cars clogged the narrow street in mid-block, wheels turned toward the curb or parked at an angle to keep from rolling downhill. The white coroner's van in front further marked their destination, a druggist shop with cheerful blue and white striped awnings over the wide front window. Three flagstone-topped wooden steps led up to the door from the street, a decorative iron railing on the open side opposite the wall.

The shop was located on a main thoroughfare that ran through a narrow maze of side streets and lanes that dead-ended. Most of the lanes were occupied by single-story cottages with red-tiled roofs and small yards. A smattering of larger houses sat at the end of cul-de-sacs. Neighborhood grocers, small storefronts, and shops occupied the main avenues. Given the number of families living here, merchants would have no shortage of trade.

Another thing went on Gabe's list of things he wanted to know. Discovering the fastest ways in and out of this tangle of homes and shops might give them an idea of which route the murderer used to escape, and who might have seen.

"Captain, do you want me to leave the car right in front with the squad cars? It's pretty crowded up ahead and I'd have to block traffic." Marshall glanced over his shoulder and back to the road. "Otherwise, I'll get you as close as I can and we can walk."

"Do what you can without blocking the entire street." Gabe slicked his hair back and put on his battered fedora. "I'm not the chief. Walking won't kill me."

They parked four doors down from the druggist's shop, blocking the entrance to a narrow lane that ran between a butcher and a milliner's shop. This lane was only five small brick cottages long, the hedges between their minuscule front gardens frost-burned and winter brown. Marshall came round the car and opened Gabe's door. Lace curtains twitched on the front window of the cottage closest to where they'd parked, confirming his opinion of the neighborhood's watchfulness.

"Go on ahead, Marshall. I'll catch up." The lanky young patrolman set off at a brisk walk to carry out his orders and find Jack. Gabe got out more slowly, using the time it took to rebutton his overcoat to stand on the sidewalk and look around.

Men from his squad had formed a line to keep curious civilians away, blocking the sidewalk on either side of the druggist shop. A few officers were still mounted on the tall, brown Morgan horses they rode on patrol, using the advantage of height to keep an eye on the crowd. Parked police cars barricaded the curb and spilled into the middle of the road. More well-dressed people gathered on the other side of the street, craning their necks and straining to catch a glimpse of what might be going on.

This was like other quiet neighborhoods he'd worked in, home to bankers and prosperous merchants, full of small storefronts that catered to their well-off clientele. He understood what drove the residents to discover why the police had arrived in force, disrupting their ordered lives. People needed to know if the block where they lived was still a safe place for their children to play or for their wives to walk after dark. Gabe could pick those men and women out of the milling crowd, read the concern and fear on their faces.

What he'd never understand was the desire some people felt to turn tragedy of any kind into a carnival. He could pick those faces out of the crowd as well: eyes too bright, smiles gleeful, expressions harboring no trace of nervousness or fear. Gabe saw those faces at every murder scene, at every raging fire. At times he got near enough to smell their excitement.

Those were the faces he studied and remembered, the faces that held joy where none should exist.

Jack waited for him at the foot of the druggist's steps, his ever-present moleskine notebook in one hand and a worn pencil in the other. His brown herringbone suit was well pressed, a common occurrence since he'd married Sadie and their housekeeper, Annie, took charge of his wardrobe. The plaid cap perched on top of his red-brown hair did a poor job of containing the unruly mess, but nothing had ever come close to taming Jack's tangle.

Gabe's partner looked calm and in charge of the investigation, directing officers to different tasks and taking brief reports of what they'd found before sending them off again. But Jack tapped his pencil against the edge of the notebook, a nervous, staccato rhythm that grew faster as soon as he spotted Gabe.

After being partners for twelve years, they knew each other's habits and signals. This was a warning. There was more going on here than Gabe knew, something worse than murder first thing on a Monday morning.

He wasn't sure he wanted to know what was worse than murder; not that he had the choice.

Gabe ignored the knot forming between his shoulders and kept the public mask he wore while working firmly in place. High-profile cases always drew the press sooner or later. The newspaper photographers with their Speed Graphic cameras mounted on tripods and the reporters scribbling notes were right up at the front of the crowd, positioned so they had a clear view. He and Jack were on display, their every expression scrutinized.

That reporters had beaten Gabe to the scene was another bad sign. "Good morning, Lieutenant. Tell me what you've found so far."

"One victim, Bradley Wells, a twenty-six-year-old white male. The victim's wife called the Columbus Street station last evening. He didn't arrive home on time and didn't answer the telephone when she called the shop. Mrs. Wells got worried and asked the police to check on her husband." Jack flipped through his notes. The tremor in his hands was slight, but Gabe saw. It gave lie to the flat, professional tone in his voice. "Captain Pearson sent two men from his squad out last night. They poked around the outside of the building, but didn't find anything suspicious or go inside. A second call came in this morning. This time the patrolmen broke down the back door."

Gabe, was beginning to understand at least part of Jack's reaction. If the coroner's report came back that Wells had been alive when the first call came in, the newspapers wouldn't hold back. But he knew it took a lot more than fear of bad press to give Jack the jitters. "Where did they find the body?"

"Mr. Wells's body is in a storeroom. No windows, only one way in." Jack snapped his notebook shut. "I thought you should see the scene before the coroner moved the body. Follow me, Captain, and I'll show you."

He followed Jack up the steps, anxious to get out of public view. With his back to the cameras, Gabe muttered quietly so only Jack could hear. "Bradley Wells . . . I know that name from somewhere."

"You should." Jack held the pine-framed door open and shut it firmly again as soon as they got inside. The shade was pulled over the window in the center, closing them away from curious eyes and cameras. "Bradley Wells is—was—Commissioner Lindsey's son-in-law. He married Adele Lindsey three years ago."

Gabe wiped a hand across his mouth. "Christ Almighty. The second phone call this morning came from Lindsey."

"You got it on the first try. I knew you made captain for a reason." Jack led the way toward the back of the shop, threading around upturned bins of penny candy and smashed apothecary jars, their contents splashed across polished oak floors. Footprints tracked through crushed peppermints and spilled white powder, spreading it further. "He called Pearson personally and got him out of bed. Lindsey ordered him to get some men over here to break down the door. I gather from the chief that threats were involved."

Gabe stopped at the back counter, trailing a finger through swirls and drifts of black fingerprint powder. The register stood open; all the money was still inside. He brushed the powder from his hand. "Since Pearson and his men aren't here, I'd say Lindsey's threats didn't work."

"Pearson didn't get around to sending any of his men out until after he'd had breakfast. He's had it in for the commissioner since Lindsey leaked details of a case. When Lindsey found out, he went straight to the mayor. The chief didn't have much choice but to suspend Pearson." Jack pulled back a bead curtain hanging over a doorway and waved Gabe through. "And that, Captain Ryan, is how we ended up drawing the short straw."

The back room was L-shaped, with an empty, narrow passage that ran from the doorway and turned a corner into a deeper, wider room. If anything, the mess here was much worse than out front. Broad wooden shelves against the back wall had been stripped bare, everything on them flung to the floor. Jars, crocks, and canisters lay abandoned, whatever they might have contained carted away.

Traces of chalky powder smudged the floor and trailed back the way they'd come, but Gabe couldn't tell if his men had tracked it in on their shoes or if the dusting of white had been there all along. Shards of broken glass crunched underfoot. Tiny slivers caught in the dark crevices between floorboards glittered under the single bulb dangling from the ceiling.

Bradley Wells's body was spread-eagled atop a long yellowed-pine worktable in the center of the room. A heavy white cloth trimmed in gold and black braid covered him from shoulders to knees. Lengths of rope looped his chest under the fabric, ends tied to the table legs. His shirt and shoes were missing, but Wells still wore socks and trousers.

Baker had set up his camera to take pictures of the body. Gabe circled around behind the camera to avoid being blinded by the magnesium flash going off. Each burst of harsh light revealed details obscured by the dim overhead bulb: Wells's peaceful expression, the outline of his hands folded and lying on his chest under the fabric shroud, the way one leg was pulled up slightly, knee bent; the gaping slash across Wells's throat.

What he saw didn't make sense.

Patrolman Baker finished with his photographs and began packing his equipment away. Gabe moved closer to the table, hands shoved deep into his coat pockets. "Baker, ask the coroner to wait outside until the lieutenant and I finish. And deliver those photos to my office as soon as they're ready."

"Yes, sir." Baker finished taking apart his tripod and snapped the case closed. He wiped sweat off his upper lip, staring at the body. "I've been on the force seven years and this is the strangest thing I've seen so far. Got any ideas about what happened, Captain?"

"Not a one." Gabe grimaced. "Not yet, anyway. Go develop those pictures for me."

Baker hurried away, leaving them alone with Wells's body. Jack walked the margins of the room, surveying the damage and nudging empty crocks with his foot. He made notes in his moleskine as he went. "Whatever the senior Mr. Wells kept in the back room was what the killers were after. They didn't leave anything behind."

"We need a list of the medicines kept in this storeroom. I want a list of the customers he dispensed them to as well." Gabe moved to stand at the head of the table. The victim's skin had the waxy sheen of death, his slightly parted lips unnaturally pale. "Some older druggists are still selling old-style patent medicines without a prescription. People will pay a lot to keep their habits secret, especially in a respectable neighborhood like this. Maybe someone found out and wanted a piece of the old man's business. Could be Bradley wasn't the one they expected to find."

"That might explain the robbery, but not how he was murdered." Jack whistled through his teeth. "The way Wells is laid out gives me the willies. Murderers don't usually drape their victims in an altar cloth."

"I just want to cover all the angles, Jack. Ask the right questions." Gabe lifted the edge of the cloth, examining Wells's hands. They were smooth and unblemished, with no scratches or marks to indicate a struggle. Bradley Wells hadn't put up a fight. He let the cloth drop back into place. "I'd really like to know if Wells was the intended victim or just got in the way. And between you and me, all this makes me nervous too. It reminds me of something Dora told me about. A ritual of some kind, but I can't remember what."

"Show Dora the photographs if you think it will help. As long as you warn her first, she'll be all right. We might get a lead about who to look for." Jack wiped a hand over a shelf and held it up. "Whoever did this was very careful to tidy up afterwards and not leave anything for us to find. One person couldn't have done this alone, not and handle Wells too."

"The way he was murdered is all too tidy, if you ask me. I can't say the same for the mess they made of the storefront or the floor in here." Gabe made a sweeping motion with his arm, taking in the empty shelves and Wells's body. "And you're right, there had to be at least two people involved, maybe more. Either they've been planning this for a long time or they've killed this way before. They knew exactly what they were doing."

The cloth draping Wells's body was almost pristine, with only the tiniest flecks of rusty brown marring the surface. Gabe glanced at his partner and gestured toward the body. "The killers cut his throat. What happened to all the blood?"

"I asked the coroner that as soon as he arrived. Dr. Gometz said that there's a slim chance Wells was already dead before his throat was cut. Bleeding would be limited if his heart had stopped." Jack scratched a few more notes. "But Gometz can't explain why there isn't any blood at all. No blood around the wound, no seeping, no blood pooling in the lower extremities or under the body—nothing. He refused to speculate until after he does an autopsy."

Raised, angry voices came from the front of the store. The bead curtain hanging across the entrance to the back room clattered and banged against the wall. Heavy footsteps stomped on broken glass, and a deep, booming voice shouted Gabe's name. "Ryan! Where the hell are you?"

He exchanged looks with Jack. "Lindsey's here. That arrogant son of a bitch thinks he's going to supervise."

Robert Lindsey loomed over almost everyone, man or woman. At six foot six, broad across the chest and broader still at the shoulder, he was an imposing figure and wasn't above using his size to intimidate people. But he'd also honed the art of politics to a fine edge. Lindsey learned early on in his career that being jolly and accommodating was the quickest way to impress those in power.

A former mayor was impressed enough to appoint Lindsey to a five-year term as commissioner of police, an administrative position that required no real experience or training. His appointment had been a huge mistake. Lindsey saw the police, from the chief down to the newest rookie walking a beat, as underlings to bully and use for his own political purposes. The present mayor, a former cop himself, longed for an excuse to fire Robert Lindsey.

Gabe intercepted Lindsey just before he turned the corner into the main storeroom. He put an arm out, blocking the way. "Commissioner, I have to ask that you wait outside. I can't allow a civilian inside a crime scene. This is an active investigation."

"Don't give me that bull crap, Captain Ryan. I'm your boss. I can go anywhere I damn well please." Lindsey's face was flushed an angry red, his voice a low growl. He tried to use his bulk to push past. "Now, get out of my way."

Gabe planted his feet and didn't budge. "You're not a cop, Lindsey, but you know the regulations as well as I do. This is my investigation and I'm not letting you inside. Don't force me to arrest you."

"Think of the headlines, Commissioner." Jack stood so that he blocked the rest of the passageway, arms folded over his chest. "'Lindsey arrested for interfering with murder investigation.' The papers will ask why you tried to force your way in. It won't take long before they start wondering if you had something to hide. Think of your daughter. You don't want to put her through that."

Lindsey glared at the two detectives in turn, shoulders heaving and fists clenching open and shut. Gabe stared back impassively, praying all the while Lindsey wouldn't force the issue.

Finally, the commissioner took a step back, signaling surrender. He cleared his throat and straightened the lapels of his overcoat, looking anywhere but at Gabe and Jack. "I am thinking of my daughter. You need to understand something, Detectives. Adele is in a delicate condition and the baby could arrive at any moment. The doctor is with her now, but my daughter has always been in fragile health. Doctor Young is worried that the strain—that her upcoming confinement so soon after losing Bradley might be too much for her heart."

"We do understand, Commissioner. Your daughter has our deepest condolences." Gabe couldn't help but feel sympathy for Adele Wells, but the simple truth was that he didn't trust her father. He stood his ground. "That doesn't change anything. You have to wait outside."

"Captain—please." Lindsey tipped his head back, staring at the ceiling and throat working. His eyes were moist when he looked back at Gabe. "My daughter needs to be certain there hasn't been a mistake. I promised that I'd identify the body."

Jack glanced at Gabe, asking permission. His partner possessed more patience and was better at dealing with difficult people, a category the commissioner of police filled to bursting. He nodded and Jack stepped forward.

"Commissioner . . . have you ever seen a murder victim before? Even if you think you're prepared, I can promise that you're not."

A muscle in the commissioner's jaw pulsed. "I remember you. You're Katherine Fitzgerald's son."

"Yes, sir, I am. We met when I escorted my stepmother to Adele and Bradley's wedding. My wife and I have friends in common with Brad and your daughter. We see them fairly often at parties or small dinners. I promise you, there's no mistake." If anyone could convince the commissioner to back down, Jack could. He kept his tone calm, soothing and sympathetic. "You don't want to remember him this way. They cut Brad's throat."

Lindsey blanched, rivulets of sweat running down his forehead. He tugged a monogrammed handkerchief from his breast pocket, mopping his face and breathing hard. "I still need to see him. I made a promise."

Gabe wasn't entirely sure what made him relent, but he did. That Adele Wells deserved to have her doubts laid to rest was partly a factor; the realization that underneath his bluster and brash man-

ner Lindsey was human another part. He hoped he didn't live to regret a moment's compassion. "All right, Commissioner. You can
identify the body and then I need you to leave. No statements without my clearing them first or revealing details of what you've seen to
the press. Agreed?"

"Agreed." Lindsey stood straighter and removed his black bowler
hat, visibly steeling himself. "Thank you, Captain."

Lindsey handled viewing his son-in-law's body better than Gabe
had anticipated. He stood looking down at Wells's face for a few
seconds, silent, shaking hands crushing the brim of his hat. Without
a word, he strode back around the corner and sagged against the corridor wall. "Dear God . . . I can't tell Adele what they did to Brad. I
can't."

"I'm sorry, Commissioner." Jack closed his moleskine and stuffed
the notebook into a coat pocket. "But there's no real need to tell her
how he died. Not yet."

"No . . . you're right. Bad enough that I know." Lindsey mopped
his face again, squaring his shoulders and standing up straight.
Blotchy pink color returned to his skin and the imperious tone to his
voice. "Captain, I'm putting you personally in charge of Bradley's
case. If there's anything you need in terms of manpower, anything at
all, let my office know."

Gabe nodded. Lindsey sounded sincere. "Thank you, sir. The
offer is much appreciated."

Commissioner Lindsey stuffed the sweat-damp handkerchief in
a breast pocket. "My daughter's waiting for me. Find the men who
did this, Detectives. I want to look them in the eye before I watch
them hang."

The coroner's men appeared at the end of the passageway, canvas
stretcher in hand. Robert Lindsey bulled past them and out into the
main room of the shop. He slammed the front door on his way out,
setting the bell over the door to ringing wildly and rattling shelves in
the storeroom.

Jack frowned and glanced at Gabe. "I don't think we need worry about him making statements to the press. He's more likely to assault any reporter who gets in his way."

"You're probably right." Gabe took one last look at the storeroom and Wells's body, setting the scene in his mind. He flattened himself against the wall, making room for the coroner's men to pass before leading the way into the front. "I never thought I'd see the day I felt sorry for Robert Lindsey."

"Neither did I." Jack pointed at the front door. The window shade hung by one bracket, and the glass was crazed with spiderweb cracks. "But don't worry. That won't last."

"As soon as we get back to the office, I want to start calling in favors. Someone on the street will know if there have been other victims in the city who died the same way as Wells."

Jack's mouth pulled into a grim line. "You mean unreported murders. Dead vagrants and any John Doe the department didn't waste time on."

"Exactly. We'd never hear about those victims unless we went looking for them." Gabe flipped up the collar of his coat and pulled his hat down low, preparing for the shouts of newspaper photographers and the gawking eyes of the crowd. He couldn't give anything away if no one saw his face. "We're looking for them as of now. How much do you want to wager we find more than one?"

"I never bet against you, Gabe." Jack pulled the door open. He gestured at the crowd of reporters yelling their names. "I leave that to those who don't know you."

CHAPTER 3

Delia

The front bell rang just before six. I opened the door to find Gabe home early, a bouquet of hothouse carnations, sprigs of fern, and baby's breath in his hand. He presented the flowers with a flourish. "For you, Mrs. Ryan."

"Oh, Gabe. These flowers are just lovely." I inhaled the sweet scent of carnations and the peppery tang of fern, delighted. "Thank you. What a nice surprise."

"I like seeing you smile. Besides, I missed you." He hugged me to his chest, held tight, and gave no sign of letting go. I listened to his heart race, the rhythm much too fast and uneven. A glance over his shoulder gave me a reason why.

A cloud of ghosts lingered in the entryway behind Gabe, ragged souls only partly in this world. Spirits churned and boiled and crowded one atop another, never holding still, never allowing me to glimpse more than a face, a hand clutching the head of a cane, or dark eyes.

Stronger ghosts thronged beyond our front step and vanished into the evening fog: soldiers and tradesmen, shopkeepers, society matrons and men in top hats, young girls and small boys. Each spirit watched Gabe attentively, eyes bright and knowing.

Ghosts often followed Gabe home. Dora maintained he had the

soul of a paladin and attracted the spirits of victims seeking a champion. The majority of the ghosts attached to him came from forgotten crime scenes or pieces of evidence stored in tattered pasteboard boxes. Most were no more than whispers of memory, names scribbled in a file and otherwise forgotten.

These faded spirits crowded around Gabe in greater numbers each time he started a difficult case. But in the nearly two years we'd been married, I'd never seen so many ghosts seek him out. The sheer number startled me; that so many of them were children was frightening. Others might encounter the ghosts of children often, but for me catching a glimpse of young spirits was rare. Children didn't cling to this world as fiercely.

Now I couldn't help but think of my nighttime visitor. Suspicion took root and spread, and the memory of bright blue eyes shining with moonlight made me shiver.

I whispered the charm Dora had taught me, forbidding ghosts and haunts or wandering spirits to cross our threshold or enter our house. The oldest ghosts wailed in despair and turned to vapor, spiraling into the clouds and becoming part of the evening fog. Newer spirits resisted, reluctant to loosen their hold on Gabe, but in the end I forced them to follow the others.

The last spirit vanished and Gabe's heartbeat slowed, became smooth and even. I relaxed as well. He was sensitive enough to feel the weight of so many spirits and the relief when they left, but not to see them as I did.

"Half the ghosts in San Francisco followed you home tonight." I stepped back, holding tight to his hand and watching his eyes. Making doubly sure no lingering traces of another soul clung to him. "Are you all right?"

"I wasn't feeling very well, but now I'm fine." Gabe raked his fingers through his hair. Tousled curls woke, making him look younger. "I've always known when you send ghosts away, but this was different. I felt them leave. What just happened, Dee?"

That he'd recovered so quickly was an enormous relief. Despite

Isadora's assurances, I still worried that my connection to the spirit realm might someday cause Gabe harm. Discovering a host of spirits hanging on to his coattails awoke all my fears. The challenge now was to find the reason why so many spirits had developed a sudden fascination with Gabe.

"I'm not quite sure. Haunts have followed you home in the past, but I'd send them away and you never noticed. What concerns me is why so many strong spirits chose to attach themselves to you today. It doesn't make any sense."

"Jack and I started a new case. There might be a connection." Gabe glanced at me, regret and what I took to be reluctance to say more in his eyes. He shut the door, hung his overcoat and jacket on the hall tree as normal, and began rolling up his shirtsleeves. "I'll tell you what I can, but maybe we should fix supper first. What still needs to be done?"

"Supper's almost ready." I took his hand and led him down the hall. "Come sit in the kitchen and talk to me while the biscuits finish baking."

The house was large for just the two of us, with three good-sized bedrooms, a bathroom, a formal parlor and a larger sitting room, and a solar off the dining room. A utility porch opened off the kitchen and led to a side yard. Windows in all the rooms let in plenty of sunlight and fresh air.

I loved our house, but often I caught myself wandering aimlessly, adrift in all that space. Once I'd thought children would fill my days and the house to bursting, but no longer.

Having lost one child, I seldom thought of more. I couldn't bear to.

We almost never ate in the dining room, saving that space for company and special occasions. Most days we ate in the kitchen, a habit that lingered from our courting days. Gabe finished setting the table while I piled chicken, biscuits, and roasted potatoes on plates. A dish of applesauce and a jar of honey already sat in the middle of the faded checkered tablecloth.

Gabe filled his plate as always, but ate next to nothing. I watched in silence as he pushed his food around the plate, reminding me of a little boy pretending to eat some much-hated dish. Two biscuits were picked apart and reduced to a pile of crumbs in the center of his plate.

This wasn't the first evening Gabe had arrived home quiet and withdrawn. I'd learned not to rush conversation too soon. But I'd also learned to tell when he was brooding and needed to talk. I had Isadora partly to thank for that. She'd taught me how to read auras. Every person had an aura, a living rainbow that changed colors in response to fear or stress.

Red and black streaks rippled through Gabe's normally placid green nimbus. Something bothered him a great deal; something that went deeper than discovering an army of ghosts had followed him home. Gabe never kept things from me for long, not unless he was unsure about where to start.

So I gave him a place to begin. I asked.

"Gabe." I put my hand over his, preventing him from taking a third biscuit. He looked up with a guilty start. "Tell me about your case. Talking may help."

He toyed with his fork for a moment, carving pathways in the pile of crumbs on his plate. I waited patiently until Gabe cleared his throat, his usual prelude to difficult conversations.

"Commissioner Lindsey's son-in-law, Bradley Wells, was murdered in his father's drugstore. We think he died sometime last night or very early this morning. I've been trying to make sense of what we found." He shoved his plate away and slumped in the chair. "Whoever killed Wells vandalized the store and stole all the medications from the back. But the cash register was sitting open, with at least a hundred dollars inside, and they didn't touch a penny. None of this feels right. I'm missing something."

"You and Jack are very good at your jobs. And following your instincts has always stood you in good stead. Don't doubt yourself." I took his hand. "But that's not what's bothering you most."

Gabe took my hand, his aura seething with dark colors. "Wells was killed in the storeroom. The way his body was laid out . . . I've never seen anything like this, Dee. I can't shake the idea there was some kind of ritual involved. Cops aren't supposed to look at the occult for a motive or a means for murder, but Jack and I agree that we need to bring Dora into this case. Quietly if possible. Wells's death is already making headlines."

I gripped his hand tighter, unsure I'd heard correctly. "A ritual killing? Are you certain?"

"I don't know what else to think." His voice cracked as he described the cloth covering Bradley Wells, how his throat had been cut and the lack of blood. "He didn't seem to struggle at all. If I didn't know better, Dee, I'd swear he let the killers cut his throat."

Now I understood why this case had shaken him so badly. What he'd described left me with an irrational need to keep looking over my shoulder. "Dora said something about ritual murders or some sort of cult sacrifices a few weeks ago. Do you remember? Jack and Sadie were late getting to the café and we were talking about the war. Dora changed the subject as soon as Sadie arrived. But I'm positive the murders Dora told us about happened in Europe nearly a century ago."

"I don't want to believe something that barbaric could happen in San Francisco. This is 1917." Gabe rubbed a hand over his face. "But I can't shake the feeling I'm right. I'm really hoping that Dora tells me the idea is ridiculous."

I couldn't bring myself to let go of his hand or stop thoughts of possible disaster. The ghosts that had followed him home frightened me, especially in connection with this case. "You're not being ridiculous, Gabe, and I'm glad you told me. Bringing Dora in is wise—she knows more about the occult than any of us. She'll help you find the person responsible. I'll help as well."

"I don't like dragging you into my cases. And I know how hard this is on Dora. If there were another way, I wouldn't put either of you through this." He leaned across the table to kiss my cheek. "But

I'd be an idiot not to know I'm in over my head. Just promise me that the two of you will be very careful. I wouldn't admit this to anyone but you or Jack, but something about this case scares me."

"We'll be careful. I promise." I stood to clear away the dinner dishes. "Annie brought a batch of apple tarts by this afternoon. We have sweet cream too if you like."

"Maybe later." Gabe took the plates and bowls from me and set them in the sink. He pulled me into his arms and nuzzled my neck. "I don't see enough of you, Mrs. Ryan. Leave the dishes for morning."

I laughed and held him tight. "We're already the talk of the neighborhood gossips. Going to bed early and leaving the dishes unwashed is for honeymooners, not an old married couple like us. Can you imagine the scandal?"

"Let them talk." He looked into my eyes, serious and sober. "I'm not willing to waste a moment with you."

Events and wandering haunts conspired to make sure neither of us ever forgot that life was precarious. Fragile. Gabe was right. Let them talk.

We turned out the lights and left the dishes in the sink. Scandalizing the neighbors was far better than living with regrets.

The parlor clock struck three, each hollow chime sounding farther away than just down the hall. I sat straight up in bed, confused and unsure about what had awakened me. Panic burned in my chest, making me nauseated and urging me to get away, to run far and fast and not look behind. I'd be safe if only I could run fast enough.

Gabe sprawled across the bed beside me, arms thrown up over his head and long legs tangled in the coverlet. He muttered nonsense and thrashed side to side, kicking at the bedclothes. "No . . . don't run . . . no. I can't follow. . . . I can't reach you!"

"Gabe, wake up." I put a hand on his shoulder. "Wake up, it's only a dream." He rolled toward the wall, still muttering, still pleading for someone to wait. Gradually his thrashing quieted, the pleas died away, and I lay back down. My panic faded as well.

A little girl's laugh and the singsong rhyme of a familiar child's song set my heart to pounding again.

> *Every night when I go out*
> *The monkey's on the table,*
> *Take a stick and knock it off,*
> *Pop! goes the weasel.*

I sat up again, panic slithering across my skin and searching the shadows for the small ghost I'd seen before. She was back, I was certain of that, even if I couldn't see her. More laughter sounded, and a man's deep, guttural voice joined in with the little girl's singing.

> *All around the cobbler's bench*
> *The monkey chased the people;*
> *The donkey thought 'twas all in fun,*
> *Pop! goes the weasel.*

Laughter and threads of melody trailed away, and I shivered at the sudden chill in the room. The same small ghost I'd seen before shimmered into view at the foot of our bed. She clutched her china doll tight and stared at me, blue eyes too wise for a child so small.

This slip of a girl was stronger than I'd guessed and, as Dora warned, older than I'd imagined. She'd evaded all my wards easily, creeping into Gabe's dreams to show me that she could. I suspected she'd chosen to use him as a way to force me to pay attention. Anger woke, fierce and determined to protect Gabe at all costs. Whatever her reasons were didn't matter. I wouldn't let her hurt him.

"Leave my house, spirit. Go now and never return." I put all the force of command I could muster into my voice, the rage churning inside lending power to the skills I'd labored so hard to learn. "You can't have him. You've forfeited any help I might've been willing to give."

She drifted closer, defying me. A red glint flickered in her eyes, anger of her own and determination to enforce her will. The chill in our bedroom deepened, and the lamp on the nightstand rattled.

Laughter filled the air again; the joyful sounds of a little girl at play replaced by a man's harsh laugh, gloating and triumphant. The little girl's voice became breathless half sobs, chanting, *"The monkey chased the people, run . . . run, don't stop . . . run run run."*

Gabe groaned, his eyes screwed shut and fingers clawing at the bedroom wall blindly. Choked sobs filled his voice. "Stop . . . oh please, you have to stop!"

"Go!" I slipped from bed, putting myself between Gabe and the ghost. "I banish you, spirit. You are not welcome in my house!"

She glared a final time, turned, and opened a bright doorway into summer. I glimpsed a pathway lined on either side with tall grass and sunlight sparking off pebbles in a burbling stream. The small ghost looked back at me with a chilly smile and vanished.

Gone for now, but I couldn't fool myself into believing this ghost was gone forever. I stood on the carpet, fists clenched and shaking, whispering charms under my breath, building new walls around our house, our bedroom, and another set around our bed. Long after all traces of the spirit's presence vanished, I kept adding more layers of charms. If I made the walls thick enough, she'd never find a crack to wiggle through. Making sure Gabe was safe, even if only for one night, was all I could think about.

The bed was still warm, a relief after shivering barefoot on icy oak floors. I rolled toward Gabe, molding my body to his and putting an arm around him. He sighed sleepily, threading his fingers through mine.

Sleep was impossible, so I lay there thinking and listened to the creak and groan of redwood trees swaying, and the hiss of wind slithering through needled branches. I couldn't keep this ghost away for long. She was too strong, too determined. All my plans to send her on and vows to keep her out of our lives were nothing more than comforting lies and foolishness. She could do what she wanted with Gabe, drive him mad or convince him to harm himself, and there was nothing I could do to stop her.

I was afraid. Afraid I'd summoned this spirit unknowingly, afraid that a lack of skill on my part would bring disaster. The thought of losing Gabe, the way I'd lost my parents in the 1906 earthquake, or the way Gabe had lost his first wife, Victoria, to the fire afterwards, truly terrified me.

Admitting that even to myself stung my pride, but I'd never been good at hiding from truth.

Feeling helpless in the face of this spirit made me angry all over again. Like Gabe, I knew when I was out of my depth. I needed to ask Dora for help.

I wouldn't allow this spirit to keep the upper hand. I'd find a way to banish this ghost for good.

CHAPTER 4

Gabe

Gabe pulled the desk lamp closer, tipping the shade so all the light shone on the open file. The early-morning fog had thinned and burned off enough not to hug the pavement, but clouds still hung low in the sky, and very little light shone through his office window. Trying to read Officer Rockwell's reports, written in a jagged, cramped script, was difficult enough under the best of circumstances. Doing so in semidarkness was impossible. He refused to go blind in order to read burglary reports.

He initialed the last page and glanced at the old clock hanging above the door. Gabe automatically added five minutes to the time, compensating for the fact the clock ran slow no matter how often he wound it. The same clock had hung in his father's office when Matt Ryan was a detective with the San Francisco Police Department. After Matt retired, he'd put the clock in the office he set up on his egg ranch, bent hands, cracked glass, and all.

If the clock had belonged to anyone else or been department issue, Gabe would have thrown it out long before. But the slow, battered-looking timepiece had been his father's, not a fixture that came with the office and his promotion to captain. As he'd done with so many things left behind after his father's murder two years before, Gabe brought the old clock back from the ranch. He couldn't bring himself to get rid of it.

His partner gave a perfunctory knock and opened the office door without waiting for Gabe to answer. Jack was whistling an old tune popular on the docks when they were rookies. The bawdy lyrics had never been suitable for polite society, but Jack liked the song for exactly that reason.

Gabe smiled and reached for a new folder. "Good day, Lieutenant. You're in a jolly mood. That's a pleasant change."

"The baby slept for six blissful hours last night. Sadie thinks the worst of Stella's teething might be over for a while. I hope she's right." Jack whistled a few more notes. Not much dampened his spirits, not even losing sleep helping Sadie walk the floor with a teething baby. "Mrs. Bourke across the street snubbed me the other morning after Stella cried all night. I'd wager she's keeping the neighbors awake too."

"Don't let that bother you. Stella's just like her mother. She'll have the entire neighborhood charmed before she's a year old." He glanced up at his partner. "They don't stand a chance against her. Neither do you."

"The poor bastards will never know what hit them. Now, close that file and lock your desk. I promised Sadie I'd make sure you ate a decent lunch today. You're buying." Jack's coat was draped over an arm and his cloth cap stuffed into his back pocket. "Your wife worries about you, Gabe, and she tells Sadie all about it. I'm under orders to see that you don't try to survive another day on cold coffee."

Gabe rubbed his eyes. "Lunch is a good idea. I might even tell Delia you thought of it if you pick up the check."

"Senior officers shouldn't engage in blackmail, Captain." Jack attempted to slick back his hair, but caused more disarray instead. "And fair is fair. I bought last time."

"When we come back, you can help me go through the rest of these reports. Looking for other robberies was a good idea." His stomach rumbled at the thought of food. Gabe flipped the file closed and settled back in his chair, making the polished oak creak and groan. After tucking the files inside the deep bottom desk drawer, he locked them away for safekeeping. "The other precincts found fifteen break-ins at small druggist's shops all over the city, all within the last five weeks. And Lindsey was as good as his word about getting us anything we needed. The files arrived by messenger this morning."

Jack tossed Gabe's overcoat to him. "I got word to the last of my contacts last night. We should start hearing back from them soon. I don't know whether to hope they turn up more murders or not."

"We may have found one already. One of the files from the Pine Street station was flagged." Gabe smoothed the brim of his battered fedora and let it dangle from his hand, taking one last glance around the office to make sure everything was secure. Satisfied, he waved Jack out the door. "A small herb shop in Chinatown was broken into. The owner, Mr. Sung, and his granddaughter were found dead in a back room."

The hallway was full of dayshift cops and detectives. Men hustled from the public portion of the station in the front and into the private areas at the back. Jack nodded to the patrolmen passing, waiting patiently while Gabe swore under his breath and fought with the sticky lock on his office door.

Gabe rattled the doorknob, making sure the bolt had caught. The frosted glass panel painted with his name, CAPTAIN GABRIEL RYAN, shook as well. Once he was sure the lock would hold, they continued toward the front desk. "Remind me to get the custodian up here to fix this. It's getting worse."

"I'll send him over if I see him first. How did Lindsey know to flag the Chinatown file?"

"He didn't. It was one of the detectives at Pine Street. The case in Chinatown bothers him the way Wells's murder bothers us. We aren't the only smart cops in the city." Gabe fought to ignore the itchy, crawling sensation on the back of his neck. His father taught him that good cops didn't believe in hunches. But the more he learned from Delia and Isadora about the spirit realm, the more certain he became that this feeling of something hidden, something he needed to *find*, wasn't a hunch in the way his father meant.

He didn't know what to call it, but he'd learned to pay attention. "The locations are miles apart. The days of the week and the times don't match up. But I can't bring myself to think there's no connection between the murders, especially with all the other robberies. I just can't see it yet."

"Maybe there's nothing to see, no pattern." Jack frowned and tugged the end of his mustache, thinking. "But I'm not a big believer in coincidence either."

Gabe stopped short of stepping out of the corridor and into the noisy station lobby. Midday was always busy, the benches arranged in front of the desk sergeant full of a mix of criminals and solid citizens who'd come to lodge complaints, sometimes loudly. The sound of motorcars, newsboys hawking papers with the latest war news from Europe, and horse-drawn cabs drifted through the open front doors and echoed off the high ceiling, adding to the noise. Once they left the relative shelter of the hallway, the din would engulf them. He'd be forced to shout to make sure Jack heard.

News of murder shouldn't be delivered at the top of his voice. The victims deserved more respect.

"We know how Wells died." Gabe leaned against the wall, scowling at the rookie who'd slowed down and appeared too curious about their conversation. The young patrolman blushed and hurried past. "Two weeks ago, an eighty-year-old shopkeeper in Chinatown, Mr. Sung, and his granddaughter were found dead in the back room of the family herb shop. The family was afraid a rival tong had ordered the old man killed and the granddaughter got in the way. They refused to involve the police."

"What changed the family's mind?" Jack pulled a stubby pencil and his moleskine out of a pocket and began taking notes. He'd filled hundreds of the little notebooks over the years and saved every one of them, a scribbled history of their time on the force. "I don't remember the last time a Chinatown victim's family or neighbors spoke with the police. Not willingly."

"The girl's fiancé went to his tong leaders to ask for vengeance on whoever killed her. No one knew anything about the murders or who might be behind them. Word spread that the killer was someone from outside the community and that the girl's parents had permission to talk to the beat cops. Mr. Sung was well respected. The tong wants his killer found. They might wage war on each other inside Chinatown, but the tongs don't like outsiders coming in and murdering their people."

Jack let out a low whistle. "Now I understand why the detective flagged the case file. How did the old man and his granddaughter die?"

Gabe settled the fedora on his head and slipped on his overcoat. He led the way into the lobby, stuffing his hands deep into his pockets and heading straight for the door. Air was as important as food. "I don't know. The family buried the victims before they reported the murder. Then they refused to tell the officers who took the report."

Jack stopped in midstride, green eyes wide with disbelief. "Wait. The tong allowed them to report the murders, but not how they died?"

"I didn't believe it either, but that's what the report says." He was rapidly losing his appetite, and the crawling sensation on the back of his neck was worse. Much worse. "I don't want to make too many guesses or draw conclusions yet. Not until we get a chance to speak to the family ourselves."

They stood in the middle of the crowded lobby staring at each other. Supposition and experience battled in Jack's eyes. Gabe waited his partner out, letting him think everything out and sort through what little they knew.

At the beginning of any murder case, they collected all the scattered details, the tiny bits of information they managed to dig out of dark places or that were handed to them. They didn't have near all the pieces yet. That took patience and time.

Jack finally nodded. "Answer a question, Captain Ryan, and then I'll let you buy me a steak. What are the chances that Mr. Sung and his granddaughter died the same way as Bradley Wells?"

They began moving toward the door and fresh air again. Gabe kept his clenched fists hidden inside his coat pockets. "I don't know. All the investigating officers could get out of the parents was that they couldn't anger the family's ghosts."

"Ghosts?" Jack pursed his lips. "We're already involving Dora in the Wells case. Maybe we should take her with us to talk to the Sung family."

"Maybe. We'll head over to Chinatown this afternoon and try talking to the girl's parents without Dora. If that doesn't work, we'll introduce them to Madam Bobet." His stomach continued to rumble, a consequence of skipping breakfast to wash dishes for Delia. If he was lucky, food would chase away the sour taste on the back of his tongue. "She might be able to convince the family their ancestors won't be angry if they speak to us."

"How is Dora, anyway? I don't think Sadie and I have seen her since we all had dinner. That was right after Stella's christening."

"I think she misses Daniel, but she'll never admit to that." Gabe shrugged. "The only one who really knows is Dora. She hasn't said much about his leaving and going home to Portugal."

"She won't. That would be admitting she's afraid he won't come back. I don't think it's much comfort to her that he's not in the middle of the fighting. Bringing Dora in to consult on a new case might be just what she needs."

"You're probably right." The idea of bringing Isadora in on the investigation soothed some of the uneasy feeling crawling over Gabe's skin. "Let's go find that steak. My treat."

It was midafternoon before he and Jack finished going through the burglary files. All the remaining shops had been empty at the time of the break-ins. Gabe found himself oddly grateful for that.

He gathered their notes and the files, locking them safely away in his desk. They hadn't found much that looked important, but the reports focused on the bare facts of the break-ins. In a city the size of San Francisco, burglary was all too common and unremarkable. Finding evidence that linked the robberies to the murders would take more digging, more questions.

Fog had moved in off the bay again, swirling in thick layers that hugged the sidewalks. A fine sheen of moisture coated Gabe's office windows. The streets would be slick with it too, making the drive to Chinatown slow.

Gabe and Jack shrugged into their heavy coats before leaving his office and crossing the front lobby. They'd almost reached the door to the street when shouting and a scuffle broke out near the desk sergeant's raised counter. Gabe glanced back, curious.

A man broke free of the knot of cops and civilians surrounding him, and dashed across the lobby. He ran hard, dodging around a patrolman and the two prostitutes in the officer's custody, and nearly knocked over an older, well-dressed gentleman. Officer Polk sprinted after him.

"Jack! Jack wait!" The man tripped over the hem of his coat and fell, scrambling to his feet again just as Officer Polk tackled him. Polk pulled the man's arms up behind his back and forced him to move toward the desk sergeant. The man kept shouting. "Jack, you have to help me! Please, Jack, please!"

"Archie? Archie, what are you—? Polk, hold off a minute." Jack wiped a hand over his mouth and muttered something too quietly to be heard. He started toward Officer Polk and the struggling suspect. "I'm sorry, Gabe, I can't leave yet. I know this man."

"Not a problem." Gabe took one look at his partner and went with him. Jack's face was chalky, ill looking. "This man is a friend of yours?"

"He was. I haven't seen Archie Baldwin in almost two years." Jack cleared his throat, subdued and serious. "He went to Europe and volunteered to fight with the Belgian army. I'd heard he was back. And I'd heard he'd changed."

Jack didn't need to say the words; Gabe saw the evidence of what the war had done in Archie Baldwin's face and wild eyes. He'd met other men with that same haunted expression, good men who'd joined the war in Europe believing in glory and an honorable cause. That belief didn't survive the horror of rats and mud-filled trenches, watching other men die on barbwire tangles, and the slaughter they couldn't escape.

"Shell shock," the doctors called it. Such an innocuous name for minds shattered on a barricade in hell.

Baldwin was unshaven, scruffy, and rough, as if he'd slept hobo-style in Golden Gate Park for days. His expensive serge suit and overcoat were filthy, shoes caked in mud or worse. His suit jacket was missing buttons, and a pocket hung half torn away.

Gabe got a good look at Baldwin's white dress shirt as Polk swung him back to face Jack. Rusty brown stains splashed the front, splatters that went from his collar to his untucked shirttails. Dark stains splashed the front of his trousers as well.

Blood. Too much blood to have come from the scratches on Baldwin's face and the backs of his hands. He spared a glance for his partner. Jack's face was closed off, careful; he'd come to the same conclusion.

"Oh thank God, Jack, thank God. . . ." Baldwin slumped in Polk's grip, sobbing. "You have to help me. I didn't know anyone else or . . . or where else to go. You're my only hope."

"I'll do what I can for you, Archie. We'll go someplace quiet and you can tell me all about it." Jack took hold of Archie's arm and gestured for Polk to let go. Baldwin sniffled and wiped his face on a sleeve, but didn't struggle or try to get away. "I'd like to speak with the officer who brought him in. Do you know who that was, Patrolman?"

Polk scowled and brushed at the front of his uniform, trying to remove specks of dried mud picked up during his struggle with Baldwin. "He's not under arrest, Lieutenant. Lewis pointed him out to me before he went off duty. Said this gentleman wandered into the station house and sat on the bench sometime early this afternoon. Officer Lewis thought the gentleman might be drunk and it'd be best to keep an eye on him. I've been watching him since my shift started. He's not drunk. I'd stake my reputation on it."

Gabe watched Baldwin from under the brim of his hat. His men were well trained. Anyone who staggered into the police station in the middle of the day and took a seat would come in for extra scrutiny as a matter of course.

That Baldwin's filthy, stained clothing drew special attention wasn't a surprise. He was dressed like a rich man who'd gone slumming on the wrong side of the tracks and found trouble.

A lot of trouble. Gabe unbuttoned his overcoat. "Did Mr. Baldwin say anything when he came in?"

"No, sir." Polk pulled a handkerchief out of his back pocket. He frowned and scrubbed at a spot on his sleeve. "Lewis asked if he could be of assistance. But Mr. Baldwin insisted he'd only speak to his friend, the sergeant. Wouldn't talk to anyone else, but he wouldn't say who his friend was either. He was quiet up until a minute ago, so we let him be. I'd have come to your office if I'd known he wanted to speak to Lieutenant Fitzgerald."

"We'll take it from here, Officer." Gabe exchanged looks with Jack and took hold of Baldwin's other arm. Two years ago, Jack had been Sergeant Fitzgerald, but Archie wouldn't know about his promotion. "Your office or mine?"

Jack made a face. "Neither. I don't want to risk that stench lingering. Let's find a free interrogation room until this gets sorted."

"Excellent idea." The stomach-turning smell was familiar, but Gabe couldn't place it. He quickly ran through a list of possibilities, from sun-rotted garbage and sewage to the stale smoke of rum-soaked Cuban cigars, and gave up. None of them matched the vague memory of smelling that same odor, an old memory from the days he and

Jack still walked a beat. Chasing it down could wait. Right now, other pieces of information were more important.

Finding out whose blood soaked Archie's shirt topped Gabe's list.

Six interrogation rooms lined a narrow corridor behind the desk sergeant's high perch. The cell block was behind a barred door at the end of the hallway, only a short walk for suspects who suddenly found themselves elevated to prisoners. They took Archie into the first open room on the left. Four plain, straight-backed chairs and a scarred pine table took up most of the space in the narrow room. Three plain lights hung on long cords from the high ceiling, casting bright spots of yellow light on the scuffed linoleum floor.

Gabe shut the door and leaned against it, arms folded over his chest. He wasn't looking forward to discovering Archie Baldwin's unpleasant secrets.

Jack steered Archie to a chair. Baldwin dropped onto the seat, staring at his shoes and hands resting on his knees. Tears slid down his chin, dripping onto the lapels of his overcoat and into his lap. He didn't look up.

"Tell me what's wrong, Archie." Jack dragged a chair from the other side of the table, flipping it around so that he straddled the seat. He gripped the top chair rail tight, knuckles bled white. "Why did you come looking for me this afternoon?"

"I couldn't think of anyone else. I need help, Jack." Archie sniffled and hiccuped. "Mandy's gone."

"Gone?" Jack's back stiffened and his tone grew fierce, insistent. "What do you mean by gone, Archie?"

"Gone . . . I don't know where she went. I can't find her."

Gabe raised an eyebrow at Jack. "Mandy?"

"Amanda Poe, heiress to the Poe and Blake Shipyards. Walter Poe died about six months ago. She's engaged to Archie. Or she was before he went to Europe." Jack swallowed, but didn't look away from Baldwin's face. "That's how I heard Archie had come home from Europe. Sadie and Amanda are friends."

Gabe briefly considered stepping in and taking over the questioning. Jack was personally involved here, maybe too involved to be impartial, but his partner was also the best interrogator on the force. No one was better at coaxing information out of a witness or a suspect. He decided to watch and wait.

And Baldwin, sitting there in his bloodstained, filthy clothing, was a suspect in Gabe's mind now. The knot that had been in his gut since he first discovered that Archie was Jack's friend tightened.

"Tell me what happened. Start from the beginning and take it slow." Jack put a hand on Archie's shoulder and gently shook him. The muscle twitching in his jaw gave lie to the soft patience in his voice. "Where is she, Archie? Where did Mandy go?"

Baldwin finally stopped staring at his shoes and looked into Jack's eyes. His face was slack, his eyes dull. "We . . . we went to a pacifist lecture. She told me to call her Effie, but the big man with her didn't like that. He told me to call her Miss Fontaine. Miss Effie Fontaine, evangelist for peace. She says God is against us fighting a European war. Mandy's wanted me to go for weeks so . . . so I'd understand. There was a reception after the lecture. I didn't want to go, but Mandy wanted to talk with Miss Fontaine again. She wanted . . . she wanted to tell her how much she enjoyed . . ."

He stopped speaking, staring blankly at the wall. Jack shook Archie's shoulder again. "Did you go to the reception with Mandy, Archie?"

"They served French wine. I thought it strange an evangelist would condone liquor, but Mandy just laughed at me. I remember her laughing. And . . . and she wouldn't stop. People were watching. Staring." He slumped back in the chair and covered his face with a hand. "Mandy's gone, Jack, she's gone. Please help me find her."

Gabe cleared his throat. "The reception was last night, Mr. Baldwin?"

"The lecture was Friday night. Downtown at a church." Archie suddenly came alive. He grabbed Jack's arm, eyes wide with fear and alarm. "What day is this? Is it Saturday? I can't remember! Oh please—tell me it's only Saturday."

"I'm sorry, I can't. Today's Monday, Archie, not Saturday." Jack's voice was soft, soothing. He pried Archie's hand off his arm and stood. "I need you to answer a question for me. How did the blood get on your shirt?"

"Blood?" Baldwin stared blankly at the dark stains down the front of his shirt and his trousers, as if Jack's calling attention to the condition of his clothing let Archie see for the first time. He brushed at his shirt halfheartedly at first, his efforts growing more frantic and violent when the blood stubbornly refused to vanish. "You're wrong, Jack. I . . . I must have spilled the wine. It can't be blood. Oh God . . . Mandy . . . please . . . it can't be. . . ."

Jack grabbed Baldwin's wrists, stopping him from ripping off his shirt. Archie surged to his feet and howled, the sound more wounded animal than man. With Gabe's help, Jack wrestled him back into the chair. "Calm down and listen to me, Archie. Listen! I'll find Mandy. She can't have gone too far. I'll find her."

Baldwin wilted as suddenly as he'd turned combative. He curled over his knees, rocking and sobbing.

Gabe opened the door and motioned the first two patrolmen he saw to come inside. Perry and Taylor were both tall and well muscled, hopefully more than a match for the shorter, slimmer Baldwin if he became violent again. "Mr. Baldwin, I need you to go with these officers. They'll help you get cleaned up and take you to a place where you can rest. Officer Perry will bring you some food if you're hungry."

Panic welled in Baldwin's eyes, but he didn't struggle as the two young officers took his arms. "Find her, Jack, please. Find Mandy. . . . I can't remember where she went."

"We'll find her, Archie." Jack clapped him on the shoulder. "You have my word. Now, go rest. I'll visit you later."

The door closed, the click of the latch a hollow echo.

"Christ, Gabe." Jack wiped his mouth with a shaking hand. He paced the length of the room, appearing as trapped and restless as Baldwin. "I don't know what to think. The man I used to know would never hurt anyone. Amanda said he'd changed, but she never let on to Sadie he was raving. If he's been this mad all along—"

"Don't jump to conclusions." Gabe dropped into the chair Baldwin had vacated. He set his fedora on the table, idly running a fingertip around the crown. "We don't know if Miss Poe is really missing or not, or if she has any notion that Archie thinks she's missing. This could all be a hallucination. Given what I've seen so far, I'm not inclined to trust his word on anything yet. We don't have any hard evidence, Detective."

"What about the blood on his shirt, Gabe?" He ripped off his plaid cap and slammed it down on the table. Jack raked fingers through his hair, looking anywhere but at Gabe. "All that blood is evidence of something heinous. It's not Archie's, we know that. The only question is whether it's Mandy's or someone else."

"One thing at a time." Gabe shoved the chair back. "Finding out if Amanda is safe at home is the first step. Where does she live?"

"Nob Hill, less than a block from my stepmother."

"That's where we look first. If Miss Poe is there, we go on to Chinatown. If not, we open a missing persons file and go to Chinatown in the morning." Gabe handed Jack his cap. "Do you want to call Sadie before we leave?"

"This isn't a conversation I'd want to have with my wife over the phone. I don't want to say anything until we know what happened to Amanda." Jack's expression was grim. He'd already resigned himself to the idea Baldwin was guilty. "I never thought I'd be praying for a suspect to be lying or delusional. And I sure as hell never thought I'd be thinking of Archie Baldwin as a suspect either. He was a good person until he went to Belgium."

"I'm guessing he's still a good person and that's why he came looking for you." Gabe waved Jack through the door. "Let's go. Edwards is still waiting with a car. Does Miss Poe have servants who might know her whereabouts?"

"A housekeeper, Maddie Holmes. Maddie's been with the family since right after Amanda's mother died. She has a daughter a year younger than Amanda. They grew up in the same house, but Lia moved away two years ago to get married." They hurried down the hallway and across the station lobby. Jack was a few inches shorter, but he matched Gabe's long strides. "Maddie keeps pretty close track of Amanda, especially since Mr. Poe died. I hope to God she'd call the station and ask for me if Amanda went out with Archie and didn't come home again. But not everyone thinks like a cop."

The tense, prickly feeling on the back of Gabe's neck returned. They threaded around patrolmen and civilians in the crowded lobby, finally pushing through the front door and reaching the fog-slick sidewalk. He buttoned his coat as they walked. Damp cold crept under his clothes, chilling his skin and digging down to the bone. Gabe flipped up his overcoat collar and quickened his pace.

Climbing into the backseat of the police car was a relief even if it wasn't noticeably warmer. Jack gave Patrolman Edwards the address. Edwards pulled away from the curb, slipping into fog-shrouded traffic slowly and carefully. Headlights on the passing cars formed glowing halos in the mist, an eerie sight, as if they traveled amongst a pack of mythical monsters.

Neither he nor Jack spoke on the slow drive to Nob Hill's mansion-filled streets, each lost in his own thoughts. Gabe's mind circled back to the same idea again and again.

No one had called to report Amanda Poe missing. That didn't mean she wasn't lost, needing to be found.

CHAPTER 5

Gabe

The house on Nob Hill was bigger than any of the neighboring mansions, large even by the standards of the rich and well off. A black iron fence that stood seven or eight feet tall closed off the entrance to the grounds and the front yard from the street. Double gates across the drive swung open at a touch from Officer Edwards. Gabe noted the ornate patterns and scrolls that formed the letter *P* in the center of each gate.

A gravel drive ran down one side of the house and continued to the back. Edwards drove the car up onto the paved crescent in front of the porch, parking near the front steps. Fog was thinner at the top of Nob Hill, a pearly mist that swirled with a life of its own but didn't obscure the view of the street and neighboring houses. The city and the bay below had completely vanished beneath a blanket of gray fleece.

Gabe climbed out of the patrol car and looked around, curious about Poe's house and the grounds. At first glance, he couldn't decide if the hulking structure was meant to intimidate or impress.

Like so many buildings in San Francisco, the Poe mansion was relatively new. Built in the first year after the quake, the mansion stood three stories tall, with rows of wood-framed windows on each floor, double-front doors, and a wraparound porch.

A riot of shrubs and trees filled the front yard, planted in clumps with islands of lawn between. Mulch-covered flower beds and winter-bare rosebushes softened the severity of the redbrick house front and edged the white columned porch. A gazebo showed at the back of the house on one side, a garage for motorcars at the end of the gravel drive on the other.

Jack came around from his side of the car. His overcoat was unbuttoned and flapped around his ankles, stirring eddies in the fog. He nodded toward the house. "Walter Poe wasn't shy about flaunting his fortune. Impressive isn't it?"

"Very." He climbed the slick stone front steps with Jack, unable to shake the feeling this had never been a home to Walter Poe's daughter, but a temple to wealth. Poe's shipbuilding empire extended up and down the entire California and Oregon coast. Gabe gestured toward the looming front doors. "How did Sadie become friends with Amanda? All this seems a bit outside her usual social circle. An heiress to the Poe fortune is someone your stepmother would cultivate. Sadie's more down to earth."

"Not all the hoity-toity are like Katherine. My stepmother is in a class by herself." Jack rang the doorbell. Chimes sounded somewhere deep inside the house. "Amanda's spent a big part of her life trying to deny she comes from one of the richest families on the West Coast. Sadie met her at a supper club. That was in 1910, if I remember right, just about seven years ago. Amanda was out with a group of friends her father never approved of, mostly because they didn't have enough money. Sadie knew some of the people in Amanda's group from school. They introduced Sadie to Amanda, and the two of them got on famously."

No footsteps sounded within the house and no one arrived to answer the door, so Gabe rang the bell again. Maybe they'd made the trip for nothing. "How much money was enough for Walter Poe?"

"If your last name was Hearst, Morgan, or Rockefeller, you might have enough money to associate with his daughter. Mr. Poe was always afraid people would try to take advantage of Amanda for her money. Occasionally he was right. She fell in with a few scoundrels." Jack peered in the narrow window next to the door and leaned on the doorbell. "I think months went by before Sadie found out who Amanda really was. They were fast friends by then."

Gabe frowned and hunched deeper into his coat. "Delia must know her too."

"She does. I think Amanda was a little too wild for Delia when they first met, but they got on well enough. By the time Amanda stopped trying to shock her father and run from his money, Delia had taken the teaching job in New York." Jack began pounding on the front door with his fist. Hollow, booming echoes rattled the windows next to the entrance. "Maddie, are you in there? Maddie! It's Jack Fitzgerald. Open the door!"

Gabe went back down the steps and surveyed the front of the house. "All the lights are on downstairs and on the second floor. Maybe we should go around to the back. It's a big house. The housekeeper might not hear us."

Jack beat on the door again. "Maddie! This is official police business. Open the door!"

A curtain twitched on the big window to the right of the door. Gabe got a glimpse of a middle-aged woman's face before the heavy lace panel dropped back into place. He took the steps two at a time, reaching the porch as the front door swung open.

Maddie Holmes's cerulean blue eyes peered suspiciously at the two of them through wire-rimmed spectacles, her gaze darting from Gabe to the car in the drive, and back to Jack. Her shoulders slumped for an instant before she caught herself and stood up ramrod straight. Bracing herself for the worst.

Amanda wasn't here. He knew without asking a single question and so did Jack. The slim hope he'd harbored that Archie Baldwin had only imagined his fiancée's disappearance evaporated, leaving a bitter taste in his mouth. Gabe put on the stoic face he wore when dealing with victim's families. The only thing in doubt now was just how terrible this would become by the time they found Amanda.

"Good afternoon, Lieutenant Fitzgerald." Maddie brushed back a strand of dark hair that had escaped her chignon. The nails on her long fingers were neatly trimmed, and small tasteful rings sparkled on both hands. "What can I do for you?"

"How are you, Maddie? This is my partner, Captain Ryan." Jack swept his plaid cap off and stuffed it into a coat pocket. "Is Amanda at home?"

"No, she went out with Mr. Baldwin." Her fingers curled around the edge of the door and she moved to stand in the small opening, blocking the way inside. "Has something happened?"

"That's what we're trying to find out, Maddie. We need to ask you some questions about Amanda." Jack smiled and moved closer, putting a hand on the doorknob. "May we come inside? These may not be easy questions to answer. The sitting room will be more comfortable for you than standing on the porch with the neighbors watching."

She bit her lip and nodded, pulling the door open wide. Once they were inside, she led them across an entryway bright with gleaming marble floors, polished rosewood tables, and gilt-framed portraits of old men wearing dour expressions. Her heels clicked softly on the white and rose-tinted marble, oddly in counterpoint to the ticking of the black walnut grandfather clock outside the sitting room door.

Gabe took the seat Maddie indicated, balancing his hat on the wide, upholstered arm of the chair. The sitting room was lavishly furnished, with red velvet cushions on brown leather chairs and a black horsehair sofa. A marble fireplace filled one wall, and tall, glass-fronted cabinets held porcelain figurines and decorated china vases. Paintings of pastoral scenes hung on either side of the fireplace, no doubt costly and done by a famous artist.

He took note of the rich surroundings, doing his job and remembering the details, filing them away in case they became important later. Most of his attention went toward studying the woman seated across from him.

A slight woman with gray just beginning to frost her temples, Maddie Holmes looked more like a society matron than a housekeeper. Her yellow silk blouse was spotless and likely expensive on a domestic's salary, her ankle-length black wool skirt freshly pressed and showing no signs of hard use. A sterling chain hung round her neck, holding a single red stone that nestled in the hollow of her throat. Gabe wasn't well versed enough in gems to tell if it was a large garnet or a small ruby.

Maddie wasn't dressed like any servant Gabe had ever encountered. She dressed like a rich man's mistress. He filed that information away to think about later.

For once Jack wasn't scribbling notes in his moleskin. Instead, he sat next to Maddie and took her hand, his voice gentle and kind. That was another skill his partner possessed that Gabe admired, the ability to know what a witness needed in order to talk. "Archie came into the police station today. He's in a terrible state, Maddie, and not making much sense. I'm not sure he's slept in days. Archie says he needs my help, that Amanda's disappeared and he doesn't know where to look for her. Have you heard from Amanda today? Can you tell us where she is?"

"I . . . I haven't seen Amanda since she left on Friday." She stared at the embroidery abandoned on the side table next to her, as if the piece of pale linen stitched with bright silk threads held the secret of where Amanda was or how to find her. Maddie took a deep breath and looked Jack in the eye. "I knew something was wrong when Amanda didn't come home. She's gone off with Archie for a night in the past, but that—that was before he came home from Belgium. Three days without a word isn't like her."

Gabe cleared his throat and leaned forward. "Mr. Baldwin said they went to a lecture together on Friday night. This lecture was being held at a church downtown, but he couldn't remember the name. Do you know which church?"

"I never heard her say." Maddie yanked her hand free of Jack's grip. "But Amanda had a handbill telling the time and place. Give me a moment, the notice should still be upstairs. I'll see if I can find it."

She ran from the room, leaving Gabe and his partner staring at each other in strained silence. Neither spoke until Maddie returned with a well-creased sheet of newsprint in hand.

"This is it." Maddie sniffled and brushed a tear from her face. She passed the paper to Jack. "The lecture was in the social hall next to the Lutheran church on O'Farrell. Amanda told me the pastor wouldn't allow Miss Fontaine to speak inside the sanctuary. Members of the congregation voted to rent the hall out instead."

Jack glanced over the handbill and handed it to Gabe. He read it just as quickly, noting the address, dates for more talks over the next few weeks, and the times each lecture was being held. Gabe tucked the handbill into an inside pocket. "Did Miss Poe tell you anything else about her plans on Friday?"

"They were going to supper first and then over to the church. Amanda was excited that Archie agreed to go with her to hear Miss Fontaine speak. Amanda's been trying to talk him into attending a lecture with her for weeks."

Gabe glanced at Jack. His partner nodded, a signal to go ahead. "So this wasn't the first time Miss Poe attended one of these pacifist lectures. How often had she heard Miss Fontaine speak?"

"Three or four times a week for the last month. She's become a devoted follower of Effie Fontaine and her message. Too devoted for my comfort. Amanda often trusts the wrong people." Maddie sat on the sofa, dragging one of the velvet cushions into her lap and hugging it to her chest. Her eyes glimmered with unshed tears. "The first talk Amanda went to was at a church hall in Oakland the week before Christmas. Miss Fontaine's message is that God doesn't want America to enter the war or fight in Europe. Amanda came home bubbling over with excitement, convinced it was God's will that she keep other men from becoming damaged the way Archie was hurt. That's all she's been able to talk about ever since."

"You've been a huge help, Maddie. This is the number where you can reach me at the station." Jack ripped a page out of his notebook and scribbled down the phone number for the sergeant's desk. "Call if you remember anything else or if you hear from Amanda. If I'm not in my office, someone will get the message to me. Captain Ryan and I can see ourselves out."

She crumpled the scrap of paper in her fist. "You must think poorly of me for not calling the authorities. But Amanda's run off before, when she was angry and quarreling with her father. I keep expecting her to come home just as she always has in the past. I keep expecting her to call."

"Thank you, Mrs. Holmes." Gabe stood. "We'll let you know as soon as there's any news."

He led the way across the entry hall and out the front door. The sun was sinking behind the cloud bank that covered the bay and stretched out to sea, leaching the last bit of fog-dimmed light from the sky. Transparent mist had become a solid wall of murky gray, smelling of salt and making it difficult to see the car parked at the base of the steps.

Jack stood with him on the porch, silent and brooding. Gabe fiddled with his cuffs and the collar of his coat, giving his partner a little time. They wouldn't find Amanda Poe tonight, not unless Baldwin suddenly regained his memory. The trail was cold. Any witnesses who might have seen Amanda on Friday night were scattered, likely unaware they'd seen anything of note.

Not many missing persons cases ended happily once families and loved ones called on the police for help. Gabe wasn't ready to give up on the idea of finding her alive, not yet, not until they knew more, but they needed a starting point. He'd been a cop long enough to understand that life didn't hand out happy endings often. As Jack and Sadie's friend, he wanted this case to be an exception.

Gabe wasn't in any hurry to start hunting for bodies. "Marshall Henderson, Dodd, and Baker are all on duty tonight. I want to send Marshall and Dodd out to see what they can uncover about Effie Fontaine and the people around her. It's long odds, but maybe they can find someone at the church who remembers Miss Poe and saw her that night before she disappeared. Baker's good at picking up gossip in taverns and on the docks. I'd like to know if there's any word on the street about the pacifist crowd."

"That makes sense. It's a good place to start." Jack peered at him. "What are you expecting to find?"

"I don't know. Maybe a zealot who believes her own message. Maybe a confidence artist after Amanda's money. I won't know until we start digging." Tendrils of damp air crept down the back of his neck, making the hair stand on end. He told himself it was just the fog and a cold January night, not anticipation of disaster. "The housekeeper made it sound like Amanda was deeply involved in Miss Fontaine's movement. Knowing how she was involved and who she associated with might give us a place to look. I don't want to risk Miss Fontaine leaving town before we get a chance to question her."

"And you can't bring Miss Fontaine in just because Amanda attended a few lectures, but she's the best lead we have." Jack glanced over his shoulder at the front door and lowered his voice. "I can't help thinking that something terrible happened to Amanda after that lecture. For the life of me, Gabe, I can't imagine why she'd stay away this long without getting word to Maddie. Not unless she can't come home."

"We don't know that." Gabe couldn't get the specter of Baldwin's bloodstained shirt out of his head. "We don't have proof of anything yet."

"What we do have is a probable suspect in her disappearance: Archie." Jack scuffed the toe of his shoe on the porch. "But I can't believe Archie Baldwin would hurt her. He just doesn't have it in him."

Maybe Archie truly was a gentle man before he went to war, but that war had changed him, changed the man he was now, today. Even Jack couldn't deny that.

But he might try, if only within himself. Gabe started down the steps. This was difficult for both of them, but more so for Jack. "If he was in his right mind, I might agree. I know he's your friend, but I can't dismiss the possibility he's responsible. If you need to excuse yourself from this case, I'll understand. I can square things with the chief too. Just say the word."

"Not a chance, Captain Ryan, I'll stick it out. I've got a stake in this case. If something has happened to Amanda, I need to find the person responsible. Even if that person is Archie." Jack swung open the car door and waved Gabe inside. "Besides, you need me. How many cases have you solved on your own?"

He let Jack's attempt at false bravado pass without comment. Gabe knew better than to take his partner's joke as a sign all was well and they'd go on as always. Things were far from well.

"Fine, you're in. But we treat this like any other case. No special treatment or considerations because Archie Baldwin is your friend. And the offer stays open. You can take yourself off the case at any time." Gabe paused before ducking into the car, studying Jack's face. "Agreed?"

"Agreed." Jack moved around the back of the car, head bowed and hands in his coat pockets, and climbed inside. He slammed the door, Edward's signal to drive away. "Once Henderson finishes digging up information on Effie Fontaine, what's our next move?"

"I want to talk to Baldwin again. Maybe his head will clear after a night in a cell and he'll remember more of what happened." Cold from the leather seat seeped through his coat. Gabe fidgeted, hoping it would warm up soon. "But I want to visit Chinatown early tomorrow morning before questioning Archie again. Lindsey's not going to let his son-in-law's murder alone for long. He wants results. And I don't want to give him reasons to start making noises about passing Amanda Poe's disappearance off to another detective. We'll figure out a way to work both cases. We've done it before."

"More times than I like to think about, Gabe." Jack pinched the bridge of his nose and sighed. "That doesn't mean I have to like working major cases this way."

"Neither do I, Jack. Neither do I." Gabe slid down in the seat, hands folded in his lap. The memory of Delia's smiling face was there as soon as he shut his eyes, a reminder. "How are you going to break the news to Sadie?"

"I don't know." The leather seat creaked and groaned as Jack shifted his weight. "How do I tell her Amanda might be dead and that Archie may have killed her?"

"You can't pretend nothing happened. Neither of us can. Tell Sadie as gently as possible and trust her not to fall apart. Delia isn't as close to Amanda, but she needs to know too." Gabe sighed and slid farther down in the seat, imagining delivering the news to Delia. "Then we hope like hell nothing we told our wives really happened. With luck, we'll find Amanda holed up safely with a new beau."

Jack cleared his throat, but his voice was still rough; choked. "Have we ever been that lucky, Gabe?"

"There's a first time for everything." Gabe burrowed deeper into his coat. He ignored the sensation of cold fingers brushing his cheek, and laid blame for the shivers rippling up his spine on the dampness in the air and the stubborn refusal of leather seats to warm beneath him. "But Amanda Poe's the one in need of luck. I'm more than happy to give her our share."

CHAPTER 6

Delia

I shaded my eyes, squinting in order to peer down our deserted street and hoping to see Dora come round the corner. My mother had maintained squinting was a bad habit, one destined to etch lines around my eyes at a young age. Undoubtedly she was right, but I couldn't help myself.

Bright sun and glittering pavement conspired to blind me, consequences of the first sunny day we'd had in a week. A brisk wind blew in off the bay. Rose canes on the trellis near the porch rattled, and overgrown frost-browned grass on neighbors' lawns rippled and swayed. Thin clouds skipped across the sky. Each cold, biting gust ripped them into finer shreds of sugar frosting spread over pale blue.

This winter had been unusually cold, with frequent frosts and snow dusting the East Bay hills. I'd kept my winter coat from the three years I lived in New York for traveling, and now I was doubly glad. My normal winter attire was much too thin for standing outside, waiting on Isadora's arrival.

Dora was late. Not an unusual circumstance with her, but I worried more since she'd acquired a Pierce-Arrow roadster and drove herself everywhere. She was an attentive driver, but mishaps happened too often on city streets. Each time she was tardy, I feared the worst.

As if my worry summoned her, Isadora's sleek black car careened around the corner. She tooted the horn and raised a hand to wave, her bright smile a serious rival for the sun. Even in brisk weather she kept the top down, claiming to relish the feel of wind in her face and hair.

I suspected that what she really relished were the admiring looks she received from those who saw her pass. Hats had a tendency to fly off as she drove, so Dora had taken to wrapping her bobbed hair in long, vividly colored scarves and letting the ends trail out behind in the breeze. Lately she'd taken to wearing brown leather goggles as well, reminding me a great deal of an aviator's photograph I'd seen in the newspaper. She looked very striking and rather dramatic traveling down the street that way.

With a slight squeal of brakes, the car slid to a halt at the end of our drive. Dora leaned and unlatched the door for me. "Hurry and get in, Dee. Matters with Mrs. Allen's poltergeist have taken a nasty turn, and I promised her we'd be there before noon."

"What happened?" Dora never tarried long at the curb. We were rounding the corner at the end of the block before I wrestled the door shut, slamming it hard to make sure the latch caught. "I spoke with her not two days ago."

Dora sounded her horn before zipping round a slow-moving furniture van. The driver of the van frowned and appeared angry, at least until he saw her smile and wave. "Most poltergeists are a nuisance, content with minor disruptions. Once in a great while, you encounter a poltergeist who harbors a grudge toward the living. Given that Mrs. Allen's has begun shattering mirrors, shaking bedsteads and flinging knives about, I'd say this ghost harbors an enormous grudge. At least one of her boarders is threatening to move out."

A gust of wind snaked down an alley as we drove past, threatening to send my hat winging toward the bay. I smashed it down and held on. Dora's habit of wearing scarves became more appealing each time I rode with her. "Broken mirrors sound dangerous."

"They are, but we spoke at length about how to deal with trickster spirits, Dee. The two of us should have no trouble with this ghost." She smiled brightly, a transparent attempt to reassure me. If anything, her attempt to calm my nerves made me more apprehensive. I knew Dora too well.

The speedometer crept up alarmingly, hovering near thirty miles per hour. I gripped the passenger door handle tighter, unsure whether this ghost or Dora's haste frightened me most. "We may have different ideas about what constitutes trouble. I'm in no hurry to face a spirit who enjoys flinging kitchen knives. I've had my fill of difficult haunts."

She glanced at me and went back to watching the road. "Did the ghost you told me about come back? The little girl?"

"For the last two nights. You were right, Dora. She's older and more determined than I'd imagined. This ghost is strong enough to evade all my protections, and to come and go as she pleases. She frightens me."

Dora stopped at an intersection, chewing her bottom lip and studying the traffic before finding an opening and darting across. We reached the other side and began climbing the hill. She looked at me again, frowning and obviously perplexed. "Delia . . . you haven't been frightened of a spirit in a long time. You've had no reason. What did this ghost do?"

"I've tried every charm and trick I know to banish her and forbid her entrance to our house. Nothing works. I might as well have flung the door wide and invited her to breakfast." I cleared my throat and swallowed. "I need your help, Dora. She forces her way into Gabe's dreams. I don't know how to stop her."

Dora's frown became a scowl. She jammed on the brakes and swerved toward the curb to park, drawing the stares of passersby and other drivers. The car rocked to a halt, shuddering from end to end as she shifted into neutral and swiveled to face me. "Tell me what happened, Dee, all of it."

She sat very still and didn't interrupt as I related all I remembered: Gabe's thrashing and muttering in his sleep each time the ghost appeared, the singsong chant, the man's voice, and the glimpse of a summer day before the ghost vanished. Each of the spirit's visits began and ended the same way. At the last, I remembered to tell her about the army of ghosts who'd followed Gabe home, not knowing what was important or what might help.

Dora continued to sit quietly once I'd finished, brows drawn down in concentration and red lacquered nails drumming a rhythm against the steering wheel. The drumming stopped and she sighed. "Did you tell Gabe he was in danger from this ghost?"

"No, not a word. I thought talking to you first and deciding on a plan of action was for the best. And I honestly didn't know what to say to him." Guilt soured my stomach. "Can you imagine the dinner conversation? 'Oh, by the way, darling, you're being haunted. I know you're not terribly keen on the idea, so I'll do my best to keep her from driving you mad.' We both know how well Gabe would take that, but not telling him feels wrong. I don't like keeping secrets from him."

"Nor should you. Your husband trusts you." Dora patted my shoulder and put the car into gear again. "Gabe believes everything you tell him about the spirit world. That gives you an enormous advantage over this ghost, Delia. On some level, he'll know the ghost is lying to him and fight her control. He won't succumb quickly or easily."

She pushed on the accelerator, and the car lurched away from the curb. I grabbed the corner of the windscreen this time and held tight. "So what do we do?"

"We carry on with what we had planned for the day. Rushing into things wouldn't be wise. We have time, Gabe's not in immediate danger. I want to consult my books and as you so colorfully put it, formulate a plan of action." Isadora gave me her best, most winning smile, but a smile couldn't disguise the anger in her eyes. "You have my solemn vow, Dee, I won't let this ghost harm Gabe. We'll find a way to send this spirit away. Now, put on a cheerful face for Mrs. Allen. She's worried enough."

The boardinghouse was just ahead on the right. Gabe and I had lived there for a few short weeks after we'd married; a way station between my moving out of the house I shared with Annie, Sadie, and Jack, and into our own. During that time I'd grown enormously fond of Mrs. Allen. She was a warm, loving woman who treated her boarders as family, not tenants.

Three shallow steps led up to a front door painted carmine and trimmed in soft white. Wooden frames surrounded the lace-curtained windows on all three floors, painted white to match the door. The front of the building was plain, weathered brick, a style that suited Mrs. Allen more than some of the garishly painted row houses on the block. Tiny bits of fuzzy green moss grew in the seams between brick and mortar, kept alive by an abundance of fog.

Dora parked in front of the house next door and gathered her things. Each stubborn ghost or haunting might require any number of herbs or arcane objects, so she usually brought along an assortment to cover most possible situations. Guesswork mostly, but she was right more often than not. She passed me a heavy basket, full of muslin bags that smelled of rosemary and nutmeg and thyme, and chunky white candles. Dora looped the handle for another basket over an arm and grabbed a canvas bag overflowing with sage and pine branches.

I put a hand on her arm to stop her from charging out the car door. "There's something else I need to tell you before we go inside. Gabe told me last night that Amanda Poe's gone missing."

"Missing?" Her mouth pulled into a hard, thin line. "She's run off before. I think it amuses Mandy to worry her friends."

"Not this time." I couldn't deny that Isadora was right. Knowing, and explaining, that this time was different left me queasy. "It's a police matter. Gabe has Archie in custody."

She appeared genuinely shocked. "He's arrested Archie? Whatever for?"

"Suspicion of murder." The words were difficult to say, bitter and awkward on my tongue. "They think Archie may have killed Mandy."

Dora scowled and waved a hand in dismissal. "Nonsense. Archie isn't capable of hurting Mandy, nor anyone else for that matter." She slid out of the car and came round to my side. "He deserted from the Belgian army because he couldn't bring himself to shoot anyone, not even the Huns. The idea of him murdering Mandy is ludicrous."

"Archie deserted?" Now it was my turn at shock and disbelief. "I hadn't heard anything from Sadie other than he was home. She and Jack must not know either."

"Very few people know." Dora removed her goggles, dropping them on the car seat. "Mandy took pains to keep the reason Archie came home and his condition quiet. I'd like to believe she did so out of concern for him, but concern for her social position is more likely."

I opened the gate and we strolled up the short walkway. The boardinghouse was set close to the street, with the majority of the grounds in the back. "From what Gabe said, Archie wasn't in his right mind. He stopped short of saying Archie was mad as a hatter, but not by much."

"I'm meeting with Gabe and Jack about the Wells murder case tomorrow afternoon. As long as Gabe doesn't think doing so will cause any harm, I'd like to speak to Archie myself." Dora reached the top of the steps first and rang the bell. "I've always been fond of Archie, much more so than Mandy. Maybe I can help sort things out."

The door opened wide. Mrs. Allen was expecting us, but her face lit up with relief. "Thank the heavens it's the pair of you. Come in, come in. I didn't think you'd ever get here, Dorrie."

I couldn't hide my amusement. Dora raised an eyebrow in warning, her stern expression promising no quarter if I dared make fun.

No one called Isadora Bobet pet names to her face. No one but Mrs. Allen. I coughed and looked away, biting my lip hard to keep from laughing.

"My apologies, Katie. We were delayed." Dora held her basket out in explanation, her expression contrite and utterly sincere. "Gathering everything took more time than I thought. Now, show me where all the trouble started. Dee and I will work out what to do from there."

Katie Allen was shorter than both of us, with wild iron-gray hair that hung loose to her knees, hazel eyes, and a kind, round face. Traces of her Yorkshire girlhood lingered in the way she spoke—as well as the way she viewed the world—even well into her fifties. She still wore full skirts that brushed the tops of her sturdy shoes, high-necked blouses, and long sleeves the year round.

"No harm done, you're here now to get this sorted. Follow me up to Mr. Baskin's room on the third floor." She lifted her long skirts ankle high and led us up the front stairs. "He's been away on business since the day all this mischief started or there'd be real hell to pay. Mr. Baskin is a meticulous man, neat and tidy to a fault. I rarely have to do more than dust his room or give it a good airing. That's how I knew right off something peculiar was going on."

I shifted the heavy basket to my other hand. Stair treads creaked with each step we climbed, a sound I'd grown used to in the brief time I lived in the house. "What happened?"

"The day Mr. Baskin left, I went in to open a window. This time of year rooms start to smell musty if they're closed up too long. Sometime in late afternoon it was, when the sun was hitting this side of the house." She frowned and clucked her tongue. "All his clothes and books were on the floor, like they'd been tossed in the air and left right where they landed. That isn't Mr. Baskin's way."

We reached the second-floor landing and I heard the sound of a woman singing scales. Her voice soared, hitting each note perfectly. I wanted to stand and listen, hoping she'd go on to something grand and wonderful, but this wasn't the time. I kept climbing stairs.

"This all started in one of the tenant's rooms, not downstairs in the kitchen?" Dora kept pace with Mrs. Allen, but her attention was focused on the upper floor. Trying to sense the ghost, as I was. "For some reason I thought most of the activity was in the kitchen. Broken dishes and such like. Was I wrong about that?"

"No, no, Dorrie, you weren't wrong. I tidy up each night before bed, but by morning I'm likely to find my kitchen a right mess. Put me in mind of my gram's stories about brownies and sprites back home in Harrogate. I even tried leaving out a bowl of milk one night as a peace offering." She unhooked a fat ring of keys from her belt and stopped in front of the room at the end of the hall. "But you asked where things started and that's right here, in Mr. Baskin's room."

A frosty wind blew under the door, twining catlike around my ankles. "Dora . . . this used to be Gabe's room."

Mrs. Allen unlocked the door and pushed it open. "Gabriel lived in this room for more than seven years before he showed the good sense to marry Delia. Mr. Baskin moved in last year."

"Really . . ." Her fingers tightened around the canvas sack and the glance she gave me was troubled, but Dora showed Mrs. Allen the cheerful face she'd urged me to adopt. "Dee and I will take care of everything up here. Why don't you make us a pot of tea? We'll join you in the kitchen once we've finished in Mr. Baskin's room."

"Don't think I can't see through what you're doing." Mrs. Allen shook her finger at Isadora, setting the ring of keys in her hand to jingling loudly. "If you want me out of the way, Dorrie, then say so. I'm not in the least ways dim. Chasing off haunts is likely something I shouldn't stick my nose into."

"You're right, Katie. I'd like you to go downstairs for your own safety." Dora set down the bag of pine branches and herbs before breaking off a sprig of sage. She rubbed the sage along both sides and the top of the doorjamb, leaving green streaks and pieces of crushed leaves on the painted wood. "Forgive me. I should have said so right off. Poltergeists are usually harmless and easily routed, but I'd rather not take chances."

"I thought as much." She sniffed and started for the stairs. "My gram was a hedgewitch. I've seen a few things in my day."

I held my tongue until Mrs. Allen was well on her way downstairs. "Tell me the truth. Do you think this is a coincidence?"

"That Mrs. Allen's haunting started in Gabe's old room?" Dora broke off a piece of pine and smeared yellowish, sticky sap over the sage. The combined scent filled the hallway, burning my nose and making me want to sneeze. "No, Dee, I'm afraid not. Coincidence happens so rarely with spirits, it might as well not exist. Most are single-minded and utterly focused on getting what they want. I wouldn't be at all surprised if Mrs. Allen's poltergeist is somehow tied to the ghost giving you so much trouble. What I can't be sure of yet is if she's determined to attract your attention or Gabe's."

"She doesn't want me. If anything I'm in the way." Any doubts vanished, replaced by the certainty that was true. All the new strangeness in our lives, from poltergeists inhabiting his old room to legions of ghosts on our front steps, revolved around Gabe. "I chase her away from Gabe and put obstacles in her path. And this spirit has never appeared when he wasn't home or given as much as a hint of her presence when I'm alone."

"I suspect you're right, but I'll reserve final judgment for now. The question I want answered is not only why this spirit appears to be focused on Gabe, but why now." Dora tossed the shredded remnants of sage and pine into Gabe's old room and pulled a clean white rag from the bag at her feet. She wiped her hands, pensive and thoughtful. "Causing trouble for Mrs. Allen is sure to lure Gabe into the thick of things one way or another. He dotes on Katie Allen, nearly as much as he adores his mother, and he'd never leave her to cope alone. He'd find help."

"Even if that help involves an apprentice and her teacher performing cleansing rituals on a Tuesday morning." I hugged the basket of candles and herbs to my chest. We'd done this a hundred times, but I was jittery and nervous. "I assume cleansing the house of spirits is what you have planned. Now would be the preferred time to tell me otherwise."

"Containment first and then hopefully some answers. Now, scoot inside before I seal the threshold."

We lugged the baskets and bag of pine branches through the door. I set mine down on the worn black and tan carpet next to the four-poster bed, grateful to be shed of the weight. The furniture was the same as I remembered: a tall, scarred oak chest; an easy chair and floor lamp under the window; a small washstand in the corner. But the personal effects on the washstand and atop the chest, the book left lying on the chair, place neatly marked with a green ribbon, all belonged to a stranger.

Nothing marked the time I'd spent here with Gabe, how comfortable and at home I'd been living in this room. I was an intruder now. That was an odd thing to contemplate.

Mr. Baskin's room was cold, but it was a natural cold, a consequence of the season. Windows had been flung open, letting in a strong breeze from outside that whipped the curtains up and down. Dora hurried to tug the sash down and shut out the wind.

"There, now the candles will stay lit. Give me a moment before we light them." She pulled off her gloves, walking the edges of the room with a hand outstretched, pausing to touch a picture frame on the wall, run a finger along the top of the chest, or brush her palm over the back of the easy chair. I stood near the door, waiting for instructions on where to place the candles.

Dora walked the circuit three times, her frown growing darker. She stopped in the center of the room and folded her arms over her chest. "Dee . . . close your eyes. Tell me what you sense and if you hear anything unusual."

I set the basket of candles at my feet. "What's wrong?"

"Maybe nothing." She sat on the edge of Mr. Baskin's bed, eyes narrowed and searching the corners of the room. "Humor me. I want to be sure before we continue."

I trusted Dora implicitly, but turning toward the windows bathed my face in sunlight and made shutting my eyes easier. The sounds of other tenants drifted up from the lower floors, a woman's laughter and the heavy tread of a man climbing the creaky stairs. Traffic noises carried from outside, a child's shout and a mother calling her son back to the yard. The smell of baking cookies chased the scent of Mr. Baskin's cologne from the room, making my stomach rumble.

"Nothing." Try as I might, I couldn't find anything out of the ordinary. I turned, Dora's sour expression confirming my instincts. "There's nothing here, not a trace of a spirit in this room. I'd swear no ghosts had ever entered Mrs. Allen's house, let alone caused the destruction she described. How can that be?"

"I wish I knew, Dee. The house is completely empty of spirits, too empty for a building of this age. Almost all old houses have at least one faded haunt hanging about. At the very least, I'd expect to sense residue of a spirit's presence before it passed from this world. I'd dearly love to know what happened to the resident ghosts." Dora stood, smoothing her skirt before pulling her gloves on again. She turned in a slow circle, peering at everything in such a way, I was certain she saw more than a shaving brush on the washstand, or a book left unfinished on the chair. "Katie Allen's not one to make things up or cry wolf just to draw attention. She's too solid and rooted in the here and now. I'm sure everything happened just as she said."

I looked around Mr. Baskin's quiet room, feeling the emptiness settle around me and endeavoring to remember if the boardinghouse had always felt so hollow. Perhaps I hadn't noticed. That I'd grown so used to the presence of spirits that a house without them felt unnatural was telling. "Dora, if it's not a poltergeist breaking Mrs. Allen's dishes and threatening her boarders . . . what is?"

"I wish all the answers that leap to mind didn't make my skin crawl. Ghosts aren't the only denizens of the spirit world. They're merely the most common and benign." Dora yanked open the windows, letting the windborne smell of salt and the sea fill the room again, and replace the dusty scent of sage and pine. "Do you remember the discussion we had on imps and fiends? Certain types of demons are said to devour older, weaker ghosts and assume the spirit's place. Demons must be invited inside deliberately, they don't wander into the realm of the living by accident. But that would explain the lack of haunts and house spirits here."

I stared. "Ghost-eating demons? You can't be serious."

Dora waved a hand in exasperation. "Of course I'm serious. But just because I used that as an example doesn't mean I'm convinced we're dealing with anything quite that dramatic. Chances are that Katie was closer to the mark in thinking something similar to brownies or sprites are at the root of her troubles. Trickster spirits are found everywhere."

The tightness in my throat eased, allowing me to breathe. I'd questioned my sanity for years before circumstances forced me to acknowledge that the ghosts I saw were real. That spirits sought me out was bad enough, but I'd learned to cope. I wasn't eager to repeat the experience. Suddenly, facing a poltergeist didn't seem all that bad. "All right. What do we do now?"

"We go down to the kitchen and have tea." Dora gathered up half the supplies we'd lugged in from the car and started for the stairs. I took the rest. "Afterwards, I'll burn some sage and sprinkle some rue and thyme on the windowsills, but that's mostly for show. Katie needs to see something tangible to believe in what we're doing. You used to live in this house, so I'll leave building wards to you. We should be able to keep out most harmful spirits."

My failure to keep one small ghost out of my home and away from Gabe still weighed on me. "I've not done well on that front of late. Are you sure?"

"Quite sure. There are methods of layering protections and weaving barriers I haven't taught you yet. I foolishly thought neither of us would ever need protections that strong. Not in San Francisco." Dora paused on the second-floor landing, shoulders tense, and looked back toward Mr. Baskin's room. "Obviously, I was mistaken. Evil has no regard for borders. The Great War is changing the world, and balances are shifting. I'd do well to remember."

A gust of icy air swirled down the stairwell from the top floor, chilling me through my winter coat and rising gooseflesh on my arms. Daniel was still trapped in Europe, subject to all the unsettling changes and dangers Dora spoke of. I refused to think of the tiny shivers rippling across my shoulders as an omen.

Open windows on a January day and a drafty old house. That's all it was, nothing more.

CHAPTER 7

Gabe

Gabe stared out the car window, struggling mightily to keep his impatience from getting the best of him. Traffic crawled along the downtown streets. Fewer horse rigs worked in the city every year, but the remaining horse-drawn cabs and delivery wagons clogged the roadways, slowing everyone down. Henderson navigated the car down side streets and shortcuts in an attempt to bypass the worst jams, but there was only so much that could be done.

That Jack hadn't said more than a dozen words since they left the station didn't lighten Gabe's mood. He wanted this trip to Chinatown over with and done.

He and Jack had met in his office early and gone to Baldwin's cell first thing. Both of them had hoped a night in a warm bed and a good meal might have helped Archie regain his senses. If anything, Baldwin was worse, cowering in the corner of his cell and whimpering each time Jack tried to speak to him.

They'd quickly given up trying to question Baldwin. Persisting was cruel, as much for the pain Jack felt as for the distress their questions caused Archie. He wasn't sure he could stomach that a second time.

Sadie had taken the news of Amanda's disappearance and Archie's incarceration hard, just as Jack feared. Any hope Sadie might have an idea of where Amanda was died pretty quickly. The two women hadn't spoken since Amanda's visit to deliver a gift for the baby. Weeks had passed since.

Henderson, Dodd, and Baker hadn't turned up much of anything on Effie Fontaine either, another disappointment. A few of the men drinking in the most popular dockside taverns had heard the name, but not much more. The same was true for the prostitutes working near the wharves. Gabe suspected Miss Fontaine didn't frequent the same social circles as Baker's and Henderson's contacts.

He and Jack had discussed other ways to track down information on Miss Fontaine and her followers before confronting her, but the Bradley Wells murder case and the trip to Chinatown came first. They'd agreed, reluctantly, to put off delving into Effie Fontaine's life until after they met with Dora that afternoon.

Secretly, he hoped Dora would put them on the road to catching Wells's killer quickly. He'd almost welcome her pointing out some obvious clue they'd missed and solving the case. Life, and police work, never resolved itself that cleanly, but he saw no harm in daydreaming.

Gabe knew which case was foremost in Jack's mind and the reasons behind his silence. He felt the same way. A strange sense of urgency—part experience, part instinct he couldn't quite explain—pushed him toward finding out more about Effie Fontaine.

Instinct and unexplained feelings were a poor basis for prioritizing investigations. They still didn't have any real evidence that Amanda Poe had come to harm or hadn't left of her own accord. Pressure from Commissioner Lindsey aside, finding the person, or persons, responsible for three murders should come first.

The stylized buildings on the edge of Chinatown, their sweeping, curved rooflines and bright colors designed to appeal to tourists, came into sight. Chinatown had burnt to the ground after the 1906 quake, leaving the residents homeless and impoverished, and on the verge of losing their place in the city. Some of the illustrious citizens of San Francisco had denied the Chinese survivors access to fresh water or food, content to let them die. Desperate times often brought out the worst in people, but he'd never understood that level of cruelty.

Gabe had heard the stories of tong elders begging to keep their homes, and finally convincing San Francisco's leaders that a rebuilt Chinatown would attract visitors from all over the world, enriching the city's coffers. Greed turned the tide in favor of San Francisco's Chinese residents, not compassion.

As they approached Sutter and Grant, his tolerance for delays and snarled traffic evaporated. He slid open the window separating the front and back seats. "Pull over and park, Marshall. We'll walk from here."

"Yes, Captain." Henderson pointed. "There's a space right over there."

He climbed out and slammed the car door, waiting for Jack to come around and join him on the sidewalk. The Sung family tea shop was dead in the center of Grant Street, at the heart of Chinatown. In 1905, still rookies and new on the force, he and Jack spent four months walking a beat in Chinatown. They'd endlessly circled up Stockton and Grant and Pine, avoiding the small alleyways and side streets that were too dangerous for a pair of rookie cops. Staying away from places they didn't belong kept them alive, and in the end, earned them a measure of respect.

Tourists were scarce this early on January mornings, visits from the police even rarer. They were the only white faces on the crowded street and garnered just as many suspicious stares as they had while walking a beat. But the whole point of walking was to be seen, to let the tong and Mr. Sung's family know they were coming. Surprising the family and their tong leader was a bad idea.

Tension knotted between his shoulders as he looked up and down the street. They were being watched, openly, with no attempt to conceal the watchers. Permission from the Sung family tong aside, someone didn't want them here. Gabe slipped his hands into his trouser pockets and worked at looking relaxed. "Stay with the car, Marshall. Keep your eyes and ears open. You have company."

"Yes, sir. I see them." Marshall Henderson pulled a battered nickel weekly out of his back pocket and leaned against the front fender. He spent so much time waiting with the car that he'd taken to carrying old copies of *Pluck and Luck* or *Secret Service* with him at all times. Other senior officers weren't so lenient, but Gabe let him read.

They set off walking and hadn't gone more than a few yards when Jack broke his silence. "Tsk, tsk, Captain. What would the commissioner say? Boredom is supposed to be a part of a patrolman's job."

"My dad always said boredom makes you lose your edge. I'll take his opinion over Lindsey any day. And we both know that Marshall never misses a thing." He nodded to the gray-haired old woman and the little boy with wide, curious eyes watching them from a doorway. She scowled and hurried the child inside. "Maybe you should try reading, Lieutenant Fitzgerald. Henderson tells me detectives in the weeklies always solve the crime. You might learn something."

"I read." Jack sidestepped two men carrying a heavy crate into a curio store. Straw sifted through the rough pine slats, leaving a trail on the sidewalk. "But my taste runs more to *Collier's* or Ring Lardner in *The Saturday Evening Post*. I get my fill of detectives and crime on the job."

Gabe smiled, grateful Jack was talking again. The car ride from the station house had been much too quiet. "Henderson is still new at this. Give him five years, and you won't be able to pay him enough to read detective stories."

Chinatown's streets were always busy, even at 10 A.M. on a Tuesday. Early-morning delivery vans lined the curbs, unloading crates of live ducks, chickens, and tubs of iced fish outside restaurants and markets. Sacks of rice, weighing fifty pounds or more, were handed down from truck beds and carried inside. Men on bicycles wove around motorcars, and women weighed down by shopping bags or small children darted across traffic.

The scent of incense wafted from open windows, mingling with the clouds of tobacco smoke that formed around the heads of old men standing on street corners. Other scents filled the air as well, a sweet, sickly odor seeping out of alleyways and drifting up from boarded-over basement windows.

Gabe stopped, staring down an alley and aware of the hostile glares from a group of young men near the opening. Memories of a nighttime raid in Chinatown when he and Jack were rookies flooded back. More than half the men they'd pulled out of that reeking maze of narrow hallways and closet-sized rooms were so deep into opium dreams, they didn't know they'd been arrested. He hadn't been able to get the smell out of his uniform.

That he'd forgotten, even for a little while, baffled him. He'd had nightmares about the stench in those rooms for weeks afterwards. "Jack . . . do you smell that? I couldn't place it before, but now I'm positive Archie Baldwin's clothes stank of opium."

"Christ Almighty. That new guy over in vice, Haskell, claims all the dens were shut down." Jack paled, his always-fair skin suddenly bleached of all color. He took a step into the alley. "Archie was gone for three days. No wonder he can't remember what happened to Amanda or where he was. He's damn lucky to be alive. Christ!"

More young men, all of them well muscled and rough, moved away from sheltered doorways and niches along the alley and toward Jack. The group near the mouth of the alley moved closer as well. Gabe took his partner's arm and hustled him down the street.

"It's one more thing to question Baldwin about. Assuming he ever regains his memory." One more piece of evidence that might damn Archie Baldwin as a murderer. Gabe looked over his shoulder. The young men from the alley clustered around the mouth, watching, but showed no interest in following them.

Certain things had changed since the 1906 fire destroyed

Chinatown. Tongs no longer waged open warfare and the days of the highbinders were over, but there were still places Gabe wasn't willing to venture and risks he wasn't willing to take. Captain Haskell could claim to have Chinatown under control all he wanted. That didn't make it so. The men he'd spotted watching him and Jack made him doubly cautious. Two outsiders—two cops—could still disappear without a trace.

For that matter, so could an heiress. Chinatown might hold more secrets they needed to unearth beyond how Mr. Sung and his granddaughter died. That thought disturbed him, as did the prospect of needing to search for Amanda Poe in hidden rooms and basements along the maze of side streets and alleys in Chinatown. He wouldn't wager much on their chances of finding her alive.

Gabe took note of the shops on either side of Grant and the names of the side streets near the alley. He'd bring the entire squad if he and Jack were forced to come back.

Two blocks later, they found the Sung's teashop. A cheap plate glass window, full of ripples and imperfections that distorted Gabe's reflection, took up the entire front of the shop. The name, BLUE TIGER TEAS, was rendered in both English and Chinese in a garish, gold script meant to catch the eye of tourists. Wooden latticework, painted a dull and faded red, framed the window.

The shop was empty this early in the day. Chairs sat upended atop the tables, the shade half-drawn on the front door. Long shelves along the back wall held rows of painted teacups, jars of loose tea, and small figurines for the tourists: good-luck cats, tigers, and dragons. A light shone behind a bead curtain over a doorway into the back room. Someone was in there.

"Do we knock or just walk in?" Jack nodded toward the silent crowd gathering across the street, acknowledging they were being watched. Two white-haired men standing at the front bowed respectfully. A third man, his short, dark hair liberally streaked with gray and a strip of black cloth tied around his shirtsleeve, started toward them. "Something tells me the family knows we're here."

"They've known since we parked the car." Gabe removed his fedora, letting it dangle from his hand. "Take off your hat, Jack. My guess is that this is Mr. Sung's son."

"Captain Ryan? My name is Sung Zao." Zao bowed his head, but didn't smile or offer his hand. He was tall and thin, his trousers and shirt hanging loosely on his frame. "My uncle Wing is head of our family now. He sent me to ask if you would meet with him about my father's death."

"Certainly." Gabe gestured toward the tea shop door. That Zao hadn't mentioned his daughter's death struck him as odd, but maybe the loss was still too raw. He'd wait and bring the girl up with the uncle. "Is your uncle inside?"

"No, Captain. This is my shop, my wife and children's home." Zao frowned. "My uncle wishes to meet you at the herb shop he ran with my father. I can take you there if you like."

Gabe exchanged looks with Jack. Neither of them had expected an invitation to the crime scene. "I'd appreciate that, Mr. Sung. Thank you."

Zao nodded and led the way farther down Grant. People stepped out of the way to let them pass, moving back to block the sidewalk once they'd gone by. Gabe glanced over his shoulder, both curious about why their visit had attracted such a crowd and wondering if he should worry. The faces looking back at him appeared just as curious about what he and Jack were up to with Zao. He stopped worrying.

He cleared his throat, gaining Zao's attention. "I wondered if you could answer a question for me, Mr. Sung. Why did your uncle choose the herb shop as a meeting place? I assumed the family—"

"Would still be mourning? We are, Captain." Grief overshadowed Zao's face, there and gone in an instant. He turned onto a small side street and then down an alley lined with a mixture of clothing shops, gambling parlors, and what Gabe guessed to be brothels. Doors slammed at their approach, and any curious faces hid behind the curtains on second- and third-story windows. This was a part of Chinatown the tourists never saw.

The alley was a dead end, terminating in a brick wall marred by streaks of black paint and scraps of faded handbills in Chinese, chips and deep gouges. Tall, burly men lounged against the bricks and sat on upturned boxes, smoking and eyeing the two cops coming down the alley. A few of the younger men studied Jack and Gabe, openly curious. The older men didn't try to hide their hostility.

Zao stopped in front of an unmarked door, the last on that side of the alley and only a few yards from the brick wall. White paper covered the front window, hiding what was inside. "My uncle is a powerful man, Captain, and well respected in our community. The only reason you're here is that he believes you and Lieutenant Fitzgerald will be of help to our family."

Water dripped from an awning above the door. A drop of cold water found its way down Gabe's collar, making him shiver. "The department will do everything we can to catch whoever killed your father and daughter, Mr. Sung. You have my word on that."

"You misunderstand me, Captain Ryan." Zao opened the door and bowed them inside. "Uncle Wing wants your help in finding my father's ghost."

That brought him up short. "Your father's ghost?"

"My uncle will explain." Zao gestured toward the rear of the darkened shop. "Please, Captain. He doesn't like to be kept waiting."

"I told you we should have brought Dora." Jack clapped him on the shoulder and strolled inside, pretending a nonchalance Gabe didn't believe. "You owe me lunch for a week."

Zao waited patiently until Gabe followed his partner in before shutting the door. The bell over the entrance jangled and fell silent. Electric lamps hanging from the tall ceiling and in fixtures on the walls shone brightly, filling the interior of the shop with light. He turned in a circle, looking for Mr. Sung. By all appearances, he and Jack were alone.

Jack kept his hands stuffed in his pockets as he surveyed the inside of the shop. He rocked back and forth on his heels, and whistled softly. "Does this remind you of anything?"

"Wells's shop." Labels on the few crocks and jars still on the shelves were written in Chinese characters, but discolored rings on the painted wood showed where many more missing containers once sat. The resemblance to the store where Bradley Wells had been killed was undeniable. Gabe nudged a half-hidden shard of pottery with his shoe, sliding it out from under the edge of a display case. "Someone made an attempt to clean up."

Jack wiped a finger over a shelf and sniffed the power sticking to his skin. He made a face. "They didn't do a very good job."

"No, Lieutenant. My neighbors didn't do a good job at cleaning. I stopped them before they could finish." An older Chinese man stood in a doorway at the back of the shop, a tray of steaming tea-cups balanced on his hands. A silk wall hanging swayed back into place as Sung Wing moved into the room, hiding the entrance once again. "They meant to spare me the pain of seeing my shop in ruins, but I needed things left as they were. Now, come, sit and share tea with me. Then we can talk."

A latticework folding screen sat near a display case to the right. Wing put the tray on top of the case and pulled back the screen to reveal a round table and four chairs under a small window. Gabe took the chair near the window. A small flower garden, no bigger than a closet and with most of the plants winter brown, grew just outside.

"That garden gave my brother great joy. Given a choice, Liang would have been very happy as a cabbage farmer in Sacramento." Mr. Sung poured pale green tea into cups and offered one to each of them. "But our family and business are here in San Francisco, so he stayed. Now I wish I'd let him buy the farm he wanted so badly."

Gabe took a sip of the sour-tasting tea and put the cup aside, politeness satisfied. Status and rank meant more in Chinatown than skill at questioning a witness, so he took the lead while Jack took notes. "Mr. Sung, I'm very sorry about your brother and your great-niece, but I need to ask you some questions about how they died. Lieutenant Fitzgerald and I believe that their deaths may be related to another murder case we're working on. Any information you give us may help bring this killer to justice."

Most Chinese men wore their hair cut short and Western-style clothing, but Sung Wing's ash-gray hair was braided into a queue that hung below his waist, and he wore traditional loose trousers and a tunic. Gabe had met a few other Chinese men who clung to tradition and the old ways, but not many. The ones who stood out in his memory were the ones who stubbornly refused to involve the police in anything, no matter what the cost.

But Sung had asked them to come. That gave Gabe a modicum of hope he might get some answers.

"Captain, I will tell you what I can." Sung Wing put down his cup and sat up, straight and unbending. "Ask your questions. Both of us need answers."

Jack shifted in his chair, drawing Mr. Sung's attention. Gabe let his partner ask the questions. "Forgive me, sir, but this won't take long. Our other victim, Bradley Wells, was found murdered in the back room of his father's drugstore. The shop had been vandalized and all the medicines in the back room stolen. Something similar happened here. What did the murderers steal?"

"Powdered seeds and herbs." Anger sparked in Mr. Sung's eyes. "They left my brother's gold and jade. Liang and the girl died for sleeping potions."

"And none of your neighbors saw anything unusual?" Jack glanced up from scribbling in his notebook. "Any strangers?"

"Nothing." Mr. Sung frowned. "Before I'd have said no one could reach my door unseen, friend or stranger. These men must be made of shadow."

"One last question, Mr. Sung, and we'll leave you in peace. Your family waited until after the funeral to go to the police." Gabe cleared his throat and looked the old man in the eye. "Why is that? How did your brother and his granddaughter die?"

For an instant, Sung Wing held his gaze, proud and defiant, and

Gabe was certain he wouldn't answer. But Sung turned away, staring out the window at his brother's garden. Despair and grief settled over his face, aging him. "My niece did not die quickly. They beat her and cut her face. I had her cremated to spare her mother and father the sight of what had been done to their child. Her mother named her Lan, orchid, and I wanted them to remember her as beautiful. But Sung Lan's spirit was still here and whole. I was able to send her ghost to be with our ancestors."

He'd heard almost the same words spoken by Delia, by Isadora, countless times. Zao had said his uncle was a powerful man. The way Gabe thought of Mr. Sung changed, twisted into a different definition of power. "And Sung Liang? How did he die?"

"His throat was cut. Then the men who murdered my brother bled him like a suckling pig and stole his ghost." Mr. Sung shuddered and gripped the edge of the table. "In China they still tell stories from long ago of sorcerers who stole souls. But China is an old land, with a long memory. I didn't think such things could happen here."

The roiling in Gabe's stomach was more than instinct, more than a hunch panning out. He didn't need to see the bodies of the old man and his granddaughter, or if they'd been laid out the same way, or the wound gaping in Sung Liang's throat. He *knew* Bradley Wells had been killed by the same people, for the same twisted reason.

And knowing shook him. Ritual killings and stolen ghosts were far beyond the boundaries of normal detective work. He couldn't avoid involving Delia and Isadora now.

Gabe pushed back his chair and stood. "Thank you, Mr. Sung. You've been very helpful. I promise Lieutenant Fitzgerald and I will do everything in our power to bring these killers to justice."

"Help me find these men, Captain Ryan. We must stop them from killing again." Mr. Sung swirled the cup and poured the rest of Gabe's tea into a saucer, leaving sodden black leaves coating the bottom and sides. He turned the cup in his hands, peering at the patterns clinging to smooth white porcelain. "Justice will take care of itself."

Gabe gestured toward the teacup. "Is that what you see in the tea leaves?"

Sung Wing looked up and smiled. "Reading tea leaves is a trick for the tourists. Good day, Captain. Sung Zao will contact you if I learn anything more."

They'd reached the front door when Sung called out to him.

"Captain Ryan." The old man still cradled the teacup, his expression grave. "Be careful."

Gabe touched the brim of his hat and nodded. "You too, Mr. Sung. You too."

They were back on the main street and headed toward the car before Jack said anything. "Tell me if I'm wrong, Gabe. Mr. Sung wants us to find the murderers so he can have them killed. He's not interested in justice."

"No, you're not wrong." He hunched into his coat, attempting to hide from the cold wind burrowing into his bones. Sung Wing might be plotting revenge, but Gabe wouldn't let him get away with it. "Let's get back to the station. Maybe Baldwin's come to his senses."

CHAPTER 8

Delia

Mrs. Allen gave us tea and then insisted on feeding us lunch. She thought it only fair after all the trouble we'd gone to in her behalf. Dora smiled and upheld the conversation, chatting with Katie Allen about what it was like to grow up in Northern England and why she'd come to America. I answered when spoken to, but otherwise I was content to listen.

In actuality, we'd done very little, but there wasn't much we could do. Yet I couldn't shake the sense that we'd deceived her and that, somehow, we should have made good on our promise to end her troubles. I'd feel worse if Mrs. Allen woke tomorrow to find her kitchen a shambles again. All through lunch I'd searched for the slightest sign of ghosts, but the house held no trace of any spirits that Dora or I could roust.

The emptiness was disquieting in light of what Dora had said about demons and ghosts being eaten. Still, I couldn't quell the faint hope all Katie's Allen's problems had ended.

We said our good-byes and went back to the car. Dora adjusted her scarf and eased away from the curb. I did my best to ignore her sidelong glances as she wove around a slow-moving ice wagon blocking the road, a horse-drawn vegetable cart, and a delivery van full of rolled carpets. Ignoring that we were headed downtown instead of

home once we'd left Mrs. Allen's neighborhood proved more difficult. "Where are we going?"

"To meet with your husband and Jack at the station. I meant to
say something before, but I got caught up talking to Katie. This
shouldn't take long." Even with her driving goggles on, Dora managed to give me a long, measuring look, gauging my reaction. "I
spoke with Jack last evening about the Bradley Wells case. Photos of
the murder scene are going to be extremely difficult for me to view,
doubly so if Gabe is right about occult involvement. Jack understands
that handling anything from the crime scene is out of the question.
It's much too soon. I promised I'd do my best, but this will be less of
an ordeal with your help."

Dora and I interacted with the spirit realm in different ways. I'd
touched ghosts before, felt the instant of death and life leaving their
bodies. Even violent death was endurable if the agony was a momentary echo.

Isadora wasn't so fortunate. A victim's pain and suffering lingered long after death, a kind of aura that clung to their clothing,
objects they'd touched, or even furnishings that had been in the
room when they'd died. That suffering engulfed Dora, forcing her to
relive every second of agony before a person's death. Putting myself
between her and evidence from a murder investigation spared her
the brunt, and left me none the worse for the experience. "You need
me to act as a buffer."

"For some of the evidence, yes. None of it will be pleasant, but I
should be able to look at the photographs. Where I'll need your help
is if faced with the cloth that covered the body. And I may be forced
to that, Dee. After listening to Jack's description of how they found
Bradley Wells . . . I'm afraid Gabe's hunch is right. An element of
the occult is involved." We turned left onto Montgomery and traffic
slowed to a crawl. Dora frowned, craning her neck to peer ahead and
spot what had caused the delay. "Whether the killers are experienced practitioners or not, the sooner we get this sorted, the better.

Just dabbling in rituals can stir up powers best left slumbering. Once set free, containing them again is difficult at best."

"Like opening Pandora's box." Traffic moved so slowly, I felt safe loosening my death grip on the door handle. I rubbed feeling back into my hand, shutting fear of the unknown away for later. "And you and I will be in the thick of everything."

Dora nodded, her smile grim. "Very good, Dee. You do pay attention occasionally. I'd dearly like to be wrong, but I suspect someone has already set things in motion. Once Gabe and Jack discover who is responsible, putting things right in terms of the spirit realm will fall to us."

Broadway wasn't far ahead and the police station only a few blocks farther along. People had gathered at the intersection with Montgomery, standing on corners and spilling into the street, blocking the roadway. The sound of cheering and music echoed between buildings, and I imagined I heard a few people booing as well. Patrolmen on horseback ranged back and forth at the rear of the crowd.

Other officers rode a ways down Montgomery to speak with motorists, pointing out side streets to either side. Cars turned down the smaller avenues as directed, but some of the drivers shouted back at the policemen, shaking their fists and obviously angry.

Dora watched the mounted officers, eyes alight with curiosity. "How odd. Did Gabe mention anything unusual happening downtown today?"

"No. Not a word. He probably didn't know." I grasped the top edge of the windscreen and stood, trying in vain to see past stopped cars and over the heads of people blocking the intersection. A gust of wind nearly stole my hat and I took that as a sign to sit down again. "I wonder if it's another peace demonstration. The organizers seldom give advance warning to the police."

We continued to inch forward. I had to admit to being as curious as Dora to know what was happening. One of the mounted officers, an older man I didn't recognize, approached Dora's car. He frowned at the sight of Dora's goggles, deepening the creases in his sun-browned face, but nonetheless tipped his hat. "Good afternoon, ladies. I'm Patrolman Delano. If you mean to watch the parade, you're too late. Speeches have started already."

A huge cheer went up from the crowd, followed immediately by a raucous chorus of hisses and boos. Whatever the subject of the speeches, the speaker drew a strong reaction from both supporters and naysayers.

The sun was directly behind Officer Delano, and I was forced to shade my eyes in order to see his face. "We're meeting my husband at his office downtown. Perhaps you could tell us why the way is blocked and suggest an alternate route."

"Oh yes, please tell us what's happening. I'm about to perish of curiosity." Dora tipped her head and peered up at him, her smile bright and guileless. "I hope you'd warn us if there was any danger."

I'd come to gauge a man's strength of character by how completely he succumbed to Isadora's smile, or if he managed to avoid being overcome. Officer Delano was sorely lacking in that regard. He flushed a deep shade of red that crept all the way up under his hat and stammered. "No, no, nothing for you to fret about, miss. Last week it was the pacifists marching up Geary. Today those suffragette girls are making a nuisance of themselves. They've blocked the streets with their floats and speaker's stands."

She acted the carefree spirit, but Isadora believed passionately in women's suffrage. Sadie and I did as well, and the three of us had attended suffrage pageants together before Stella was born. California had given women the right to vote years before, but the fight still raged in other states. Dora's smile faded. "Really . . . You don't think women should be allowed to vote, Officer Delano?"

"No, miss, I don't hold with ideas like that. And I won't allow my daughters to vote either. Not while they're still living under my roof." He pulled his horse around, putting some distance between his mount and the car. "You best be on your way before the crowd breaks up. The next street on the right runs the same as Broadway. It should get you where you're going."

A storm brewed on Dora's face, one that promised to break over Patrolman Delano if we lingered much longer. I touched her arm. "We really should be on our way. Gabe and Jack are waiting."

"You're right, we should leave. I've heard enough." Dora gave Delano a final, chilly glare and shifted the car into gear. She drove around the corner slowly and carefully, a measure of how angry she was. "If we ever have the misfortune to encounter Officer Delano again, remind me to tell him the tale of Pandora's box."

Dora possessed enormous amounts of knowledge about the world and the evil people were capable of, yet the stubbornness of closed minds continually surprised her. In some ways, I felt more worldly. "Perhaps we should recruit his daughters to instruct him. The lid is already off the box in his household."

Afternoon clouds were beginning to blow in off the bay, transforming cheerful blue to dismal gray and adding more of a damp chill to the air. Huge vees of brown and black Canada geese, pale snow geese, and pintail ducks flew toward the wetlands around the bay. The leaders' raucous cries were answered by all the birds following behind, a call and response designed to keep any in the flock from becoming lost. Yet lost and alone was how geese always sounded to me, searching endlessly for someone or a place never found.

I pulled the fur collar of my coat up under my chin, determined not to give in to a sudden onset of melancholy. "How did your visit with Sadie go yesterday?"

"Well enough. Sadie's always tired and she's still not up to much socializing in the evenings, but that's to be expected. I cooed and made eyes at the baby while Sadie looked on proudly. The entire time, Stella smiled angelically and did her best to win my affections. She seems to have inherited her mother's irresistible charm." Dora gave me a sidelong look, the weight of unsaid things in her eyes. "Sadie misses you, Dee. I gathered that Jack and Annie have both tried to smooth things over, but she knows you're avoiding her even if she doesn't understand the reason. To be honest, neither do I."

"That makes it unanimous. I'm not entirely sure I know why or that I can explain, but staying away seems best for now." Sadie had taken to motherhood and caring for Stella with the zest she'd once reserved for conquering high society or collecting gossip. She was completely and deliriously happy. I didn't want anything to spoil that for her. "Each time I think about visiting Sadie, I grow uneasy about being near the baby. Telling myself it's foolish and trying to go anyway makes me queasy. I want to see Sadie, and the baby too, for that matter, but I'm afraid to."

"Afraid?" She gave me a startled look. "Whatever are you afraid of?"

"Disaster." I tugged my coat tighter around, fingers growing stiff and cold inside my kid gloves. "That I'll be the one to bring tragedy down on Sadie and Jack's heads . . . or lead calamity to them. And I'm perfectly aware this feeling doesn't make any sense. Knowing hasn't helped in the slightest."

"This isn't at all like you, Delia." The corners of her mouth turned down slightly, her usual expression signifying deep thought. "Is this feeling tied to the dreams you told me about earlier?"

"About the little girl? I'm not sure. Let me think." Placing blame on the small ghost was tempting, but certainty was more important. I tried to remember, going back over the last few times I'd seen Sadie. "The need to stay away came over me gradually. It wasn't as if I woke up one day knowing I should avoid Sadie and the baby. But I can't remember when the dreams started either, not for sure. The two could be tied together."

"My guess is that one emanates from the other. An unusual amount of spirit activity is centered on you and Gabe right now. And a touch of fear over aspects that you don't understand might be perfectly reasonable and wise." Dora waved back to a little boy waving from a street corner, her bright expression at odds with our grim conversation. "All things considered, I'm not inclined to dismiss your aversion to seeing Sadie out of hand. I can't say with any certainty that you're jumping at shadows. The strong possibility exists that all this strangeness originates from one source."

I sighed, shaky and uncertain as any tragic heroine in a dime novel. "If that was meant to reassure me, I think you fell short of the mark. Perhaps I should go back to questioning my own sanity. At least that's familiar ground."

"You know I won't varnish the truth." Dora's tone was stern and matter-of-fact, but the amused gleam in her eye spoiled the effect. "We need to look at all the possibilities if we're to ferret out what's really going on. Now, buck up. We still have to deal with the unpleasantness of your husband's murder case. And as long as we're here, I'll attempt to check for any signs of that nasty little ghost's influence on Gabe. He'll be too distracted by your presence to notice a little hocus-pocus on my part."

I flushed, heat creeping up my neck and burning bright in my cheeks.

Dora laughed. "Gabe notices very little when you're in the room. I'm not above using that to my advantage."

We'd passed the tail end of the parade and resulting crowd, and made our way over to Broadway only two blocks short of our destination. Dora parked the car a few doors down from the police station. The intersection near the station was always busy. Motorcars passed through in a constant stream, and the policeman operating the rotating traffic signal couldn't let his attention flag for an instant. Newsboys stationed on each corner shouted out headlines for the afternoon papers, each vying to attract the most customers.

I stood beside the car and waited quietly for Dora to gather her things, struggling against the pull to watch ghosts keep pace with the living, or tread paths that ran through walls or parked cars. More new ghosts roamed San Francisco each day, confused and lost young men who'd died in the Great War. Many didn't realize they were dead and continued to fight an enemy that wasn't there. Others had died in horrible pain, drowning as gas ate away their lungs.

All ghosts carried markers of their death. These phantom soldiers were tainted by terror and the horrors they'd endured. I desperately wanted to lay them to rest and ease their passage, but there were far too many.

London and Paris must be thick beyond imagining with wandering spirits. I counted myself lucky to be in San Francisco. Living in Europe would drive me mad.

A flash of light drew my attention to a spot across the street. Ghosts clustered in a doorway, staring at the front entrance of the police station. Another bright flash, and another, and more knots of ghosts appeared along the curb, against the walls, and in other doorways across the street. Mixed among the patient dead were the ghosts of far, far too many children, none older than seven or eight.

Sick certainty settled in my stomach and I couldn't look away. These ghosts had no interest in me or Isadora. They wanted Gabe.

Dora took my arm, breaking the trance. "Don't let them hold you like that, Dee. You know better. That rather dramatic manifestation was staged for the sole purpose of attracting our notice. They have our attention now, but acknowledgment is all I'm willing to give them. I don't want to anchor them here with no hope of sending them on again."

"They're waiting for Gabe." I looked again, searching the throng of ghosts for the little girl I'd seen before. A part of me hoped all the haunts would fade if I muttered banishing charms and attempted to send them away. If anything, they grew more solid and tangible. Dora was right; attention gave them a stronger hold on this world. "They think they can use Gabe to get something they want. I won't let them."

"At a guess? I'd say these ghosts want justice. That's what Gabe does, Delia. Finding justice for victims is his job. Frankly, I'm not surprised the spirits of victims would choose to haunt him. I'm only surprised at the numbers. And if they meant him harm, we likely wouldn't see the spirits at all." She put an arm around my shoulders.

"Come inside. Helping Gabe solve this case is the best thing you can do for him right now."

Turning my back and walking toward the entrance was the most difficult thing I'd done in a long while. The gaze of each waiting ghost was a physical pull, trying to drag me back so they could tell me something, something I desperately needed to know. Ghosts lied more often than not and used any means to get what they wanted, I knew that, but the desire to listen grew stronger. This plea had the taste of truth. Only Dora's arm around my shoulder kept me from giving in.

"Gabe's case, the ghost in our house, even Mrs. Allen's vanishing poltergeist . . . they're all woven together. I'm right about this, Dora. I know I am." We reached the entrance and I glanced across the street again. The smallest ghosts were all I could see: big-eyed little girls, braids unraveling or hair ribbons untied, young boys with dirty faces and holes in the knees of their trousers, a brother and sister holding hands. "So many children . . . like the little girl in my dreams. That can't be a coincidence."

"Probably not." Dora sighed and gave my shoulders a squeeze. "Two things I could accept as coincidence, but matters have progressed considerably past that. But if I seem hesitant to wholeheartedly agree with you, I have good reason. We talked about this not long after you married Gabe."

"I remember." We made our way past the stream of people leaving the station and entered the lobby. As soon as I crossed the threshold, pressure from the ghosts to turn and look at them vanished. I could think of other things again. "Both of us saying that something is true could make it so. There's power in belief."

"Exactly. There are unscrupulous practitioners who use belief to achieve their ends. I'd rather not call new problems into existence. As things stand, we have more than enough to deal with and far too many questions." Dora patted my arm. "What we need are answers, preferably ones Jack and Gabe can work with."

"We'll find them." I tried to feel sure. Tried to believe. "I know we will."

"Your faith is inspiring, Delia, but you're also right. If viewing the evidence doesn't work, I have other means at my disposal." Strain already pulled at the corners of Dora's mouth and bled the color from her cheeks. Being closed in with groups of people always took its toll, but the anger and emotions trapped inside a police station made the experience far worse.

That didn't stop her from smiling at the sight of a handsome young officer near the front desk and sidling over to him. A flash of something else crossed her face, something that appeared more serious than flirting, but vanished too quickly for me to be sure. "Perhaps this nice young man will escort us to Gabe's office."

He tipped his hat and blushed, confirming my guess that he hadn't met Dora before. Meeting Isadora for the first time had become a rite of passage for the rookies in Gabe's squad. Some survived the shock better than others. "Officer Dodd, miss. Are you looking for Captain Ryan?"

"We don't need an escort, thank you." Dodd's dazed expression proclaimed I'd already lost the argument, but I plowed ahead. "Captain Ryan is my husband. Both of us know perfectly well where Gabe's office is located."

Isadora smiled prettily before taking Dodd's arm and leading him away. "Now, where's the fun in that? Come along, Dee. Perhaps I can think of something else for Officer Dodd to do other than walk us down the hall."

I rolled my eyes and followed. Experience had taught I couldn't stop her. Dora was being herself as always, fiercely determined to act outrageous and bohemian in public, no matter what her true aim might be. And it was an act, a role she played to cover nerves or uncertainty. Strangers never looked any further, but her friends knew Madam Isadora Bobet was more than a dilettante.

Dora's fun would end at Gabe's office door. But I'd no doubt she knew that as well as I.

CHAPTER 9

Gabe

Gabe roamed his office, too restless to sit or do paperwork while waiting for Isadora. He made the same circuit each time, pausing to straighten the calendar over the file cabinet and study the map on the wall, fussing with the shade on the window or pulling out a book from the shelf and putting it back again.

Jack sat in the desk chair, rocking while tossing a baseball up and catching it again. His partner was just as restless, but the room was too small for both of them to pace.

They both avoided the pasteboard box in the middle of Gabe's desk and the file folder of photographs sitting on top. The box held the cloth that had covered Bradley Wells's body, a broken crock from the back room where Wells died, and the doorknob they'd removed from the shop's front door. Removing the doorknob had been Henderson's idea, a damn good one. Long odds to be sure, but Isadora might be able to detect some trace of the killer clinging to the crystal and brass knob. He and Jack would take that chance.

Nerves over what Dora would find in his paltry stack of evidence was part of why he couldn't stay still. This was all he had to go on in the Wells case, other than the absolute conviction Mr. Sung and his granddaughter were killed by the same people. He and Jack both put word out on the street asking about similar killings, but no one had come forward yet. If Dora came up empty, Gabe didn't know where to start looking.

And if he was honest, the necessity of bringing Isadora into the investigation nagged at his conscience. Official policy had no tolerance or place for the kind of expertise Dora brought to his cases. The chief was thoroughly charmed by Isadora Bobet and turned a blind eye, but Gabe still walked a fine line. He often imagined he heard his father's voice saying a good cop would find another way, one that didn't bend regulations.

What helping him cost Dora made his guilt all the stronger. No matter how many precautions they took, just being in the room was bound to cause Dora pain. Gabe couldn't escape the conflict between friendship and duty. That he'd no better choice didn't help, nor did knowing she'd readily agreed.

A knock rattled the glass set into his office door, and a muffled voice called out. "Captain Ryan? It's Randolph Dodd. You have visitors, sir."

The door opened and Isadora breezed past the flustered young rookie holding it open for her. Delia followed close behind.

Gabe's entire day brightened at the sight of his wife. He crossed the room to take her coat. "This is a welcome surprise. I didn't know you were coming with Dora."

"Neither did I." Delia stood on tiptoe and kissed his cheek. She smiled and handed him the coat, but he knew her too well to miss the worry in her eyes. "Dora convinced me coming along to help was the wiser choice. She didn't quite threaten to abandon me on a street corner if I refused, but it was a near thing."

Dora kept her distance from the desk, eyeing it from just inside the door, but slowly moved closer. Her mouth pulled into a harsh, narrow line. She was already in pain.

The driving goggles she insisted on wearing dangled from one hand and she'd unwound her scarf so that it hung off her shoulder and trailed along the floor behind, regal and strangely dignified. "Don't be silly, Dee. Gabe and Jack know I'd never leave you to walk home from Mrs. Allen's. I'd drop you at the nearest trolley station or call a cab."

Randolph Dodd cleared his throat, still red-faced from his first encounter with Isadora and poised to flee as soon as permitted. "Do you need anything, sir?"

Jack had moved out of Dora's way to lean against the file cabinet. He answered, but never took his attention off Isadora. "Not right now. You can go, Patrolman."

Dora glanced up, looking Dodd straight in the eye. "No, stay. I need your help. Come all the way inside and shut the door, please."

"Do what she asks, Officer." Gabe finished hanging Delia's coat, taking an extra second before he turned around. The request had taken him by surprise, but he wouldn't let his newest rookie see. He cleared his throat and went to stand with Jack. "I'm sure Miss Bobet will explain in a moment."

She smiled, arch and knowing. Dora held her hand over the file folder containing the photographs, but stopped short of picking it up. "Since we're going to be working together on this case, you should call me Dora. Do you mind if I call you Randy?"

"No, I don't mind, Miss Bob—" Dodd was backed up against the closed door, more flustered than ever at the attention paid him by Dora. He swallowed and wiped his hands down the front of his coat. "I meant Dora. And I still don't mind."

Gabe had seen Dodd only in passing before now, but he understood why the older men teased the squad's newest rookie about being a pretty boy. Still, he knew Isadora well enough to believe her reasons for wanting Randolph Dodd to stay were more noble than his broad shoulders, wavy dark hair, blue eyes, and cinema-star good looks. She was too much of a professional to drag the boy into a murder case just to flirt. Something else drew her to him.

"Marvelous. Come over here, Randy. You too, Delia." They stood on either side of Dora, both of them appearing apprehensive but for different reasons. She pulled her hand back, unthinkingly wiping it on the tail of her scarf. "We're going to alter the plan a bit,

Dee. I want to try using Randy as a conduit to bleed off some of the energy generated by Mr. Wells's death. That could prove vital, especially given the ritual involved and the violence. If he can channel some of the worst away, this encounter won't be as devastating for either of us."

"Use me as a conduit? What does that mean?" Dodd looked between Gabe and Dora. His fair skin blanched and the spattering of freckles across his nose looked dark in comparison. "You talk about channeling energy as if I should understand or it's something that happens every day. And I'm sorry, but I don't understand any of this."

"Your part is actually very simple. Nothing at all difficult nor dangerous." She traded looks with Delia. Gabe knew this was anything but simple when his wife developed a sudden interest in studying the toes of her shoes. Dora peeled off her gloves, shoving them into her pockets before shrugging off her coat. Scarf, coat, and driving goggles ended up in a pile under the desk. "The energy will find its own path without you even needing to think about it or realizing what's happening, I promise. Follow my instructions and you'll be fine."

"No, not until you explain what this . . . this energy is and where it comes from. I don't mean any disrespect, but I've heard talk about you." Randy pulled himself up straighter, his jaw setting in stubborn lines, and pushed back against Dora's assumptions of obedience. Gabe's estimation of the boy went up a notch. He wouldn't interfere; Dodd could hold his own. "They say you see ghosts, that you're some kind of spiritualist . . . or medium. Is that what you're talking about, helping you communicate with the dead? I'm not sure I want any part in anything that disreputable."

"You shouldn't pay attention to rumors, Officer Dodd." Delia smiled, appearing serene and utterly normal, and looked the young rookie in the eye. "The people spreading gossip are only half-right. Dora is a spiritualist, a very knowledgeable one with years of experience in dealing with the spirit realm. I'm the one who sees ghosts."

Randolph Dodd gaped, mouth working like a carnival goldfish in a bowl of cloudy water. He managed to get his mouth closed and stammer an apology, but the shocked expression remained. "Mrs. Ryan, I'm sorry. I didn't mean—You see ghosts?"

"I do. And please, call me Delia. Most days I wish that weren't true, but I've come to accept that the spirits aren't going away. I've learned a lot from Isadora. More importantly, I trust her. She believes you can make handling the evidence in this case less difficult for her." She sat in Gabe's desk chair, hands folded in her lap. "Any death generates spiritual energy, but the energy from a violent death includes all the victim's pain and suffering. Items from a crime scene, even photographs, absorb all the energy generated. Dora feels everything from a victim's last moments as if it were happening to her right now."

Randy wiped a hand over his mouth. "That sounds hellish. Again, no disrespect intended, Dora, but if that's all true . . . why put yourself through that? You're not a cop."

"Trite as it may sound, because someone has to help Gabe and Jack catch the villains. Not that they need my assistance all the time." Dora's smile was tight and brittle, but that didn't stop her from winking at Gabe. "But I have knowledge that falls beyond the bounds of normal police work. Occasionally one of their cases drifts outside those boundaries and into the realm of the occult, and they ask me to consult. I'm more than happy to help keep them safe under those circumstances. A detective's job is dangerous enough."

Jack raked fingers through his disheveled curls and sighed. "I understand why Patrolman Dodd is hesitant. This is all new to him and he doesn't know you. But I've seen you examine evidence a hundred times, Dora. If you need to bring in someone other than Delia for this case, let me try. At least I'd know what I'm getting into."

"That's very sweet, but I'd have asked you or Gabe long ago if either of you were suited. And much as I enjoy corrupting impressionable young men, that isn't why I need Randolph to help us." Cats circled garden snakes the way Dora approached the evidence on

Gabe's desk, wary and mindful of being bitten. "Spiritually neutral people are rare, but they do exist. The best way to explain what makes them different is that they always have one foot in the spirit realm and one in the land of the living. Energy of all sorts can pass through them from one plane to the other and cause no harm."

Gabe frowned. "And you're saying Patrolman Dodd is spiritually neutral? How do you know?"

"His aura, Gabe." Delia watched Randolph Dodd with the same distracted, faraway expression he'd grown accustomed to seeing on Isadora's face. How alike they'd become frightened him at times. "The nimbus surrounding Randy shimmers with mother-of-pearl rainbows. All the energy in the room, good or bad, flows through him. It's really quite beautiful."

"And very distinctive." Dora pushed a strand of hair behind her ear and sighed, the sound weary enough to worry Gabe. She was uncomfortable at the very least, but she'd never say so. "Given what we suspect about this case, finding Randy in the lobby was either a stroke of luck or divine providence. I'm not willing to prod that idea too hard, but I'm grateful to have found him, whatever the reason. Now, be a dear and let us work. Assuming Randy is willing and agrees to trust me."

She offered her hand to Dodd. He hesitated another instant, uncertainty flickering in his eyes, before grasping her hand firmly. "If the lieutenant and the captain trust you, I guess I can too. Tell me what to do."

"We'll start with the photographs. I think this will work best if you handle them first before I see the image. That should siphon off a great deal of the pain." Dora turned on the desk lamp and adjusted the shade so the light shone on the dark green blotter. "Lay them faceup so the light hits them."

Under other circumstances, Gabe might have found Randy Dodd's obvious relief over not bursting into flames or being struck by lightning comical. But nothing about this case was comical. His stomach soured watching his wife work side by side with Isadora, partners the way he and Jack had always been. He didn't find that the least bit funny.

Dora studied the photos, holding tight to Delia's arm for support with one hand, her other hand hovering over the photos. For some of the images, she used Delia as a buffer between her and the photographs. Even with Randy running interference and absorbing the worst, she took a lot of punishment.

Lines, each one a marker of pain, formed around Dora's eyes. "You were right, Gabe, this was a ritual. A particularly nasty one, given the way Mr. Wells was bound and his throat cut. I can't say what the purpose was, not with any certainty, but I've no doubt this was a blood sacrifice. Bradley Wells was made a victim in more ways than one."

Jack whistled through his teeth. "That's not something a San Francisco cop hears very often. I'm not doubting your word, Dora, but how do you know? You can't have seen this before, you said as much."

She swayed for an instant, but Randy put a hand on her arm, bleeding away whatever force caused her pain, and some of the color returned to her face. Gabe's view of the world and people shifted again, leaving him unsettled.

Dora squinted at the photos. "No, Jack, not exactly like this, and not anything that's occurred in our lifetime. But there are texts and drawings, some that date back hundreds of years that describe these types of rituals. I was very young when I first delved into the spirit realm, but my teacher believed in showing me the dark things as well as the light." She rested a hand on Randy's arm and passed the other over the assembled photographs, still careful not to touch them. Dora shut her eyes, trembling. "He didn't struggle."

"No. We couldn't find any signs that Wells put up a fight." He and Jack had gone over what to tell her beforehand and what to hold back. Influencing a witness was bad police work, and Isadora was a witness of sorts, even if it was long after the crime. Gabe cleared his throat. Telling Isadora and Delia the rest of what they knew would help clear away the last of his doubts about the connections between his cases.

Telling them made what he had to say true. "Before Wells died in his father's shop, there were two murders in Chinatown. Sung Liang and his granddaughter, Sung Lan, were killed in the back room of his herb shop. The girl fought her attackers and according to Liang's brother, Sung Wing, she didn't die easily. But her spirit was intact and Sung Wing was able to send her ghost to be with their ancestors."

Dora sank into the desk chair, drawn and pale. "Really . . . Wu Mai died nearly four years ago. She was the last in Chinatown with that much power or skill, or so I thought. I've not heard of Sung Wing before now."

"I'm not surprised. Lieutenant Benson's squad works Chinatown full-time. I spoke with him and some of his men as soon as we got back to the station. None of them have heard of Sung Wing either." Gabe stuffed his hands deep into his trouser pockets and leaned against the file cabinet. "At least one of the beat cops should have heard Mr. Sung's name before. He's a tong leader."

"I suspect he's much more than that, Gabe." Dora frowned and gripped the arms of the chair, fingers white. "Tell me the rest."

"Liang's throat was cut. The bodies were cremated, but from Sung Wing's description, his brother died the same way as Bradley Wells. He never mentioned his brother fighting his attackers." Gabe traded looks with his partner. "Mr. Sung was very angry about his brother's death and what happened to his great-niece. But what upset him the most is that his brother's ghost vanished. He thinks the killers stole Sung Liang's spirit."

"Oh dear God." Delia stared, owl-eyed and breathing too fast. "Dora . . . they took his ghost. That's what they wanted all along."

"Let's finish this before jumping to conclusions. Sung Wing could be mistaken. And remember what I said about belief making it so." Dora stood, bracing herself against the edge of the desk. "Randy, open the box, please. We'll do this the same way, with you handling everything first. Perhaps seeing what's inside will help me determine what's going on."

That his wife and Dora knew, or at the very least, suspected, something he didn't was obvious. He wouldn't press for an explanation yet. The pasteboard evidence box looked mundane, harmless, but he knew that wasn't true. Not given its effect on Isadora.

Gabe stood next to Delia and took her hand, trying not to be obvious about hovering over Isadora. Jack moved to stand on the other side, positioned where he could catch Dora if she fainted, something Randy Dodd wouldn't know to expect.

"I'll make a bargain with you, Captain Ryan." Dora scrubbed her hands up and down her skirt and watched Randy lift out Wells's white shroud through narrowed, pain-filled eyes. "I promise not to swoon if you and Jack let me breathe. Step back, please."

Jack stood his ground, arms folded over his chest. "Not a chance. Daniel made me promise to take care of you."

"I'm perfectly capable of taking care of myself, despite what Daniel thinks. You men are all so stubborn. If you insist on crowding me, don't complain if I tread on your toes." Dora went back to studying the cloth covering the desktop. She skimmed a hand over the top, barely avoiding touching the fabric itself. "Has Mr. Wells been buried yet?"

"This morning." Gabe put an arm around Delia's shoulders. "Why?"

"Pity. Confirmation would have been nice. I'll have to make do without viewing the body directly." Her frown deepened. "I thought maybe it was the lighting, or the angle of the photographs. But there really isn't a trace of Mr. Wells here. Nothing at all."

"Nothing?" Jack looked from Gabe to Dora. "You've been in pain since you came in. How can there be nothing here?"

"I didn't say that nothing lingered, just nothing of Mr. Wells." Dora sat in the desk chair, tipped her head back, and shut her eyes. "Be a lamb and put everything in the box, Randy, and close the lid. Then take it down the hall to another room."

Dodd did what he was told, casting sidelong, concerned glances at Isadora the entire time. He closed up the box, but paused before leaving. "Will you be all right?"

"I'll be fine. Thank you." She opened her eyes and smiled. "I may need your help again later. Captain Ryan will send for you when the time comes."

Gabe waited for the door to close behind the rookie before asking the obvious question: "If you're not sensing Wells, what is it?"

"Remnants of the ritual and the power generated. It's rather foul, somewhat like being closed in a closet with a sun-ripened corpse." Dora pushed herself up straight in the chair and dropped her head into her hands long enough to take a shaky breath. "But none of that foulness is connected to Bradley Wells. His pain and suffering, the essence of who he was is all gone. They drained that from him along with his blood."

Delia shuddered and he pulled her closer. "They took his ghost. Just like Sung Liang."

Isadora rubbed her temples. "Much as I hate to admit it, Dee's right. Whoever performed the ritual took his spirit. That was their aim all along."

There were a hundred questions in Gabe's mind, all clamoring to be asked. But the haggard lines newly etched in Dora's face stopped him from interrogating her. He asked only one. "Can you find who did this from the traces they left behind?"

She winced and shut her eyes for an instant before answering. "No, I can't, not directly. But those who practice blood rituals and embrace the darker aspects of the occult are marked. I can see those marks. I suspect Dee can as well. And unless they leave San Francisco entirely, their identity won't stay hidden for long. Raising power that way makes you hungry for more. A trail of corpses will lead you to Sung Liang and Bradley Wells's killer."

"Damnation, Dora." Jack tugged his notebook and pencil out of a back pocket and began scribbling notes, scowling. "If anyone else told me a story like that, I'd call the asylum and have them committed. But this is you. It makes my skin crawl, but I believe every word. And that scares the hell out of me."

"Good." She kept rubbing her temples, peering bleary eyed at Jack. "Being scared will make you more careful. That goes for you too, Gabriel Ryan. Dee and I will do what we can to protect you, but being cautious will keep you alive."

A rap on the door was followed by Dodd calling his name. "Captain Ryan?"

He hugged Delia's shoulders and stepped away. "Come in."

Dodd pushed the door open, looking and sounding as if he'd run back to the office. "Captain, the desk sergeant sent me to get you. A woman's body washed up at the construction site north of the Ferry Building an hour ago. Officer Henderson told the sergeant that you and the lieutenant need to come to Pier 3 right now. A car and driver will be waiting out front by the time you get there."

Dora looked up, her attention focused on Randy. "Do they know who this woman was or her name?"

He gave Dodd credit for looking to Jack for permission and waiting for a nod before answering. "No, the officers on the scene haven't been able to identify her. Marshall said the body's been in the water for days. Unless someone can identify her clothing or belongings . . . he said we may never know her name."

"Oh dear God." Delia hugged arms over her chest. "Could it be Mandy?"

"No, it's not Mandy." Jack helped Dora to her feet, the twitching muscle along his jaw the only hint he wasn't as confident as he sounded. "Chances are it's a girl from the streets or one of the taverns near the docks."

"He's right. It could be anyone." Gabe wanted to hold tight to Jack's certainty that only a stranger spent days floating on the shifting currents of the bay. But believing only strangers came to violent ends—or would fetch up against mussel-encrusted pilings—was a lie, and he tried very hard not to lie to himself.

Gabe fetched Delia's coat first, helping her slip it on before getting his own. Jack did the same for Isadora, dragging her coat and scarf out from under the desk. Dora braced herself against the back of the chair once her coat was on, shaky and unsteady on her feet.

The clammy caress of fear along his spine was a warning, one he'd do well to heed. Sending the two women home alone suddenly struck Gabe as a bad idea. "Do you drive, Patrolman Dodd?"

"Yes, sir." Randy's eyes flickered to Isadora and back to Gabe. "I drove my mother to town every week when I lived in Indiana. I can drive."

"Good. I want you to take Mrs. Ryan and Miss Bobet to my house. Use Miss Bobet's car. That will be easier all around." He kissed Delia on the cheek, running a finger along her chin before stuffing his fedora on. "And I want you to stay with them until Lieutenant Fitzgerald and I arrive. Is that understood?"

"Yes, sir. You can trust me to get them home safely." Dodd was new to the force, untested and unscarred, brimming with the confidence of youth. The last time Gabe remembered being that young and sure was long ago, before the quake and fire; before Victoria died.

Victoria's death had changed him. Gabe didn't know if he'd survive losing Delia. He'd do everything in his power to keep from finding out.

"Make no mistake, Patrolman, I am trusting you. Don't let me down." He exchanged smiles with Delia and left the office, not quite at a run, but close. Gabe's heart sped up, traitorous and threatening to make him as breathless as the rookie he'd entrusted with his wife's safety. Henderson wouldn't send for them unless he had good reason.

And the only reason that came to mind was that Amanda Poe's luck had run out.

Delia

I couldn't fault Dora for leaning heavily on Randy Dodd's arm, nor accuse her of making a pretense of fatigue as an excuse to flirt. Even with Randy's help, the lingering residue of the ritual surrounding Bradley Wells's death brought her near to collapse. Leaning on him would likely help draw away the strong emotion threatening to lay her low, or so I hoped. I'd not seen her tremble quite this hard in the past, her face pale and drawn to the point she resembled one of the ghosts wandering the police station's halls.

We'd gone more than halfway across the lobby when Isadora suddenly stopped and looked back at the desk sergeant's station. She frowned and shut her eyes for an instant, appearing even more wilted once she opened them again. "Dee, I need to see Archie. You can wait in Gabe's office if you like, but I can't in good conscience be here and not take a moment to speak with him. This won't take long, I promise. I'm sure I can count on Randy to escort me through the cell block."

"Captain Ryan didn't say anything about visiting prisoners." Randy licked his lips and pushed his hat back, peering down at Dora. He was a good eight inches taller, long limbed and lanky, with the kind of frame that would no doubt gain muscle with age. "He told me to take both of you right home and stay with you. Even if he didn't explain why, there's a reason he didn't want you left alone. I'm not sure he'd approve of us traipsing through the jail with you on my arm, Dora. Matter of fact, I'm positive Captain Ryan would be pretty angry about me ignoring his instructions."

"I wouldn't dream of doing anything that might get you in trouble with Gabe. All I'm asking is that we delay leaving a bit until I talk to Archie. This is important. I have to see him." Dora's eyes had that faraway, searching quality that said she wasn't looking at the physical world, but beyond the top layer and into the realm beneath. We both saw manifestations of ghosts everywhere, echoes of who they'd been wandering amongst the living, unwilling to move on and let go. But that was all I saw, echoes of how they'd looked in life or at the moment of death. I'd no doubt what she saw was far deeper, more disturbing.

"I understand why you want to speak with Archie, but be reasonable. You're very tired." I tightened my grip on Dora's arm, doing my part to ensure she wouldn't slide to the floor. Randy stood on her other side, completely in the dark about why she'd taken a fancy to visiting cell blocks. I doubted he knew why Archie Baldwin was being held or what it meant. "We can visit tomorrow after you've rested. Besides, Gabe never gave his permission. Showing up unexpectedly might make things much worse for Archie."

"Oh posh, Dee. I don't plan on holding a séance in his cell or anything outrageous. I just want to speak with him. Perhaps today he'll remember more of what happened or where Mandy might have gotten off to. And if I'd had the presence of mind to mention this before Gabe and Jack left, we wouldn't be having this discussion." She gently pried my fingers off her arm and stood straight. "I've been down that hallway before while working on a case. I'll go alone if need be and ask Gabe's forgiveness later."

She'd do just that too, drawing on some hidden well of strength kept against time of need. Dora was the strongest person I'd known, but even the strongest have limits. I'd rather she didn't find hers.

"If I can't make you see reason, then it's probably best if I give in gracefully and go with you. That way I can at least try to keep you from pitching onto your face." I threaded my arm through hers and gestured toward the hall leading to the back of the station. "Are you coming, Randy? We really won't change her mind."

"Mrs. Ryan . . . Delia, I'm not sure this is a good idea." He looked between us, searching for the smallest sign we'd relent. "But the captain ordered me to stay with you, so I really don't have much choice. What's the prisoner's name?"

Isadora leaned on me now, small tremors rippling through her at odd intervals. Recovering from viewing the evidence was taking her longer than in the past, making me uneasy, but I'd no way to know how much to worry. Neither of us was used to dealing with rituals of any sort. "Archie Baldwin. We'll be on our way in two ticks if you ask Sergeant Morgan what cell Archie slept in last night."

He obtained the number and led us past interrogations rooms and into the area occupied by prisoners. The cell block was oddly quiet when we entered, most of the cells either empty or the occupants sleeping. Those who were awake stared or made rude comments. A few men watched Dora and me pass with a flat, emotionless expression that made my skin crawl. The feel of eyes on my back lasted until Randy led us around a corner and through a door that opened into a long, bright corridor.

"Sarge said Mr. Baldwin is the only prisoner in this section." We were out of sight of watching eyes, and Randy took Dora's other arm, holding her up. A faint flush of color returned to her cheeks. "Baldwin's in the big cell at the very end. I can't let you inside, but you won't have any trouble talking through the bars. Just promise me neither of you will get close enough he could grab you."

Dora patted his arm. "You have my word. Based on Jack's description, it's possible Archie might not be in his right mind. I don't think he'd harm either of us, but best not to tempt fate."

We turned a corner onto the row of cells where we'd find Archie. The sound of heartbroken sobbing and incoherent muttering filled the corridor.

Randy frowned. "I need to make sure everything's all right before I take you any closer. The two of you wait here. I'll be right back."

We did as he asked, watching as his long, rapid strides took him down the empty hall. The light was murky at the end holding Archie's cell, and filled with what I first took for shadows. Randy moved right through them, but the shadows deepened around him and took shapes that grew more distinct.

Soldiers' ghosts packed the corridor in front of Archie's cell—so many, I couldn't begin to count the dead men crowded up against the bars and spilling inside. Helmets and gas masks dangled from phantom fingers, their rifles slung over a shoulder and rucksacks strapped to their backs. Most of the blood-splattered uniforms and insignia were Belgian, a few were French or British, fewer still were German.

All of them watched Archie tossing restlessly on the cell's hard cot, whimpering and crying out in his sleep.

"They're haunting him. There must be hundreds of soldiers, Dora . . . hundreds . . ." The truth of what was happening struck me, awaking horror. "His unit must have been under attack when he deserted. They blame Archie because they died."

"And they hate him for still being alive." Dora's mouth pulled into an angry line. "No wonder Archie's raving. None of us will get any sense out of him until we clear this lot out. We won't be leaving as quickly as I'd planned."

"Are you sure you're strong enough for this?" She was already pale and sweating. I worried that banishing so many ghosts would cause her more harm.

Dora sighed and held my arm tighter. "I've little choice."

Spirits on the outer edge of the assembled host turned toward us, their hostility slamming into me, cramping my stomach and leaving no doubts about their intention. They meant to keep us from Archie or attempting to banish them. They meant to keep tormenting him.

I took a step back. Something here was very wrong.

Isadora stepped back as well, fingers digging into my sleeve. She called out, voice strained. "Randy, is it possible for Archie to be brought to an interrogation room while I speak to him? Or moved to either Gabe or Jack's office?"

"Not without either the captain or the lieutenant giving permission to move him." He glanced at Archie, hesitating for an instant, before coming back down the hall. "What's wrong?"

"I'm not feeling as well as I thought." She stared down the corridor at the ghost army, shivering violently, and took hold of Randy's arm. "Dee was right. We should wait and visit tomorrow. Take us home, please."

He didn't question her. We went back the way we'd come, past leering inmates and silent men with soulless eyes. The hostility radiating from the ghosts haunting Archie lessened with distance, but never disappeared. As strongly as I felt the spirits, I couldn't imagine the effect on Dora.

Randy left us on a bench near the front door and went to fetch the car. Dora leaned against my shoulder, a hand covering her eyes, pale and much too quiet. How drained she was frightened me. "Are you all right?"

"No, Dee, I'm far from all right. My pride has taken a mortal blow. I don't remember the last time a spirit forced me to back down." She pinched the bridge of her nose and sat up straight. "In addition to feeling rather foolish, I have a splitting headache. Given time and enough whiskey, I'll recover from both. I'm also trying to work out what happened in there."

"Oh." I wrapped my fingers around the edge of the bench, holding tight to something real and solid. Cold from the iron frame seeped through my gloves. "I was hoping you knew and could tell me."

She stared across the lobby, but I knew she didn't really see the crowded benches or the people coming and going. "Not yet. The only thing I can say with certainty is that the spirits around Archie acted very strangely. I can't recall any ghosts I've run across working in unison. Spirits are selfish, single-minded. It's not in their nature to form packs or cooperate."

"And the odds of hundreds of ghosts all deciding to haunt Archie are vanishingly slim. I'd say the same was true of the spirits following Gabe." I spotted Randy coming back into the station. Relief that we hadn't wandered away or disappeared brightened his face at the sight of us, making him look very young and making me feel so much older. I got a hand under Dora's elbow and helped her stand. "I'm finding it difficult to credit anything that's happened of late to chance."

"Nor should you. Too many odd circumstances have come together around us. And I don't just mean you and me. I include Gabe and Archie in that as well. Dismissing the idea that these things are connected somehow could be courting disaster." Dora wrapped her long scarf over her hair and tucked the ends inside her coat, preparing for the cold car trip home. "Even putting the ritual aside, everything about this feels orchestrated. Someone is setting up a deliberate pattern of some sort, gathering power. Don't ask me how Archie became entangled, but I've little doubt that's what happened. The trick will be to free him without breaking Archie's mind completely."

"You think it's one person, not a group."

Dora nodded. "Ultimately, yes. Others may be involved, but one person is the driving force behind whatever is going on."

I let the idea settle around me, accepting without question that Isadora was right. She'd taught me to trust my instincts. Even if I couldn't see the whole of this pattern yet, I knew one existed. "This person can't have been here long or you'd have seen evidence before now."

Randy reached us, cheeks flushed from the cold. Dora took his offered arm and we strolled toward the door. "Your faith is touching, Dee, but an hour ago I'd have sworn the last shaman and sorcerer in Chinatown was dead. But I know to watch now, and it's only a matter of time before this person tips his hand."

Men and women dodged around us, intent on whatever mundane business brought them to the police station, people blissfully ignorant of blood rituals, unaware of hauntings and hostile ghosts. A very small part of me longed to go back to living life on one plane, grounded in a world that always made sense, and where evil was spoken of only in Sunday's sermon.

But I'd shut that door years ago. No sense dwelling on what-if and might have been.

CHAPTER 10

Gabe

Cold wind hit Gabe in the face as he got out of the car, each biting gust brimming with the smell of fresh creosote and salt water. Hordes of keening gulls and terns wheeled in interlocking circles against the cloudy afternoon sky, riding the wind to spiral upward. Gulls broke the pattern every so often, watching for the opportunity to dive from high above and steal fish from brown pelicans or cormorants that didn't guard their catch.

Back when he and Jack walked a waterfront beat, he'd spent hours watching the birds' antics. Gulls were consummate opportunists and unabashed thieves, not above stealing a young patrolman's lunch if given the slightest chance. At least the birds were honest about their intentions. You learned not to turn your back on a seagull.

Gabe surveyed the construction site, observing faces, the way men stood in tight groups, restless and muttering, or alone, scowling and still. Knowing when not to turn your back wasn't always an easy call.

Fresh-cut pilings, big around as a man's body and twenty feet long, were stacked on the landward side of the construction site. Vans and flatbed trucks were parked near the timbers, each painted with the name POE'S CONSTRUCTION. He refused to believe that was an omen. Walter Poe's company had won most bayside construction contracts for more than twenty years.

They'd sunk pilings for the pier out two or three hundred yards from shore, topping all but the last dozen yards or so with green-brown, creosote-stained planks. This was one of the last new piers under construction near the Ferry Building, all slated to open sometime in 1918. At least one pier would be dedicated to ferries carrying passengers through the delta and all the way upriver to Sacramento. Others would be devoted to freight and transporting crops from Central Valley farms to ports up and down the coast.

Timber-framed and stucco-covered buildings opening onto the Embarcadero would go up last, the public face of the working piers. He'd seen a drawing of the design in the *Examiner,* a caption beneath stating that the two-story arches facing the street were similar to those at the Chelsea Piers in New York. All in all, a great deal of money had gone into the project, but over the long term, even more money and jobs would flow into San Francisco and the state as a whole. Most people saw that as a good thing.

According to the newspapers, work had gone well until now, keeping to or even a little ahead of the announced schedule. Progress had been helped along by relatively mild weather, no major accidents, and a ready supply of labor.

Finding a body tangled in a set of winch cables put an end to the site foreman's perfect record of not missing a day.

The construction crew stood idle and watched his squad work, grim faced and appearing decidedly unhappy. It was a small crew of no more than ten men, all older, settled, and no doubt experienced. Losing a day's pay could mean the difference between a workman's family having enough to eat or not. Gabe sympathized, but he didn't have a choice. Finding evidence they could use would be difficult enough. Maybe impossible.

But the longer he watched, the less sure he was that a lost day was the crew's only source of discontent.

Men in suits circulated among the coverall- and dungaree-clad construction workers, likely supervisors sent out by the head office. One carried a megaphone to make sure the orders he gave were heard. Scowls blossomed in the supervisors' wake, accompanied by angry muttering.

A heavyset man in a brown plaid jacket climbed onto a stack of planks, loudly proclaiming that work was halted until the police sorted out their investigation. He ordered the crew to go home, but no one made a move to comply.

Jack came around the front of the car, hands stuffed in his pockets. He hunkered down into his overcoat, whistling tunelessly and studying the scene. Gabe waited for his partner to reach his own conclusions. It didn't take long.

"The construction company seems to be in an awful big hurry to get its employees to leave. Securing the site or stowing their gear doesn't seem to be a priority." Jack tugged the end of his mustache. "I wonder what they have to be so nervous about?"

"Other than a dead body?" Gabe gestured toward Marshall Henderson facing down one of the suits a few yards away. An older man, dressed in patched coveralls and a grimy denim work coat, stood just behind and to the left, poking his finger at the company official and shouting. Wind and noise from adjacent piers carried most of his words away, but Gabe didn't need to hear. Marshall's presence between the two of them was all that kept the men from coming to blows. "I'm going to guess it's us. They don't want their men talking to the police."

"The crew doesn't seem in any hurry to leave." Jack pulled his notebook and a well-chewed pencil out of an inside pocket. He pointed at a knot of four workers standing near the stack of pilings. "I'll see what I can find out from that bunch."

Raised voices came from the rowboat bobbing underneath the half-built pier. They'd freed the woman's body from the cables and gotten it into the boat. Gabe had seen bodies after they'd spent days in the water, exposed to the uncertain mercy of sun and birds and ravaged by hungry fish. He wasn't in a hurry to see another. That the

dead woman might be Delia and Sadie's friend only added to his reluctance.

Instead he joined Patrolman Henderson. A year before, he might
have seen relief in Marshall's eyes at having a senior officer there to
back him up. Now all Gabe saw was the stubborn determination not to
let anger get the better of him and to keep the situation under control.
Even so, a little of the tension went out of the young officer's stance.

Marshall gestured at the man in coveralls. "Captain Ryan, this
is Michael St. John. He's been a foreman on site for more than five
years. Mr. St. John feels he might know something that could aid us
in our investigation. His boss here, Mr. Edwards, wants a company
lawyer to hear the story first and threatened to fire Michael if he
talked to me. I've tried to get him to explain why a lawyer is necessary, but Mr. Edwards doesn't feel an explanation is in the company's
best interest."

"And why is that, Mr. Edwards?" Gabe stared at Edwards, unsmiling and businesslike, and didn't offer his hand. He wanted no
doubt of where he stood. "I can't think of a reason one of your employees wouldn't be free to make a statement to the police if they
choose. Not unless the company is liable in some way for this woman's death. Is that the case?"

Edwards was not quite as tall as Henderson, with thinning
blond hair and a pained, pinched expression. Gabe guessed he was
more than forty, given the maze of wrinkles in Edward's face and
neck, and the telltale stoop to his shoulders that spoke of years bent
over a desk. He'd likely spent his life working for Walter Poe's company, offering loyalty in exchange for a promised pension.

"No, no. Of course not." Edwards pulled a handkerchief out of
his pocket, using it to wipe his wire-rimmed spectacles. His voice
was calm and his manner self-assured, but sweat glistened on his
forehead. On such a cold day, Gabe could only see that as a sign of
nerves—or guilt. "I didn't mean to give that impression. But it's my
job to protect company assets and our good name. Surely you can

understand that, Captain. Poe Construction can't afford to have its name bandied about in the newspapers. Especially not in connection with such an unfortunate incident."

Rather than set him at ease, Edwards' glib explanation made Gabe doubly certain more was at stake here than the company's reputation. He hid clenched fists deep in his overcoat pockets. "Death is always unfortunate, especially in these circumstances. But that still doesn't explain why you'd threaten to fire your foreman over speaking to Officer Henderson. Make me understand, Mr. Edwards. Otherwise, we can continue this conversation at the police station. It shouldn't take more than an hour or two for me to finish here."

Edwards slipped his spectacles back on and used the handkerchief to dab his face. "I'd hate for you to embarrass the department, Captain. Our attorney should arrive at any moment, and we can settle the matter."

"Oh to hell with it. And to hell with you, Angus." Michael St. John scowled and unhooked the large ring of keys attached to his belt. He flung them at Edwards's chest. The keys bounced off, landing in the street between the two men. "Fire me if you want. No job is worth not being able to sleep at night."

Gabe caught Marshall's eye as the patrolman started to interfere and shook his head. He wanted to see how this played out.

Fear flashed in Edwards's eyes, quickly hidden again behind outrage and bluster. "Think carefully before you say anything, Michael."

"You can't threaten me with Tommy's job no more. I sent him up to Seattle to work with my brother." Michael St. John planted a hand in the center of Edwards's chest and shoved, forcing him back a step. St. John was near the same age and a good five inches shorter than Edwards, but years of hard work had left him well muscled and much stronger. "I won't keep your dirty secrets, Angus. Neither will the rest of the men."

Gabe cleared his throat and put a hand on St. John's shoulder.

"Feel free to say anything you like, Mr. St. John. No one here will stop you."

"I shouldn't have let Angus and his threats stop me before. Stupidest thing I ever done." He shoved Edwards again, and this time Henderson did step between them. St. John threw his hands up in disgust. "This ain't the first body to wash up at the job. I made the mistake of sending for Angus when my son found the first. Thought he should be here as the site overseer. I should have sent Tommy running for the police first."

"How long ago was that?"

"Close to three, four weeks now." St. John glared at his boss, fists opening and closing at his side. "Angus gathered up the whole crew and said not to go to the police or talk outside of work if we wanted our jobs. He did the same thing when the second body showed up. Only that time he said the police would find a way to blame one of us. He was looking at my boy when he said it."

"That's not how it was, Michael." Edwards's expression was haughty and defiant. "You know that's not how it was."

"Ask any of the men here, Captain. Not one of them will tell you a different story." St. John pointed to the group of men gathered round Jack. His voice was harsh, rasping. "We all got families to take care of. Twice this bastard made us choose between doing right and putting bread in our children's bellies. He'd have done the same again, but I'd had my fill. I sent one of the boys to find the beat cop."

"Twice before today?" Marshall looked ill. "What happened to the bodies?"

St. John jabbed a finger in Edwards's direction.. "You'll have to ask Angus. Company men took them away once it got dark. We'd come to work the next day and they'd be gone."

"I warned you." Edwards's face flushed. "I warned all of you. You and your crew are fired, Michael. I'll have your pay sent tomorrow."

Gabe had more practice than Henderson in keeping his public face in place, hiding shock and astonishment no matter what a witness said. St. John's story sickened him, but not as much as Angus Edwards's lack of remorse. "Let me see if I finally understand, Mr. Edwards. You threatened your employees, failed to report two deaths, and then disposed of the bodies. All to keep the company's name out of the papers. Now you're firing them for not looking the other way and doing the decent thing. Do I have that right?"

"Captain . . . we're one of the biggest companies in the city. If we were forced to cut the number of people we employ, either due to scandal or loss of business, those jobs would be sorely missed." Edwards's mouth worked, as if trying to rid himself of a bad taste. He waved a hand toward the officers hauling on ropes, lifting the tarpaulin-wrapped body from the boat and up onto the pier. "These were street girls, doxies from the taverns. No one was going to miss them."

Something in Gabe's face made Edwards blanch and step back. Not far enough.

Gabe grabbed the front of Edwards's coat, twisting the fabric in his fist, and hauled the man off his feet. Edwards dangled with his toes just brushing the ground, face turning scarlet. "You don't know who they were or where they came from. You sure as hell don't know if anyone missed them."

Giving in to his temper was an indulgence, but Gabe couldn't bring himself to regret it. He let go of Edwards and pushed him toward Henderson. "As of this moment, you're under arrest for failure to report a suspicious death. If I had an ounce of evidence, the charge would be accessory to murder. Officer Henderson, find someone to take Mr. Edwards to the station. And I want statements from all the men on Mr. St. John's crew."

Henderson tightened his grip on Edwards's arm. "I'll take care of it, Captain."

He nodded to St. John and went to join Jack. His partner was pacing near the edge of the pier, waiting to view the body. He wouldn't let him go through that alone. Amanda Poe was Jack's friend too.

Deputy Coroner Sal Rosen waited too, fingers flexing around the handle of his doctor's case. Rosen was near fifty, short and blocky-looking with thick, straight gray hair and piercing black eyes. Sal was one of three deputy coroners working for the city, but he was the best in the department, hands down. He also lacked any political ambitions. Finding Sal here was a relief. Politics and unexplained death never blended well.

The dead were beyond knowing the indignities visited upon them. Ropes tied around the woman's body to haul her up the ten feet from the rowboat to the wood-planked pier didn't cause her pain. She didn't feel the jolt as they dropped her, slick, wet tarpaulin weighed down by water-soaked clothing slipping from his men's hands.

That didn't stop Gabe from cringing or feeling that he owed her an apology.

Unwrapping the tarp fell to the deputy coroner.

She was dressed in a green linen dress and a short, beaded black jacket, stockings shredded and both shoes lost to the shifting tides. A small garnet ring on her right hand caught the sun, glittered with bloodred sparks. Her face was a ravaged mess, swollen from water and sun, mauled by birds and fish. Seaweed tangled in her long black hair.

"Oh God." Jack wiped his mouth, his voice hushed and shakey. "It's not her. It's not Amanda Poe."

Gabe looked from the woman's ruined face and back to Jack. "You're sure?"

His partner nodded. "Very sure. Amanda's hair is red, not black. This is someone else."

He clapped Jack on the shoulder, sharing a moment of guilty relief. Neither of them would have to break bad news to their wives. But this woman was someone's friend, someone's daughter, wife, or sister. That she wasn't Amanda Poe didn't make her death less important.

"Ryan, take a look at this." Rosen had been with the coroner's office longer than Gabe had been a cop. The clues he followed were different, but Rosen was as much a detective as any investigator on the force. And Sal never flinched, no matter what condition they found a body in. Gabe couldn't make the same claim.

Sal pulled a fountain pen from his pocket and traced a line on the dead woman's wrists. "See this? It's hard to be sure with all the swelling and tissue damage, but my guess is that both her wrists were slit. I won't know until I get her to the morgue, but you're probably looking at the cause of death right here."

Gabe crouched down, barely able to make out the wounds Rosen said had killed a young, well-to-do woman. "Are you thinking suicide?"

"I don't think so, not dressed like that. She looks ready to go out to supper, not bleed her life into the washroom basin. And if the clothes were intended to send a message to someone, we'd have found her at home. Probably in her bedroom." He bent her arm at the elbow. "Rigor's gone. Given the temperature, my guess is she's been in the water for five to seven days. All of which raises the question of how she ended up in the Bay to begin with."

"Leave finding the answer to us." The scent of sun-rotted fruit and spoiled meat grew stronger, turning Gabe's stomach. Sal kept poking at the body, seemingly oblivious. "And you're sure she didn't do this to herself?"

Rosen turned one of her arms so that her wrist was more exposed. He leaned in and squinted. "The edges look too smooth and the depth of the wound too even to be self-inflicted. Even the most determined suicide flinches from the pain. The cuts get the job done, but they tend to be ragged and uneven."

Jack scribbled furiously in his moleskine. "Could she have drowned?"

"Anything's possible. But there's very little postmortem lividity visible." Rosen shrugged. "Call it a professional hunch if you like, but I think she was dead from blood loss before she hit the water."

Sal's hunches weren't offered lightly and usually turned out to be fact. If Rosen said the girl bled to death, Gabe accepted that as fact.

Isadora had told them to follow the trail of bodies. Thanks to Edwards and his concern with Poe Construction's good name, they might have missed two along the way.

He stood, brushing off his hands before shoving them deep into his coat pockets. The clouds were thickening, bringing a deeper chill to the air and the promise of rain before morning. "I need to ask a favor, Sal. The body's in pretty rough shape, but if you find evidence of other wounds, would you let me know right away? I've got a hunch of my own that this might tie in with another case."

Sal paused in his examination of the body, squinting up at Gabe. "Before I write my formal report?"

Gabe nodded. "That would be a big help."

Rosen motioned two of his men over. They lifted the woman's body off the tarpaulin and onto a canvas stretcher. A nondescript gray blanket covered her for the trip in the back of the coroner's van.

"I'm not going to make any promises, Ryan. I'll see what I can do." Rosen pulled off his rubber gloves and replaced them with worn, brown leather ones retrieved from a coat pocket. He packed everything away and shut the doctor's case at his feet. "Anything in particular I should look for?"

"One thing. Pay close attention to the injuries on her neck." He knew Sal well. Telling the deputy coroner what to look for wouldn't send him down the wrong trail. "Find out if her throat was cut before she died."

Rosen quirked an eyebrow. "This must be some case you're working, Ryan. Be careful. You too, Jack."

The deputy coroner settled his hat down tighter and followed his men to the waiting van. Jack watched him go, pencil idly tapping on the side of his notebook. "Now what?"

"We wait to hear from Sal. I don't see where we have much choice with this victim. We don't know who she was or have much of a place to start to find out."

Henderson and Flynn had split St. John's crew into groups of two to take statements, keeping the men being questioned separated from the rest. The squad was doing their job, including keeping bystanders away from the pier and speaking to anyone who came forward offering information. Most of that information was worthless, prompted more by a person's need to feel they'd helped solve a crime than by any real knowledge. No malice was involved, no intent to steer the investigation away from the guilty, just the desire to be useful.

Every so often they got lucky and someone who really did possess information stepped out of the crowd, or showed up at the station later. That was why his men had standing orders to listen to everyone and take each person seriously.

Gabe flipped up his coat collar, attempting to stave off the feel of cold fingers tickling the back of his neck. Not everyone with information came to them. "You and I are going for a walk down the Embarcadero. Three bodies have washed up on the waterfront in the last month, all unreported. Even odds say that if three dead women showed up here, there are more bodies we don't know about."

"That's a cheery thought." Jack tucked away his notebook and fastened his overcoat buttons up to his chin. "That might also explain why my contacts couldn't turn up any word on the street."

"Mine haven't found anything either. But we sent them out looking for stories of people who died the way Bradley Wells and Sung Liang were killed." They'd wasted time hunting for a pattern that didn't exist. He led the way down Embarcadero, past the Ferry Building and the wharves that serviced bigger cargo ships, and toward the fishing docks, taverns, and rooming houses that faced the harbor. "This area is full of transients. What we need to find are stories about people who vanished and their absence was unusual enough someone noticed. Noticing a person isn't around doesn't mean anyone reported their disappearance to the police."

"Like that poor woman Sal took to the morgue. I'm sure someone must have noticed she was gone." Jack tipped his hat to an older woman and stepped off the curb to let her pass, a reflex of politeness. His expression remained distracted, but he still took in everything around them. "I'm not sure how Mandy fits into that description. Before her father died, I'd have been sure. Now . . . Sadie says she's changed. Losing her father and taking care of Archie made Mandy steadier."

"People grow up, Jack. Even spoiled rich girls."

Walking along the waterfront together was a lot like walking a beat again. Neither of them said much, occupied with looking for people and things that seemed off-kilter, noting details and how people reacted to their passing by. They weren't in uniform, but men with hard eyes watching from shadowed doorways knew they were cops without the uniform or being told. The hunted always knew the hunters.

Gabe let those men know he saw them too, going so far as to nod if a man didn't look away. The city was changing, poorer districts and neighborhoods becoming dangerous even for a cop. He blamed a great deal of that on the war. The time wasn't far off when a police officer wouldn't venture out on the streets without a sidearm.

A cold wind blew from behind, each gust a fist in the back pushing them along a few more steps. The prospect of turning around and walking against the wind made Gabe huddle deeper into his overcoat and keep going. They'd gone nearly three miles when Jack stopped and pointed across the street. "I wonder what's going on over there."

A young man dressed in workman's dungarees, a gray wool coat, and a black cloth cap shouted and waved a stack of handbills at a greengrocer standing in front of his corner store. He kept the hammer in his other hand at his side, but that could change if anger got the better of him. The grocer was white haired and much older, but that didn't stop him from shouting back and swiping at the young man with his cane. If anything, the older man was angrier.

Gabe checked for traffic and darted across the street, Jack a half step behind. "I don't know. I think we better find out."

"Hoodlum!" The old grocer whacked the younger man on the shoulder. "Get away from my store! Nail your notices up somewhere else."

"I've the same rights as anyone else, Mr. Glibert." He deflected the old man's cane with his forearm. "If others can nail up handbills on the electric poles, so can I."

Jack shoved his badge in the old man's face and grabbed the cane with his other hand before it came down a second time. "Hold on there, Mr. Glibert. I'm Lieutenant Fitzgerald of the San Francisco Police. This is Captain Ryan. Why don't you explain to us what's wrong."

Mr. Glibert glared past Jack, all the while yanking on his cane, trying to get it back. "Joey Harper is the problem! He wants to scare people away before they ever come inside my store. I told him yesterday not to put those notices up, but he doesn't listen."

"This doesn't have anything to do with your business, Mr. Glibert. Everyone posts handbills on this corner." Joey's face was red and a vein in his neck throbbed, but he was much calmer than the grocer. He held up the sheaf of papers. "People in the neighborhood have a right to know what's happening. And maybe this will help me find my brother."

"Joey, isn't it?" Jack glanced Gabe's way. He nodded and let his partner ask the questions. "How old is your brother?"

"Thad's going on twenty-six, a widower with a little daughter. He hasn't come home for more than a week." Joey clutched his flyers tighter. "He's not the kind who'd run away and leave her."

"Grown men up and leave all the time." Mr. Glibert started to cough, the sound wheezy and liquid. That didn't stop him from waving his fist and continuing to scold. "You'll make everyone afraid to walk the block, that's what your notices will do."

Gabe took an empty crate from the stack near the door, upending the wooden box. "Sit down and try to relax, Mr. Glibert. Let the lieutenant and me sort this out."

He walked Joey a few feet away, out of reach of the grocer's cane but not out of sight. They'd set out looking for stories of people who were missed. Thad Harper fit that description all too well. "Tell me what this is about. Start with your brother and why he might not come home."

"Nothing would keep Thad from coming home if he was able." Joey pulled off his cap, freeing wavy, chestnut hair. He looked younger that way, closer to sixteen than the twenty that was Gabe's first guess. Freckles were sprinkled across his cheeks and the bridge of his nose, and dark circles underneath shadowed his green eyes, adding a haggard look to his face. "Nothing would keep him away from work either, and he hasn't shown his face. He's got a good job at the cable car barn. Something happened to him, Captain. I know it."

Wind swirled around them, threatening to rip away the paper in Joey's hand and howling round the corner of Mr. Glibert's store. Dozens of handbills tacked to the pole on the corner fluttered, edges shredding and pulling loose. A fanciful man might think the scraps of paper waved, seeking his attention.

Gabe wasn't prone to fancy. He pulled his mind back to the young man in front of him. "When was the last time you saw your brother?"

"He came home last Friday and fed Lizzie supper. Thad said he had a chance to pick up an extra job for a few hours that night. He asked if I'd mind Lizzie and get her to bed." Joey swiped at his eyes and cleared his throat. "We need the money. Thad's still paying doctors from when Lizzie's mama died."

Jack frowned and tugged on his mustache. "And your brother hasn't come home since?"

"No, sir. And it's long past time." Joey held one of his handbills out to Jack and another to Gabe. "That's why I'm going around putting these up. Maybe someone else in the neighborhood went on the same job. If nothing else, they might remember the men promising two dollars to anyone who met them in Mr. Glibert's store."

The grocer's reasons for being so angry became clearer.

"Two dollars is a lot of money for a night's work." Gabe held out Joey's handbill. "Is what Joey says true? Did these men meet in your store?"

"What if they did? Everyone within ten blocks knows me and my store." Mr. Glibert started coughing again and Gabe waited him out. The grocer spit on the sidewalk, glaring at all of them. "Gathering a work crew's not against the law, last I knew. And it's not like the people paying were socialists or union organizers. The job was honest labor."

The old man believed what he said; honest men had offered honest wages for a night's work. That Thad Harper hadn't come home again afterwards didn't shake Mr. Glibert's belief in the slightest.

"I'd still like to talk to these men, Mr. Glibert. One of them might remember something important." Gabe stuffed Joey's handbill into his coat pocket. Hope kindled in the boy's eyes. The police were on his side. "Do you know their names or where I can find them?"

"Jonas and Max are the names they gave. Never heard a last name for either of them. They posted notices of their own." The old man pointed his cane at the tattered papers fluttering on the electric pole. "Find the woman they work for, and you'll find them."

Jack ripped a familiar-looking yellow handbill off the pole. He read the notice over, doing a poor job of hiding surprise. "Well son of a . . . it's her. You need to see this, Gabe."

Across the top of the handbill were printed dates and times for meetings and lectures, and an address for a church on Clement Street. The name of the speaker was printed in neat block letters underneath: EFFIE LADIA FONTAINE.

The color of the paper, the typeface, and the information were the same as the handbill retrieved from Amanda Poe's bedroom. But that's where the similarity between the two advertisements for Miss Fontaine's lectures ended. The differences were what struck Gabe hardest.

In the center of the page was a color photograph of a rather plain woman dressed in a crimson choir robe, arms outstretched as if to gather someone into an embrace. She smiled broadly, a garland of pale blue flowers crowning unbound dark hair. Even reproduced on cheap paper, the colors were bright and the image lifelike.

Officer Perry had explained about Lumière Autochrome plates after showing Gabe some color photographs in a *National Geographic* magazine. He'd confirm his hunch with Perry later, but he was dead certain this photo was taken the same way. The process was much more expensive than hand-tinting black-and-white photos, putting it out of reach of most amateur photographers. Reproducing images taken with Autochrome plates was expensive as well.

Effie Fontaine couldn't be more than a step up from a tent-show revivalist. That a traveling speaker would have that kind of money to throw away on handbills gave him pause.

Amanda Poe had attended Effie Fontaine's pacifist lectures, and Thad Harper had signed on for a night's labor with two of her followers. Both of them had gone missing. Miss Fontaine was the only link between the rich society girl and the struggling widower, a tenuous connection at best, and one that most people would consider a coincidence. But Gabe wasn't most people.

He stared at the picture, memorizing the face, trying to read who this person was from an image captured by a camera. Effie Fontaine's expression was pure sincerity and belief, her smile full of compassion. A camera wouldn't be able to capture the life in a person's eyes, nor the spark of personality that ink-and-paper photographs deadened. Still, the pose in the photograph was artful, designed to draw people in and inspire trust.

Gabe trusted the revulsion that shivered up his spine. "Mr. Glibert, have these men come around offering jobs in the neighborhood more than once?"

"Three, four times that I know of. Found men willing to work for them every time." Glibert scratched his neck, leaving long, red welts on pasty skin. "They've been putting handbills up for weeks, but they met in my store only the one time."

Jack looked up from scribbling notes. "Is Thad Harper the only man not to come home again?"

Glibert planted his cane firmly and struggled to his feet, arms shaking and eyeing Jack. No one would mistake his glare for anything but what it was, thinly veiled contempt. "I couldn't say, Lieutenant. Not my job to keep track. Now, if you're done with me, I've got work to do."

Gabe moved to block Glibert's way inside. "One last question. Were you paid for the use of the store?"

The old man snorted. "Course I got paid. That's not against the law either. Now, unless you intend to arrest me, get out of my way."

He tipped his hat and stepped back, letting Glibert hobble inside. The grocer stopped short of slamming the front door in their faces, most likely out of fear of breaking the glass and not out of any show of respect for officers of the law.

"Joey, do you have access to a phone?" The boy nodded and Gabe tore a blank page from Jack's notebook. He wrote out the address and phone number of the police station, and handed the paper to Joey. "Call us at the station if there's any news of your brother or you hear of anyone else who's missing. If Lieutenant Fitzgerald or I aren't there, someone will get a message to us."

"Thank you, Captain." Joey carefully folded the scrap of paper and tucked it into his shirt pocket. "A neighbor's minding my niece, but I promised to be home before supper. I best get the rest of these handbills posted and get back. With luck, Mr. Glibert won't rip them all down before people get a chance to read one."

Curtains on the window nearest the door twitched shut. Gabe looked pointedly at the front of the store and took a step closer, certain the old man was watching. He raised his voice, wanting to make sure Glibert heard. "Don't worry about Mr. Glibert. I'll make sure he won't bother you."

He and Jack waited until the boy had nailed up three notices on the pole outside Glibert's store, standing guard. Once Joey moved down the block, they started back the other way on Embarcadero, toward the construction site. The wind had died away to a fitful breeze, not a cold gale that blew full in their face. They made better time as a result.

Neither of them said much, but talking wasn't really necessary. Gabe and Jack both saw the yellow handbills nailed on every electric pole, fence post, and notice board they passed. Some were faded to the point the paper was almost white, victims of sun and age. Bright, fresh notices with new meeting dates were layered atop the old, splashes of sunshine against weathered wood. He couldn't begin to count the tattered pieces of paper or explain why he hadn't noticed before.

Now he couldn't stop seeing. Effie Fontaine's smiling face was inescapable.

CHAPTER 11

Delia

I'd put Dora to bed in the spare room as soon as we reached the house. She'd made a token protest, but I knew her well enough to recognize that was all show. Exhaustion dragged at the corners of her mouth, and her eyes were narrowed with pain, all signs she'd pushed herself too far. How quickly she'd fallen asleep proved I'd been right to insist. Gabe and Jack might not arrive until suppertime or later, and I saw no reason for her not to rest until then.

Convincing Randy Dodd there was no need to patrol the outside of the house or stand guard at the front door was more difficult. He was an earnest young man, determined to fulfill Gabe's trust. We'd settled on him dragging a sitting room chair into the front hall, a vantage point that let him watch the front entrance and the doorways into most of the house. Seeing him comfortably seated and reading *The Saturday Evening Post* eased my conscience.

A part of me viewed Randy's staying here as unnecessary, an overreaction on Gabe's part. Isadora and I had viewed evidence from dozens of murders, consulted on Jack and Gabe's investigations for more than two years. Hints of the occult had crept into cases in the past, not as strong nor so gruesome, but undeniable. This was the first time Gabe had felt Dora and I needed protection just because we'd viewed a set of photographs, or handled a piece of evidence.

That in itself was disturbing. And if I was honest and paid heed to the disquiet that dogged my steps, the urge to roam room to room, peering into dark corners, I had to admit that having Randy in the house was a comfort. I couldn't talk myself out of the certainty that something was there and that if I just looked hard enough, I'd see.

Not knowing what—if anything—might be hiding ate at me. The possibilities kept unreeling in my head, ghosts and spirit creatures I'd learned of from Isadora, but had never seen. Walking always helped me think, even if the longest distance I walked was up and down the hall. That more than anything kept me from sticking to any one task.

After the fifth or sixth time I went between the sitting room and the kitchen, and peered into the bedroom checking in on Isadora, Randy glanced up from his reading and frowned. "Is everything all right, Delia?"

"Everything's fine. I'm a little restless and having a hard time settling down. That's all it is, nothing dire." A flush crept up my neck and a bright, hot spot burned in my cheeks. Randy didn't know me well yet, certainly not well enough to recognize my quirks and habits. Jumping at the thinnest of shadows had concerned him for no reason. "Nothing to worry about, I promise."

He looked me in the eye, making sure. Randy might not know what kind of threat he'd be called upon to protect me from, or if indeed there was a threat, but he took Gabe's charge to watch over us seriously. Once reassured that all was well, he went back to his reading.

I wandered into the parlor, determined to settle and be quiet until Dora woke. The kitchen was my workroom and where I was most comfortable, but our parlor was my second favorite room in the house. I spent a great deal of time there while Gabe was working. Large bay windows looked out over the side garden, ensuring the parlor was bright even on cloudy, overcast winter days. Summer gave me a view of the garden in full bloom, black and yellow bumblebees happily gathering pollen.

That wasn't the only reason I loved this room. The fireplace mantel was filled with family photographs, many of them gifts from Gabe's mother. After Matt Ryan was killed, Moira sold the egg ranch and went to live with her sister in Boise. She'd given me most of the photographs she had of Gabe as a child, portraits of Matt in uniform, and a photograph of Matt pinning Gabe's lieutenant bars on his dress uniform while Moira looked on, smiling and proud.

I'd added my own photographs of Esther, Sadie, and Annie to the collection. The 1906 fire took my parents and destroyed everything in our house, leaving me with only memories. That left me doubly grateful for the line of silver and walnut frames along the mantel and on the wall above. Not everything was lost.

My knitting bag was tucked into the corner of the parlor sofa, an activity that usually kept me well occupied. I pulled out the nearly finished carriage blanket I was making for baby Stella and set to work. Picking up a dropped stitch proved to be a challenge and concentrating on setting it right bled away most of the restlessness.

The line of frames on the mantel rattled and danced. Minor earthquakes were common, most so small and swiftly over, they passed nearly unnoticed. That was my first thought, but a glance toward the lamp on the sofa table showed the shade's beaded fringe hanging straight and still.

Laughter and a child's high-pitched singing filled the room, chasing away all thoughts of an earthquake.

A penny for a ball of thread,
Another for a needle—
Ask her where the money goes,
Pop! goes the weasel.

I stood, searching the room for the little girl ghost. She still evaded all my layers of charms and barricades, and crossed my threshold as she pleased. I refused to believe any spirit was so strong, she couldn't be shut out of my house.

She couldn't be allowed to have her way. By necessity, my will must be stronger. "You're still not welcome here, spirit. Twice I've told you to tell me what you want or to leave and not come back. This is the third time and the third time binds. Say your piece or go."

She laughed again, grating and brittle, not at all like a child at play. A cool wind ruffled my hair, lifted the curtains on windows shut tight for the winter.

Every night when I go out,
The monkey climbs the steeple,
Take a stick and knock her off,
Pop! goes the weasel.

A large walnut frame over the fireplace slid down the wall and crashed to the floor, sending shards of shattered glass and splintered wood flying. Two more frames, a photo of Esther and one of Gabe's parents, jumped off the wall as I watched. They landed at my feet, showering the tops of my shoes with broken glass. That sent me scrambling away from the sofa and toward the other side of the room.

Frames flew across the parlor too quickly to dodge, driving me toward the wall and away from the door. I huddled against the pale yellow wallpaper, arms wrapped around my head. One by one, the photographs I'd cherished crashed into the wall next to my head, tearing the wallpaper and gouging holes in the plaster. Others smashed on the floor around my feet.

"Delia! What's going on?" I heard Randy's voice calling me and the note of alarm when I didn't answer. Not everything the ghost threw hit me directly, but she kept me pinned in place.

Two sets of running footfalls in the hall promised help. "Delia! Answer me!"

Not being able to escape proved both painful and terrifying. The backs of my hands stung with tiny cuts and pieces of glass lodged in my cuffs, threatening to slide down my sleeves. Blood matted my hair and trickled down the back of my neck.

In and out the corner store,
The monkey chased the people,
Ask her where the children go,
Pop! goes the weasel.

Mrs. Allen's poltergeist and the little girl ghost were one and the same. That was the only thought I could form and hold. Charms to send away harmful spirits, cantrips to seal entrances and forbid ghosts from crossing the threshold: all the words evaporated before I could utter a one. Fear was a small part of it, but the ghost's power to use my fear against me was a bigger factor. The ghost wanted me afraid and silent; that was clear. I just didn't understand why.

A tall curio cabinet tipped over, shattering the glass-paneled front and blocking the doorway. Large, razor-edged pieces of glass slid across the oak floor, coming to rest in the carpet fringe. A smaller fragment bounced and pain spiked up my leg. I screamed.

"Oh dear God . . . Dee!" A quick glance showed Isadora framed in the doorway, hair disheveled and clothing rumpled from sleeping on the guest bed. She planted both hands against the curio cabinet and pushed, but it wouldn't budge. "Randy, go help her. Hurry!"

Randy scrambled over the toppled cabinet, ripping his uniform pants on a jagged hook of glass still hanging from the front. He curled over me, providing shelter and blocking the rain of broken glass and splinters with his body. The ghost had run short of framed photographs and made a start on flinging books, vases, and small knickknacks. Sharp intakes of breath and a quickly stifled groan told me the ghost wasn't holding back or deliberately missing now that he was between us; she hit Randy more than once.

The barrage stopped as unexpectedly as it began. A large, heavy-bottomed vase hovered for an instant before settling to the floor and spinning in a circle. Books tumbled off a shelf, but nothing else flew toward me.

The clock in the front hallway chimed five o'clock. Randy waited a few more seconds, gasping, before he stood straight. He got a good look at me and his eyes went wide. "We should send for a doctor, Delia, just to make sure you're all right. I'm going to call the station and have them hunt down the captain. He'll want to come home right away once he hears."

Dora searched the corners of the room, eyes narrowed and her mouth set in a scowl. "We'll call Gabe soon enough, but first we need to get her out of this room. Quickly now. Help me get her to the kitchen."

The curio cabinet moved easily enough this time. Randy shoved it to the center of the room, leaving the doorway clear. Dora looked me over quickly, concern and relief warring in her eyes, before wrapping an arm around my waist to hurry me down the hall. My kitchen was swaddled in wards, a necessity to protect my workroom. I'd be safe there if I was safe anywhere in the house.

That the home I'd made with Gabe might not be safe, not for me or for him, struck me hard. Falling into despair would be so easy. I shut my eyes, swallowing tears and nursing a stubborn spark of anger inside until it grew into a raging flame that drove away fear. The ghost thought she'd won, but I wouldn't let her. I refused.

Dora settled me into a kitchen chair and began giving orders. "Randy, close the door into the hall and find me a basin for water. I know Dee has a bowl or something in the cupboard by the stove. You should find clean napkins or towels in the sideboard. And don't open the hall door again unless I say. The seal is stronger with it shut."

I sat quietly and let her fuss over me, shaken but unable to stop my mind from circling endlessly. Fear and pain receded into the background. All I could focus on was the question of why the little girl ghost attacked me and why she'd spent so much time causing trouble for Mrs. Allen. "Why" was important.

Isadora took stock of my injuries, giving me a running list. Her hands were steady even if a tremor had crept into her voice. "The cut on your cheek isn't very deep. I don't think you need worry much about scars on your face. Your hands and your calf are worse, but nothing is bleeding much. I'd feel better all the way around if a doctor took a look at the gash on the back of your head. I'm so, so sorry, Dee. Damn sneaky poltergeist attached itself to you and I didn't notice."

"You couldn't have noticed, Dora, and there's no need to apologize. She was already here." Powdered glass covered my clothes, razor-edged diamond dust that caught the light and warned not to touch. I held tight to the chair seat to keep myself from brushing at my skirts, an old habit born of nerves. "The little girl ghost I told you about was responsible for wrecking my parlor and all the trouble at Mrs. Allen's boarding house. This is all her handiwork, I'm certain of it. I'm equally sure she's not a poltergeist."

"A ghost did all that damage?" Randy set a basin of warm water and one of my best tea towels on the table. His hands shook, sloshing water, and a dark, wet ring spread across the tablecloth. "When you told me you saw ghosts—I mean, well, I thought you saw spirits like they show in the cinema. I never imagined real ghosts could tip over pieces of furniture. You can practically see right through the ghosts in *Old Scrooge* and that new movie. What's it called? The one with the mad king and the witches."

"It's called *Macbeth*. And you weren't wrong." Dora patted his cheek fondly and smiled. She dipped the tea towel in warm water and began wiping blood and layers of dust off my face. "It's very rare for a ghost to be able to move or influence physical objects. But this ghost has already proved to be exceptional. I'm beginning to doubt that she's a ghost, at least not in the way I normally think of spirits. She doesn't follow the rules."

He flipped another chair around and sat backwards, the way he straddled the chair reminding me a great deal of Jack. My husband had more than his share of rookie cops looking to be just like him, imitating Gabe's mannerisms and the way he worked. I could easily imagine the same type of hero worship directed toward Jack.

Randy laid his arms along the back of the chair, studying Dora's face. "What do you mean?"

"Just what Dora said, this ghost doesn't follow the rules spirits are normally bound by. Ghosts normally manifest in one way, take one form." I flinched, fighting back tears. Isadora smiled an apology and went back to scrubbing cuts and scrapes on the back of my hand. "That form can be as solid and real as they looked in life, thin as a cloud of steam, or somewhere between. A poltergeist is always a poltergeist and a haunt is always a haunt. This ghost had proved she can change form as she pleases. Act as it suits her to act."

He looked between us, not confused or frightened as I'd expect from someone encountering spirits for the first time, but truly curious. "So what is she?"

"A problem." Dora's smile was bright, guileless. Randy didn't know her well and I doubt he saw the momentary uncertainty in her eyes, but I did. "I need to resolve this soon before anyone else gets hurt. Now, be a darling and go call Gabe for me. The telephone is in the sitting room. Make sure he knows it's nothing terribly serious, but tell him to fetch the doctor on his way home."

He left, shutting the door again without prompting.

"He's gone. Tell me what you're afraid of." I twisted in the chair, ignoring the sting of cuts pulling open again. Looking Dora in the eye was more important. "And don't you dare try to be coy with me, Isadora Bobet, or try to wheedle out of telling me everything. I don't need to be coddled or cosseted because this spirit singled me out."

Dora sighed and tossed the tea towel onto the table. She dragged Randy's chair over, sitting knee to knee with me and taking my hand. "But she did single you out, Dee, and that has to mean something. I wasn't lying when I said this spirit was a problem. You said yourself that you were in her way when it came to getting at Gabe. Maybe she thinks she can drive you away, and the attack today was only the beginning. It's not coddling for me to be extra cautious in the face of that. I can't say for certain how malevolent this spirit is or begin to guess what she'll do next. I'm not even sure what she is."

I'd learned that unless she was telling fortunes or holding a séance at a society party, Dora wasn't given to theatrics or exaggeration. If the little girl spirit frightened her or made her unsure of her ground, I had every right to be terrified.

That I wasn't frightened, especially after what I'd just been through, probably said something about my sanity. Instead, I was furious. The things she'd destroyed—photographs of people I'd loved and lost, wedding presents and small remembrances of Esther— couldn't be replaced. This ghost in little girl guise continued to seek ways to come between me and Gabe, and I was just as determined she wouldn't have her way. What she'd done to Katie Allen just added more reasons to be angry.

Anger had carried me through rough spots more than once. "Solving the mystery of what this spirit is seems to be the logical first step. We can deal with her once we know. This might be a good time to dig into that witch's bag of tricks you've mentioned a time or two. I'm keen on discovering what you're hiding in there."

She smiled, genuinely amused. Doubt left her eyes. "At least one of those tricks is better tried in my house. Have Gabe bring you for supper tomorrow night. I think Randy may prove useful as well, so I'll include him in the invitation. My housekeeper will adore having someone to cook for that appreciates her efforts."

"What do you have in mind?"

Dora carried the basin of dirty water to the sink and rinsed it under the tap. "I want to try a tarot reading for both you and Gabe to discover why this spirit is so focused on your husband. The spread that comes up for Gabe will be of special interest. I'm hoping to find a hint as to who this ghost was in life."

"And that in turn will give you an idea of what she is now." I brushed the damp tea towel over the front of my blouse and down my skirts, attempting to remove the worst of the glass slivers that clung to my clothing. "Why include Randy?"

"Because having him there will make me feel better about your safety. There's always a chance this tarot reading could stir our puzzling ghost into action again." She leaned back against the sink, staring at the kitchen door as if she expected it to fly off the hinges at any moment. "This spirit relented because Randy came into the room and siphoned off the psychic energy. Otherwise, I'm sure she would have been quite content to pummel you for much longer. I don't want to think about what might have happened if he hadn't been here."

I stared at the cuts on my hands and the blood splattered on my dress. "You actually believe Randy stopped her from killing me."

Dora sighed. "Yes, Delia, that's exactly what I think. He saved your life. I won't be leaving tonight until I've taken steps to keep her from entering your house or attacking you again. Wards and charms haven't held this ghost at bay, but salt should do the trick."

"Salt?" I stared at her openmouthed, unsure if I should laugh or cry. "You could have told me before now. I've been at my wit's end. Knowing I could send this spirit packing with a saltcellar would have been a huge help."

Dora did laugh. "It will take considerably more than a saltcellar to shut her out, but we'll manage. I'll send Jack to call on a grocer I know over on Polk Street. Two or three fifty-pound bags should be enough." She held out a hand. "Let's get you out of those clothes. Gabe will bring the doctor soon. Better he doesn't see you like this."

"Very wise." I stood, grateful for her hand as the room spun for an instant and then righted itself. "I'd hate for Gabe to get the idea that dealing with ghosts might be dangerous at times. That would never do."

"It's too late for that, Dee." She smiled and put an arm around my waist. "I'm fairly certain he already knows."

CHAPTER 12

Gabe

Gabe switched off the desk lamp and slumped back in his chair, rubbing his eyes. He couldn't focus on the reports littering his desk. The image of shattered glass on the parlor floor, broken furniture, and dusky bruises on Delia's arms and back overlaid the words each time he tried.

He'd spent many a strange night on foot patrol or working cases, but nothing so outlandish as what he'd done last night. Two hundred pounds of brining salt ringed the foundation of their house, sealed the thresholds and casements. He and Jack had spread the salt according to Dora's instructions while she followed behind, muttering charms to make the barrier tight.

Remembering the relief on Delia's face when they'd finished roiled his stomach. That she believed this ghost meant to kill her made him believe too. He'd kept an arm around her all night, starting awake at the smallest sound.

Gabe didn't know how he'd protect her from a vengeful ghost, just that he'd do anything to keep her safe. He wouldn't lose Delia that way. He couldn't.

A cursory rap on the door was all the warning Jack gave before waltzing in, arms full of more report folders. The neat creases in his trousers and freshly starched collar were Annie's daily contributions to making him look the part of a police lieutenant. Not even Annie could disguise that his partner looked as worn and harried as Gabe felt.

Jack dumped the folders on the existing pile. "You look like hell, Captain Ryan."

"So do you." He covered his mouth, attempting to stifle another yawn. "It was a rough night. I kept waiting for the monster to crawl out from under the bed. Any progress?"

"Depends on what you mean by progress." Jack dragged the visitor's chair to the side of the desk and sat. He riffled through the folders, finally pulling one up to the top and handing Gabe the paper inside. "At least ten, maybe fourteen people went off with Effie Fontaine's men and never came back. All but the two young women on that list signed on for a night's work. Leanne Schaffer and Greta Taub told the boardinghouse landlady Mrs. Jacobs that they were going to attend one of Fontaine's lectures. That evening was the last time she saw them."

Gabe scanned down the list, noting names and ages. Looking for a pattern. "Their landlady didn't report them missing?"

"Mrs. Jacobs saw a well-dressed man help Leanne and Greta into a car and drive off. Henderson said she went on at length about there being only one reason for them to drive off with a man." Jack made a sour face. "She apparently didn't think much of the girls' virtue. Rent was due by the end of the week. Leanne and Greta still hadn't shown up by then, so Mrs. Jacobs boxed up their things and rented the room to a new boarder. Neither girl has any family that the landlady knows of."

He looked the list over one last time. Names alone didn't tell him much, but he could guess. They were all alone in the world, people no one would miss or wonder where they'd gone. Unlike Thad Harper, they had no one counting on them to come home again.

"We can connect ten of these names to Fontaine for sure." Gabe rocked back in his chair, fingers steepled on his chest. "What about the other four?"

Jack frowned and tugged another piece of paper out of the pile. "All of them were part of a work crew hired by Fontaine's men sometime in the last two or three months. They vanished later, not the same day. That makes connecting their disappearance to her harder."

"But not impossible."

None of what they knew made any sense, and each time Gabe tried to think of a possible motive, or what Effie Fontaine had to gain, he came up short. All he was certain of was that the scattered facts and bits of evidence disturbed him in a way he couldn't explain. And Gabe dearly wanted an explanation for all of it. He tossed the list of names on the desk and stood. "I think it's time for us to pay Miss Fontaine a visit. People who cross her path have a bad habit of disappearing. I want to hear her tell me why."

Jack stayed where he was, arms folded over his chest, and stared out the window behind Gabe's desk. The window was set high in the wall, giving little more than a view of the sky and the rooftops of buildings across the street. A brisk wind blew thin white clouds across that small, visible patch of sky, a gauzy veil rippling over the deeper blue. Gabe waited for his partner to speak, dead certain Jack wasn't cloud gazing. The wait wasn't long.

"Sorry." Jack sighed and scrubbed hands over his face. "I can't help thinking about Amanda. Her name should be on this list too."

Gabe cast about for the kindest way to say Amanda was dead, that she'd been gone too long to hold out hope. But he didn't need to say the words.

His partner was a good cop. Jack already knew. "If she was able, Mandy would have come home by now. Archie didn't kill her, something happened after Fontaine's lecture. All the people on that list are dead. I don't know how, but Effie Fontaine is in this up to her neck."

"You're not going to get an argument from me, Lieutenant. I think you're right." Gabe locked the report folders in his bottom drawer, checking twice to make sure nothing had been forgotten. "But right now it's only a wild guess, a theory. We need proof and a solid connection to Effie Fontaine or the people around her. The only way to find out what happened to Amanda is to keep looking for evidence. We will find it."

Jack stood and cleared his throat. "I'm game. Even if Amanda is dead—knowing for sure one way or the other will be better for Sadie. This is tearing her up, Gabe."

"Then let's start finding proof. Maybe we can uncover a motive while we're digging." He clapped his partner on the shoulder. "Get your overcoat. I'll have the desk sergeant arrange for a car."

Gabe grabbed his coat and hat. He yanked open the office door to find Patrolman Rockwell outside, arm poised to knock.

"Captain Ryan, I'm glad I caught you." Lon Rockwell's face was blotched and sweaty, and he fidgeted with his collar. Gabe was startled to see Rockwell so rattled and drew back a step, on guard. The tall, beefy patrolman was normally calm in the face of almost anything. "You have a visitor, sir. She insisted on being escorted to your office. I hope you don't mind."

The woman in the hallway didn't wait for an introduction or an invitation. She swept around Rockwell and into Gabe's office, two men in well-tailored black suits a step behind. Bodyguards. The show of force ratcheted his sense of caution up another notch.

He recognized Effie Ladia Fontaine from her photograph. She wasn't more than an inch or two over five feet tall, and Gabe doubted if her head reached any higher than Delia's shoulder. Compact and square shouldered, hints of gray showed at her temples, Miss Fontaine wasn't at all what he'd expected from a woman delivering pacifist lectures in church halls.

Part of that was the fashionable dark green suit she wore and the emerald and jade choker at her throat, an outfit more suited to a society luncheon than to preaching peace from the pulpit. Her small handbag was dyed a greenish black, big enough to hold a comb and a compact, but not much more. The entire ensemble was obviously chosen to set off her striking green eyes.

What really struck him was the way she strutted into the room, utterly in command and certain that all eyes were on her. Dora moved in that same confident way, but Isadora was playful and flirtatious. Effie Fontaine was sultry, arrogant.

Gabe and Jack traded looks, a question asked and answered. His partner saw the same thing. He cleared his throat and smiled, but kept his hands buried deep in his trouser pockets. "What can I do for you, Miss . . . Sorry, I didn't get your name."

Miss Fontaine took a turn around his office before acknowledging his greeting. She studied the newspaper articles and old telegrams pinned to the soft pine board on the wall, glanced at the small stack of books on the file cabinet, and idly leafed through the papers in the tray on his desk. Anything more important than a duty roster was locked away, but he had a hunch she knew that. He reined in his temper, determined to win whatever game she played.

He was slowly counting to a hundred for the fifth or sixth time when she turned to him. She tugged off her glove and held out her hand, unsmiling and direct. "Effie Fontaine. I hear your men are asking questions about me, Mr. Ryan. That needs to stop immediately."

Rockwell looked up, startled by the implied insult. He opened his mouth to say something, but a look from Gabe stopped him. "You can go back to your duties, Officer. The lieutenant and I will handle things from here."

He didn't take Miss Fontaine's hand until after Lon closed the door. A hot, blue spark snapped between them. She flinched hard, trying to yank her hand back, but Gabe held on for another few seconds. He didn't let his smile drop, gritting his teeth against the feel of grabbing a bare electric wire.

Something similar happened with Isadora on occasion. Dora had explained the spark and flash by saying she was the lightning rod that grounded him, draining away the negative energy that just doing his job attracted. The worst he'd ever felt with Isadora was a mild shock, akin to scraping his shoes on the carpet before touching a doorknob. This was burning, painful, and left a dusty taste on the back of his tongue. And he'd never felt the need to scrub his skin raw after touching Dora's hand.

That left him wondering who Miss Effie Ladia Fontaine really was and what she might be hiding. She definitely wasn't just the peace evangelist she claimed to be. Every instinct he'd honed as a cop and every bit of hard-won experience said the face she showed the world was a lie.

Anger, irrational and unprovoked, bubbled up as he let the handshake end. Gabe found himself fervently wishing Dora were there to tell him what there was about this woman he couldn't see. He was out of his depth and he knew it. "It's Captain Ryan. This is my partner, Lieutenant Fitzgerald. Why don't you have a seat?"

"I'll stand if you don't mind." She studied the reddened palm of her hand, frowning, and put her glove back on. Miss Fontaine was still frowning as she looked him in the eye. "I don't plan on wasting your time or mine, so I'll come straight to the point. Call off your dogs, Captain. People opposed to my message have tried to intimidate me before and failed. And I certainly won't allow myself to become entangled in malicious gossip or some trumped-up scandal. The questions your men are asking are certain to do both."

Jack stepped forward, his face a study in polite puzzlement. "I don't understand, Miss Fontaine. We're conducting an investigation, not spreading gossip. What makes you think otherwise?"

Gabe stayed in the background, waiting to see how she'd react. Jack had used the same ploy in the past, both to survive his stepmother's social circles and to coax reluctant witnesses and suspects to talk. Being overly polite and concerned often irritated them into revealing more than they'd planned, especially if they were angry to begin with.

That tactic wasn't going to work on Effie Fontaine. Her frosty smile and exasperated sigh left no doubt she knew what he was doing. "Really, Lieutenant, don't play the fool with me. The role doesn't become you."

Knowing when to change how he approached a witness was one

of the reasons Jack was so good at his job. And at least for now, Miss Fontaine was only a witness.

"All right. I was hoping to keep this polite and civil. But we can do it your way." Jack folded his arms, glancing at the two bodyguards in turn and openly dismissing them as beneath notice. "The captain and I have no interest in intimidating you or causing a scandal. All we want to do is bring Thad Harper home to his family. Asking questions that might help us find him is our officers' job."

"If asking after a missing day laborer were all your officers did, I wouldn't be here. The reports I've had say your men are implying that anyone who comes to work for me vanishes into thin air." She waved a hand dismissively. "That's a preposterous allegation and you know it."

Gabe perched on a corner of the desk, coat draped across his lap. He kept his cool, impersonal detective expression in place, hiding how much this small woman irritated him. She set his teeth on edge, and for the life of him, he didn't understand why. "No one is making any allegations yet, Miss Fontaine. We're investigating a missing persons report filed by a member of Thad Harper's family. The last place anyone saw Mr. Harper was on one of your work crews. And preposterous or not, your name keeps coming up in connection with other people who've gone missing. Other men who joined your work crews have disappeared."

"I can't be held responsible for every man who collects his wages and falls into a whiskey bottle afterwards." She stood ramrod straight and looked Gabe in the eye, arrogance replaced by injured sincerity. "My benefactor is very generous in funding my travels, Captain, and believes wholeheartedly in my message of peace. I try to be just as generous with the men I hire. Setting up tables and chairs or serving food at my receptions isn't hard work, but it is honest labor. I don't inquire into what they do with the money or where they go once they leave. That's between them and their conscience."

Gabe picked a thread off the overcoat draped across his lap, watching the bit of string twirl and float to the floor. Thinking.

Trying to sift truth from lies. "That's very generous of you. Who is your benefactor, Miss Fontaine? Anyone I might have heard of?"

"I promised not to reveal his identity." The apologetic smile she gave him was brief and insincere. "He prefers to remain out of the public eye. You understand. Now, if you'll excuse me, I must get back and prepare for my lecture tonight."

He didn't understand, and from the scowl on Jack's face, he didn't either. Gabe cleared his throat and stood. "One last question before you go. Not all the missing persons reports we've taken are for day laborers. When was the last time you saw Amanda Poe?"

Effie Fontaine's smile dimmed. He saw the initial surprise in her eyes and the calculation that quickly followed. "The shipping heiress? I've read about her in the society columns, but I don't know her personally. What possessed you to ask?"

Gabe heard Jack's muttered curse and the creak of floorboards as he moved behind her to stand near the window. Her bodyguards watched him, eyes flat and faces emotionless, but Miss Fontaine took no notice. He added finding out who her bodyguards were, and why she needed them, to his long list of unanswered questions about her.

Number one on that list was why Effie Fontaine chose to lie about knowing Amanda.

And Gabe had no doubts that she was lying. He knew what Amanda's housekeeper, Maddie Holmes, had said about how obsessed Amanda was with Effie Fontaine. Of the two women, Maddie was the one with no reason to lie.

Gabe gave Miss Fontaine a different name to attach to the housekeeper's story, someone he knew she couldn't reach—Archie Baldwin. That was important. He could almost hear his dad's voice saying that if Effie Fontaine couldn't reach Archie, she couldn't hurt him.

Provoking a reaction from her, whether anger or indifference, was important too. A reaction might lead him closer to the truth. "I asked because Miss Poe hasn't been seen by any of her friends or family for over two weeks now. Her fiancé, Archie Baldwin, told me that Amanda went to quite a few of your lectures. They attended one of your talks together the night she disappeared. As a matter of fact, he said Amanda introduced him to you at the reception afterwards. Mr. Baldwin gave me the impression that Miss Poe knew you quite well."

Effie Fontaine's laugh was harsh, mocking. "Come now, Captain. According to the newspapers, Amanda Poe is one of the richest women on the West Coast. I think I'd remember if she was deeply involved in the peace movement or sought me out for conversation. Her fiancé is mistaken."

Jack turned round from the window, the flash of anger in his eyes quickly hidden again. He hadn't forgotten their conversation with Maddie either. "So Miss Poe never attended any of your lectures?"

Miss Fontaine fished out a small mother-of-pearl compact from her handbag and began preening in the mirror, not sparing Jack so much as a glance. "I can't say for certain. She might have come to one or two. But the halls are packed with the cream of San Francisco society every night, Lieutenant, and very few have any real interest in keeping this country out of the European war. To be brutally frank, they're slumming. I'd be hard-pressed to tell one socialite from another."

He'd heard enough. Vague suspicion became a hard lump of cold certainty. She knew what had happened to Amanda, Thad Harper, and all the other names on their list.

Effie Fontaine was in this up to her chin. The only question he had left was why.

"I expect our investigation will wrap up shortly, Miss Fontaine." Gabe stood and slipped on his overcoat. The tallest bodyguard eyed him warily as he opened the office door and stepped back so she could get past. "Now, if you'll excuse us, the lieutenant and I have an appointment."

A raised eyebrow and tapping the mother-of-pearl compact

against her hand, an action quickly stilled, were the only signs he might have irritated her in turn. Effie Fontaine struck him as eerily calm. Madness often brought that kind of calm.

She sighed and tucked the compact back into her handbag. "I take it that I can expect your men to keep asking questions, Captain?"

Gabe pulled the door open wide, his smile polite and professional. He wasn't giving her an inch. "Would you like an officer to see you out?"

"Thank you, no. I think we can manage." She stopped on the threshold and smiled, one hand resting lightly on the doorframe. "Very well played, Captain. I hope next time we meet it's under more congenial circumstances."

She strutted down the corridor, one bodyguard going ahead and the other close on her heels. Gabe didn't quite slam the door behind the second bodyguard, nor did he give in to the impulse to lock it after her. Neither response was rational, but nothing he felt about Effie Fontaine was rational.

Gabe turned to find Jack sitting in the visitor's chair next to the desk, frantically scribbling in his moleskine notebook. Recording what happened as he recorded all the cases they worked together.

His partner glanced up when Gabe dropped into his chair. Jack wrote another few lines before snapping the notebook shut and stuffing it into a jacket pocket. "Christ Almighty, Gabe. How could she look you in the eye and lie like that?"

"She doesn't know about Maddie Holmes. I'd like to keep it that way if at all possible." Gabe opened the shallow top desk drawer, shifting the clutter inside until he uncovered his tattered Woolworth five-and-dime-store notebook full of names and phone numbers. He thumbed through until he found the page with Commissioner Lindsey's name and number scrawled down one side. "But what she said about society folk slumming at her lectures made me wonder who else might have gotten involved with the peace movement. Do you think your stepmother, Katherine, has heard any gossip regarding Effie Fontaine?"

"Katherine doesn't indulge in gossip, and she'd be insulted if I implied such a thing. I doubt she'd tell me even if she had heard any talk. We get along worse than ever since I had the nerve to make her a grandmother." Jack tapped the edge of the desk with his pencil, frowning. "Sadie, on the other hand . . . I'd wager lunch that she's heard something. Nothing keeps my wife from knowing all the gossip, not even our daughter. I'll ask her tonight."

"Make it clear that she's not to go hunting for stories or asking questions. I'm not sure that's safe."

Jack wiped a hand over his mouth and frowned. "That would be just like her too. I'll make sure Sadie understands to stay clear. Fontaine and her bodyguards give me the willies. I don't want Sadie anywhere near that woman or doing anything that might be noticed."

"Good. I've got another angle I want to try too. Maybe we can figure out what's at stake for Miss Fontaine. There has to be a reason people who have contact with her turn up missing and presumed dead." He scribbled Lindsey's number on a piece of paper. "I'm going to give the commissioner a call and see if his daughter Adele is well enough to talk to us."

"Why bother—?" Understanding bloomed on Jack's face. "Bradley and Adele Wells aren't the cream of society, but they're damn close. Bradley might have gone slumming for a lecture or two."

"Maybe. Right now it's only a hunch, but I want to play it out. We've got a long way to go before we can connect Fontaine or the people around her to any of these cases." The cold itch on the back of his neck said this was more than a hunch. Gabe didn't understand where his certainty came from, but he knew in his bones that Bradley Wells had fallen under Effie Fontaine's shadow. He closed up his desk for the second time in an hour and stood. "I'll use the phone in the chief's office to call Lindsey. Even if Adele is too ill to speak to us, she might be able to tell her father what we need to know. And even if Wells did attend her lectures, connecting Fontaine to the murder is still a long way off. Let's go."

The call to the commissioner was brief. Lindsey was eager for any kind of progress on his son-in-law's murder and agreed to let them speak to his daughter. Having her father there would make things easier for Adele.

They stopped at Jack's office for his coat and plaid cap before leaving the station. The two of them didn't speak on the way out. Questioning grieving relatives was part of a detective's job, a duty that never got easier. Neither one of them relished causing Adele Wells more pain or reminding her of all she'd lost.

Most days, Gabe believed finding justice for victims was paramount, no matter what the cost. Other days, he wasn't so sure.

CHAPTER 13

Delia

Isadora showed up at my front door not long after ten. As always, she was dressed to turn heads and ensure she was the center of attention. Dora did a little twirl in the entryway to show off her fashionably short watered-taffeta skirt and matching sea green jacket. A single strand of pearls at her throat matched the cream silk blouse underneath the jacket.

Her hat was utterly outrageous, with puffs of rumpled black silk and bows all around the brim, all of which made it absolutely perfect for her. The peacock plume on the crown was so long, it had brushed the top of the doorframe as she swept inside.

"Delia, hurry up and get dressed to go out." She appeared much more chipper and cheery than I'd seen her in weeks, positively brimming with good humor. "I woke up this morning with the most marvelous idea! Go on now, I have a driver waiting."

Her smile was sunny and utterly guileless, and I didn't believe it for an instant. I'd no doubt that this was all a ruse for my benefit, an attempt to take my mind off vengeful ghosts and my ruined parlor. "Good morning, Dora. Perhaps you should tell me about this marvelous idea before I commit to going out. I'd a full day planned before the tarot reading tonight."

She took both my hands, fond smile still firmly in place. "Did you really think I'd leave you here alone to brood all day? Get dressed. I promise this will be fun."

"All right, but I'm holding you to that promise." I looked her outfit over again and shook my head. "Between you and Sadie, I always end up looking dull as dust."

"Nonsense. I have to dress this way to get any attention at all. And still, no one has ever looked at me the way Gabe looks at you." She squeezed my hand. "Wear your blue silk. You look lovely in that shade. I'll tell you where we're going once we're in the car."

I did as I was told and got dressed after finding the blue silk dress in the wardrobe and sorting out gloves, a handbag, and shoes to match. Dora chatted about things she'd read on the society page that morning, reminding me of Sadie at her best, full of gossip and stories of amusing scandals. By the time I was ready, I felt much better about our mystery outing.

A long black car sat at the curb, a uniformed driver waiting patiently by the rear door for Dora's return. I stopped on the front steps and stared. "Please say you didn't hire a car just to pamper me. If anyone needs pampering, it's Gabe. He's much more shaken than I am."

Dora laughed and put her arm through mine. "The car belongs to Daniel. He rarely drives, so the car sits in a rented garage, gathering dust. I promised him I'd take it out every so often while he's in Europe." She leaned close to whisper, laughter in her voice. "The driver comes with the car and leaves the garage about as often. I think he might have gathered a bit of dust as well. Nathan is rather stodgy, but a day with us should loosen him up a bit."

I eyed Nathan, taking in his stiff posture and frosty demeanor. "Thawing him will be a challenge even for you. You might need more than an afternoon."

"Then perhaps we should make taking the car out a weekly event. Never let it be said I shrink from a challenge." She gave him her most beguiling smile, the sort that normally turned men's knees to jelly on the spot.

Nathan didn't melt; if anything, the way he stood became more rigid. He bowed stiffly as I got into the car, but never so much as gave a hint of a smile. I slid across the cold, leather seat to make room for Dora, fairly certain she'd finally met someone she couldn't charm.

Dora got in and he shut the door, moving quickly around the front of the car to the driver's seat. A moment later we pulled away from the curb.

Dora and I had spoken about her going to see Archie again this morning, and making an attempt to banish the ghosts tormenting him. I'd had nightmares of Archie Baldwin all night long, watching him cringe at the feet of vengeful soldiers, each gas-ravaged and bloody face full of hate. "Did you get the chance to see Archie today?"

"No, I'm afraid not. Gabe and Jack had just left the station. Something to do with the Wells murder investigation." Isadora rooted around in her handbag, frowning until she found her compact. She checked her hat in the small mirror and dropped the compact back in her bag. "Your husband's men are too well trained. No one would let me into his cell without Gabe's permission. I'll make arrangements with Gabe and Jack to see Archie first thing tomorrow."

"I'll go with you. Knowing beforehand what we'll face will make a world of difference." Just the thought of Archie suffering for another day made me intensely uncomfortable. "We'll be prepared this time."

"I've already prepared. But I'll more than welcome your assistance." Dora patted my hand and smiled, doggedly determined to be cheerful. "We'll help Archie, you've my word on that. But I've gone to a lot of trouble arranging this surprise, and all my efforts will be wasted if you spend the day fretting. Try to enjoy yourself."

A small picnic hamper sat on the floor at my feet. I opened the lid, and the smell of roast chicken, fresh bread, and chocolates filled the backseat. "A picnic is a wonderful idea, Dora, but I'm afraid eating outdoors in mid-January is a bit chilly for me."

"Don't be silly. I'm better at planning surprises than that." She leaned back and fussed with the beads on her jacket, smug as a cat with a saucer of cream. "We're going to the Conservatory of Flowers for our picnic. With the exception of a few hearty Minnesotans, not many tourists go to Golden Gate Park in winter. It's much too cold. We'll be quite warm inside the conservatory while we eat and likely have the orchids all to ourselves."

"Dora . . . that's perfect." Tears filled my eyes. "My father used to go there to paint the water lilies and the roses when they were in bloom. He'd take me with him whenever I wanted to go along. I haven't been there in years. Not since he died."

"You told me." She squeezed my hand. "And since I've never been to the conservatory, this is the perfect opportunity for you to teach me about the plants grown there. You never know when some exotic herb or flower buds might come in handy."

Golden Gate Park wasn't far and it didn't take long before the tall redwood and eucalyptus trees, thickets of rhododendron, and sweeping green lawns came into view. Even in winter, the three-mile-long park was an oasis in the middle of San Francisco, quiet and green.

Most of the pathways that crisscrossed the park were designed for strolling, not for cars. Nathan found a place to park not too far from the conservatory, and Dora and I set off, picnic hamper swinging between us.

Few ghosts wandered the park anytime I'd visited, something that had always surprised me. I'd expected to see men from the gold rush years, women from Barbary Coast saloons, or whalers from long ago, but I never did. Those few spirits I saw were faded, little more than tattered remnants of people living here before San Francisco was founded: Spanish explorers and Russian fur trappers, and members of the Ohlone Tribe, the people who lived here first of all.

Occasionally I caught glimpses of young men in muddy uniforms wandering between the trees, rifles at the ready, or crawling across the grass on their bellies. The city was filling with haunts of those recently dead in the Great War, their spirits returning home or to places they remembered fondly. Given the headlines and the number of spirits I saw anytime I ventured downtown, there weren't near as many soldiers' ghosts in the park as I'd feared.

What I feared most was finding the little girl ghost had followed me here, far outside the protections ringing my house, or finding legions of ghostly children staring at me from between the trees. Neither of those things happened. The few children I saw were very much alive, bundled tight in heavy coats and holding fast to a mother's or nanny's hand, or playing tag on the lawns, cheeks flushed with cold and laughter.

We strolled around a curve in the path and the conservatory came into view. Spread atop a slope and overlooking a small valley, the building looked enormous even from a distance. The greenhouse's central dome soared sixty feet over the entryway, a delicate bubble of glass and painted wood silhouetted against the sky, glittering in thin winter sunlight. L-shaped wings with arched roofs extended more than a hundred feet in each direction on either side of the central pavilion. Moisture condensed on curved walls and fogged the inside, leaving the glass looking perpetually rain-washed.

Dora stopped in the middle of the path, staring, and a smile slowly spread across her face. She set the picnic hamper on the walkway between us. "No wonder you and your father were drawn here so often, Dee. This might be the most beautiful place I've seen in San Francisco. The palaces I visited in Europe weren't nearly so striking. Was the building rebuilt after the quake?"

"No—surprisingly, the conservatory survived almost unscathed." I pointed to the top of the dome and a wall to the left of the entrance. "A few glass segments broke there at the top, over there and a few places around the back. It was rather miraculous how little damage the quake caused."

"Really . . . for a building like this to survive an earthquake that size would be a bit of a miracle." Dora studied the conservatory through narrowed eyes, frowning slightly. She turned in a slow circle, taking in the slope, the valley, and the trees growing all around the rim. As soon as she got back round to facing me, a bright smile wiped concentration from her face. Isadora took my arm and picked up the picnic basket. "I can't say for certain if other forces are at work here, so we'll leave things at miraculous for now. Let's get inside, Dee. I'm ravenous."

Dora wouldn't tell me what she suspected until she knew for sure, if for no other reason than to keep me from imagining monsters lurking behind the begonias. I trusted her to warn me of danger and wasn't overly concerned. Still, I looked at my surroundings with a fresh eye.

We hurried up the path to the front door, a fitful wind rattling winter-bare tree branches and stirring the shrubbery. Isadora's peacock plume bobbed up and down, but didn't seem any the worse for suffering the wind's attentions. We paid the entrance fee and went inside.

The building was a marvel, but the plants and trees the conservatory held were a wonder. Warm, moist air filled the pavilion under the dome, brimming over with the sweet scent of flowers, the spicy smell of ferns, wet leaves, and the dusty odor of tree bark. Bright splashes of color filled planting beds anywhere I looked: deepest reds to brilliant blue, soft shell pinks and sunburst yellow.

Quiet filled the space as well, broken only by the faint trickle of water and the crunch of footfalls on the gravel paths. People spoke as they moved past the lily ponds and admired trailing orchids, but the sound was swallowed by the dome overhead, muffled by flower petals and leaves. If I'd closed my eyes, I might have thought us the only people there.

Dora and I made our way down the wing off to the right, settling on a bench near a cluster of orange trees for our picnic. Fat yellow and black bumblebees flitted from blossom to blossom, intent on gathering orange nectar and pollen, ignoring us. We covered the bench with a red-checkered cloth and set out the food.

The chicken was still warm; a matter I decided was best left unremarked. I'd learned not to question many things involving Isadora Bobet.

Isadora was positively beaming when we'd finished eating. "This is utterly delightful. I can see why you loved coming to the conservatory with your father. Next time let's see if we can bring Sadie and the baby."

"If we make plans in advance, Gabe and Jack can come as well. Maybe in early spring when the roses begin to bloom, but before most of the tourists arrive." She'd forgotten my case of nerves concerning Sadie and the baby, but I hoped by spring I'd have no reason to be nervous. I finished packing leftovers back into the picnic hamper, full and content. "I'd love to show Gabe the spots my father set up his easel and tell him about watching Papa paint. Papa loved the rose gardens best of all, so spring would be perfect."

Something soft and warm twined around my ankles, startling me and making my heart race. I started to jerk my leg away, but stopped just in time. A tiny gray kitten, no more than nine or ten weeks old, peered out from under the edge of my skirts.

"Oh dear . . . where did you come from?" I scooped the kitten up, confirming my guess she was a little girl, and held her at eye level. Golden green eyes gazed into mine, utterly trusting and fearless. "You shouldn't be out here all alone."

Dora scratched behind the kitten's ear with a long red nail. "It's entirely possible she wandered away from her mother. A warm, sheltered place would be just the spot a mother cat would find for her litter. But the more likely scenario is that someone didn't want her and she's been abandoned. Not everyone is fond of cats, Dee. She's lucky you found her."

"Or perhaps she was looking for you." An older Chinese man, wearing a brown serge suit and a bowler hat, stood on the path a few feet away, leaning on his cane and watching us. Two heavyset Chinese men stood behind him, both of them taller and younger, and dressed in cheap-looking black trousers and coats. The older man smiled. "If so, you are indeed favored. We tell children the story of

Yifan Zhang, the Cat Goddess, and how she led an army of cats to restore righteousness to the emperor's kingdom. She will bring luck to your house and help ward off evil spirits, Mrs. Ryan."

"How do you know my name?" I pulled the kitten close, feeling a need to defend my claim to her. Her soft gray fur tickled my neck and she began to purr loudly.

Dora stood, visibly agitated to anyone who knew her, and likely to those who didn't. She folded her arms, the fingers on one hand tapping an angry rhythm against her elbow. "I'd like to hear the answer to that. How do you know Mrs. Ryan's name?"

"My apologies. I didn't mean to frighten you. Forgive me, Miss Bobet, Mrs. Ryan." He bowed. "My name is Sung Wing. Captain Ryan and his partner visited me at my business in Chinatown. They're searching for the people who killed my brother and his granddaughter."

"Captain Ryan told us about the case and what happened to your family, Mr. Sung. Your family's death is a tragedy, but that still doesn't explain how you knew Delia's name—nor mine, for that matter. And since I've a fairly good idea of who and what you are, I need to hear that explanation." Dora took a step closer, not at all pacified. "Try again."

"Isadora Bobet is well known in Chinatown. Stories about you taking an apprentice, a police captain's wife, spread quickly. A teacher and her apprentice spend much of their time together. I guessed at who the little cat had chosen." Mr. Sung smiled, appearing not at all put out by Dora's being so forward. "Wu Mai was my teacher and spoke of you often. She considered you an equal, worthy of friendship and respect. I'd be foolish not to do the same."

"You'd be foolish to underestimate me, yes." Dora's stance softened, but only slightly. "I had a great deal of respect for Mai. Since I'm committed to helping Captain Ryan solve his more difficult cases, one could say you and I are on the same side. I'm sure that's as strange for you as it is for me. Hopefully we can remain cordial."

Mr. Sung bowed deeply. "That is my hope, Miss Bobet. We both seek to find these people for our own reasons. I've sent my niece's ghost on to our ancestors, but my brother's spirit is lost to us. I need to find Liang's ghost so he can rest."

The little cat snuggled tight against me. Her purring echoed in my chest, vibrated in my bones. I was taking her home, no matter how she came to me. That much about my day was certain. "Is that why you followed us, Mr. Sung? To ask for help in finding your brother's ghost?"

"My being here is a fortunate accident, Mrs. Ryan. I was on my way home from a business meeting and while passing the park, I asked my driver to stop." Sung Wing gestured toward the orange trees and the lily ponds with his cane. "I come here often. This place reminds me of my grandmother's garden in China. I was only five when my father brought our family to San Francisco, but I remember grandmother's house smelled of orange blossoms."

One of the younger men with Mr. Sung leaned toward him and quietly said something in Chinese. Mr. Sung answered, his reply sounding crisp, abrupt. The younger man scowled and began speaking rapidly, his irritation obvious even if I couldn't understand what was said. Dora's curious expression was doubtless a twin for my own.

A snapped word from Mr. Sung ended the strange argument. The younger man's anger drained away, his face pale and sweating heavily. He whispered a few words, bowing again and again before turning and walking toward the entrance.

Mr. Sung turned back to us. "Forgive me. Li doesn't think I'm safe here and wants me to go back to Chinatown. I had to make it clear that I'm not ready to leave." His smile was touched with regret. "Li is young. He hasn't learned that always doing the safe thing can feel like a cage. Safe or not, a man must step outside his cage once in a while."

Dora raised an eyebrow. "Do you have that many enemies, Sung Wing? Mai would be disappointed."

"Not so many that her spirit would return to scold me, Miss Bobet. Any man in my position acquires enemies, but Li doesn't fear them. He's afraid that those who killed my brother will come back and take me as well."

I unbuttoned the first button of my coat and tugged off my scarf with one hand, with an eye toward wrapping the kitten in soft wool before leaving the greenhouse. "That seems like a reasonable thing to fear, Mr. Sung."

"Perhaps." He stared across the lily pond. Frogs leapt between flat green leaves the size of dinner plates, or dove into the water, but I didn't think Mr. Sung saw. "But first I'd have to believe Liang's killers knew he was my brother or mistook him for me. And I don't believe, Mrs. Ryan. They slaughtered my brother for reasons of their own."

Dora frowned and looked away for an instant, staring toward the entrance. She shook herself and took the picnic basket. "We should go, Dee. There's a lot to prepare before the boys arrive for supper."

"Give me a moment." I wrapped the kitten in the pale blue scarf, swaddling her in layers to keep out the chill wind and the damp. Only her head showed in the cocoon I'd made for her, but she didn't appear to care. If anything, she purred louder. "There. She should be warm enough now for the car ride home."

Mr. Sung stepped forward, a hand extended for the kitten to sniff his fingers. A tiny pink tongue licked his thumb and he smiled. "What will you name her?"

"I hadn't thought yet." I looked to Dora and back into the kitten's eyes. "Finding the right name is important."

Someone opened a door at the far end of the greenhouse, sending a gust of cold wind roaring from one end of the conservatory to the other. Glass tiles overhead rattled, rivaled by the sound of leaves rustling in the wind. Interwoven with the wind's voice, faint and very far away, I thought I heard a little girl singing.

The kitten lifted her head, eyes tracking the passage of the wind, and growled. Such a deep, fierce sound coming from a tiny ball of gray fluff was amusing. I should have laughed and thought no more of it. Instead my heart sped up as my eyes strained to see what this tiny cat saw.

Dora shivered and pulled her wrap tighter, but all she'd noticed was the cold creeping into our warm haven, not my reaction to a stray breeze. But Mr. Sung saw.

He reached out and scratched the kitten's ears, smoothing down ruffled fur on the top of her head until she began to purr again. "Even the smallest cat is born with a hunter's spirit. This one believes she's a tiger."

Wrapping her in my scarf was certainly enough for the short walk to the car, but I pulled the front of my coat around her as well. The degree that I worried about keeping this tiny cat out of the wind likely bordered on insanity. "Too bad she doesn't resemble a tiger. Naming her would be miles easier then, if not very imaginative."

"There is an old story that says if you listen closely, a cat will whisper its name in your ear." The twinkle in Mr. Sung's eye gave the lie to his solemn expression. "She will give you her name, Mrs. Ryan."

With that, Mr. Sung tipped his hat and walked away, his young guard following close behind. Dora and I watched until he was out of sight.

Dora started for the exit and I followed at her heels. She put on her public face, cheerful and appearing as if she didn't have a care in the world. I knew better. She was as mystified by our encounter with Sung Wing as I.

At the entrance, Isadora stopped and looked back down the path we'd just come from. Searching for Mr. Sung or one of his men. The vacant expression she'd worn disappeared, replaced by speculation. "Well, well . . . I wonder what that was all about."

"Mr. Sung?" I held the door for Dora, stepping back so she could maneuver the picnic basket past an older couple going inside. "I don't have the first idea. But I'm not at all convinced his being here at the same time was a coincidence. I find it very difficult to believe."

"So do I, Dee. He wants something."

The brisk wind shuttled rain clouds toward the East Bay hills, piling gray swirls against the slope until the clouds overhead grew thick and dark. Raindrops splattered intermittently on sidewalks and spotted the dust-dry mulch blanketing flower beds. We walked even faster, attempting to reach the car before the rain began in earnest.

We sprinted the last few yards to the car. Nathan waited next to the passenger door, rain dripping off the brim of his chauffer's cap and beginning to soak his uniform, his manner as stiff and unbending as ever. He handed us into the car without uttering a word.

The big car pulled away from the curb and Dora peeled off her hat, shaking beads of rain off the silk. "I've been thinking about our encounter with Sung Wing. I don't for a moment believe the most powerful tong leader in Chinatown just happened to be taking a stroll through the conservatory during our picnic. That he's a sorcerer as well makes me even more suspicious. Sorcerers always have a reason for anything they do."

"So do certain spiritualists of my acquaintance." That made Dora smile, but teasing her didn't quiet my nerves about why he'd seek us out. "Seriously, what do you think he wanted?"

She stared out the rain-streaked window before turning back to answer. "At first I thought he wanted information. He probably believes that the two of us are privy to all the details of Gabe's cases, including his brother's murder investigation. But the more I thought, the less likely that seemed. Sung Wing is too savvy and experienced to think we'd reveal those details in casual conversation. Then I remembered. He appeared just as you found the cat."

"You think he had something to do with my finding the kitten?" I'd transferred her from inside my coat to my lap, unwrapping the scarf to make a warm nest. She was curled up sleeping, one paw covering her eyes. "Whatever for?"

"The timing of his arrival is awfully suspicious, Dee. I may very well be wrong, but yes, I think he may have brought the cat with him. As for why?" Dora shrugged and took her cigarettes out of her handbag. She lit one, inhaling deeply before going on. "Mai told me that story about the Cat Goddess. We were sitting above the restaurant her family ran, drinking tea in her parlor. Mai owned half a dozen cats, and there were always kittens running loose. She offered to give me one, but Daniel had already brought the blasted parrot home. I distinctly remember all her cats were the same pearly gray as the little one sleeping in your lap."

"He brought me one of Mai's cats." Dora nodded, but the last of my doubts had already fled. I stroked the kitten's head, unsure if where she'd come from made a difference anymore. She belonged with me. "Mr. Sung must have a reason, but for the life of me, I can't think of what that might be."

"You're still too much the innocent at times, Delia. I haven't managed to bleed that out of you yet." She cranked down the car window a crack, flicking her half-smoked cigarette out into the rain. "Unfortunately, I can think of far too many reasons, most of which don't put Sung Wing in a very good light. But because this kitten appears to have come from Mai's household, I'm inclined to think he meant well."

"I'm glad you think so, because I hadn't planned on giving her up." The kitten stretched, flexing tiny claws, and promptly went back to sleep. "Now that we've established she's definitely coming home with me, perhaps we can get on to useful things, like naming her."

Isadora smiled, but a trace of worry still clouded her eyes. She stroked the kitten's head with a finger. "Mai maintained her cats were ghost hunters. She truly believed her cats kept spirits with ill intent from entering any house they lived in. That's why she offered me one, for protection."

Cats of various sorts had lived in our house when I was a child, orange tabbies, calicoes, a gray and black male with markings that reminded me of an ocelot, and a white cat with one blue and one green eye. All of them watched things on the ceiling I couldn't see, sprang at empty corners, or chased phantoms down the hall. That cats might see into the spirit realm wasn't difficult to believe.

"I certainly have an abundance of ill-tempered spirits in my life lately. Heaven knows Gabe needs more protection than I can give him. A cat that hunts malicious ghosts might not be such a bad thing." Imagination can be a terrible thing when let run wild. The way this tiny scrap of fur had growled at the wind rushing through the conservatory suddenly loomed large. If my hand trembled slightly as I pulled her closer, that wasn't surprising. "And Mr. Sung was right. I know the perfect name for her. She wants to be called Mai, after your friend."

"Are you sure that's wise?" Dora fiddled with her hat, frowning at finding water spots on the silk. "The cat's origins are problematic as is. Naming her after a powerful Chinese shaman is just begging for trouble."

"I'm willing to risk it. I'm willing to risk almost anything to keep that little girl ghost out of Gabe's dreams." Mai nestled against me, purring loudly even in her sleep. She was still very small, but that wouldn't last, and I wasn't sure her size mattered when it came to hunting ghosts or even demons. How fiercely she pursued her prey in the spirit realm likely counted more.

And if Mr. Sung was right and she thought herself a tiger, all the better.

CHAPTER 14

Gabe

Rain was falling heavily when Gabe and Jack started the drive from downtown to Noe Valley. Moisture fogged the car windows inside and out, blurring the view of brightly painted row houses and dripping trees. Henderson maneuvered cautiously along the slick streets, doing what he could to avoid sliding on the thin sheen of oil glistening on the pavement. Wipers swished back and forth on the windshield, their metronome ticking marking time.

The dreary skies matched Gabe's mood. Commissioner Lindsey had moved his daughter into the family home on Elizabeth Street and had promised Gabe he'd meet them there. That the commissioner wanted to be present while they questioned Adele was understandable, especially given her fragile health. Neither he nor Jack would object.

Running down the list of questions he needed to ask Adele Wells made Gabe's stomach hurt. He wished there were another way to find out what he needed to know, a way that wouldn't cause a grieving woman more pain.

He wadded the lining of his overcoat pocket in a fist and muttered to the raindrops. "If wishes were horses, then everyone could ride."

Jack turned from his own contemplation of the rainy landscape. "What did you say?"

"Something my grandmother used to say when I wanted things I couldn't have." Gabe sat up straighter, easing the knot between his shoulders. "Gram used to recite old rhymes or sing songs while washing the breakfast dishes. She wanted to pass on what she'd learned while growing up in Ireland to me and Penelope. I couldn't have been much older than three at the time."

"You're lucky, Gabe. I never knew either of my grandmothers. Neither will Stella." Jack gave him a sidelong glance. "What made you think of that now?"

"I'm not sure. I didn't think I remembered much of anything from the year my sister died, other than my mother crying." Gabe shifted in his seat, strangely uncomfortable remembering his mother weeping in the bedroom and his father's bright, red-rimmed eyes as he held her. Even at the age of three, he knew he'd intruded on something private between his parents. A large part of his discomfort was how close the memory hit home. He'd held Delia the same way after their baby had been stillborn. "I'm not even sure I told Delia about my sister. It's not something I think about, but lately I've been waking up with pieces of Gram's rhymes going around in my head."

"Maybe that's part of the dreams you told me about. Remembering." Jack pulled his plaid cap out of a pocket and shook it out before stuffing it over his hair. "Lindsey's house is in this block. If we're lucky, Marshall can park right out front."

"A little rain won't hurt you, Lieutenant Fitzgerald." Gabe put on his own hat and buttoned his overcoat. "We walked a beat in worse weather than this more times than I care to remember."

"Reminding me of our rookie days always makes me feel old. And old men are allowed to grouse about going out in the rain, Captain Ryan." Jack pointed to the empty stretch of curb down the block. "Looks like we got lucky. The blue house is Lindsey's."

Marshall parked, sending up sheets of water from the rain-filled gutter. Jack dashed from the car, soaking his shoes and the cuffs of his trousers in a puddle. Gabe didn't need to hear to know his partner swore all the way up the front steps and into the shelter of the porch.

"Wait in the car and stay dry, Marshall. I think the lieutenant is wet enough for all of us." Gabe flipped up his coat collar and opened the car door. "We won't be long."

Henderson grinned and pulled a folded nickel weekly out of an inside pocket. "Yes, sir."

He took his time getting to the front porch, looking up and down the street, getting a feel for the neighborhood. The houses were well kept, each with neat front yards and flower gardens that stretched from the curb to the front door, but not nearly as rich or posh as he'd expected. Lindsey was Commissioner of Police, but he lived in an area not far removed from working class.

Bradley Wells likely lived and grew up in an area like this, running from yard to yard with the other boys, or sitting in the porch swing after dark on summer nights, watching for fallen stars. That was how Gabe had grown up, and the kind of childhood he wanted for his children. But Wells would never get to watch his child grow up.

Gabe shook off feelings of regret and the beginnings of anger. He couldn't change what had happened. The best he could do was catch the killers and find a little justice for Bradley Wells's child.

Once under the porch roof, he took off his hat and shook off as much rain as possible. He disregarded Jack's grumpy expression. "Are you ready?"

"Let's get this over with." Jack knocked on the door. "I hate questioning widows about their late husband's activities. Given half a chance, I'd give up this part of the job."

"I know." Heavy footfalls sounded from inside, drawing closer to the door. Gabe stood up straight, bracing himself for what was to come. "Don't worry. I'll take care of it this time."

Jack frowned and gave him a sidelong glance. "Not a chance, Gabe. We both know I'm better at this, and I know Adele at least. I feel as if I owe her."

Lindsey pulled open the door, cutting off their conversation. This was the first time Gabe had seen the commissioner outside of the police station or some city function. He was still large and imposing dressed in suspenders and rolled-up shirtsleeves, and the damp dish towel clutched in one hand didn't diminish his blustering air of authority.

The fear in his eyes accomplished that.

"Ryan, Fitzgerald, come in. Hang your coats and hats in the entry. No need to drip all the way through the house." Lindsey waved them in with the dish towel, closing the door quickly once they were inside. "Adele is in the parlor, resting. I trust you'll keep this short."

Gabe handed his overcoat and fedora to Jack, who hung up both coats on a wood and brass coatrack mounted on the sidewall. "We'll do our best to make this as easy on Mrs. Wells as possible. If this wasn't necessary, we wouldn't be here. You have my word on that, Commissioner." He traded looks with Jack. "Does she know to expect us?"

"Of course she knows. I told her you'd called and let her decide whether to answer your questions or not. She insisted on seeing you." Lindsey's face reddened and he twisted and untwisted the towel in his hand. "Addie's not worried about speaking to you, but I'm worried about her heart and the harm more stress will cause. Her doctor would skin me if he knew I'd allowed this."

Jack stepped forward. "Robert, we'll be very careful. And I'm sure Adele wants Brad's killer caught as much or more than any of us. There's a good chance getting the answers to these questions will bring us closer to catching his murderer."

"All right. Let's get this over with." Lindsey tossed the dish towel on a side table. "But if I call a halt, you're leaving right then."

That parlor was just down a short hallway. Family photographs hung on the walls, including pictures of Robert Lindsey as a young merchant seaman, and posing with his wife on their wedding day. Tall and willowy, radiant in the way happy brides were, the top of her head barely came to the top of her new husband's shoulder. Gabe remembered reading in the papers about Ida Lindsey's death, but that was before Lindsey had been appointed police commissioner. He hadn't paid more than passing attention to how she died.

Adele Wells was propped up on a stack of pillows in the corner of a brown chesterfield sofa, a book in hand. Gabe's first impression was that she looked a great deal like her mother. Her dark russet hair was tied back with a green ribbon that matched her housecoat. The housecoat in turn was an attempt to match the color of her big, blue green eyes, but ended up being shades lighter.

Stark, dusky shadows bruised the fair skin under her eyes. Blankets and a coverlet swaddled her from the chest down, but Gabe didn't think that was an attempt to hide how hugely pregnant Adele Wells was. If so, the camouflage failed. He traded looks with Jack. Lindsey hadn't exaggerated how close to confinement his daughter was nor how fragile.

"Jack! I haven't seen you since Katherine's party last spring." Adele's smile lit her face, taking away some of the tiredness. She held out a hand. "Daddy didn't tell me you were one of the detectives coming to talk to me. I'd have been less nervous if I'd known."

Jack took his cue and sat on the floor next to her. He held the offered hand, cradling it between both of his, and smiled. "Hello, Adele. It has been a long time. I can't tell you how sorry I am about Brad. Is there anything Sadie and I can do for you?"

Gabe pulled up a chair near the foot of the sofa, out of the way, but where he could see Adele's reaction to Jack's questions, or ask his own. He didn't miss how tightly Adele gripped Jack's fingers.

"You can catch the people who did this." Her voice caught and her lower lip trembled, but she didn't cry. She looked between Jack and Gabe. "That's why you're here, isn't it? You think I know something that will help you find Brad's killer."

"We hope so, Mrs. Wells." Gabe leaned forward, hands folded and arms resting on his knees, and smiled. "I'm Captain Gabe Ryan. Jack and I won't keep you long, but if you feel strong enough, I'd like to ask you a few questions. If you want to stop at any time, just say so."

Adele kept hold of Jack's hand, but she looked Gabe in the eye. "Ask me. I'll be fine."

"All right." Her heart might be weak, but Gabe wouldn't make the mistake of thinking of Adele Wells as anything but strong. "How often did your husband work in his father's store?"

"Not often." She fingered the blanket stretched over her lap, mouth quirked to one side as she thought. "Not often at all. It's been more than six months, maybe as long as eight, since Bradley—He hadn't worked in the shop in a long time, Captain Ryan."

"So no one outside the family knew he was going to be there that day."

She looked him in the eye. "No one. I found his note when I woke up that morning. He'd propped it on the night table before going out."

Gabe thought for an instant before asking his next question. He didn't want to plant ideas in Adele Wells's mind. "Had your husband joined any new social clubs, or started any new business ventures in the last few months? Anything at all you can think of that might have attracted the notice of strangers?"

"Bradley was an accountant, Captain, with a well-off clientele. His business ventures were limited to taking on new clients occasionally, but most of the people he worked for had been with him for years." Adele swiped at her eyes with the back of her hand. She looked exhausted, more drawn than when they'd started. Lindsey stood behind the sofa at Adele's head, fingers curled and digging deep into the tufted leather. He kept quiet and didn't interfere, something Gabe gave him a great deal of credit for. "And I'm afraid doing sums in a small office doesn't attract the notice of strangers or garner invitations to social clubs."

Gabe sat back in the chair. "Did your husband socialize with clients often?"

"I'm afraid not, Captain. Other than church functions and the occasional party with friends, neither of us went out in the evenings. We lived a fairly quiet life."

"Adele." Jack had been sitting on the floor, listening and chewing his lower lip. He half turned to look at her directly. "Brad was on your church board, wasn't he? I remember him saying last year that he booked the church hall for wedding receptions and special events that couldn't be held in the sanctuary. Was he still responsible for doing that?"

Anticipation coiled tight in Gabe's chest, waiting for Adele's answer. He saw the possible connection to Effie Fontaine, just as Jack did, and one connection would likely lead to more.

"I'm surprised you remembered, but yes, he still worked for the church in his off hours. Over the last few months, he'd been working with our pastor to raise money for a new sanctuary. The old one survived the quake, but needs to be replaced." She winced and pressed a hand tight against her side. "Pastor Scott and Brad hit on the idea of renting the church hall out evenings. Choral groups and ladies' sewing circles mostly, but Brad found a very popular speaker too. Fees for using the hall three nights a week for several months was a tidy sum. Pastor Scott says they've raised almost half the builder's price already."

"Mrs. Wells . . . did your husband mention the name of this speaker? Or the name of anyone who might work for this person?" Gabe's cop mask stayed firmly in place, calm and professional, hiding how fast his heart beat, or that sweat trickled down the small of his back.

He knew the answer. He needed to hear her say a name.

"I remember the men who came to the house to give Brad the deposit and pick up the contracts." Adele wrinkled her nose in distaste. "Bradley introduced them as Conrad Lang and Jonas Wolf. I didn't care for how either of them spoke to me, so I excused myself as soon as was polite. I'm sorry, but I don't remember who they worked for."

The creeping itch on the back of his neck grew worse, transforming guesses into certainty. One of the men hiring laborers for Effie Fontaine in Mr. Glibert's grocery had been called Jonas, an uncommon-enough name that the chance of two popping up in a short amount of time were very slim. Gabe was sure this had to be the same man. He knew where to start looking for these men and who they worked for, but building a solid case took time. Too much time.

That Jonas Wolf had been in Bradley Wells's home bothered him a great deal. Adele was already in danger. The more he and Jack poked around Effie Fontaine, the more the danger increased. They needed to move as quickly as possible.

Gabe refused to frighten her, so instead he chose a somewhat lesser evil. He lied. "We can find their employer if need be, Mrs. Wells. Just knowing their names is a big help. There's only a slim chance that these men had anything to do with your husband's death, but we need to follow all possible leads."

Jack's glance acknowledged he knew what Gabe had done and why. He lied just as glibly. "Gabe's right, Adele. We'll follow up with Pastor Scott, but not all leads pan out. Don't get your hopes up."

Telling the commissioner he was placing guards on the house, and why, wouldn't be pleasant, but he knew Lindsey would agree once he heard him out. Robert Lindsey was a blowhard, but Gabe was sure he'd do anything to keep his daughter and grandchild safe. He stood to leave, meaning to speak to the commissioner on the way out.

The front bell rang, drawing a scowl from Lindsey.

"Blast. This better be important. I'll be right back, Addie." He stalked out of the room.

Jack squeezed Adele's hand and stood. "Thank you, Adele. You've been very helpful. If you need anything from me or Sadie, please let us know. Gabe and I will let you rest now."

"I'll try." She pressed a hand to her side again and grimaced. "This baby doesn't let me sleep much. I'm sure Sadie went through the same thing."

He smiled. "She did. Those last weeks before Stella was born might be the only time I've seen Sadie grumpy."

Lindsey appeared in the parlor doorway, his posture oddly stiff and formal. Gabe saw Marshall Henderson standing in the entryway near the open front door, hair soaking wet and plastered to his head, his coat sluicing water all over the oak floor.

Marshall wouldn't leave his post without reason. His heart caught in his chest for an instant, afraid that something had happened to Delia. But Marshall was watching Jack, his distress clear. That didn't make Gabe feel any better.

The commissioner cleared his throat. "Lieutenant, one of your officers needs to speak with you. I gather it's urgent."

Jack saw Henderson waiting and hurried to meet him in the entryway. They kept their voices low and the conversation was brief, but after listening to what was said, Jack was ashen and visibly shaken. He grabbed his coat and ran out the front door.

Marshall stared out into the rain after him, but didn't follow. The sound of a car door slamming and an engine coming to life carried into the parlor from outside.

Very few things would cause Jack to leave so abruptly without saying where he was going, or telling Gabe why. The list was short and utterly terrifying.

Gabe retreated behind the shield of professionalism and pulled himself together. "Thank you again, Mrs. Wells. Commissioner, can I have a word before I go?"

They stepped into the hall. "Commissioner, I want to put an around-the-clock guard on your house. Hear me out before you object." Gabe outlined why he felt the need to put guards around Adele, giving her father reasons that he hoped didn't sound like the ravings of a man jumping at shadows. The entire time he was patiently answering Lindsey's questions, Gabe's attention was tugged toward the open door. He couldn't help stealing glances at Marshall fidgeting in the doorway, watching Gabe anxiously and impatient to leave, but knowing he couldn't interrupt.

Lindsey finally ran out of steam. He ran a hand over his face. "I'll trust your judgment on this one, Ryan. I don't want to take any chances with my daughter's life. But I want your guards inside the house, where they can do some good, not out in the yard or standing on the street. I'll think of an excuse for Addie."

Gabe shrugged on his coat and buttoned it before plucking his hat off the rack. Rain still speckled the gray wool, glistening in the lamplight. "Expect Officer Rockwell and at least two other men within the hour. I know Lon is on duty tonight, but I'm not sure who else is available. We won't let anything happen to your daughter."

"Make sure of it, Ryan." Lindsey eyed the parlor door and lowered his voice. "Catch these bastards. I don't care how you do it, just get them. I'll take the heat from the press if necessary."

Gabe nodded. "My men will be here soon. Good afternoon, Commissioner."

He followed Marshall onto the porch, pausing to pull his hat down tight and flip up his collar before they dashed to the car. Rain fell straight down in sheets, soaking yards and flower beds, and creating shallow rivers that ran downhill in the center of the street. Even with his collar turned up, large cold drops found their way down his neck, making him shiver.

Once inside the car, he gave Henderson almost no time to catch his breath. "What happened, Marshall?"

"Polk brought a message for the lieutenant from the station, Captain. He waited to take the lieutenant back with him." Henderson twisted around to look at Gabe in the backseat, wide-eyed and face ashy with shock. "It's Archie Baldwin. He's dead."

"Baldwin's dead." Gabe stared, numbness filling his chest and slowing his thoughts. He'd tossed her a name, but Fontaine couldn't get to Archie, not locked away in a jail cell. She couldn't; that wasn't possible. "How?"

Marshall looked away and cleared his throat. "He hanged himself, Captain. Stripped the sheet off the bed and tied it to the bars."

They sat there for a few seconds, neither of them saying a word. Henderson recovered first, starting the car and heading back toward the station without waiting for orders. Thinking for himself.

Gabe slumped against the seat, hat pulled low and staring out the rain-splattered window, fighting his guilt and losing. He kept circling back to the idea that Fontaine couldn't be responsible for Archie's suicide. She couldn't reach him.

Yet, somehow, she had. He knew she'd found a way to get to Archie, felt the truth of that knowledge nestle into his bones, even if he couldn't explain how.

But he'd find the answer. Then he'd lock Effie Ladia Fontaine away for the rest of her life.

CHAPTER 15

Delia

Isadora's home was both a haven and a fortress. Entering her house always lifted a weight from my shoulders, one I hadn't known I carried until it vanished. The protections woven around the house were designed to keep the spirit realm at bay, as well as block strong emotions from the people living around her. As sensitive as Dora was to pain and suffering, and the anger of spirits who resented leaving this world, she'd have gone mad long ago without a place to retreat.

She'd lived in the house seven years, and no ghost had been powerful enough to cross the threshold without her permission, or unless deliberately summoned by Dora. I counted on that holding true well into the future. Tarot readings sometimes stirred up unwelcome attentions in the spirit world.

We'd settled in her sitting room to wait for Gabe, Randy, and Jack. Rain pounded the side of the house, but the room was warm and snug, and bright enough I could perch on the window seat and read. The light dimmed as afternoon wore on, taking on the heavy gray cast of clouds and rain. I'd be forced to turn on a lamp soon or forgo my book.

The kitten was sleeping in a wicker basket Dora had pulled from a closet, content in a nest made from my scarf. Mai appeared to be comfortable in Isadora's house, likely for the same reasons I was.

She'd lapped up most of a saucer of cream and promptly fallen asleep afterwards.

Dora sat at a round table in the center of the room, fussing with her tarot deck. She shuffled the tarot cards for the fourth or fifth time, mixing them well, squaring them up, and laying the deck atop the black silk cloth covering the table. Then she closed her eyes, head tipped to the side, and listened. Also for the fourth or fifth time, she frowned at the gilt-edged stack of cards once she'd opened her eyes, fingers drumming a slow rhythm on the tabletop.

"I don't understand this, Dee. The cards have never been angry before." Dora stood abruptly, pacing over to the shelf in the corner that held her cigarettes and matches. She took a cigarette from the case, waving it around unlit as she talked. "Once or twice I've needed to coax them to cooperate, but this is different. They positively vibrate with rage."

If I concentrated very hard, I heard an angry buzz, low and just within hearing. The noise was akin to the sound that came from a hornet's nest knocked to the ground by the gardeners, furious at being disturbed and hunting a target. There was a time I'd have thought I'd imagined hearing. Now I attributed very little to flights of imagination.

"Perhaps I should try. The cards might cooperate for someone else." I moved away from the window seat and took the chair opposite Isadora's. "You said yourself that the tarot reacts differently to me."

She lit the cigarette and sat at the table again, eyeing the cards. "You've done readings with this deck in the past. I suppose letting you handle the cards and lay them out can't do any harm. Perhaps if we concentrate on Gabe's reading first, the energy will calm down. But if they don't settle or become more agitated, we'll have to cancel and try the reading another day."

"Perhaps I should have worn my fortune-teller robes. That might have made the cards happy." Dora's raised eyebrow and exasperated expression made it clear she wasn't in the mood for levity. I laid my hand over the deck, half-expecting more than the feel of smooth paper against my skin. "Shouldn't Gabe be here for a reading? I thought the point was to find out why this ghost is so fixed on him."

"Normally I'd agree, but a reading isn't going to give us many answers about who this ghost is or why she's attached herself to Gabe. A little guidance about directions for the future and what this all means is what I'm really hoping to find. If we're fortunate, the cards will point us in the right direction. I'm trying other methods to discover more about this spirit."

Dora rested her cigarette on the sand-filled ash stand next to the table. She left the room briefly and returned to her chair with a rather large glass of whiskey in hand, and a book tucked under one arm. "Normal haunts are fixed on one person, almost always to the point that others in the world of the living don't exist for them. But this one has gone out of her way to involve other people, including her attack on you and disrupting Mrs. Allen's house. It's very clear to me she wants Gabe's attention and will go to any lengths to make sure he can't ignore her. *Why* she's so desperate is important and interests me a great deal."

I shuffled the cards, cut them three times, and paused before laying out the first one. The angry buzz was gone, replaced by a sense of quiet eagerness. I'd never have attributed awareness or purpose to a pile of printed paper before meeting Dora. That time seemed far distant, a past that happened to someone else. "You've said from the beginning she doesn't behave like a normal haunt. Whatever this little girl spirit might be, I want her out of our lives."

"I agree. Banishing her is for the best, no matter what her true nature." She took a long drink of her whiskey, and another, all the while watching raindrops slide down the windowpanes. Dora set the glass aside and opened the book she'd brought back, flipping through pages. "I've spent my evenings going through books, looking for other possibilities. Some of what I found confirmed my first guess, that this spirit might be a kind of ghost-eater."

My fingers tightened around the tarot deck. "You mean a demon."

"In one sense of the word, yes, she might be. We spoke about that after our failed attempt to find Katie Allen's poltergeist. But even demons have limited degrees of power and a strict hierarchy. A mere ghost-eater wouldn't manifest the way this spirit does, nor would she be able to invade Gabe's dreams." She glanced up from the book. "Ghost-eaters deal strictly with the dead. They have no purchase in the world of the living."

Dora viewed most conversations about ghosts, haunts, and denizens of the spirit realm as opportunities to teach me something. As a result, she often took the longest road. Most days I didn't mind, as eager to learn as she was to pass on knowledge.

Today I held tight to my patience. The need to be shed of this spirit, to be certain Gabe was safe, was all I cared about. "We've established she's not an everyday ghost nor a poltergeist, and your research tells you that she's not a ghost-eating demon. So what is she?"

"I'm afraid I still don't have an answer. She's a puzzle and a conundrum." Dora's smile was small and tight, but she did smile. "Her behavior doesn't fit any one type of spirit I can find. Attacking you and destroying Mrs. Allen's kitchen would be classical imp behavior, but doesn't fit with her nighttime activities in regard to Gabe. I've read about cunning folk and their familiars, about fallen angels and wind demons, and a spirit child sent from a long distance to wreak havoc. In the end, all I'm left with is a guess, Dee. A shaky guess at that, based on a partial passage written over two hundred years ago."

I shuffled the cards and cut the deck one last time. "Go ahead and fess up. You're not going to tell me your theory until after the reading."

"And run the risk of looking foolish when you prove me wrong? Of course not." Isadora beamed at me, appearing inordinately pleased. She toasted me with her glass and took another sip of whiskey. "You lay out the cards. I'll try to wrestle meaning from the spread."

The first card was the King of Cups. He held a short scepter in his left hand and a great cup in his right. His throne was set upon the waves of a restless sea, a dolphin leaping on one side and a ship sailing on the other. I glanced at Dora. "This card represents Gabe."

"Yes. Most interpretations refer to the King of Cups as a fair, responsible man, often involved with the law. That sums Gabe up neatly." She tapped the table. "Now the covering card. That will help tell us what hidden influences or events have entered into Gabe's life."

I stared at the next card, uncertain what the Ten of Swords covering the king meant. The image of a man lying facedown, impaled by the ten swords that gave the card its name, was ominous. But I'd learned enough about the tarot to know that the meaning behind any image wasn't straightforward or obvious. Still, the way Dora studied the cards gave me more reason to worry. As if I didn't have ample reason already.

She tapped the side of her glass with one slender finger. "Ten of Swords reversed. Profit, power, and authority are at stake. The person opposing Gabe has the advantage for now."

The next card went above the king's head, crowning him, and Dora's shoulders relaxed a bit. "The Queen of Cups is said to be a woman with the gift of vision and who isn't afraid to act. This could represent you, Dee, or even me. The queen's goal is to help Gabe achieve the best outcome. I interpret that as a hopeful sign. Now lay out the next three cards to finish the cross. Try not to think about what they might mean."

Dora watched me lay the two side cards, naming each one as I went and what the card might mean. "Nine of Swords. The weeping woman represents loss and utter desolation, most often from sometime in the past. Gabe may not know about this loss or be able to link it to the present. The card can also mean deception in the present. Seven of Wands, sometimes called the dark child. One reading of this card is of a combatant at the top, his enemies unable to reach him. This could be the ghost, but I think there's a stronger possibility it refers to the person opposing Gabe." She put a hand over mine long enough to stop me from laying out the next card. "This spread seems to relate more to the murder cases Gabe is working on than why the ghost chose to haunt him. The cards seem to be pointing in that direction so far."

"Or perhaps it's pointing toward both." All the faces of child ghosts I'd seen over the last few weeks, big eyed and expectant, came back to me. Legions of dead children waiting for Gabe outside the station were impossible for me to dismiss as meaningless. A glimmer of certainty flared to life, growing larger. "Maybe this little girl ghost is connected to these cases somehow. A victim, or perhaps tied to other victims. It wouldn't be the first time a spirit sought to right a wrong."

Dora folded her arms and stared at the cards. The kitten woke suddenly, leaving the basket and leaping into my lap. I waited patiently for Isadora to come to a conclusion, petting the cat and doing my best to ignore the storm winds beginning to howl around the corners of the house. The deck lay to one side, vibrating with what I perceived as eagerness.

Isadora reached for her whiskey, gesturing towards the cards with her glass. "No, I don't think that's quite right. The tie is to Gabe. He's the focal point and what ties the spirit to the cases and the cases to her. Without him, there'd be no connection." She arched an eyebrow and smiled. "Keep trying. A few guesses closer to the mark, and you'll demolish my theory entirely. Finish the cross. The sixth card signifies what lies ahead."

Even I knew what The Tower meant. I swallowed the sour taste of panic and tried to make light of it. "There's a cheery card for the future. I thought we'd reached our quota of calamity, ruin, and disaster."

"The Tower can also represent new beginnings, even if starting again is by necessity and not by choice." She drained the last of her whiskey from the tumbler. "But your decision to avoid Sadie and the baby may have been more prescient than I'd guessed."

The bell on the telephone jangled, three long rings and one short.

"That's my ring." Isadora pushed her chair back and went down the hall toward the parlor. "We'll finish the spread after I take this call. I'll be right back, Dee."

Her ring was repeated three more times before I heard Dora say hello. I laid the tarot deck aside and snuggled the kitten under my chin. She purred loudly, the sound filling my ears and coming close to drowning out storm howls and Isadora's voice both. I closed my eyes, shutting out the sight of cards that might prophesy catastrophe.

Opening them again to find Dora sitting across from me was a surprise. Even more startling were the changes made by her phone call. Tears glistened in her eyes, and her normally rosy skin had paled to a sickly ivory.

"Gabe wanted us to know that he and Jack are delayed at the station. He said not to wait supper on them." Dora picked up her glass, staring at the melting ice in confusion. She put it down again and cleared her throat. "Gabe is sending Randy Dodd and Thom Russell over to sit with us. I told him that would be fine."

"Dora, what's wrong?" Now I was truly alarmed. I set the small gray cat on the tabletop and went to kneel next to her chair. Dora's hand was ice cold and shaking. "Are Gabe and Jack all right? Tell me what happened."

She looked toward the window and angrily swiped at the single tear sliding down her cheek. "Gabe and Jack are fine. It's . . . Archie's dead. I didn't make it back in time to help him. He hanged himself." Dora stood abruptly, pulling her hand free from mine. "I need more whiskey. Would you like something?"

I stared, unable to speak around shock and the taste of fear. Not knowing why Gabe felt we needed guards in light of Archie's death was frightening. But if he'd hanged himself as Dora said, the two of us needing protection made no sense. More was going on here than I knew, dangers I couldn't see.

When words finally came, they sounded far off, as if spoken by someone else in a voice I didn't recognize. "Yes. A glass of sherry, please."

Isadora nodded and left. I stayed sitting on the floor, pulling my knees up and wrapping my arms around my legs. Rain pelted the windows, and the light faded in increments, much as I imagined

Archie's sanity had trickled away under the onslaught of dead soldiers' ghosts.

Mai scampered across the tabletop, scattering the tarot cards. I let her play. Twice she peered at me over the edge before turning to run the other way. Cards slid off the table, drifting to the ground.

One landed in my lap: the Devil. I tossed the card away, unable to bear looking at the image.

Dora returned and sat on the floor next to me, passing over a half-full sherry glass. The room grew darker and we sat in silence, waiting for Randy Dodd and Thom Russell to arrive.

Isadora had agreed to teach me about the occult only once I understood that knowledge and power brought great responsibility. Part of that burden was to protect those who couldn't protect themselves, to keep hostile spirits and haunts from harming the living.

Neither of us said the words aloud, but we both knew. We'd failed Archie Baldwin.

CHAPTER 16

Gabe

The end of the hall near Archie's cell was sweltering, the air close and beginning to smell of sweat and death. Gabe paced the cell block in his shirtsleeves, impatiently waiting for Deputy Coroner Sal Rosen to finish his examination of Baldwin's body. They couldn't move the body until Sal finished and gave the word.

Sal was taking too damn long.

The torn sheet was looped around Archie's neck twice and tied to the crossbar at the top of the cell wall. Archie's face was blue gray, swollen hands hanging stiff at his sides and feet dangling a foot off the ground. Gabe's best guess was that Baldwin had tipped the iron bed frame on its side and wedged it against the bars, climbed up, and then kicked the bed away.

More than anything, he wanted Archie cut down. No matter where Gabe stood, he couldn't escape Baldwin's glassy, staring eyes, or avoid seeing his startled expression. Members of his squad had gathered near the cell block entrance, speculating in hushed voices on why Baldwin killed himself. Opinions were split between outright madness or guilt over having killed Amanda Poe.

Every scrap of experience gained over the years told Gabe his men were wrong. Death took Archie Baldwin by surprise. Proving that was something else entirely.

Marshall Henderson came back into the cell block, snaking through the knot of officers near the entrance to reach Gabe. The young red-haired officer glanced at the body and looked away quickly, face blanched and sweating. Gabe didn't blame him for looking ill. He wanted to be sick himself.

"I spoke to the men on duty, Captain." Marshall pulled a battered dime-store notebook out of his back pocket, flipping pages until he found what he wanted. He'd picked up the habit of writing everything down from Jack. Between the two of them, very little was forgotten or overlooked. "Burke brought meal trays to all the prisoners. He said Mr. Baldwin was quiet when he came in, but that he was awake and sitting up. Alan said Mr. Baldwin thanked him when he left the meal tray. I guess he hadn't done that before, so Alan remembered."

Sal was packing up his bag. Two big, burly officers, Reid and Tyler, crowded into the cell to cut Baldwin down.

Gabe looked away. If they dropped the body before loading Baldwin on the stretcher, he didn't want to see. "Who collected the trays?"

Henderson consulted his notes. "A new man, Eli Marsh. He just transferred in from Captain Pearson's squad."

"Marsh?" Gabe raked fingers through his sweaty hair, thinking hard, trying to match the name with a face. Men from Fade Pearson's squad had been dispatched to investigate Adele Wells's call the night her husband was murdered, but reportedly never entered the shop to look for Bradley. The knot forming in his guts tightened. "I don't think I've met him. Any relation to Sergeant Marsh?"

"Not that I know of, Captain. Officer Marsh came to the station three days ago." Henderson shrugged. "This is the first time I've spoken to him. He's a little brusque and not overly friendly, but he seemed a nice-enough fellow. Marsh said Mr. Baldwin was sleeping when he collected the trays and never woke up. No one else came back here until shift change."

"I need you to do me a favor, Marshall. I'd like you to see what you can find out about Eli Marsh. Get to know him if you can." They stepped back out of the way so that Reid and Tyler could carry Baldwin's body out. Sal Rosen stood framed in the open cell door, waiting. "And I'd appreciate it if you'd keep this between us."

A muscle in Henderson's jaw twitched and his eyes widened for an instant, the only outward signs he gave that Gabe's request was out of the ordinary. Gabe let him think it through and sort out the implications, prepared to accept whatever Marshall decided.

Marshall swallowed hard and nodded. "Yes, sir. I'll talk to him and see what I can find out. And just so you know, Lieutenant Fitzgerald did go home. Rockwell and Polk went with him. Jefferies and Perry will take the next shift watching the lieutenant's house."

Gabe had formally ordered Jack to go home within minutes of getting back to the station. That Jack wasn't in any condition to be involved with the investigation, even from the sidelines, wasn't a surprise. Their argument over bringing Effie Fontaine in for questioning immediately was short, but loud and very public.

Their suspicions about Miss Fontaine weren't common knowledge, and the longer they kept that quiet, the better their chances of getting proof. But nothing would stay secret with Jack yelling at full volume. He hadn't left Jack a choice about going home to cool off, nor about accepting a guard on the house. His partner's heated reaction only confirmed that Gabe had made the right decision.

Knowing he'd made the right choice didn't make him feel any better.

"Thank you." Gabe clapped Marshall on the shoulder. "We'll talk tomorrow. I need to speak with Doctor Rosen before he leaves."

Rosen wasn't even sweating when Gabe shook his hand. If the heat bothered the deputy coroner, he hid it well. "Thank you for waiting, Sal. Let's go to my office. It's cooler there."

"Good idea." Sal shifted his bag to the other hand and eyed the assembled cops. "I was on my way to see you when the call came in. We need to talk privately."

Gabe's office was on the other side of the station. The two men crossed the crowded lobby in silence, Sal managing to keep up with Gabe's longer stride without too much of a struggle. Conversations between patrolmen ground to a halt, the buzz of voices fading away. Every officer on duty watched them cross the dirty and chipped linoleum floor.

But every man in the station knew Archie Baldwin was Jack's friend, and by this time they'd have passed around the story of Gabe and Jack yelling at each other. He pretended not to see them staring, acting as if this were any other case and that his heart wasn't pounding.

Closing his office door was a relief. He sat behind his desk, gesturing toward the guest chair. "Have a seat, Sal. I can send for coffee if you like."

"No thanks. I have a social engagement in about an hour. One of my wife's charity fund-raiser dinners." Rosen set his black doctor's bag on the floor and tossed his overcoat over the back of his chair. He unbuttoned his expensive-looking gray dinner jacket before taking a seat. "Drinking station house coffee might keep me awake all the way through the mayor's speech. This won't take long."

Gabe leaned forward, hands steepled on the desk, acutely aware of how anxious he appeared. But he was anxious. He needed Sal to confirm his hunch. "Any surprises with your examination of Baldwin?"

"Only one. That he succeeded." Sal stared at the floor, frowning, before looking back at Gabe. "Don't get me wrong, a really determined man will find a way to kill himself. But he was tied to the bars with knots done behind his head. Tying those knots so they'd hold his weight, or without falling and tipping the bedframe over before he'd finished looks damn hard. And if he was raving the way you said? That would make hanging himself that way twice as difficult."

He cleared his throat and asked the obvious question. "You don't think he could have managed on his own?"

"I don't know, Gabe. Officially, I can't say it's impossible." Sal shrugged and fussed with the crease in his trousers. "Unofficially? I can't rule out someone helping him along. I might know more once I do the autopsy."

Gabe's heart thudded and quieted again. He'd known Baldwin hadn't committed suicide, but hearing Sal say it brought an odd sort of relief. A fresh onslaught of guilt followed almost immediately. Not letting Miss Fontaine know about Maddie Holmes had been the right decision; mentioning Archie Baldwin might have condemned him. He couldn't say one balanced out the other.

And on the heels of guilt came full-blown rage. Someone, maybe one of the men working in his station, had killed a prisoner under Gabe's protection. That one of his officers might have betrayed his trust was a sickening thought.

Gabe wanted that person found, to look him in the eye and make sure he'd never have the chance to hurt anyone again. Then he and Jack would find a way to lay the blame where it ultimately belonged, at the feet of Effie Fontaine.

For all of this they needed evidence. And if Archie's death showed him anything, they needed to be careful. His decision to follow his instincts and place guards on Sadie and the baby, as well as Delia and Isadora, had been the right choice.

"Fair enough, Sal. I'll wait for the autopsy." Gabe leaned back in his creaky chair, already making a list of longtime members of the squad, men he was certain he could trust. "You said you were coming to see me."

"I brought you a copy of the autopsy report for the girl who washed up under the pier. You asked me to tell you if her throat was cut." Sal pulled out a large manila folder from his bag and passed it across the desk. "There was too much tissue damage for me to be able to tell for sure if her throat had been cut or not. But I can say for certain that blood loss was the probable cause of death. I don't think there was more than a cup or two of blood left in her entire body."

Gabe flipped open the report, reading the typed sheets and Sal's neat, handwritten notes. His father had taught him that once was chance, twice a coincidence, but three times was a pattern. Three murders in a little over a month, corpses drained of blood, was definitely a pattern.

Where there were three, four would follow. He swallowed down the queasy feeling welling in the back of his throat. "I'm guessing that you didn't find anything to tell us who she was."

"If you mean her name, no." Sal stood, gathering up his overcoat and bag. "I can tell you she was in her late twenties or early thirties, well nourished, and that there was no evidence of serious illness. No scars, no birthmarks. She'd had at least one child in the past, so she might have been married at one time. Still might have been. She wasn't wearing a ring."

"Thanks, Sal." He pushed back his chair, coming round the desk to offer his hand. "How soon before you have the report on Baldwin?"

"Not for two or three days. My wife would never forgive me if I bowed out on her big night for work, especially after I swore nothing would keep me away. The *Examiner* promised a big write-up in tomorrow's paper. Pearl wants me in all the pictures too. She thinks it will be good for my career." Sal gave him a wry smile. "That reminds me of the second thing I came to tell you. The press has been nosing around some of the boys from the morgue, asking questions about the Wells case. I thought you'd want to know that your name and Jack's have come up more than once."

He wasn't surprised. Bradley Wells's murder had made front-page headlines for days. Murders in poor neighborhoods rarely got attention from the papers, but high-profile cases always saw a rash of editorials demanding the police find the killer quickly. The Wells's case wasn't any different.

Asking questions and digging for the next big story under those circumstances made sense. A half-decent reporter wouldn't need to look far to find more of Gabe and Jack's open cases.

A really good newspaper man might start making connections,

just as he and Jack had. That worried Gabe. The number of victims tied directly or indirectly to Effie Fontaine was already too high. "Any reporter in particular?"

"A new kid over at the *Call*. Samuel Clemens Butler is his name." Sal pulled a pasteboard card out of an inside pocket and passed it to Gabe. "Claims to be second cousin to *the* Samuel Clemens, but I don't know how seriously to take that. Butler left that card with the grave-yard shift and made it known he'd like to meet you. He hasn't been in town long, but he's already starting to make a name for himself."

"Thanks for the warning." Gabe read the calling card and tucked it into his shirt pocket. "And if Butler shows up again, your staff can tell him I'm not in the habit of passing out information on my cases or discussing police business with reporters. Let me know if he gives you any trouble."

"I will." Sal gave him a long look. "Be straight with me, Gabe. Any particular reason you want to scare this kid away?"

"Keeping him alive is the only reason I need." He stuffed his hands deep into his trouser pockets, hiding his clenched fists, and smiled. "Butler has no idea what he's stepping into. I'd like to keep it that way."

"Your cases, your rules." Sal opened the door. "I'll get my report to you as soon as possible."

Gabe waited for a moment or two after Sal left before dropping heavily into his desk chair. He slid down in the seat and covered his face with his hands, craving darkness and quiet, even if just for a few minutes. No one could fault him for taking time to think.

And he needed to think, to breathe and sort through all he knew so far. He'd never figure out how to catch Fontaine without taking the time to lay the bits and pieces of information all out, building a trail that led back to her. The only way to get ahead of her was to backtrack.

Fontaine's connections to Amanda Poe, Baldwin, and Wells were all too clear. The link to Thad Harper and others missing from the neighborhoods near the docks was through the men who worked for her, but he'd be a fool to think she didn't know what was going on. Tying her to the murders in Chinatown or the bodies washing up under the docks was a problem, but Gabe knew that somehow, Effie Fontaine was responsible.

Not knowing her reasons bothered him a great deal. Gabe spent a long time trying to figure out why an advocate for peace and non-violence would murder people. Money was a possible motive, but Fontaine claimed to have a benefactor and hadn't demanded money from the Poe estate or from Adele Wells. Thad Harper and the people living on the waterfront who'd vanished certainly didn't have any money.

No matter how he approached the subject of what Effie Fontaine might have to gain, he came up empty. Gabe rarely considered insanity alone as a motivation for crime. He considered it now.

A knock on his office door startled him. Gabe sat up abruptly, blinking his eyes against the bright glow of the desk lamp. He took a second to steady himself. "Come in."

Sergeant Bailey stuck his head around the edge of the door. "Lieutenant Fitzgerald's on the phone, Captain. He's changed his mind about staying home tonight. He wanted to know if you'd pick him up on the way to Miss Bobet's house or if he should meet you there. The lieutenant's holding on the line for an answer."

The fight with Jack had eaten at him, overshadowing all his thoughts about Effie Fontaine and their interwoven cases. Now some of the dread camping out in his chest vanished. He'd thought Jack would take longer to cool down and come to his senses, but he hadn't factored in Sadie's influence or her ability to make her husband see reason. Those who thought Sadie was flighty didn't know her well at all.

"Thank you, Sergeant. Tell the lieutenant I'll pick him up on the way." Gabe checked to make sure his desk was locked. "And have a car brought around front, if you would."

Bailey bobbed his head. "Yes, sir. Should I find Henderson to drive you?"

"Not tonight." He grabbed his coat and fedora off the rack in the corner. If things were going well, Marshall Henderson was working his way into Eli Marsh's good graces. "I won't be coming back to the station tonight. I'll drive myself."

Sergeant Bailey hurried back toward the front lobby. Out of habit, Gabe surveyed the office one last time. He reached for the chain to turn off the lamp and hesitated, thinking hard. Deciding.

He bent and unlocked the shallow top right-hand drawer of the desk, the drawer he almost never opened. Gabe lifted out the pistol and the shoulder holster resting inside, heart hammering loud in his ears. The pistol didn't show once he'd donned his suit jacket again.

Carrying a gun wasn't something he was used to or that felt natural. He'd needed a weapon once in all his years on the force, chasing down and apprehending the man who'd killed his father. The weight of the pistol dragged at his shoulder, the metal pressed against his side icy through his shirt. Ominous.

Second thoughts crowded in, but the cold shiver on the back of his neck was too strong to ignore. Gabe buttoned his jacket and left.

He could always put the gun back in the drawer tomorrow.

CHAPTER 17

Delia

I'd eaten enough supper to be polite, taking a small bite or two of everything before pushing my plate away. Isadora's cook—a stout Swedish woman named Ella—noticed my lack of appetite but did little more than frown. No doubt she was used to the way Dora picked at food and rarely ate.

Randy and Officer Russell both took seconds of roast beef, yams, and yeast rolls, and then thirds, alleviating some of my guilt. The two men ate large slices of chocolate cake as well. I didn't see how Ella could feel her efforts had been slighted after their show of enthusiasm.

We helped clear the supper dishes away and went back to the parlor. Dora took a pack of playing cards from a drawer, holding them up to Officer Russell. "You owe me a rematch and a chance to win back my two dollars, Thom. Five-card draw this time, I think."

"If you insist, Miss Bobet." Thom unbuttoned his uniform jacket and draped it over the back of his chair. He rolled up his shirtsleeves, grinning broadly. "Never let it be said I didn't give you a fair chance at getting even."

Dora's lip stuck out in the pretty little pout that meant she was flirting, but wasn't at all serious. "Well, I've been practicing. Taking my money might not be quite so easy this time. Randy, Delia, would you like to play poker with us? It will be scads of fun, I promise. Gabe and Jack may not break free for hours."

Her lightheartedness was all for show, a ruse designed to hide how deeply Archie's death had shaken her. Randy and Thom would never guess, but I saw right through her charade.

That didn't stop me from playing along. If Dora could put on a brave face, so could I. "I'd love to, but someone needs to mind the kitten and keep her inbounds. I'll cheer you on from the settee."

My weak excuse earned a skeptical look and a raised eyebrow, but Dora didn't comment beyond that. She turned to Randy with a small, hopeful smile and laid a hand on his arm. "Please say you'll play."

Randy Dodd blushed furiously, right up to the roots of his hair. "You'll have to teach me how. I've never played poker before."

"Really . . . Never?" Dora's face lit up. "Poker's not at all difficult, I promise. You'll pick the game up in no time."

Thom was already shuffling the cards, whistling cheerfully in anticipation. She hooked an arm though Randy's and walked him to the table. He was an innocent being led to the slaughter and I thought about warning him, but I trusted Dora not to let Thom go too far. Better Randy learn about losing at poker here and now, in the safety of Dora's parlor, than from some of the older men at the station.

And there was always the chance Randy Dodd possessed hidden depths of skill. He might surprise both Thom and Isadora.

I collected Mai from her basket and curled up on the settee with the kitten, starting at each gust of wind that rattled the windows. Imagining the long, low creaks and groans of roof timbers to be footsteps of the ghosts that had tormented Archie, come to confront me with my failures, was all too easy. That I knew real ghosts would never cross Dora's barriers didn't matter in the slightest. Guilt seldom respected boundaries.

Mai purred under my hand, fuzzy and warm and totally unconcerned by the storm noises, while I pretended to read a book. I turned pages, but I couldn't have said what words were written there.

Brooding was closer to the truth. I couldn't stop mulling over everything that had happened outside Archie's cell and trying to make sense of what I'd seen. The ghosts surrounding his cell were much too aware of me and Dora, and bent on driving us away. In many ways, the encounter reminded me of visits from the little girl spirit that had invaded my life, an idea that chilled me. I'd thought her an aberration.

But I'd never doubted the dead soldiers were ghosts, real ghosts, despite their strange behavior. The recently dead all have a look about them, as if pieces of the life they'd left still clung fast. I couldn't say the same of the little girl spirit, and my puzzlement about what she truly was grew daily.

One thing I knew without question: Ghosts played by certain rules in the world of the living, respected boundaries. Passing into death left them little choice in the matter. That didn't mean spirits couldn't cause great harm, even go so far as take others into death with them, but ghosts had little in the way of free will. Once set on a path, they followed that road until they accomplished their task or faded out of existence.

Dora and I were able to send spirits on or keep them from haunting someone by forcing them onto a new path. Haunts could resist commands from the living, but they couldn't say no. Not for long.

That was one thing that had perplexed me about the little girl spirit, back when I thought her nothing but a ghost. She'd said no and made it stick.

The clink of whiskey glasses and hoots of triumphant laughter came from behind me as Dora won a hand. I glanced over and smiled. Thom's scowl made it clear Isadora's revenge was well under way.

I turned another page, still thinking about ghosts and commands, and the control exercised over the dead by the living. Commanding spirits for a séance took a great deal of effort, and a spiritualist's hold never lasted long. Part of that was by design. The dangers to everyone involved increased as time passed and the spiritualist grew tired.

Dora had mentioned during one of my early lessons that other ways to command large numbers of spirits had existed centuries ago. The gathering of dead soldiers who'd tormented Archie Baldwin were all focused on making him suffer. Their numbers were frightening enough, but the idea that they might be acting under someone's control was both terrifying and revolting. Torturing a person that way was excessively cruel.

But Isadora had also made a point of saying all the texts containing knowledge of how to raise an army of ghosts were destroyed. The danger to the living and the potential for abuse were too great, and the keepers had ordered the books burned. Now I wondered.

Isadora and Randy were taking turns fleecing Officer Russell at poker when the front bell rang, announcing Gabe and Jack's arrival. By the time I disentangled myself from cushions, my book, and the cat, Gabe was already standing in the doorway.

When Gabe was first promoted, the wife of an older police captain sat me down and instructed me on the proper way to conduct myself as a captain's wife. Her instructions involved a great deal of stiff, prim, and dignified behavior, and most of all, maintaining a proper distance from my husband in the presence of others. I'm sure she'd have been horrified to see me fling myself into Gabe's arms, and equally shocked to see how tight he clung to me in return.

I was in no hurry to let go. Neither was Gabe. I rested my head against his chest, listening to the steady beat of his heart. The two of us spent far too much time surrounded by death to take our life together for granted.

Jack edged past us, going straight to the settee and taking a seat. He was worn-looking and haggard, more subdued and down-spirited than I could ever remember seeing him. The loss of a friend was never easy and the circumstances of Archie's death were heartrending. That he'd taken things hard was to be expected. Archie had been his friend, a true friend, as Amanda Poe had been Sadie's.

That I thought of Amanda as dead and not just missing saddened me. She'd been gone too long for me to hold out hope she was off on another one of her escapades. Gabe didn't need to tell me she was never coming back. I already knew.

Mai pounced into Jack's lap, batting at his necktie. He scratched the kitten behind the ears, smiling for the first time and obviously bemused. "I never imagined you with a cat, Dora. Especially after Daniel went to Europe and left his parrot behind."

"Don't be gauche, Jack. The parrot belongs to me as much as to Daniel." Dora lounged back in her chair, a whiskey glass in one hand and a cigarette dangling from the other. "And you know perfectly well that I adore cats. In any case, the kitten isn't mine. She belongs to Delia. Dee found the cat at the conservatory this afternoon. Or maybe the cat found her. I'm not at all clear on the sequence of events."

I gave Gabe a hug and moved to rescue Jack from Mai's sneak attack on his fingers. She snuggled into the crook of my arm, purring loudly and watching Gabe. I could almost imagine she knew who he was and that charming him thoroughly was in her best interest. "Don't exaggerate, Dora. We both know what happened. The kitten was a gift from Mr. Sung."

Gabe looked from the small gray cat in my arms and back to me, wide-eyed with surprise. "Sung Wing? The tong leader?"

"Dora tells me he's apparently the resident shaman of China-town as well. One kind of power would feed into the other, I imag-ine." I held the kitten up to Gabe. "Her name is Mai. Isadora and I talked over why Mr. Sung might have come to the conservatory at the same time we were having our picnic. We came to the conclusion that Mr. Sung was there to bring me the cat, not out of any need to look at flowers. Why he felt the need to give me a kitten is still a mystery."

He turned to Isadora, his expression stormy. She ground out her cigarette and made the effort to appear somewhat apologetic. "The conversation we had was a little more involved, but yes, that's the gist of it. I'm reasonably certain I know where the kitten came from inside Chinatown and the family involved. Otherwise, I'd never have let Mr. Sung leave the cat with Dee."

"Keeping a present from the most powerful man in Chinatown doesn't strike me as a good idea at any time. The timing right now couldn't be worse." Gabe crossed his arms and dragged a toe across the Persian carpet, watching the pile change from dark to light. He looked me in the eye, frowning. "Aside from anything else, Sung knew right where to find you and Dora. That scares me, Delia. I have to wonder how long his men have been watching you and worry about what he'll do next. What if he thinks he can use you as leverage against me? A man like Sung Wing doesn't do anything out of the goodness of his heart. He wants something in return."

Thom coughed and pushed back his chair. "Come along, Dodd. We should let the captain and Mrs. Ryan talk in private. Let's see if Miss Ella's got any more chocolate cake out in the kitchen."

Dora gave me a look as they left the parlor, but didn't say anything. Jack watched keenly, bright-eyed and attentive, but he didn't interject himself into the conversation either. I'd no way to know how he felt.

I was on my own. "Frankly, Gabe Ryan, I don't care who Mr. Sung is or what he thinks I can do for him. He's doomed to disappointment on that score. And even a powerful man can do a good deed without expecting payment." I ran my hand over Mai's back, stroking fur softer than eiderdown. "I'm keeping her. We belong to each other."

He watched me, conflict and worry clear in his eyes. "I don't ever want you to be hurt because of my job or a case I'm working on. But all right. If you want the kitten that badly, then we'll keep her." Gabe offered Mai his hand to sniff. She smelled him quite thoroughly before licking the ends of his fingers. That made him smile. "One small cat really isn't much of a bribe. Just promise me that you'll let me know right away if Mr. Sung contacts you again."

"I promise." I stood on tiptoe and kissed his cheek.

Dora tapped her long nails on the side of her glass, rattling the ice inside. "I share your concerns about Sung Wing and his motives, Gabe. I can't say I was very kind once I discovered he knew who

Delia was. But in the end we are talking about a very tiny cat, not a jade necklace. I don't see how any harm can come from this." She glanced at me, her smile secretive and conspiratorial. "Cats are useful creatures. Give Mai a little time to grow, and she'll be a formidable hunter."

I hadn't said anything about Dora's belief that Mai might hunt ghosts or keep spirits with ill intent out of our house. Coming from a long line of ghost-hunting cats wasn't why I wanted to keep Mai. And I needed to be certain about what my small gray cat could or couldn't do before I told Gabe, perhaps raising his hopes. We'd all had enough upset for one day.

Dora drained the last drop of whiskey and held the glass out to Jack. "Be a dear and pour me another one. If Gabe and Delia are quite finished making eyes at each other, we can confront the unpleasant subject staring us in the face. I'd like to hear what happened with Archie."

"Only for you, Dora." Jack leaned over to kiss her cheek as he retrieved her empty glass. He pulled open the doors on the rosewood and black lacquer bar cabinet, lifting out several bottles and reading labels before choosing one. "I could use a drink too. This has been one hell of a day. Can I get you something, Gabe?"

Gabe put an arm around my shoulders and pulled me close. "None for me, thanks. Maybe later. If we're going to talk about what happened with Archie at the station, I want Dodd and Russell to hear this. They need to know."

Jack handed Dora her drink. "I'll go get them."

By the time Randy, Jack, and Thom returned from the kitchen, I'd settled down on the settee again. The kitten perched on my lap, calm and quiet, making no effort to run and play. She watched Randy move into place, purring in an odd rhythm I'd not heard before, and shut her eyes once he'd taken a seat next to Isadora. I wondered at that.

Gabe paced the center of the room, shoulders held stiffly and hands stuffed deep into his pockets. I knew my husband well. He was working up to telling us unpleasant truths.

He stopped pacing, looking at each of us in turn, and cleared his throat. "I wanted Dodd and Russell to hear what I have to say about how Archie Baldwin died. Thom Russell's been on my squad for years. I know him pretty well. I know his family and the kind of man he is. And Randy's been at the station just a few months, but Delia and Dora trust him. That means I can too."

"Gabriel." Dora leaned forward, blue eyes narrowing and the newly lit cigarette in her hand forgotten. "Let me make certain I understand. Are you saying you can't trust all of your men?"

"That's exactly what he's saying, Dora." Jack leaned on the wall behind Dora's chair. He swirled his glass, watching pieces of ice careen off the sides. "Archie didn't commit suicide. He was murdered."

Thom's face went slack with shock. "Murdered in the cell block? Are you sure, Captain?"

"I'm as sure as I can be until I get the coroner's report. Sal says that will take a few days, but based on what he found today—he agrees with me." Gabe raked fingers through his hair, looking exhausted and utterly defeated. "Baldwin didn't hang himself. I'll spare my wife and Dora the details, but Archie couldn't have managed on his own. He had help."

"So it had to be one of our squad." Thom wiped a hand over his mouth and shook his head. "I'd never have believed that, not in a fistful of years."

"Christ Almighty!" Jack slammed his glass on the tabletop, sloshing whiskey onto his hand. His voice was rough and ragged, and his face grew red and blotchy. "How the hell did she get to one of our men? Fontaine struts into the station bold as brass, and two hours later, Archie's dead. Explain that to me, Gabe. How did that happen?"

Dora laid a hand on Jack's arm. She winced at the strength of his emotion, but didn't pull away. "Sit down, Jack. Please. Let Gabe tell the rest of us what happened."

He sank into the chair next to Dora, staring at his shoes. She kept an arm looped through Jack's, offering what comfort she could, and endured the pain his grief and anger forced upon her. I knew what that cost her.

I caught Randy frowning as he studied Isadora's face. That he understood she was in a great deal of pain was clear, but then again, he'd helped Dora endure the agony of handling evidence the first day they met. Randy reached for her free hand, holding tight, and much of the strain left Dora's face. His ability to channel away her pain was a true blessing.

We sat quietly listening as Gabe explained who Effie Ladia Fontaine was and recounted her unannounced visit to his office, and all that he and Jack suspected about her. His voice broke as he told us about mentioning Archie's name and how that may have been the reason Archie was murdered. Gabe cleared his throat and went on, giving us the details of Miss Fontaine's connections to Archie, Bradley Wells, and a young man named Thad Harper, and how devoted Amanda Poe had been to the pacifist cause.

Those were ties he and Jack could prove, the first links in a chain. All the people Gabe had mentioned were dead or missing after crossing Miss Fontaine's path. The facts they knew for certain made a damning case in my mind, but lacked legal proof.

The list of horrors Gabe laid at her feet went on: bodies of young women washing up under a pier, men recruited for a day's labor and never coming home, young women vanishing. He and Jack suspected Miss Fontaine of somehow being a party to the murder of Mr. Sung's brother and niece, a ruthless killing much too like the way Bradley Wells died for them to ignore the similarities. Gabe couldn't prove Effie Fontaine was directly connected, not yet, but he knew. Listening to him speak, I became certain as well.

As the story unfolded, I'd begun to understand why ghosts were flocking to Gabe, looking for a champion and seeking justice. Remembering the child ghosts in that throng of haunts, each big-eyed, small face frightened and confused, made me heartsick. I couldn't imagine anyone wanting to hurt children deliberately. Nor could I grasp how a mind became depraved enough to murder a child.

But as I listened, the certainty that I knew the truth became stronger. Each small ghost was somehow connected to Effie Fontaine, more links in the chain—more victims—stretching back far too many years. That was a horrific thought, one I couldn't put aside.

And I couldn't help but think of the little girl spirit and wonder what part she played. I didn't believe for a moment her appearance was a coincidence.

Gabe finished speaking and no one said anything for a long while. I needed time to think, to sift through all the things I'd learned and see how they fit with what I already knew. From the expression on Isadora's face, she was doing the same.

Thom was the first to break the silence. "I'm not doubting what you said, Captain, far from it. But I can't deny the whole thing makes little sense to me. Why would someone like Miss Fontaine take up murder? She must be well respected or all those churches wouldn't let her speak. Even traveling the way she does, seems like someone would have noticed if she was leaving a trail of bodies behind."

"Not necessarily." Randy glanced at Gabe, seeking permission to speak. "Depends on the towns she visited. Strangers were always passing through the little town I grew up in. No one paid much attention if a drifter was there one day and gone the next. We only kept track of people who'd lived there all their lives. Things are different here."

"Dodd's right." Jack shifted in his chair. "Things are different here. She attracted the attention of San Francisco society, for one thing. People notice if the society pages fill up with stories about socialites being murdered. And Archie had enough sanity left to come looking for me after Mandy disappeared. I don't know if we'd have noticed Effie Fontaine or made connections to the rest of these cases otherwise."

Thom rolled down his shirtsleeves, forehead screwed up in thought. "There's a lot of truth in that, Lieutenant. But even if she'd paid a gang of rowdies to do her dirty work, I still can't see the logic or what she'd have to gain. No offense, ladies, but most women don't have the stomach for murder. And it takes a pretty cocksure person to reach inside a jail cell to silence someone."

"No offense taken." Dora let go of Jack's arm. She drained her glass, the remaining whiskey watered down and pale with melted ice. "You're right. Few women have the stomach for that type of cold, calculated murder. The ones who do are all the more dangerous."

My earlier thoughts about spirits and control returned, blossoming into hard, jarring conviction. I knew what had happened to Archie Baldwin.

"Effie Fontaine has the stomach for murder and much worse. She drove Archie to the brink of insanity before she had him killed." Randy and Thom traded looks, unsure what I meant. Gabe and Jack peered at me quizzically, waiting for me to go on, but they'd had a good taste of Archie's raving. I sat up straighter and spoke before I thought better of it. "The spirits surrounding him weren't random haunts. Dora and I both saw that. She sent those ghosts after Archie."

"Oh dear God. Archie escaped her somehow." The same stark and horrible realization I'd come to sat in Dora's eyes. She slumped back in her chair, hands limp in her lap. "No one listens to the ravings of a lunatic. She kept him quiet and in a cage until she could dispose of him."

Jack left the room, his footfalls sounding farther away as he headed toward the front door. Gabe started after Jack, but Thom stepped in front of him. "I'll look out for the lieutenant, sir. Stay with Dora and Mrs. Ryan. The three of you can work out what we do next."

I made room for Gabe to sit next to me. He looked ghastly, the combination of anger, worry, and lingering guilt over Archie's death leaching the color from his face. My own guilt over Archie weighed on me as well. I leaned against Gabe, knowing that nothing I did would make things better, while fervently wishing I could.

He slipped an arm around my shoulders. "What are we going to do, Dora? You and Dee understand what's going on better than I do. Tell me where to start."

"I'd suggest burning Effie Fontaine at the stake, but supporting a witch hunt of any sort might be hypocritical on my part. I'm only half-serious in any case." Dora tried to stand, but her feet got tangled and she ended up sitting heavily instead. She waved away my frown and Randy's startled expression. "Please don't look so outraged. Be a pet and pour me another drink, Randy."

"No, I don't think so. You've had at least five since dinner. That's enough." Randy stayed in his chair, jaw set and hands braced on his knees. "This is serious, Dora. The captain just asked for your help. You won't be any use to him if you're too full of whiskey to stand up."

Dora arched an eyebrow, her smile icy and controlled. "Are you calling me a drunk, Officer Dodd?"

"My granddad had a saying, Miss Bobet." Randy stretched out his long legs and sat back, arms folded. "If the cap fits, wear it."

Gabe's arm tightened around my shoulders, a warning I didn't need. Neither of us was foolish enough to get between Dora and Randy until it proved necessary. The two of them stared at each other, engaged in a silent duel of wills. I'd not seen anyone other than Daniel or me stand up to Dora this way. I'd thought Randy an Indiana farm boy trying to find his footing in San Francisco, but now I revised my opinion. There were depths to Randolph Dodd that I'd not guessed.

Her close friends all knew Dora drank more than she should. We watched over her, but we'd also given up direct attempts to get her to stop. She'd explained to me from the onset of our friendship that she much preferred the numbness alcohol brought to experiencing another person's suffering. Put that way, I couldn't say I blamed her.

Daniel was usually able to keep her drinking in reasonable check, but he'd been gone for months. I was so used to seeing her with a glass in her hand, or adding whiskey to her tea, that I seldom paid attention. She might be drinking more and I just hadn't noticed.

The standoff between them didn't last long. Dora sighed and

pushed her glass away, giving in gracefully. "Perhaps coffee would be best after all. Cream and two sugars, please."

He wasn't gone more than a few minutes. Randy returned from the kitchen with a tray full of coffee cups, cream pitcher, sugar cubes on a saucer, and a plate full of ladyfingers. Randy handed Isadora her cup, offered coffee to the rest of us, and took his seat again.

Dora looked Randy in the eye and smiled brightly, as if they'd never had a disagreement. "Do you own a good suit? I realize elegant tailoring might be too much to ask, but a nice coat and vest, and decent trousers will do. Just as long as it's appropriate for a night on the town."

"I have a good suit. My family pitched in and had one made for me before I came to San Francisco." Randy looked to Gabe and me for help, but we were just as much in the dark. He eyed Dora, understandably cautious. I didn't blame him in the slightest. "I don't have the need to wear it often. Why?"

"Because it occurs to me that before we know where to start with Miss Fontaine, we need to know what she is. I'm not at all certain about that right now. Once I know, I can determine what she's capable of, aside from murder." Dora tasted her coffee, made a face, and dropped in more sugar. "The best way to do that is to attend one of her lectures. Think of it as braving the lion in her den, if you like. Dee and I will need an escort, someone she doesn't know and can't influence. You fit that role perfectly."

"Dammit, Dora." Gabe took his arm away, moving to perch on the edge of the cushion, stiff and tense. "I don't want you or Delia anywhere near Fontaine. Something about her makes my skin crawl. You're the one who taught me not to disregard those feelings. And this feels much too dangerous, especially after what you said about Baldwin. There has to be another way."

Dora blew a cloud of blue-tinted smoke toward the ceiling before laying the cigarette aside, all the while studying Gabe's face. Her expression softened. "I believe you. But unless you have sensitives tucked away in your squad room, Delia and I are the only ones qualified to ferret out Effie Fontaine's secrets. If she's able to marshal armies of spirits and send them after people, we need to know. What happened to Archie makes it even more imperative. I won't presume to know if either Dee or Randy is eager to undertake this spying mission. They can decide for themselves, but I'm going regardless of their decision. There is no other way."

I tucked the kitten into the crook of my arm and moved to rest my head on Gabe's shoulder. He held himself still and rigid, as if moving or even reacting to my presence would cause him to shatter. I'd never thought of Gabe as being afraid of anything, mostly because he'd never said as much or acted fearful. But he didn't need to say it aloud for me to know he was afraid for me and Isadora right now. "Dora's right, Gabe. She has to go and I have to go with her."

He sagged a bit then, resigned. Gabe knew both of us too well. Dora and I had decided on a course of action and he'd never talk either of us out of attending Effie Fontaine's lecture. Now that the die was cast, he wouldn't belabor the point.

Gabe took my hand and glanced over at Randy. "Dodd? What about you?"

"I'll escort them to the lecture." He looked at Isadora, and something flashed across his face, quickly hidden again. Randy Dodd wasn't the first to fall in love with Dora or become wildly infatuated, but those hidden depths of his would complicate matters. "The two of them shouldn't go alone. I won't let anything happen to them, Captain. You've my word on that."

"Don't make promises you can't keep, Officer. And don't worry about being a hero if something goes wrong. I don't expect you to protect them alone." Gabe rubbed a hand over his face. "I'll post other officers I trust at the lecture to help keep an eye on things. Give me a day or two to line them up. I need to make sure I find men who didn't have any contact with Fontaine when she was at the station."

"Not trying to argue us out of this was the right choice, Gabe." Dora finished picking apart a ladyfinger and left it lying on the plate. "Make certain that Jack understands the dangers Miss Fontaine poses, both spiritual and physical. He's very angry right now. Don't let him do anything rash or leave Sadie and the baby unprotected."

"I'll do my best with Jack. I've already placed guards on Sadie and Stella." Gabe stood and offered me his hand. "Let's go home, Mrs. Ryan."

I handed the kitten to Gabe and gathered my coat and scarf, and the basket she'd slept in earlier. Mai seemed very content with Gabe, purring with eyes closed and settling against him. We said our good-byes and started down the hall.

Gabe stopped at the front door to tuck Mai into the top of his overcoat, sheltering her from the rain and cold as I had. "Dee, I forgot to ask, but what came of Dora's tarot card reading? Did she find what she was looking for?"

"I think so, but by then it was too late. She couldn't have changed what happened." Cards predicting overwhelming sorrow and disaster weren't what she'd expected, but that was what we'd found. And it truly was too late by then; Archie was already dead. I took Gabe's arm and leaned into him, fighting back fresh grief and tears. "Take me home, Gabe. I'll explain on the way."

I put the kitten's basket in our bedroom near the large chest of drawers, out of drafts and hopefully clear of mischief, and shut the bedroom door. Mai settled in right away, purring softly. She appeared content, and I imagined she knew she was home.

Gabe and I fell asleep in each other's arms. Life was uncertain and perilous, and each of us needed to know the other one was there.

I wasn't certain what woke me, the chiming of the parlor clock or Mai's low growl, but I sat up quickly and groped for my dressing gown. The small gray cat was a shadow on Gabe's pillow, crouching next to his head and staring into the darkness, green eyes glowing in faint moonlight.

Laughter chased around the edges of the room, growing louder and fading again, as if a carousel full of children spun on the ceiling.

Mai growled again, but didn't move away from Gabe. She was protecting him; I'd no doubt of that, and less doubt of where the danger lay. The little girl spirit was back.

Pieces of frantic melody replaced the laughter.

Round and round the city streets,
The monkeys chased the people,
Find them now before they die
Dancing with the weasel.

She binds them with a ring of iron,
She beds them in the steeple,
That's the price the people pay
For dancing with the weasel
Dancing with the weasel
Dancing with the weasel. . . .

Mai continued to stare at the ceiling, growling fierce as a lioness guarding her kill. I couldn't see the ghost, but the cat saw. Laughter and singing faded away, replaced by the sound of rain pounding the roof and hissing through winter-bare trees outside our windows.

Once Mai relaxed and shut her eyes, I lay back down, heart pounding. Rain had washed away most of the salt ringing the house, weakening Isadora's boundaries and allowing the little girl spirit closer. That she couldn't manifest so strongly as before was a blessing.

And I was doubly grateful to Mr. Sung for his gift of Mai, no matter the motive or what hidden intent he'd had. She'd protected Gabe and likely kept the ghost at bay.

I drifted back to sleep slowly, convinced that guarding Gabe from harmful spirits may have been Mr. Sung's plan all along.

CHAPTER 18

Gabe

Gabe rocked back in his chair, frowning at the pair of typed lists sitting side by side on his desk. Staring at columns of names all morning wasn't going reveal secret connections to Effie Fontaine. Hoping for and actually finding an association between the missing people on his list and Fontaine's organization were two different things.

And even if he'd found a link, that wouldn't stop Isadora and Delia from attending Miss Fontaine's lecture on Friday. Their arguments still held true.

He'd been lucky to get his wife and Dora to agree to wait a week, both to let some time pass after Archie Baldwin's death, and for him to try to discover which of the men he could trust. Gabe's stomach churned each time he walked through the station. He hated looking at the men passing him with suspicion, wondering. Hated having to come in to work each day, pretending nothing was wrong.

A quick rap on the door was all the warning he had before Jack waltzed in, a bakery bag in hand and whistling gaily. Jack was better at pretending.

Pretense ended once the office door was closed again. His partner pulled a bulging file folder from under his jacket and dropped it on the desk. "These are the personnel files for Eli Marsh, Thomas Walsh, and John Luther. All of them transferred over from Pearson's squad in the last six months. Marsh and Luther made the move just after Bradley Wells was murdered. Walsh came over the month before."

Gabe flipped open the file, skimming through the pages rapidly. "All three joined the force at about the same time two years ago. It doesn't say so here, but I'd guess they were rookies together in Fade Pearson's station. No commendations or disciplinarily notes for any of them, no special training or performance evaluations on past assignments." He read a few more pages and shut the file again. "No notations about sick leave or being late for a shift either. When was the last time you saw a two-year-old personnel file without a single note?"

"As I recall, Sergeant Marsh was leaving bons mots in our files in less than a month." Jack ripped open the bakery bag, revealing waxed paper–wrapped ham sandwiches and a half-dozen sugar cookies. He dragged over the visitor's chair and took a seat. "I knew we wouldn't make it out for lunch. Don't let Annie know I'm eating bakery cookies. She wouldn't speak to me for the next month."

"Annie wouldn't forgive me either." He took a bite of salty ham and thick sourdough bread, eating because he needed food but not really tasting anything. "So we have three cops that started in Pearson's squad, all with spotless official records. Or no record, depending on how you look at their files."

Jack shrugged. "No record is closer to the truth. That doesn't mean the three of them are clean. And you haven't heard the best part. I double-checked the duty rosters. Marsh and Luther were both collecting meal trays the day Archie died."

"The trick now is to figure out if three San Francisco cops got bought by Effie Fontaine. And when. Marshall hasn't had any luck trying to make friends with Marsh or Luther. He says Eli Marsh cuts him dead if he tries to strike up a conversation in passing." Eating food he couldn't taste was about as appealing as gnawing on the file in front of him. Gabe took another bite anyway, chewing methodically and thinking. "What about the taverns? Did Marshall or Randy turn up more names?"

Henderson and Dodd had gone out dressed in street clothes every night for the last week, visiting small cafés in working-class neighborhoods and dockside taverns where they weren't known. Trying to find more of Effie Fontaine's tracks.

"Not yet." Jack divided the cookies between them, giving Gabe two and keeping four for himself. Not much affected his partner's appetite. "A few rumors, but nothing solid. Marshall had one place he wanted to visit again tonight. One of the men sweeping up started to talk to them, but the owner yelled for him to stop wasting time and get back to work. He wouldn't talk to them again after that. I guess the old man was scared of losing his job."

"Tell Henderson and Dodd to keep at it. It's only a matter of time before we get lucky and she makes a mistake." Gabe brushed crumbs off his lap. He flicked a few more off the personnel file before slipping the folder into the deep, bottom desk drawer. His mouth twisted into a thin, bitter line. "I'm looking forward to that day. I'll sleep better at night knowing she's locked up."

Jack tipped his head to the side, a quizzical expression on his face. "I don't think I've ever seen you react to a suspect this way. You really don't like Effie Fontaine."

Gabe rocked back in the desk chair.. "The truth is that Fontaine sets my teeth on edge and makes my skin crawl at the same time. Even more so after what Dora's told me. Aside from all that, she's made this personal, Jack. Effie Fontaine's first mistake was storming into my office making demands and thinking she could intimidate me. A bigger mistake was having Archie Baldwin murdered in my jail."

Jack looked at the half-eaten cookie in his hand and set it aside. "Has Sal finished Archie's autopsy report yet?"

"I spoke to him last night. He apologized for taking so long, but he had other cases ahead of Archie's, and there were some things he needed to be sure about. I'm hoping that means he found evidence we can use to link Fontaine or someone working for her to Archie's murder." He held the trash can up, and Jack dumped the last of the debris from lunch inside. "He wouldn't tell me over the phone either. You know how Sal is. He promised to bring the final report over late this afternoon. If something comes up, he promised to call and let me know."

A knock at the door made Gabe's heart race. He traded looks with Jack and swept all the papers on his desktop into his desk drawer. Locking the drawer left him feeling foolish, but that didn't change the fact they needed to keep what little they'd discovered secret. The last time they talked about Effie Fontaine, she'd walked into his office. He couldn't take the chance.

Lon Rockwell's voice called out, adding to Gabe's moment of déjà vu. "Captain Ryan? You have a visitor, sir."

"Christ Almighty, Gabe." Jack eyed the blurred silhouettes glimpsed through the glass in the door and kept his voice low. "Maybe Dora's right, and saying Effie Fontaine's name summons her."

"You shouldn't believe everything Dora tells you. It's not her. Fontaine's not reckless enough to show up here again, not after what happened to Baldwin." And Effie Fontaine had made her point the first time, driving home the fact she was untouchable. Or that she thought she was. Gabe straightened his shirt cuffs and buttoned his jacket before coming around to stand in front of the desk. "Come in, Rockwell."

He was right; the person ushered into his office wasn't Gabe's prime murder suspect. A tall, rawboned young man with sandy blond hair and an engaging smile stood just behind Rockwell. Dressed in a new-looking straw boater hat, white shirt, and a tan suit that had seen better days, the stranger had light green eyes that swept what he could see of the office from the doorway, seeming to take in everything at once.

Rockwell nodded toward the man in the hallway. "Captain Ryan, this is Samuel Clemens Butler. Mr. Butler is a reporter for the *Call* and he wants to speak with you and the lieutenant. Normally I wouldn't have brought him back, but he says he has information on one of your cases. I can show him out again if you're too busy to speak with him."

"He can stay for now. Go back to the front lobby, Rockwell." Gabe sat on the corner of the desk, arms folded over his chest, sizing up the young reporter. "I'll call you when I need you to escort him out."

Rockwell nodded and turned to leave, squeezing past Butler and giving him a dubious look. Samuel Butler stood just inside the door, barely acknowledging the big officer's presence—or anyone else's, for that matter. He was too busy gawking. Butler's eyes swept the room again. Gabe guessed he was looking for anything that might make good copy.

Locking everything away didn't feel so foolish now. Gabe cleared his throat. "Come all the way inside, Mr. Butler, and shut the door. Sal Rosen said you'd been asking questions about me down at the morgue."

"The deputy coroner got that wrong, Captain." Butler closed the door and stood square in front of it, appearing relaxed and at ease. "Asking about unsolved cases isn't the same as asking questions about you. Not unless you and Lieutenant Fitzgerald are the only detectives in the city with unsolved murder cases. If so, you've got a lot bigger problems than my asking questions."

Gabe had dealt with a lot of reporters in his years on the force. Butler was cocky and overconfident, but he was young too, probably no more than twenty-two or twenty-three. Growing older had a way of deflating cocky young men. "I don't have a lot of time to spare, so let me get right to the point, Mr. Butler. Lieutenant Fitzgerald and I don't share details of our cases with the press. I'm afraid coming here was a waste of your time."

Butler flashed a toothy grin. "And that's where you're wrong, Captain. I didn't come here looking for information. I came to share what I've dug up on Effie Ladia Fontaine. A very interesting woman." He stuck his long hands deep into his trouser pockets and strolled over to the bulletin board, looking over the newspaper clippings pinned there. The smile was gone when he turned around again. "Dangerous as hell, but interesting."

Jack frowned and moved around to the front of the desk to stand near Gabe. "Who told you we want information about Miss Fontaine?"

"Word gets around. For starters, you have men asking about her in every tavern up and down the waterfront. And according to my informants, she came to your office and told you to call off your dogs. Given what I know about her, my guess is that something you're doing makes her nervous. At the very least, you got her attention." Butler sat sideways on the visitor's chair, one arm draped casually across the back. "Don't try to give me the bum's rush, Lieutenant. I've been in San Francisco for months, tracking down information about Fontaine and waiting for my chance. This is it. I want her stopped even more than you do."

"All right, Mr. Butler." Gabe went back to his chair, his curiosity aroused. The nod from Jack was slight and easily missed by anyone who didn't know him, but he'd learned to read his partner years ago. "We'll hear you out. Why don't you start with explaining why you think Effie Fontaine is dangerous."

"You've met her, Captain. Do I really have to explain?" Butler turned to face them, his casual demeanor replaced by one that was tense and completely earnest. "Two years ago, I was living in Upstate New York and working on my uncle's newspaper. I helped him set type, wrote obituaries, and helped deliver papers three days a week. Uncle Walter hadn't opened the office one Saturday morning, so I went by the house to check on him. My cousin Rose had gone to a meeting in the church hall the night before. Rose never came home. My uncle was out looking for her."

"A meeting?" Jack's tone was impatient, pressing Butler. "What kind of a meeting?"

"Lieutenant Fitzgerald." Gabe didn't take his eyes off Samuel Butler's face, but the warning note in his voice was clear enough. Jack was the best interrogator on the force, able to put witnesses at ease with only a few words. Attacking Butler showed how far off his game Jack was. "Let Mr. Butler finish his story."

Jack looked at Gabe, startled, and his eyes widened at the realization of how badly he'd misstepped. "My apologies, Mr. Butler. I shouldn't have interrupted. Go on."

Butler waved the apology away. "We're all in the business of asking questions. That's our job. The meeting Rose attended was a talk on the dangers of the United States becoming involved in the European war."

Gabe's hands clenched into fists. "Let me guess: Effie Fontaine was the speaker."

"Good guess, Captain. She'd made arrangements to speak at the church hall four nights running. Rosie went all four nights." Grief flashed across Butler's face. "That was the first I'd heard of Fontaine. It was far from the last."

"I'm sure it wasn't." Gabe straightened the stack of duty rosters on the corner of his desk, suddenly unable to sit still. Fontaine had been giving her lectures for two years. For two years, people had not come home afterwards. *Two years.* The urge to hit something, anything, was almost overwhelming, but he couldn't give in to that. He aligned the corners on the stack of files, waiting for the need to lash out to pass. "What happened to your cousin?"

"Rose and one other girl, Cassie Adams, disappeared on Friday night. My uncle and the sheriff organized a search party and questioned everyone who'd been at the meeting. No one even remembered seeing Rosie." Butler took off his hat and slicked his hair back, anger glittering in his eyes. "There was a traveling carnival set up on the edge of town that same week. Fontaine suggested that maybe the girls had lied about where they were going and had gone to the carnival instead. I was there when the sheriff questioned Miss Fontaine. I kept watching her, wondering why the hair on the back of my neck stood up. And I *knew* Fontaine was lying. I knew it."

"Mother of God." Jack traded looks with Gabe. "Did they ever find your cousin?"

Butler set his hat on his lap. "The sheriff's men never found a trace of Rosie. She just vanished. Cassie's body turned up in an old barn less than half a mile from the carnival. They arrested one of the carnies for her murder. Fontaine left town and went back to New York City the next morning."

Gabe rocked back in his chair, staring at the ceiling. Thinking. "And you've kept track of Fontaine ever since."

"As much as I could. Being a reporter means most people don't think twice about me asking questions. Sometimes she'd give me the slip for weeks, then I'd catch word of her again. The pattern's always the same. People disappear when Fontaine's in town. People die." He toyed with his hat, one long finger smoothing the brown and tan ribbon around the straw crown. "She never stays in small towns more than a couple of weeks. Big cities like Chicago and San Francisco have more people and it's easier to avoid being noticed. She was in Chicago five months, Seattle for three. Fontaine's been in San Francisco close to four months now."

"And if she holds to the pattern, Miss Fontaine won't be here much longer." They needed to act soon, before she left his jurisdiction. Gabe sat up, leaning across the desk toward Samuel Butler. "Explain something, Mr. Butler. You've been following Effie Fontaine and collecting information for two years. Why haven't you gone to the police before now?"

Butler's laugh was harsh and bitter sounding. "What makes you think I haven't? The head constable of a little town in Georgia threw me out for spreading slander about her. Another chief of police in Iowa put me in jail for two nights. I looked like a better suspect for murder than a well-dressed woman preaching peace from the town pulpit." He tossed his hat onto Gabe's desk. "You're the first police officer I've come across who didn't think Effie Fontaine was destined for sainthood. I figured I stood a reasonable chance of you believing me, Captain Ryan."

"Call me Gabe. And I have reason to believe you." He rooted around in his desk, hunting for paper and a pencil, and doing his best to ignore the imagined sensation of cold fingers caressing his cheek. He found the tablet he'd been hunting for and passed it to Jack. "What I need is for you to tell me everything you can remember from the last two years. Names, dates, places, anything I can use to build a case. I mean to put Miss Fontaine in a cell and keep her there."

"And both of you can call me Sam." He pulled a thick sheaf of papers out of an inside jacket pocket and smiled. "I was hoping you'd feel that way, so I came prepared. A good reporter takes lots of notes. The rest I can fill in from memory."

Jack tugged the second spare chair from the corner to the side of the desk. He sat and flipped the tablet to an empty page, pencil poised to write. "I have a question before we get started. Did Miss Fontaine ever come after you directly, Sam?"

"No, she never did. That used to keep me up nights, but then I figured it out." Sam stretched out his long legs and crossed his arms, papers gripped tight in one hand. "Or I think I did, anyway. All those people who went to Fontaine's lectures and disappeared believed in her, and in every word of her message. My aunt told me that Rosie believed. But I don't. I see right through Effie Fontaine to the lies. For some reason, that keeps her from coming after me. That probably sounds pretty strange, but it's the best explanation I can come up with."

"Not so strange, Sam." Gabe could understand and even see how that worked. He'd had long conversations with Dee and Isadora about belief and the power that brought. Even a flicker of belief could wedge open pathways best left sealed shut. "I'd even wager you're right. Now, let's get to work. We've got a lot of ground to cover and not much time."

Gabe hadn't lied. Two years was a lot of ground to cover. Samuel Clemens Butler talked for almost three hours, outlining a zigzag course of murder and mysterious disappearances all across the country, and filling in the details his notes missed. The list of names Jack wrote down grew longer: men who'd signed on for casual labor, mothers who believed Effie Fontaine would keep their sons out of battle, grandmothers, young women, and men looking for a cause.

Children's names were included on the list of victims as well: sons and daughters of well-to-do merchants who vanished from front yards, working-class children who never arrived at school, and street urchins scrambling to find enough to eat. Butler had stumbled upon the name of the first missing child by accident, but once Sam started looking, he found more in each city and town Fontaine visited. He'd never been able to discover why.

None of what they knew made any sense to Gabe. Sticking pins in a map didn't reveal a pattern for her travels nor give them a possible motive. Everything she did, each town she visited and the people who fell victim to her, might have been chosen by tossing a coin. Effie Fontaine was the one constant in their laundry list of small towns and big cities.

That and the fact that Miss Fontaine returned to New York City for one or two weeks every few months.

Gabe tapped the map pins clustered around New York City. "Sam, did you ever find a reason for why Fontaine goes back to New York so often? She said something while she was in my office about having a benefactor who funds her work, but refused to name him. Could she be going back to report to him?"

"That makes as much sense as anything she does. She has family there too." Sam dug through his stack of papers, finding what he wanted scribbled in the corner of a faded sheet of newsprint. "An uncle, Henry Mertz, who runs a secondhand shop on Second Avenue. I went to his shop more than a year ago. He has some news clippings with Miss Fontaine's picture hanging up behind his counter. He's a nice-enough old man, close to eighty if he's a day. I doubt he knows much more about his niece than what he reads in the paper."

Jack set down his pencil and loosened his tie. "He might know more than you think. Any chance the uncle could be her benefactor?"

"Not if that shop is all he's got. I poked around in there almost an hour, trying to get him to talk." Sam shrugged. "People came in, but they didn't buy anything. Mr. Mertz seemed to be doing all the buying."

"I know a precinct captain in New York, Theo Watson. If there's any information we should know about Henry Mertz, Theo will find it for us. I'll ask him to see what he can find out about Fontaine's visits when he questions Mr. Mertz." Gabe rubbed a hand over his face and turned away from the map. He glanced at the clock, surprised to find it was after four. "It's already after seven in New York. I'll send Theo a telegram first thing in the morning."

Butler tidied up his stack of papers and stuffed them into the deep, inside pocket of his jacket. He stood and picked up his hat. "I have to get back to the office and file my story for tomorrow's paper. You know where to find me."

Gabe offered his hand. "You've been a big help, Sam. Jack and I appreciate it."

"Just don't let her get away, Gabe." Sam clapped him on the arm. "And the two of you take care. Fontaine is dangerous, and so are the thugs who work for her."

"You be careful too, Sam. She hasn't come after you yet, but that could change."

He stood looking at the door after it closed behind Sam Butler. Thinking. Trying to devise a way to stay a step ahead of Effie Fontaine and keep her from leaving town.

Gabe turned back to find Jack flipping through the notes he'd made. "There must be seventy or eighty names here, Gabe. We should arrest Fontaine now. Tonight."

"A lawyer would have her out before morning, and she'd be on a train an hour later. You know that just as well as I do. We have to be smarter than that." Gabe stuffed his hands into his trouser pockets, pacing because he couldn't sit still. He glanced at the clock again, vaguely bothered by the lateness of the hour. Sal hadn't called about the autopsy report, and he wasn't sure how long to wait before giving up and going home. The deputy coroner was a busy man. Too busy. "All we have so far is a list of names from other cities and other states, and Sam's word. Proving our case here in San Francisco is what's going to put Fontaine behind bars. We have to catch her here."

Jack tapped his pencil against the table edge, a slow fast, slow fast rhythm. "Which case do we concentrate on? We can't link Fontaine to the bodies that washed up under the pier, not unless we can identify them and prove she had contact with those women. Mandy and Archie attended her lectures, but we haven't uncovered an eye-witness who saw them there. Hell, we haven't found Amanda's body or Thad Harper's. And if anyone asked me what Miss Fontaine's motive is for killing people, I couldn't say."

"Dora has a theory or two."

"All her theories give me the willies. Even if I wanted to believe Dora's ideas of rituals to raise power, do we want to take that in front of a judge?" Jack's pencil tapped faster. "I wish I didn't feel like time is running out. Fontaine could leave town tonight, and we'd be no closer to making an arrest stick."

"We can prove that Bradley Wells rented the church hall to her staff. That's solid at least and something Miss Fontaine can't deny." Gabe stopped in front of the map again, staring at the small knot of pins representing San Francisco. He didn't want the number of pins to increase. "I'll charge her as an accessory to Wells's murder if she makes a move to leave town. That will buy us time. As much press as the Wells case received, her lawyer would have a tough time with bail. If need be, I'm sure Commissioner Lindsey would hold a news conference."

"That sounds reasonable. What else do you have in mind?" Jack tipped his head to the side, studying Gabe, and stopped tapping the pencil. "I know you too well, Captain Ryan. You're plotting something."

"Plotting is what the villains in Henderson's nickel weeklies do, Lieutenant Fitzgerald." He touched the pin representing the murders in Chinatown before going back to his desk. "First I want to talk to Sung Wing again. Having a hunch that Effie Fontaine was somehow involved in his brother's murder isn't the same as proving it. Then I want to find out where she's staying in town. What Sam said about her avoiding hotels explains why we haven't tracked her down yet. Fontaine might be living with a supporter."

"Or she could be holed up in a rooming house. All right." The long, weary breath Jack let out wasn't quite a sigh. "Where do we start?"

"You start by going home to your wife and daughter. I'm sure Sadie would love to have you home in time for supper." He nodded toward the perpetually slow clock hanging over the door. "If you leave now, you'll make it on time. I'm going to Chinatown alone."

"What about going home to your own wife?" Jack tucked away his pencil and closed up the tablet containing his notes, frowning. "And I'm not wild about you going to Chinatown alone. Mr. Sung's every bit as dangerous as Effie Fontaine."

"Dee is out shopping with Isadora and won't be home until later. I'll probably be home before she is." Gabe unlocked his desk drawer and took out the pistol sitting inside. He didn't carry a sidearm inside the station, but he'd quickly gotten into the habit of having the gun with him each time he left the office. Too quickly. "I'll have a patrolman with me. Everything will be fine."

"I'm holding you to that, Gabe. I'm too lazy to break in another partner." Jack paused before opening the office door. "Do you really think that Sung Liang had a connection to Effie Fontaine?"

"I don't know." Gabe slung his coat over his arm and grabbed his fedora. He pulled open the office door, waving Jack out. "But it won't hurt to ask."

CHAPTER 19

Delia

I'd never understood Dora's obsession with fur coats. Her closets were full of mink jackets, fox stoles, and wraps trimmed in ermine. As sensitive as she was to the lingering pain of death, wearing the fur of dead animals struck me as oddly out of character. I'd told her so more than once. Each time she'd smile, pat my hand tolerantly, and mutter some nonsense about my not understanding the small sacrifices made to stay in fashion.

She was largely right about my not understanding the need to own the latest styles, especially in regard to furs. I'd borrowed one of Sadie's fox stoles for a special occasion years ago and felt enormously silly the entire night. The furrier had left the fox's head attached, and I couldn't get over the feeling that its glass eyes were leering at me. Perhaps they were.

We'd visited five furriers so far, not one of which had met Isadora's high standards. Each shop smelled slightly of mothballs, even though valiant attempts were made to cover the aroma with the scent of hothouse flowers in crystal vases and discretely placed saucers of potpourri. Dora was always unfailingly charming and polite to tradespeople, but she was also very firm about what she wanted. Watching shopkeepers scramble to find something in their stock that might catch her fancy had amused me at first, but that had lost its charm rather quickly.

Too many ghosts wandered these shops. Not the ghosts of small animals, unbearable as that might have been, but the spirits of stylish young women wearing mink stoles and older women in beaver coats. Scantily clad ladies from saloons along the Barbary Coast, a fox wrap draped over their shoulders, passed through the walls on a regular basis. The faded haunts of trappers and the traders who bought their pelts wandered through as well, each ghost following pathways they'd trod before passing into death.

Like called to like. A storefront full of dead animals attracted the restless dead, especially those who'd had an attachment to furs in life. Dora didn't appear to notice or, if she did, pretended otherwise. I found the parade of ghosts harder to ignore.

Gazing out the window didn't help. Dora had kept to her promise to take out Daniel's car more often and leave her car at home. Nathan, the hired driver, stood stiffly at the curb waiting on Dora's pleasure. He seldom blinked and never smiled, nor tipped his hat to passersby. Storefront mannequins displayed more expressions.

What troubled me was that every soldier's haunt on the street went out of its way to approach Nathan. Young men with bloody faces and horrendous wounds surrounded him, touching his cheek or his arm, or stared into his eyes. Their expressions were angry and accusing, offended by more than the fact he was still one of the living. I tried to imagine what Nathan might have done to draw the ire of so many dead men.

Nathan never noticed, never flinched. Unseen and unacknowledged, the spirits eventually wandered away.

Going downtown was difficult enough without watching ghosts flock to him. More spirits of dead soldiers wandered the streets each day, lost and confused. The daily papers were all filled with news of the Great War, while photos of towns shelled and prisoners of war forced to pose for news photographers splashed across the front page.

Other photos showed the aftermath of battles, bodies of men and horses strewn across the ground, broken and lifeless.

Ghosts sometimes gathered on the battlefield as well, fuzzy, indistinct images in the background of the photographs that Gabe never saw, but I did. Spirits near enough to the camera were often clear enough to recognize faces. Far too often these men stared at their own lifeless bodies, expressions a mix of shock and puzzlement. I'd stopped reading the papers as a result.

"Dee?" Dora held up a sleek, honey brown mink jacket. "What do you think of this one?"

"The color's very nice." I stepped closer, grateful to be distracted from my maudlin thoughts. Maybe with enough encouragement, she'd buy this one. "I think that shade compliments your hair and your complexion well enough."

She held the jacket up under her chin and stood in front of the full-length mirror, peering at her image with a slight frown. The shop owner, a short, square, and balding man named Mr. Hopkins, hovered behind the glass-topped counter, blotting his upper lip with a handkerchief while awaiting her decision. "The color is nice enough. But I'm not at all sure that the yellow tones go well with my skin. You don't think this shade of brown makes me look a bit sallow?"

"Never, Miss Bobet. Your complexion could never be described as sallow." Mr. Hopkins's face was ashen and his hands trembled, making me fear for his health. Isadora had been nothing but pleasant since we came in, yet he acted more nervous by the minute. The effect Dora had on complete strangers frequently baffled me. "Your friend is right. This mink is the perfect golden brown for you."

Dora's frown deepened. "The cut is very pretty, I grant you that. I hate to be such a bother, but mink might not be at all right for me this year, no matter what shade. Perhaps I should try something else entirely." She turned to Mr. Hopkins, all dimples and charm, and smiled. "Do you know what might really be lovely? Chinchilla."

"Oh. What a marvelous choice." Mr. Hopkins's manner brightened, and he put away the handkerchief. "Yes, chinchilla would be lovely with your eyes. I have just the coat in the back. One moment."

He disappeared through an ivory damask curtain into the back room. Dora toured the displays in the showroom, fingering ermine hats and fox fur muffs, and studying a case of pearl necklaces. I sat in a chair near the mirror, resigned to waiting until she'd found the perfect coat.

Mr. Hopkins pushed back through the heavy curtain, a full-length coat over his arm. He smiled and held it open for Isadora to slip into. "Try this, Miss Bobet. I think this might be the perfect coat."

The showroom lights played over alternating shades of dappled gray fur, so that it appeared as if Dora were donning a shadow. A small smile showed how pleased she was. The coat fell below her knees, softly flared at the bottom and held closed by a single rhinestone button at her throat. A wide shawl collar framed her face, and the sleeves ended in narrow cuffs that seemed tailored for her small wrists. The color did bring out the blue of her eyes.

She preened and twirled in front of the mirror, reminding me a great deal of Sadie. The two of them took the same joy in clothes and turning heads. And I'd little doubt that Dora would turn heads in this coat. She looked stunning.

"I'm totally delighted, Mr. Hopkins. This coat is exactly what I'd hoped to find." Her reflection in the oval cheval mirror was bright and cheerful in a way I'd not seen since Daniel left. A bit of my perpetual worry for her lifted. "If you'd be kind enough to prepare a bill, we can settle up. I'll wear the coat home."

The bell over the front door sounded. I saw a broad-shouldered man in a gray suit, a crisp white shirt, and a red bow tie reflected in the mirror. He was very tall and had to duck slightly as he came in the shop door to keep from hitting his head. The stranger wore a felt fedora much like Gabe's, but newer and more expensive. I noticed a small black ring on the little finger of his left hand as he removed his hat. His short straw-colored hair was slicked back with pomade.

Mr. Hopkins muttered an apology to Dora and hurried to the counter near the door. "What can I do for you, sir?"

"My employer left a coat here to be mended. I've come to collect it for her." The man laid his palm on the glass, fingers splayed wide. "You promised the repairs would be finished this evening."

I pretended to watch Isadora in the mirror, but I was really watching the stranger. There was something vaguely menacing in the stranger's stance and the tone of his voice, and I flinched from looking at him directly. Everything about the way he approached Mr. Hopkins was oddly out of tune with coming to collect a repaired coat.

Still, I didn't fight the compulsion to eavesdrop and not let on. More than mere curiosity prodded me to listen. This stranger hadn't done more than walk into the room, hadn't so much as glanced in my direction, but I was wary of him. That merited paying attention.

"What was the name on the order, sir?" Mr. Hopkins was sweating again, handkerchief balled in one hand, but he stood rock steady behind the counter, order book open before him. "I have quite a few coats and jackets waiting for pickup."

"The name is Fontaine."

Dora stiffened, her gaze flying to the man's reflection. She put a trembling hand on my arm, a warning I didn't need. I couldn't say whether she meant to caution me not to turn and stare, or if holding my arm was to keep from doing so herself. She continued to fuss with the drape of the coat, but her smile turned brittle, forced.

I smoothed her coat collar, stealing glances at the stranger in the mirror, and leaned close to whisper. "Who is he?"

She gave me an imploring look and flipped the collar up to cover most of her face. "Not now. We'll talk later."

"Effie Fontaine." The tall man glanced toward me and Isadora, but took no further notice of us. "She left a fox coat two days ago. Your girl said the small tear in the lining would be simple to repair."

Mr. Hopkins ran a finger down his list. "Oh yes, here's the notation. I'll fetch the coat from the back. It won't take but a moment."

The curtain swayed softly as Mr. Hopkins hurried away. For the moment, he appeared to have forgotten about Dora and me completely, but I couldn't say as I blamed him. Ridding his shop of the tall, rather threatening man at the counter seemed like the wisest and safest course of action for all of us.

I should have known Dora would veer far from the safe and wise. She gripped my arm firmly and steered me to a display of fur hats in the corner of the showroom farthest from the counter. "Stay here, Dee, and ignore anything that goes on. Pretend to be selecting a hat or spend time staring at the paint on the wall. I don't care which you choose, just don't turn around." Dora glanced over her shoulder. "I don't want him to get a good look at your face. I'll explain later."

"Isadora Bobet—"

"Do as I ask, Delia." Her voice hissed in my ear. "I don't have time to explain. Trust me."

Trusting Dora often required a significant leap of faith, but I did what she asked and stayed put. Angling the small vanity mirror on the display table allowed me to see Dora and not reflect my face into the room. I took a mink cloche from a stand, keeping up the charade of shopping. Running my fingers through silky fur didn't stop my heart from roaring loud in my ears. Something was very wrong here. Dora's silence rendered me even more anxious.

Dora sauntered up to the counter, crowding in next to the man who worked for Effie Fontaine. She smiled her brightest, most guileless smile, confirming that I wouldn't approve of what she planned to do. "Excuse me, but will Mr. Hopkins be much longer?"

The stranger stared down at her, stone-faced and cold at first, but before long the merest hint of a smile appeared and his expression became more cordial. "I hope not, miss. Bringing a coat from the back room shouldn't take too long."

"No, I suppose not." Dora leaned against the edge of the counter, a fingertip idly tracing patterns over the smeared mark his hand had left on the glass top. Patterns that looked vaguely like warding glyphs if I concentrated on the way her hand moved, but from across the room, I couldn't be sure. "And please forgive me if this is too forward, but I couldn't help but overhear what you said to Mr. Hopkins. You work for Effie Fontaine? The pacifist lecturer?"

"Miss Fontaine is my employer." His smile broadened, but if anything, that made me more leery of him. I could imagine a snake's eyes glittering in just that way before swallowing a mouse. "You've heard of her?"

"Of course! She's the talk of San Francisco social circles. Everyone who is anyone knows about her lectures and the work she's doing to keep our boys out of the war." Dora sighed dramatically. "I've heard so many good things about Miss Fontaine's cause. You must be proud to work for her."

Dora wielded charm like a battle mace, bashing away until all defenses crumbled. The set of her shoulders, the tilt of her head as she gazed into his eyes, and her coquettish smile were all familiar, and I'd no doubt that Isadora had a legitimate reason for pretending to flirt with him. But there was an edge there as well, and she never stopped tracing patterns on the glass.

She was afraid of this stranger, careful and guarded, but didn't want him to know. That worried me most of all.

His reflection darkened the mirror suddenly, startling me. I wasn't certain what I saw clinging to the stranger like a half-shed skin and looming over Dora: remnants of a haunting spirit, smoky shreds of living shadow, or a manifestation from another plane that I didn't have a name for. Whatever surrounded this man was a part of him, yet separate. Watching it writhe made gooseflesh rise on my skin.

Turning to look at him directly made the shadowy nimbus fade to an indistinct blur clinging to his skin, almost as if this second self knew I watched, and made an attempt to hide. What I saw wasn't a dark aura, but something else entirely. A person's aura was a reflection of their inner self and could be dark or light, but auras didn't vanish viewed head-on. They grew stronger, more distinct. Perhaps the patterns Dora had traced again and again were the key, allowing me to see his true nature.

Glancing at Dora and seeing the way her free hand twisted in the expensive coat assured me that what I'd seen was real. The symbols were meant as protection against that dark, second self dwelling within the stranger. If I recoiled from a reflection, the darkness would hit her ten times stronger. I turned my back and watched them in the mirror again, all the while cursing the fact I didn't know what Dora was doing or how I could help her. All I was certain of was the way my throat tried to close and sweat trickled down my sides.

The stranger cocked his head, still smiling, but now there was a different kind of appraisal in the way he looked at Dora. "Effie does important work, yes, and she's a good, dedicated person to partner with. Have you been able to attend one of her talks yourself?"

Dora laid her hand flat on the counter, grounding herself in the wards she'd drawn. Her smile was the perfect blend of dazzling femme fatale and lost waif. "No, and I'd dearly love to. It seems that each time I try to obtain tickets, they've already sold out."

"Then it's fortunate that we met. My name is Maximillian Roth. Allow me to remedy your lack of tickets." He fished in an inside jacket pocket and pulled out a creased and worn-looking envelope. "Is one ticket enough, or will you be bringing your shy friend over there along?"

Her eyes flicked toward me and back to his face. "Would three tickets be too much to ask? My beau has been dying to hear Miss Fontaine speak."

"By all means, bring your beau." Mr. Roth laughed, but whatever amused him failed to warm his pale blue eyes. He pulled three rusty red paper tickets from the envelope and held them out to Dora. "Her next talk is Friday night at the Baptist church on Clement Street. The man at the door will know to watch for you and that you and your friends are my guests. You're all invited to the private reception Effie holds afterwards as well."

"You're much too kind." Dora tucked the tickets into a coat pocket. "I wonder what's keeping Mr. Hopkins so long?"

The shopkeeper rushed out of the back room as if Dora's question had summoned him. Mr. Hopkins's face was bright red, and crimson blotches ran down his neck.

"I'm so sorry for the delay, sir. The repairs were finished, but the girls hadn't put the coat into a muslin sleeve yet. Getting the stains out without damaging the mink took longer than estimated." Mr. Hopkins passed over the wrapped coat and quickly stepped back, putting the counter between him and Maximillian. "Miss Fontaine settled the bill when she left the coat."

"No harm done. Waiting gave me an opportunity to have a pleasant chat with this charming lady." Maximillian bowed shallowly before donning his hat. "I hope to see you on Friday. I'm looking forward to introducing you to Effie."

Dora looked him in the eye and offered a hand for him to kiss, a mannerism that lingered from her time in Europe. I so rarely saw her touch strangers that seeing her do so with this man came as a shock.

His smile was rather smug as his lips brushed her knuckles, becoming more so when Isadora didn't let go of his hand.

"I quite enjoyed our conversation as well." Dora favored him with her most fetching smile and touched the ring on his little finger. "Can I impose on you to answer one last question? My German is a bit rusty. What does the inscription on your ring say?"

Maximillian gave Dora a considering look. "Do you have German blood, Miss—?"

Mr. Hopkins spoke up, likely thinking he was being helpful. "Bobet. Miss Isadora Bobet."

A muscle in Dora's jaw twitched, but she kept smiling and didn't let go of his hand. "My family is Welsh, but I spent several years on the continent. I managed to pick up bits of the language in several countries. I know *Das Vaterland* means 'the Fatherland,' but beyond that I admit I'm lost."

"I should have guessed a lady like yourself was well traveled. Allow me to translate, Miss Bobet." He ran his finger over the inscription on the ring. "The words say 'Loyalty to the Fatherland to evidence, gave I, in troublous time, gold for this iron.' It's an old sentiment, dating back to the war with Napoléon. My grandfather wore a ring like this, and his father before him. Some family traditions shouldn't be broken. Now, if you'll excuse me, I must be on my way."

The bell over the front door jangled, signaling his departure. I turned in time to see Maximillian through the window. He'd stopped to speak with Nathan, but hurried away in less than a minute. I wanted to think it innocent, to imagine he'd just asked directions of Nathan or inquired as to the time, but I couldn't. Nothing about this man was innocent.

"Dee, take these." Isadora held out the three tickets with a shaking hand. "Seal them in your handbag before I disgrace myself by being ill."

I did as she asked and set the handbag aside. She was sagging against the counter and looked near to sliding to the floor, so I put an arm around her waist and held her up. "Are you all right? Should I call Gabe to come get us?"

"I'm far from all right, but I will survive." She gave Mr. Hopkins a wan smile. "I shouldn't have worn this coat so long indoors, it's much too warm. Would you be so kind as to fetch me a glass of water?"

"Oh, yes." He looked startled, but stopped wringing his hands. "Of course."

With my assistance, Dora slipped out of the coat and I helped her to a chair. She batted my hand away as I tried to loosen her collar. "Don't fret so, Dee. Once I get some air and my stomach settles, I'll be fine. Nathan can take us straight home once I've paid Mr. Hopkins for the coat."

"Nathan's not taking us anywhere. I'm sending Mr. Hopkins out to dismiss him for the day." Twilight had deepened to full dark, but I could still see Nathan standing ramrod stiff under the streetlight.

I gestured toward the window. "That man, Maximillian, spoke with Nathan before he left. I have no idea what they said, but I'd feel safer telephoning Gabe or Randy to take us home. If I can't reach either of them, I'll summon a cab."

"He spoke with Nathan? How interesting." Dora studied the driver through the window and frowned. "Your instincts are the equal of mine, Dee, often better. I won't second-guess you about this. We'll send for Randy."

Mr. Hopkins returned with Dora's water and was dispatched to send Nathan away. I watched their heated exchange, a silent pantomime viewed from my side of the window glass. Mr. Hopkins had no trouble being firm with those he considered below his station, and it didn't take long before Nathan stomped around to the driver's door. Mr. Hopkins stood at the curb, a fierce scowl on his face, and made sure Nathan was well and truly gone. I breathed a small prayer of thanks as the car pulled away.

I settled in next to Dora after using Mr. Hopkins's telephone to call the police station, prepared to wait patiently for Randy's arrival. She sat with her eyes closed and head tipped so that it rested against the chair back, but I knew she wasn't sleeping. "Mr. Hopkins is still outside, and Randy will be here soon. You can tell me now."

She opened one eye to peer at me. "Tell you what?"

"Why you took such a risk. I thought the plan was to spy on Effie Fontaine from a distance, without her knowing who we are or that we were part of the crowd. Now we're specially invited to her reception afterwards." I hugged my handbag to my chest, needing to hold tight to something. "And I can't believe you let that man touch you. Not after what I saw. That was very foolish, Dora."

Dora shut her eyes again, hands resting on her stomach. "My my, the worm has turned. Not long ago I was the one scolding you for taking too many risks. I'm not certain if I should be proud you're such an apt pupil or wounded. That you're right doesn't help at all. But in my defense, I was very careful. I'm reasonably certain he didn't mark me."

"Oh, that makes me feel much better, Dora. I shan't worry then until you keel over or break out in large spots." Mr. Hopkins was visible through the shop window, speaking with a beat cop and pointing down the street. Perhaps Nathan hadn't gone far after all. That would serve to make me all the more suspicious. "Now that we've established you acted foolishly, tell me what Maximillian is and what being marked means. I like to know what I'm frightened of."

"Don't settle for half measures, Dee, be utterly terrified. Maximillian is a hunter for the rituals Fontaine uses to raise power. He's still a man, but participation in blood rituals has left him—tainted. Less than completely human." Dora groaned and pushed herself upright in the chair. A touch of color had returned to her face, pinking her cheeks and making her look somewhat less drained. "My guess is he hunts for people who already believe wholeheartedly in her cause or that are weak-willed enough to convert fully. Once he finds someone, he singles them out for special attention. Belief in anything is a potent force on its own. The stronger a person's faith, the more power their death yields."

"Mandy believed, but surely not all the people who've disappeared were that passionate."

"No, of course not. They didn't need to be." She pulled her burnished gold compact from her handbag and studied her reflection in the small mirror. "Faith that someone has told you the truth or means to keep a promise can be enough. The men hired for day labor all thought the job was real and that they'd be paid. The yield in power is smaller, but still tangible."

Fear tasted acrid, burning the back of my throat and making it difficult to swallow. I'd spent two years learning about the occult from Isadora, and she'd never glossed over any of the dangers we might encounter, or that evil was a real, true thing. Neither of us had anticipated someone like Effie Fontaine arriving in San Francisco. I don't think we could have.

Being afraid didn't mean I could walk away. "How do we stop her?"

"With a great deal of caution. The forces at work here are ones I've only read about. There's a strong possibility that Fontaine is in thrall to some sort of demon." She glanced at me, making sure I listened, and went back to studying her reflection. "The teacher I studied with in Europe had me read translations of ancient Babylonian and Greek texts as part of my training. He wanted me prepared for anything, no matter how improbable. One text spoke about night and wind demons, and what I'm seeing reminds me a great deal of that section. That would also explain Maximillian."

"All right, you've won. I'm terrified now." I didn't bother asking if Isadora was joking. "We've banished our fair share of ghosts together. I assume there are ways to banish demons."

"It's not quite so simple. But yes, if my theory proves to be true, there are ways to rid the city of their influence." Dora tucked the compact away again and leaned back in the chair. "I still need to get a look at her during one of her lectures. That will tell me a great deal more about her alliances in the spirit realm and what steps I need to take. Simply arresting Effie Fontaine isn't enough. We need to sever her ties to those allies. What happened to poor Archie and Maximillian's transformation, for lack of a better word, are proof of that."

"Convincing Gabe and Jack that we need to go through with this mad plan won't be easy, but I don't see another way either. They can't stop her on their own." A car pulled up outside, drawing the beat cop's attention. Randy Dodd climbed out of the driver's side, dressed in street clothes but with his badge in hand. "Randy's arrived. We can pull him into our conspiracy on the drive to your house. Perhaps we should leave out the parts involving Maximillian's being less than human."

"I wouldn't even attempt this without Randy. Daniel's neutrality isn't as strong, but he's accustomed to shielding me. This will be Randy's first encounter with occult forces, hostile ones at that. He deserves to know what he's walking into." Dora stood, looking much steadier than I'd feared. "At least now I have a glimmering of why Fontaine is involved in such filthy practices. The ring Maximillian wears is a symbol of loyalty to the German throne. Within European spiritualist circles, the Kaiser is notorious for being involved with unsavory aspects of the occult. Given the stories I heard when I visited Austria, blood rituals aren't out of the ken of possibility."

Isadora didn't often shock me, not in the way she had when we first met. She'd shocked me now. "You can't seriously think the Kaiser is behind Effie Fontaine committing murder. What would he have to gain?"

"Victory in the Great War. Power. Think about what's at stake, Dee, and what message Effie Fontaine preaches. She finds people who already believe in pacifism on some level and whips their belief to a fevered pitch. Then she harvests the power generated by that belief to spread the message further." Dora slipped her arm through mine and we started toward the door. "If President Wilson declares war on Germany and our troops enter the fighting, that will likely decide the outcome of the war. Given that scenario, the Kaiser will almost certainly lose. If the United States remains neutral? A German victory is almost assured."

A part of me wanted to dismiss the idea, but I couldn't reject it out of hand. What Dora had said held the ring of truth. "Converting more people to the side of pacifism will rob the president of the support he needs. The United States will never enter the war."

She patted my arm. "Exactly. Matters in Europe are at a critical point and could go either way. Preventing America from ever entering the fray is actually a very clever plan on Kaiser Wilhelm's part. Who would ever give credence to the idea that an evangelist advocating peace was the Kaiser's invading army?"

"Gabe will." I pulled open the shop door and held it for Dora. "Jack as well."

"Others will be harder to convince, if not impossible. What we need right now is evidence that Fontaine or the people working for her were involved in Bradley Wells's murder or Mandy's disappearance. Involvement in a conspiracy will be enough to arrest her." She frowned. "I can deal with the occult aspects and disregard legal niceties. Gabe needs something to take to court. Something a judge won't consider lunacy."

Randy came forward to take Dora's arm. She leaned more heavily on him, but her smile was brighter too. I was glad for that. His presence helped cure the ill effects her encounter with Maximillian had caused.

Dora paused next to the car to apologize to Mr. Hopkins for leaving without the coat. He took it well, but I'd never met a shopkeeper Isadora couldn't charm. She'd just handed him a calling card and promised to return when movement across the street caught my eye.

The ghosts of sad-eyed children and soldiers, women in fancy dress and laborers in oil-stained coveralls shimmered into view, row upon row lined up along the sidewalk. As intently as they stared, I'd no doubt they'd been waiting for me.

A glance told me that Dora didn't know the spirits were there. They hadn't come for her help; they'd come for mine. I shut their emotions out as best I could, but their anger and sadness over all they'd lost still filled me to bursting. They expected me to bring them rest, justice, and peace.

Most of all, they looked to me for vengeance. From the smallest child to the oldest woman and man, Effie Ladia Fontaine had a hand in their deaths. They hated her and wanted her to suffer as they had, to feel the same pain.

At the back of the throng was the little girl spirit, clutching her bedraggled porcelain doll. Her familiar singsong rhyme filled my head.

Up and down the city streets,
Hunters search for people,
Round them up to steal their souls
And feed them to the weasel.

She binds them with a will of iron,
She binds them in the steeple,

They bleed, they cry, and then they die,
Believing in the weasel
Believing in the weasel
Believing in the weasel. . . .

"Delia, did you hear me? We're ready to leave." I looked away, startled, to find Randy peering at me worriedly.

Dora was already settled in the backseat. She leaned so she could see me through the open door, more curious than concerned. "Are you all right?"

The ghosts were gone, including the troublesome little girl spirit. Strong haunts were always difficult to understand, especially ghosts that harbored a great deal of anger and hostility. A part of me wanted to believe that she'd meant to lead me to Effie Fontaine all along, but that kernel of belief was very small and couldn't explain why she'd tried to kill me.

Nothing explained this ghost and her actions. The reasons why she'd sought me out in the first place puzzled me more than ever. I needed to speak with Isadora before drawing any conclusions.

"Yes, I'm fine." I pulled my coat closed, suddenly chilled. "Let's go home. Gabe will wonder where I am."

"I almost forgot. Captain Ryan asked me to deliver a message." Randy offered me a hand into the car. "He'll be home later than planned. The captain is paying a visit to Mr. Sung in Chinatown. He said not to wait supper and not to worry."

He shut the door and went round to the driver's side. The car jerked away from the curb, and Dora and I traded looks. "Well? What do you think that's about?"

"I've no idea, Dee. At a guess, I'd say Gabe wants to speak to Sung Wing about the investigation into his brother's murder." She frowned and stared out the window into the dark, one long nail tapping against the door handle. "Gabe was searching for a connection between the Chinatown murders and his other cases. I know he was hoping to implicate Fontaine."

I shivered. Clear, late January nights were always icy, and the cold air twining round my ankles was just that, an ordinary winter draft. Or so I told myself. "Perhaps he found what he was looking for."

"Perhaps." Dora flipped up her collar and hunkered deeper into her coat. "I just hope Gabriel took my warnings seriously. The less Sung Wing knows about Effie Fontaine, the better."

CHAPTER 20

Gabe

The brightly lit streets of Chinatown were filled with people, far more than normally went out after dark. Mothers and fathers strolled down the block with their youngest children in hand, the entire family dressed in their finest clothes. White-haired men and women sat in chairs on the sidewalk, watching the parade of their neighbors and handing out red envelopes to young members of their families. Gangs of older children ran and dodged around groups of adults, pretending to be lion dancers or tossing firecrackers to scare away evil spirits.

Few people paid heed to the patrol car slowly driving down the street or the police captain brooding in the backseat.

Back in his foot patrol days, Gabe would have known exactly when Chinatown celebrated the New Year, but he'd been gone too long. Now the crowds were a forcible reminder, one that made him briefly consider postponing his visit to Mr. Sung for another day. He dismissed the idea again almost immediately. This couldn't wait.

"Bradford, park somewhere along here." He tugged his hat down tight. "I'll walk the last block or two."

Officer Bradford came round the car to open Gabe's door. He stood next to the car, looking around. The scent of gunpowder and pork dumplings brought back memories. Red paper lanterns hung above every shop door and on ropes strung between streetlamps, adding a rosy cast to faces and the front of buildings. Good-luck pictures and symbols hung in windows. Drums sounded in the distance, a sure sign that a lion dance troupe was performing on another street.

A group of giggling young boys no more than eight or nine years old tossed a string of lit firecrackers and ran. The firecrackers landed on Patrolman Bradford's shoe as they went off, causing him to jump back. Bradford swore and lunged for the smallest boy, catching him by the arm before the child could get away.

"What the hell do you think you're doing?" Bradford shook the child hard, jerking him off his feet and making him cry. "I'll teach you some respect for your betters, you slanty-eyed little bastard."

"Bradford!" Gabe forced the patrolman back against the side of the car and twisted his fist in Bradford's jacket. "He's a little boy, not a thug. Let him go. Now."

The adults within sight of the patrol car had stopped talking, good cheer and smiles rapidly changing to anger. Several of the scowling younger men watching moved closer.

Bradford looked between Gabe and the weeping little boy dangling from his hand. "Captain, you saw what he did—"

"It's a game boys play at New Year's. Now, I gave you an order, Patrolman." Gabe leaned close, his voice a low growl. "Let the boy go."

The ruddy-faced cop finally loosened his grip on the child's arm, face screwed up in disgust. Gabe walked the boy a few steps away and got down on one knee, straightening the boy's hat and wiping tears away with his handkerchief. "I'm sorry he scared you. Do you speak English?"

Big-eyed with fright, the boy remained mute and stared into Gabe's face. Few of the younger children in Chinatown spoke English, but he'd had to try. If nothing else, taking care of the boy kept him from giving in to the impulse to shake Bradford until his teeth rattled.

A woman stepped out of the crowd, hesitating until Gabe waved her forward. "Your son?" She nodded, but didn't speak, likely thinking the boy was in trouble. He took a silver dollar out of his pocket and pressed the coin into the boy's hand. "Some luck money for him. Please apologize and tell him I'm sorry my man behaved so badly. Tell your son I'll make sure it never happens again."

She put an arm around the boy's shoulders and led him away, leaning close and speaking rapidly. The boy looked back at Gabe before they disappeared into the crowd. Fear had been replaced by confusion.

He stood, brushing dust off his knee. The boy had every right to be confused. "We'll discuss your actions later, Bradford. Consider yourself under disciplinary review from this moment on. I want you to get in the car and stay there until I come back. Don't talk to anyone. I'd suggest not looking at anyone either." Gabe nodded toward the knot of scowling men a few yards away. "If you're lucky, they'll just let you sit here."

"Captain, you can't be serious." Bradford's flushed face was a rusty brick color in the paper-lantern light. He lifted a hand and let it drop again, not even trying to hide his frustration and anger. "You saw what happened. The little brat deserved a lot more than I gave him. If you don't teach these chinks a lesson when they're pups, they never show any respect."

Gabe looked away for an instant, striving for calm. Bradford was far from the only cop on the force who thought that way. He couldn't control everything they said or did while out of his sight, but he wouldn't tolerate one of his men mistreating a child right in front of him. "Get in the car, Officer. I'm finished here."

He shoved his hands deep into his coat pockets and started down the block toward the Sung family tea shop. That was the most likely place he'd find Sung Wing, passing out red envelopes to children and giving New Year's wishes to members of his tong.

Word of his arrival and the incident with Bradford had raced ahead, but he'd known it would. Gabe ignored the stares, grateful so few were hostile. A small number of the oldest men even smiled and nodded to him, smiles he returned.

Sung Wing was holding court in front of the family tea shop, sitting in an elaborately carved high-backed chair that would have served well as a throne. Dragons and tigers with gilt eyes, snakes and monkeys curved around the back behind his head, and the arms were openmouthed, roaring lions. A black velvet throw covered Mr. Sung's lap, holding a pile of red envelopes he handed out to the long line of children waiting their turn.

Two young men, guards, stood behind the chair to either side, each holding a carved ivory basin containing more red envelopes. Wing's nephew, Sung Zao, stood at the tea shop door, exchanging greetings with the people passing behind his uncle or going into the shop.

Gabe stood to the side, knowing he'd been seen and waiting to be acknowledged. Any doubts he'd had about Sung Wing's position in Chinatown vanished. The old man smiling at youngsters and saying a word or two to each one was far more than head of the Sung family. Everything Isadora had told him came back with a rush.

"Have you come to collect your luck money, Captain Ryan?" Mr. Sung smiled at the tiny girl in front of him and touched her head, but the amusement in his voice was all for Gabe. "Or are you here to scold me over gifting your wife with a kitten?"

Sung Wing's unprompted admission was surprising. Gabe couldn't begin to guess what game the tong leader thought they were playing. He smiled and let the remark pass.

"The cat makes Delia happy. Even if I do question your motives, I can't argue with that. I came to see you on police business." He glanced at the two stony-faced young guards and leaned close to speak quietly in Mr. Sung's ear. "I'd like to ask a few questions about someone your brother might have known or had business dealings with."

Sung Wing's shoulders stiffened for an instant, but he continued speaking to the children and passing out luck money. He gave Gabe an apologetic smile. "Forgive me, Captain, but I need to ask your patience. I must do my duty to the living for a little while longer."

"I understand. Take your time." Gabe stepped back into the overhang that sheltered the tea shop window, still close but out of the way. He kept an eye on the street, noting who made a point of watching him and Mr. Sung in the midst of the celebration, or who passed by without paying attention to either of them. Most of all, he looked for faces that seemed out of place. Faces like his own.

Thinking like a suspicious cop was a bad habit, but Effie Fontaine and her crew made Gabe nervous. He didn't know what to expect from her or what was outside the realm of possibility. Dora didn't know either, which doubled his need to be cautious. Jumping at shadows wasn't unreasonable if the shadows concealed a monster.

The tide of children waned. Mr. Sung waved his nephew Zao over to take his place in the chair.

"Come with me, Captain." Mr. Sung motioned Gabe inside the crowded tea shop. "We can talk in my nephew's office. No one will disturb us."

Conversations ground to a halt as Gabe followed Mr. Sung between tables and behind the counter. A glass bead curtain swayed and clattered as the two men passed through and into the narrow hall leading to the back.

Zao's office was bigger than Gabe expected, with a large, polished mahogany desk, glass-fronted curio cabinets full of porcelain figurines, and a window overlooking a walled courtyard behind the shop. Photographs hung on the walls, scenes from a mountain village in China and pictures of the family. One photo showed Zao as a younger man sitting with his wife and son, and a gray-haired man who had likely been Liang. A tiny, bright-eyed little girl leaned against Zao's knee, her small hand held securely in his.

The lacquered oval frame was draped in mourning crepe. Gabe looked away quickly, an unwitting intruder on Zao's private grief.

Mr. Sung shut the door and took a seat in the swivel chair behind the desk. Gabe settled into the smaller chair opposite him, taking off his hat and holding it on his lap. Sung Wing eyed him, hands folded on the desktop and lips pulled into a tight line. "Ask your questions, Captain Ryan. I will do what I can to help catch my brother's killers."

"I want you to understand from the beginning that I'm not certain about any of this. I need to be certain before I make an arrest." Gabe shifted his weight, causing the chair to creak alarmingly. "Another man, Bradley Wells, was murdered not long after your brother and niece. Mr. Wells was the police commissioner's son-in-law."

"This is why you came to see me." Mr. Sung leaned forward, his frown deepening. "You think there is some connection between the people who killed Mr. Wells and Liang."

"Right now it's only a theory. The two cases have similarities." He fiddled with the crown of his fedora. Planting certainty in Mr. Sung's mind was the last thing he wanted to do. Not until he had proof that would stand up in court. "Mr. Wells was murdered in the back room of his father's druggist shop. The men who killed him left all the money in the till, but took all the medications stored in the back room. We're still not certain what they took. The senior Mr. Wells didn't have a list."

Mr. Sung muttered under his breath, swearing in Chinese as near as Gabe could guess. "There are things I should have told the police from the start, Captain. Forgive me. The men who killed Liang and my niece stole herbs and medications from his shop, yet left all his money and jade behind. Zao has a list, but most of what they stole was dried jimsonweed, poppy juice, and opium."

"Poppy juice and opium?" Gabe's eyes widened. Archie Baldwin's clothing had reeked of opium when he first arrived at the station looking for Jack. "Was it normal for your brother to have those in his shop?"

Sung waved Gabe's comment away. "My brother mixed medicines, Captain. A drop of opium takes pain from the old, the sick and dying. Poppy juice helps them sleep. If you ask Mr. Wells's father, I'm sure he'll tell you he had poppy juice and opium in his back room."

He'd been too focused on the men who'd been murdered and

lost sight of their surroundings. Where someone died could be as important as who they were. Both an herbalist and a druggist would have need for basic ingredients to mix medicines. It made sense that they'd have those items stored in their back rooms.

Gabe thought about that now, thought hard. The string of burglaries involving small druggist shops before Wells's murder made more sense now. He added robbery to Effie Fontaine's list of crimes. What still puzzled him was what use she had for opium and poppy juice.

Memories of Bradley Wells's serene expression brought an answer, or at least the start of one. That Wells hadn't struggled when he was killed made sense if he'd been drugged, likely with poppy juice from his own back room. Gabe would be willing to wager that all Fontaine's victims were drugged before being killed.

That didn't explain the cruelty the killers had shown toward Sung Zao's daughter, Lan, before they murdered her. He'd probably never know why she'd been singled out for punishment. Not all his questions had answers.

"Captain Ryan?"

Mr. Sung's voice pulled him up short. Sheepish at being caught woolgathering, Gabe cleared his throat. "Yes, sorry. What did you say?"

The tong leader folded his hands on the desktop, his expression tense. Expectant. "I asked how Bradley Wells died."

Sung Wing knew already; Gabe saw the knowledge stark in the old man's eyes. But that made looking Mr. Sung in the eye and telling him the truth more difficult, not less. "They cut his throat and bled him. Miss Bobet—Isadora says his spirit is missing as well."

"Ah. Now I understand why you came to me." Mr. Sung turned his chair toward the window. Fireworks went off outside, bathing the room in bursts of red, gold, and silver light. The sounds of children laughing and chattering to their parents, and the whistle of sky-rockets came in from outside. "This person my brother may have known or done business with, what is his name?"

Something in Sung Wing's voice made Gabe hesitate. He thought about leaving without saying Fontaine's name, but he'd already gone too far to back away. "Do you know if your brother had any business dealings with a woman named Effie Fontaine or her associates?"

Mr. Sung turned his chair to face Gabe again, anger glittering in his eyes. "Business dealings? No, Captain, but I know her name. This is the person you think murdered Mr. Wells?"

For an instant, Sung Wing's scrutiny pushed Gabe back into his chair before the intensity eased and let him breathe again. He didn't want this man for an enemy, but he wouldn't compromise his case either. "All I can say is that Miss Fontaine and her organization are under investigation, Mr. Sung. What do you know about her?"

"She tried to take people from my streets. I sent my men to turn her hunters away." The old man eyed him, considering. Sung Wing pulled a key tied to a satin cord from a pocket and unlocked a desk drawer. He rummaged inside before pulling out a stack of familiar-looking handbills and passing them to Gabe. "The people working for her posted these on every corner and building bordering Chinatown. My men were kept very busy taking them down."

The handbills were like the others Gabe had seen, with Effie Fontaine's photograph in the center and dates and times of her lectures printed above. Smaller type scrolled across the bottom, written in Chinese.

Mr. Sung pointed to the Chinese figures. "These promise jobs and good wages to anyone willing to work. She offers to pay more for a day's labor than some of my people make in a month as houseboys and maids. Something else hides in the words, something that vanishes when I look closely. Her men gave up when the posters were torn down again and again and they couldn't lure my people to them."

Gabe handed the flyers back. "How long ago was that?"

"Months now. The end of summer." He locked the handbills back in the desk drawer. Sung Wing gestured toward the photograph of

Zao's family, eyes full of regrets. "My brother and I quarreled over this woman. Liang thought I should take stronger measures to frighten her away. If I'd listened, he and Lan might still be alive."

"You can't know that, Mr. Sung." Gabe stopped short of saying that Fontaine might have killed more of the family, but experience and instinct told him that was true. She was unpredictable, extreme. "No one can know the future."

"Perhaps not, but one should be cautious. Is this woman why policemen guard the lieutenant's family and Miss Bobet?" Sung Wing arched an eyebrow. "Something frightens you, Captain. It frightens you enough, you feel the need to be armed."

"As you said, one should be cautious." The gun didn't show under his jacket, he'd made certain of that. That Mr. Sung somehow knew didn't surprise him overmuch. Gabe stood, trying not to feel the weight of the pistol against his side. "Thank you. I'll let you know if we need more information."

Mr. Sung nodded. Gabe turned to leave, but the tong leader called to him. "Captain, one more question to satisfy an old man's curiosity. What did your wife name the kitten?"

"Delia maintains the cat chose her own name." Gabe smiled. "I'm not going to tell her she's wrong. The cat's name is Mai."

"A wise and fitting choice." Mr. Sung's solemn nod was formal and dignified, suitable for someone in his position. That didn't contradict the warmth in his voice or hide the pleased glimmer in his eyes. "Give Mrs. Ryan my best wishes. And please, Captain, be as careful with your wife's safety as you are with others'. Guard her well."

"I will. Good night, Mr. Sung." Gabe took a last look at the photograph of Zao's family, making sure he'd memorized Lan's face. He didn't need Sung Wing's reminder of what was at stake.

He already knew.

Gabe stared out the car window, relishing the relative quiet. Businesses were closing for the day, owners and customers hurrying home in the yellow glow of streetlamps. Newsies shouted the latest war headlines from corners, their voices fading almost as soon as the car passed. The continual hiss of tires on damp pavement struck him as a sound too ordinary and peaceful for a world at war.

Most people found comfort in ordinary things, but he wasn't most people, and his life was far from peaceful. He shifted in his seat, restless and struggling to hold in the anger that kept bubbling to the surface.

Feeling helpless always made him angry. What Gabe knew and what he could prove were two different things. He didn't have enough hard evidence to arrest Fontaine for murder, let alone hold her for trial. She could leave town now tonight, and he couldn't stop her.

Of all Effie Fontaine's victims, Sung Lan's death haunted him most. He couldn't forget the photograph of her, a solemn-eyed little girl holding her father's hand. The thought of Fontaine just walking away unpunished, free to go to the next town to claim more victims, and the next, left him wanting to punch something. Or someone.

Officer Bradford glowered at Gabe in the driving mirror occasionally, but was smart enough to keep his mouth shut. That was for the best. They'd had another confrontation when Gabe got back to the police car and discovered Bradford had ignored his orders, a confrontation that led to him shouting the patrolman down.

His squad needed to work as a team. He didn't demand unquestioning obedience, but he wouldn't tolerate officers who thought they were above following orders or treating people decently. The paperwork necessary to bring Bradford up on charges was the only reason Gabe was going back to the station. As long as he was in the office, he'd check to see if Sal Rosen had delivered the promised autopsy report on Archie Baldwin.

Gabe slid down so that his head rested against the cold leather seat back. What he really wanted was to go home to Delia, to hold her close, surrounded by the faint scent of lilac water that always clung to her hair. A lifetime of those moments wouldn't be near enough. He didn't resent his job or duty often, but tonight he couldn't help himself.

The car jerked to a halt in front of the station, yanking him back to the here and now. Officer Bradford scowled in the mirror again, his voice grating. "Anything else?"

"What did you say, Officer?" Gabe's level stare made Bradford blanch. He could almost see the man thinking and working out what he'd done wrong. "I don't think I quite heard you."

Bradford's fingers clenched around the steering wheel. "Anything else, *Captain?*"

"No, Patrolman. Nothing else tonight." Gabe plucked his fedora off the seat and opened the door. "Report to Sergeant Rockwell first thing in the morning. He'll have your orders."

He held Bradford's gaze until the patrolman looked away. Gabe got out of the car, striding into the station without a backward glance.

The front lobby was nearly deserted. Just after suppertime was too late for most citizens coming in to make a complaint about barking dogs or to report petty thefts, and too early for the drunks and rowdies that would fill the rows of benches after midnight. He nodded to the officers who greeted him, but kept his head down as he hurried toward his office.

His door was ajar and the lights on, the low murmur of voices carrying into the hall. Gabe kept one hand on his pistol and pushed the door open wide, unwilling to walk all the way inside until he saw who was waiting.

Marshall Henderson and Sam Butler, the reporter, looked up, their expressions both anxious and relieved. They didn't need to say anything. Something was wrong.

Henderson stood right away. He was dressed in street clothes and nervously smoothing down the front of his suit coat, further putting Gabe on his guard. "Captain! I was hoping you'd get back soon."

"I wasn't coming back at all, but something happened to change my plans." Gabe shut the door and hung his coat up. He sat across the desk from them, his old chair creaking under his weight. "What's so important the two of you are loitering in my office?"

Butler looked to Marshall, who nodded. Appointing Sam spokesman. "Captain Ryan—Gabe, this must be difficult for you. I know Doctor Rosen was a friend."

He straightened his desk blotter, only half-listening. "What must be difficult?"

"You didn't get my message." Marshall tugged the bottom of his suit jacket and looked away.

Gabe sat forward, hands folded on the desk, and put on the professional mask he wore while working. Hiding the wave of panic that threatened to carry him off. His voice sounded oddly calm. "If you have something to tell me, Marshall, just say it."

"Captain . . . I sent Patrolman Finley to your house. I thought you came back to the station because you got my message." Henderson raked long, skinny fingers through his hair. "Doctor Rosen and his wife are dead."

He stared, momentarily numb. Gabe tried to talk himself into believing that Sal's death had nothing to do with Fontaine or Archie Baldwin, and that his friend hadn't been murdered. He couldn't do it.

The cop part of his mind began ticking off lists of people to check on, including his mother and Mrs. Allen.

People he needed to protect.

Gabe cleared his throat. "What happened?"

"They were hit by a car." Marshall scrubbed his hands on his trouser knees. "Sam and I were making the rounds of the taverns together, poking around and looking for anyone talking about Miss Fontaine. We were headed down Kearny when we saw the crowd. Both Mrs. Rosen and Sal were dead before the beat cop got there. We have witnesses. At least a dozen people saw it happen."

"Holy mother of God . . . Sal." Gabe swung his chair around to face the window, struggling to keep from falling apart. He could ask questions—*do his damn job*—if he couldn't see the pity in their eyes. Sal deserved that much and more. "Did anyone get witness statements?"

"I did. Marshall and the other officer had their hands full dealing with the crowd." Butler pulled a notebook out of his jacket, flipping through pages until he found the right one. "I spoke with two witnesses, a Mr. Brian and Mr. Lynch, who saw the car pull away from the curb as soon as Doctor and Mrs. Rosen came out of a little café on Kearny Street. The Rosens got as far as the corner and were waiting for traffic to clear before crossing the street. A car went over the curb, hit the Rosens, and kept going. Three different people told me that they didn't think what happened was an accident. No one else was on that corner. The driver meant to hit them."

Murder was always ugly, leaving ugly things in its wake. He needed to write telegrams to Sal's son in Oregon and Pearl's mother in San Diego. Somewhere in his desk he had a Boston address for both of Sal's sisters. He was the officer in charge. Informing next of kin was his responsibility.

The guilt landing on Gabe's shoulders threatened to crush him. He'd gotten Sal involved, pushed him to dig for any scrap of evidence that might implicate Fontaine. Effie Fontaine was guilty, but he was responsible. He turned his chair back around. "Did police on the scene find the driver or could any of the witnesses give a description?"

"The driver was gone long before officers arrived. None of the witnesses saw the driver's face, but they all got a good look at the car." Sam flipped to the next page in his notebook. "They all told me it was one of those big, black fancy cars you see on Nob Hill. A separate compartment up front for the driver, chrome trim, and a leather-covered spare wheel on the back. A woman, Mrs. Stoll, thought there was something written on the spare wheel, but she couldn't make out what."

Something about the way Sam described the car triggered a

vague memory. He chased after it, trying to remember, but gave up quickly. Nob Hill was full of fancy black cars, the new favorite toy of the very rich. The car could belong to anyone.

"Marshall, have Rockwell call the other stations and tell them what to look for. Make sure all the foot patrols get that description too. Remind them that the car will be damaged." He dug in his top drawer for paper, pen, and ink. The paperwork bringing Bradford up on charges could wait until morning, but he wanted it done and over. "Has anyone spoken to Lieutenant Fitzgerald?"

"No, sir, not that I know of." Marshall kept rubbing his hands on his knees over and over. Gabe suspected he was trying to wipe away the feel of death. "Do you want me to call the lieutenant too?"

"No, I'll call him." Pain pounded over his left eye in time with his heartbeat. Gabe massaged his temple, trying to wipe away his growing headache. "Deliver those messages and then go home."

"Gabe, this might not be the best time, but there's something else you need to hear." Sam leaned forward, hands resting on his knees. "We ran into a man, a Bill Woodman, at McGrooty's Tavern. Mr. Woodman had been drinking whiskey all evening, which probably explains why he was so willing to talk. He was angry too. Woodman told me and Marshall some interesting stories about Fontaine and one of the men working for her, Jonas Wolf."

Cold brushed Gabe's cheek and traveled down the back of his neck. His signal to pay attention. "What kind of stories?"

"Stories about Jonas Wolf mostly. Wolf likes to throw his weight around, intimidate people. Woodman's been a target a few times, including earlier today. That's why he was so angry." Sam frowned. "This isn't the first time I've heard tales of Wolf bullying people who couldn't fight back. But what surprised me is that Woodman claims that Fontaine and Wolf are really husband and wife."

"They're married?" He started scribbling on the paper he'd meant to use for Bradford's charges. Jack wasn't there to take notes; he'd have to record the conversation on his own. "What made Mr. Woodman say something like that?"

"He works at the German embassy downtown. Some kind of clerk's job they hire locals to do, filing and helping people fill out forms. Most of the low-level staff was sent back to Germany when the war heated up. That's where he ran afoul of Wolf." Sam's face was carefully deadpan, but sly excitement glittered in his eyes. "Woodman swears he saw the paperwork. Effie Fontaine is Effie Fontaine Wolf. She's a German citizen, Gabe."

. Gabe stopped writing in mid-word and looked Sam Butler in the eye. He had to ask the questions even if he already knew the answers. "Are you saying the self-styled evangelist for peace is loyal to the Kaiser?"

Sam didn't flinch. "Looks that way from where I'm sitting. My guess is the mysterious benefactor funding her travels is the German emperor. Think about it, Gabe."

"I am thinking." The calm clarity of knowing he was on the right track and pieces clicking into place settled around him. He didn't know yet where murder, blood rituals, or the rest fit into Sam's theory, but he'd find out. "Makes as much sense as anything else we know about her. Can we find Woodman again?"

"We can." Sam pulled a card out of his shirt pocket and passed it over. "His work information is printed on the front. I wrote his home address on the back."

"Keep this up, Butler, and I'll be forced to deputize you." Gabe studied the little pasteboard card, tempted to haul Mr. Woodman in right then. Instead he locked the card in a desk drawer for later. He didn't want to tip his hand. "You just handed me the leverage and time to build a murder case. Holding Fontaine as a flight risk before a deportation trial is the perfect excuse to arrest her."

Henderson folded his arms over his chest and frowned. "Deportation? Isn't that the same as letting her go free?"

"Not if Judge Alger issues an arrest warrant for treason. Given what we know, I don't think he'd have a problem with that. I'll talk to him in the morning and start laying the groundwork." Effie Fontaine's travels and pacifist lectures were common knowledge, something she'd never tried to hide. What would damn her in the judge's eyes was hiding her German citizenship.

Gabe pulled out more clean paper. He'd write out Bradford's charges and go home to Delia. At home he could mourn his friend. "Deliver those messages before you leave, Marshall. We're finished for the night."

Butler and Henderson gathered coats and hats, preparing to leave. Sam hesitated at the door, his hand on the knob. "I'm really sorry about your friend. From all I've heard, Doctor Rosen was a good man."

"He was a good man, Sam. A very good man." He tried to smile, to acknowledge Sam's sympathy, but he couldn't do it. "Good night."

The office door closed and Gabe sat there staring at the frosted glass bearing his name, brooding over the loss of good men like Sal and his father. When his old clock chimed nine o'clock, he picked up his pen to write out the charges against Bradford. By nine fifteen he'd finished.

He dropped off the paperwork at the front desk and asked the sergeant to call a cab. The air outside was damp and full of the promise of fog, but the night was clear and awash in misty stars. He leaned against the station wall, watching the sky. Deep breaths of cold air cleared Gabe's head and made it easier to think beyond the empty ache in his chest.

Treason was an easier charge to prove against Effie Fontaine than murder. He'd do what was necessary to find justice for Sal and Sung Lan, Archie Baldwin, Thad Harper, and all her unknown victims. It really didn't matter if she was convicted of murder or treason. Fontaine would go to the gallows either way.

Maybe then he could sleep at night and the nightmares about his sister would stop.

The cab pulled up. He straightened his shoulders and crossed the sidewalk to the curb, muttering to himself. "If wishes were horses, Ryan, then all could ride. Go home."

CHAPTER 21

Delia

The night Sal and Pearl Rosen died, Gabe and I slept in each other's arms. We both needed comfort and to know the other one was there, warm, alive and safe.

That someone could snatch Sal and Pearl's lives away in an instant shook me as deeply as it did Gabe. We'd talked for hours before finally giving in to exhaustion and the need for sleep. Gabe told me about discovering that Miss Fontaine was a German citizen, and I told him all about our encounter with Maximillian. Neither of us had any doubt that Effie Fontaine was behind the Rosens' so-called accident. The reason why she'd had them killed was a question we couldn't answer.

For the first time since we'd been married, Gabe left his pistol on the nightstand, in plain sight and near to hand. I knew that fear wasn't what made him leave the gun out, but caution. Our house wasn't ringed in policemen standing watch the way Jack's and Dora's homes were. Neither of us knew what Fontaine would do next or how far she'd go. He wouldn't take the risk of not having the gun within reach.

Mai crouched on the pillow near our heads, blending into the shadows near the wall. Her green eyes were wide in the dark, watching the corners, and low growls woke me twice during the night. I'd no doubt she was guarding us, driving away nightmares and phantoms of Gabe's guilt come back to haunt him.

Gabe was up and making breakfast when I stumbled into the kitchen the next morning, still bleary eyed and half-asleep. Mai was perched on the spare chair we rarely used, watching him intently. I'd grown somewhat used to seeing him put on the gun holster shortly before leaving for work. Today the pistol already hung at his side.

He smiled and gestured toward the table with a spatula. "Toast is ready and your eggs are almost done."

I stood behind him and wrapped my arms around his waist. He smelled of shaving soap and gun oil, a combination that was familiar and foreign at the same time. "How are you? Don't try to pretend everything's fine, Gabe Ryan. I know you better than that."

"Nothing is fine, Dee, nothing at all. I'm not trying to pretend otherwise. I'm furious about what happened to Sal and his wife, but scowling at you won't bring them back. And I still have to do my job." Gabe slid two eggs onto a platter already loaded with bacon and sliced potatoes. He cracked two more into the pan, breaking the yolks with the edge of the spatula. "I've already talked to Jack twice this morning. Judge Alger won't issue a warrant for Fontaine's arrest. He wants time to study the charges and make sure this isn't a vendetta of some kind. Fontaine could be out of our jurisdiction by the time he gets around to answering. I never should have mentioned Commissioner Lindsey's name in the warrant request or suggested the judge talk to him. There's bad blood between them."

I hugged him tight before finding butter and jam, salt and pepper and setting them in the center of the table. "I think there's bad blood between Robert Lindsey and half the officials in San Francisco. You can't let that keep you from going after her."

"I won't. But Judge Alger's refusal means I have to let Dora go through with her crazy scheme of spying on Fontaine's lecture. I'd feel much better if Jack and I could go inside with you." He set the platter of eggs and potatoes on the table and held my chair, letting me get settled before sitting down himself. "This is one of those times I wish I didn't believe everything that Dora tells me. Treating this as nothing but a police matter would be so much easier."

"But you can't and we all know that." Toast crunched in my mouth, sweet with the taste of last summer's strawberry jam. The pensive expression on Gabe's face worried me. Maybe he'd decided to talk us out of going. I washed the toast down with tea and rushed to plead our case. "Dora and I have to get a look at her in order to understand what she does and how to stop her. Leaving things as they are is much too dangerous. Until we know what's involved or what forces Miss Fontaine is tapping into, we won't know where to begin."

Gabe held a hand up defensively. "I know all that and I'm not trying to argue you out of anything. But that man you met with Dora, Maximillian, will be there too. Isadora's afraid of him even if she doesn't come out and say so. Anyone Dora's afraid of worries the hell out of me. I don't know how to protect you."

The kitten leapt to the back of my chair, perching just over my shoulder and studying Gabe. Dora had begun jokingly calling Mai my familiar. I'd stopped thinking of it as a joke.

"You can't protect us." I took his hand, holding tight. "But Dora and I can find a way to protect ourselves. We'll be all right, Gabe, I promise. Having Randy along will be an enormous help."

"I'm allowed to worry." He kissed my fingers before letting my hand go. "But I have to trust your judgment when it comes to ghosts and spirits. Just promise me that the three of you will stay together and leave as soon as possible. Don't let Dora go off exploring on her own."

"That's an easy promise to make." I spooned potatoes onto my plate. "And I can't imagine Randy allowing Dora out of his sight."

Gabe chewed his eggs slowly, gazing out the kitchen window and watching clouds blow in from the sea. He still finished everything on his plate and carried it to the sink before I'd half begun. That he was eating again was a good sign and made me worry less. He sat across from me again, keeping me company while I finished my breakfast.

"Jack and I will be just down the block from the church hall, and Henderson will be across the street, where he can see the side entrance. I'm trying to arrange the duty schedule for Finlay and Polk so I can station them in a car around the corner. I can trust them." Gabe picked another slice of potato off the platter and popped it into his mouth. "My grandmother used to make fried potatoes like this every Sunday after church. I remember one week Gram caught Penelope trying to talk me out of my share before we even sat down for lunch. Gram scolded her for being greedy, but somehow Penelope ended up with an extra portion on her plate anyway."

"Who's Penelope?" He didn't answer. I touched his arm and asked again. "Gabe, who is Penelope?"

Gabe jumped, red-faced and sheepish. He'd been staring out the window again, far away and lost in memories. I'd seen the same wistful longing in his eyes when he thought about his father. "Sorry. I don't know why I never told you before. Penelope was my older sister. She died when I was three. Pen was five, nearly six."

"You had a sister?" I sat back, twisting the napkin around my fingers and sternly telling myself not to make too much of this. Mai huddled against the back of my neck, purring softly. "How did she die?"

"To be honest, I'm not sure. We were visiting relatives back East and there was some kind of accident. I don't remember much, other than my mother crying and Dad telling me Pen wasn't coming home with us. Mom was so sad, I didn't ask any questions." Gabe drummed his fingers on the tabletop, frowning. "I've been dreaming about my sister the last few weeks. Nightmares mostly. I don't remember anything about them when I wake up."

I bit my lip, not wanting to say what leapt to mind and make it real. The little girl spirit who'd invaded Gabe's dreams and proved so insistent on gaining my attention might be his sister, but it was just as likely that she wasn't. The spirit who'd attacked me and caused so much chaos in Mrs. Allen's boarding house felt older, more canny, and she harbored secrets five-year-old Penelope Ryan couldn't know.

Still, I'd no way to be certain, no proof of what was true or who this ghost had been. Perhaps that didn't matter in the end. Her actions and what she wanted from Gabe and from me were more important.

Asking why this spirit had chosen now to drive a wedge between me and Gabe was the same snare I'd been caught in since she first appeared. Effie Fontaine was the answer I kept coming back to, but I wasn't entirely sure I'd found the right question. If this ghost was Gabe's sister, Penelope, I couldn't conceive of a way her death could be tied to Miss Fontaine. Too many years lay between. Still, I'd speak to Dora.

"You'll sleep better when this case is over." I stood to clear the table, oddly reluctant to continue this conversation. The last thing I wanted to do was inadvertently summon the little girl spirit. "The lecture starts at seven thirty. Dora and Randy will call round just before six to pick me up. She sacked that strange little man, Nathan, last night, but Randy's sure he can handle Daniel's car. He swears it can't be any bigger than his father's farm truck."

"He's probably right." Gabe carried the last of the breakfast dishes to the sink. He leaned against the edge of the drain board, rolling down his sleeves and watching me fill the sink with soapy water. "Why did Dora fire her driver?"

"That man, Maximillian, stopped to speak with Nathan outside the furriers." I hid the shiver that rippled through me with the memory. "They were a bit too familiar for comfort. Dora decided it was safest to send Nathan away with the car. We waited inside the shop until Randy came to drive us home."

"I'm suspicious of anyone with a connection to Fontaine, however slight. I'll see what I can find out about Nathan." An odd expression flashed across Gabe's face, come and gone before I really saw it. He straightened his cuffs and took his jacket off the hook near the back door. "Has Dora heard from Daniel?"

"Not a word. She maintains she's not worried, but I don't believe her."

"Neither do I." Gabe brushed his fingers across my cheek before slipping on his jacket. "Does Dora have any inkling that Dodd's falling in love with her?"

"No, I don't think so. She takes adoration as her due, not as anything lasting or serious. She wouldn't flirt so outrageously if she thought there was a chance of hurting someone." I took his hand and walked him to the front door. "Isadora might be the only one who doesn't know how Randy feels."

"That will be rough once Daniel comes home. I hope Dodd's prepared." He studied my face, his expression far too solemn and serious, and kissed me good-bye. "You have a few hours before Dora arrives. See if you can come up with a foolproof plan that lets me arrest Fontaine without putting you in danger. I can think of better ways for us to spend an evening, Mrs. Ryan."

"I'll do my best, Captain Ryan, but last time I checked, you were the brilliant detective." Sheer will and stubbornness let me smile. I refused to say good-bye as if I'd never see Gabe again. "Perhaps you'd do well to pull your weight and concoct a clever plan or two of your own. Or assign schemes to Jack as the junior officer. He must have picked up a trick or two from Sadie."

He smiled, amusement filling his eyes, and opened the front door. "I'll give that some thought."

Two police cars sat at the curb. Gabe climbed into one for the drive to the station. The other car containing Perry and Taylor remained behind. Perry waved and smiled, letting me know they were watching over me until Gabe came home later.

I waved back and shut the door again, grateful that Gabe's men were outside. That I deeply resented the necessity of being guarded and having my life disrupted wasn't their fault.

The blame for that rested squarely on Effie Fontaine.

Dora and Randy arrived precisely on schedule. I couldn't recall the last time Isadora was less than a fashionable ten minutes late. No doubt Randy Dodd deserved credit for her promptness.

"What do you think, Dee?" Isadora posed and turned in a slow circle, the scent of her perfume filling my sitting room. The chinchilla coat she'd bought was draped over an arm. "Will this fool the rubes?"

She was dressed to the nines as always, but there was an added air of understated wealth to the black silk taffeta skirt and jacket she'd chosen to wear. Diamonds and opals sparkled in the brooch pinned to her jacket, and the matching spray of gems pinned to the crown of her hat. Small rings—moonstone, lapis, and pale blue sapphires—glimmered on each finger of her right hand. A diamond graced the ring finger on her left.

Strangers who looked at her would see exactly what she meant them to see, a socialite with too much time to dabble in whatever caught her fancy, and more than enough money to indulge her whims. They wouldn't see Dora as a threat nor guess at what she was capable of. And I doubted that anyone but Dora and I would know that every gem she wore had a purpose. They were part of her armor, another layer of protection and a source of strength.

"I think you look utterly stunning and elegant. Miss Fontaine will be quite upstaged." I'd made my peace long ago with blending into the background while Dora and Sadie attracted all the attention. Their charm had a way of disarming people, making the most guarded person more open and willing to talk. Watching the reactions of those around us gave me a great deal of amusement.

And at times, like tonight, blending into the background served a purpose. I overheard and learned more if people took little notice that I was nearby.

Randy stood to one side, watching Dora and pulling at his starched collar. He looked decidedly uncomfortable with his hair slicked back and wearing an expensive suit, but dressed that way, Randy appeared much older, closer to Dora's age. No one would think him a farm boy from Indiana. He made the perfect escort for Dora, tall and handsome, dignified and reserved.

"How long ago did the captain leave?" Randy grimaced as Dora tried to straighten his tie, but overall, he submitted with good grace. "I don't want to arrive before he has everyone in place."

"A little after five. Gabe wanted to allow plenty of time before the lecture started." Mai sat on the back of the settee next to my coat, alternating washing her paws and her tail. The cat took no notice of me gathering my belongings in preparation of leaving, or that I'd checked my bag twice to make sure I had house keys. Her nonchalance was a stark contrast to the quivers in my stomach and the thunder of my pulse. "I don't know how long it takes to reach the church, but I'm ready now. We can leave anytime."

"One last thing before we go." Dora pulled a small diamond horseshoe pin out of her bag and pinned it to my collar. She beamed at me fondly, an expression that, given the circumstances, put me on guard. I knew her too well. "I want you to wear this tonight, Dee. Obvious symbolism aside, diamonds bring clarity and dispel illusion. Given what we might be walking into, the clearer things are, the better."

"Thank you. It's beautiful." I ran a finger over the pin, feeling the facets of the diamonds and searching for patterns not readily visible. Seldom were Dora's gifts as simple as they appeared. "I assume you've explained everything to Randy. Or is that why we're loitering?"

"Of course I explained. I wasn't going to let him come along until he knew all the facts." She preened for a few seconds, fussing with the placement of her own diamond pin. "But there is one last instruction that involves both of you. I felt it best to wait and tell you together."

"All right." Randy cocked his head to the side and studied Dora's face, his expression closed off and cautious. He'd learned quickly. I was glad he didn't let his fondness for Isadora interfere with his judgment. "Tell us and we'll go."

"I need a promise from the two of you." Dora stood up straighter and faced us. Her expression wasn't exactly grim, but she wasn't pretending to a cheer none of us believed. That struck me as both better and worse. "Miss Fontaine attracts a considerable crowd for all her lectures. She must have some method or means for isolating those singled out as victims. I'd rather we got through the evening without one of us falling prey to her. No matter what happens or what you imagine you see, don't let Fontaine or her men separate us. We stay together at all cost. Promise me."

Randy and I exchanged looks before he turned back to Dora, arms crossed over his chest. His face set in stubborn lines. "I don't need to promise. Frankly, I'm insulted you asked, Dora. Short of being forced away at gunpoint, I'm not letting the two of you out of my sight."

"She knows that, Randy, and you shouldn't feel insulted. Isadora's often overcome by the need to state the obvious. Eventually her friends learn to forgive her idiosyncrasies or ignore her pronouncements." I scratched behind Mai's ears, ignoring Dora rolling her eyes heavenward. "In any case, she's right. We don't know what might happen and it's best to be prepared."

"Pointing out when to ignore her would be a big help. You've had more experience." His expression became less tense and his stance not so stiff and angry. He'd forgiven her already, but wouldn't say so too quickly. Randolph Dodd wouldn't really need my help; he was more than a match for Dora.

The parlor clock chimed the quarter hour. Randy offered Dora his arm. "We should go. The captain will worry if we're late."

A strange motorcar sat at the curb, more than large enough for the three of us, but I'd expected to see Daniel's car. "Dora . . ."

"Nathan didn't return to the storage garage last night, and the proprietors claim not to have seen him or Daniel's car. The truth is that I'm more than a little worried about where Nathan's gone with the car. And only heaven knows what he might be doing."

Randy cleared his throat. "Given his connection to Maximillian and Effie Fontaine, you should worry. Did you file a police report? I'd feel better if the captain had men out looking for Nathan and the car."

"He's right, Dora." I checked that the front door lock had caught and dropped the key into my bag. "I'd feel much safer knowing some of Gabe's men were hunting for Nathan."

She frowned slightly, but waved her concern away immediately. "I can't worry about that tonight. I spoke with Gabe earlier and he promised to pass the word along to the squad to watch for the car. That will have to do for now. I'll file a formal police report if Nathan hasn't returned Daniel's car by morning. A friend lent me her touring car for the evening. This is posh enough to make an impression, don't you think?"

"Oh yes. A strong impression." I linked arms with Dora, putting her between me and Randy. The sudden impulse to hold tight to Isadora was a sure sign of how uncertain I was about this evening. What we were about to do should give any sane person an attack of nerves.

But perhaps the question of our sanity was best left for once we were home again, safe and whole.

Randy found a parking space in front of the house next to the church—a real surprise, considering the crowd outside. The line of people waiting to enter the church hall wound down the front walk and a considerable way down the block. People chatted with others around them, those who had attended lectures before telling newcomers how much they'd enjoyed Miss Fontaine's talks, and preparing them for the treat to come. We crept close enough to overhear most of what was said, but avoided being pulled into their conversations. That there were three of us clustered together helped.

Dora eyed the crowd dubiously. "My my, Dee. I hadn't counted on so many of the upper crust attending the same night. Based on what I'd read in the papers and conversations with your husband, I'd pictured more of a mixed crowd. These aren't the type of people who could vanish without causing an uproar. I wonder how many are invited to the private reception afterwards."

The line moved forward by inches, people filing toward the

church hall and surrendering their tickets to the men standing on either side of the door. Neither of them was Maximillian, a huge relief. Avoiding him completely was likely impossible, but I'd put off facing him for as long as possible.

"Do you know many of these people, Dora?" Randy walked between us, trying not to be too obvious about hovering protectively. "If that's going to be a problem, we'll leave."

She craned her neck to look at those waiting in line ahead of us. "Not at all. The people I recognize aren't friends, and the majority of them won't acknowledge me in public. I'd be very surprised if anyone speaks to me. I'm a society medium, a fortune-teller hired to entertain at parties. That keeps me from being entirely respectable. The fact Daniel and I live together without benefit of marriage makes me positively scandalous."

"You're joking." Most of Dora's friends went through this stage, fueled in large part by her outrageous behavior. He'd known her just long enough to be poised on the brink of skepticism and belief, and unsure about which way to fall. Sadly, I knew.

"No. I'm not." Dora arched an eyebrow, patently amused. "Surely you don't think they'd consider me an equal? The only reason I'm not called a whore openly is because Sadie and I are such good friends."

Randy stopped in the middle of the sidewalk, staring at Dora. Horror and shock played across his face, but that quickly gave way to anger. "If anyone so much as whispers a word against you, I'll make them regret it. I mean that."

I think that was the moment Dora got an inkling of how Randy Dodd felt about her. The sly, teasing edge left her smile and she touched his hand. "Thank you, but I don't need a champion. I've learned to watch out for myself. As a matter of fact, I'm quite good at that. What I could use is another friend."

Randy didn't look away, searching Dora's face. He swallowed and cleared his throat. "All right. You've got another friend."

The three of us had blocked the sidewalk while Randy and Dora worked things out, and caused a small scene. People glared and shoved past, stepping onto the grass or into the street on either side, and muttered about our lack of manners. How frantic they were to get inside to hear Miss Fontaine speak was more than a little disconcerting.

"So much for not standing out in the crowd. Come along, Randy. We need to get inside." Dora tugged him into motion. "All the seats will be gone if we don't hurry."

People handed their tickets in once they entered the foyer, and were directed to seats inside the hall. As we got closer, I saw that the tickets came in different colors, yellow and blue in addition to the rusty red slips clutched in Randy's hand. There were far fewer people turning in red tickets. Blending into the crowd unnoticed grew more unlikely.

The balding, square-shouldered man who took our tickets from Randy looked us over and smiled. A large, shadowy gap showed between his front teeth. "Guests of Maximillian sit up front. Take any seat in the first five rows."

Randy nodded and took my arm as well as Dora's, making sure we wouldn't be separated in the crush near the door. The hall was much larger than I'd imagined, more like a good-sized theater or auditorium than a room to hold box socials or quilting bees. A raised stage with heavy velvet curtains as a backdrop filled one end of the room.

People milled about, hunting for seats and blocking the way forward. Dora took the opportunity to look for empty chairs near the back and the exit, but the man in the foyer frowned and watched us keenly. When he moved toward us, Isadora relented, letting Randy lead us to the front. She leaned and murmured in my ear. "I'm beginning to feel herded, Dee, and that makes me leery. Maybe we should leave after all."

Big double doors slammed shut, closing off the foyer, a hollow, final sound that set my heart pounding. The men who'd admitted people to the hall were joined by two others. All of them took up places blocking the exits, arms crossed and looking less than friendly.

Given the smiling, eager faces all around, I was certain that I was the only one who'd noticed.

"I'm not sure we can leave. Miss Fontaine seems to prefer a captive audience." I moved down the fifth row of chairs to the far end, taking a seat next to the wall. Dora came next, then Randy. We were as isolated as we could get in a hall brimming with people, but I took little comfort in that. Once Effie Fontaine took the stage, we'd be practically under her nose.

"We'll just have to hope the risk I took with the hunter pays off." Dora's smile was brittle as she looked around, feigning the excitement sweeping the room. Lines of strain deepened around her eyes and pulled at the corners of her mouth. Even I could feel the energy in the room grow stronger, thicker. "If you'd hold off saying I told you so until we're safely out of here, I'd appreciate it. All my attention is spoken for right now."

Organ music filled the church hall, soaring upward from a half-hidden alcove to the left of the stage. The energy in the air grew stronger, thick and strangely still as a thunderstorm about to break. Ghosts shimmered into view: rows of men and women, farmers, merchants, and shopgirls hovered near the ceiling, lined up along the edge of the room and crowded at the back of the stage, half-submerged into the walls.

Churches were often full of ghosts, but I suspected this gathering wasn't made up of departed members of the congregation. They were connected to Fontaine, almost certainly victims. I couldn't tell if these spirits had been summoned by the power in the room, or come to watch Effie Fontaine of their own accord.

A blue velvet curtain parted at the back of the stage, allowing a double row of men and women dressed in dazzling white robes to march through the murky opening. They split the line at the front of the stage, half going left and the other half right. The choir was already singing a hymn and clapping their hands as they moved into place, voices blending in harmony. People in the audience began to sing and clap as well, caught up in the pageantry.

And it was a pageant, a show not unlike the revivals held in the church I attended as a child. I'd always appreciated the showmanship and fire of the pastors who traveled from town to town, and how they pulled people deeper into the fever of belief until they couldn't help but join in and shout hallelujah. The mildmannered reverend who spoke from the pulpit Sunday after Sunday believed just as deeply, but his sermons inspired little in the way of passion.

Dora and I traded looks. Passion and belief were a potent source of power unto themselves. Effie Fontaine knew all the tricks.

A second hymn was nearing its end when I saw the man from the furrier's shop, Maximillian, slip from behind the left side of the curtain. If I'd been as enraptured as the rest of the audience, I'd never have seen him. He kept to the shadows at the rear of the stage, appearing to watch everyone at once and looking at no one in particular. I knew I didn't want him to look at me.

Another man, dressed in a gold-trimmed black robe and grinning broadly, stepped through the same center opening as the choir used. He strode to the front of the stage, roaming from side to side and clapping in time to the music. Tall and broad shouldered, and with his dark hair slicked back, he reminded me a great deal of the revivalists from my childhood. As the hymn ended and the music died away, he stood precisely center stage, still smiling and leading the applause.

"Brothers and sisters!" His deep voice had a slight Southern lilt and carried easily over the noise, his words so clear that it struck me as unnatural. People grew quiet, leaning forward in their seats to listen. He pointed at the crowd, picking out people in different parts of the hall. "I'm gratified to see so many people here tonight. While I see old friends, I see lots of new faces as well. Praise God, brothers and sisters, our campaign is working. The rightness of keeping our boys home where they belong is taking root in the hearts and minds of San Francisco. Effie's message of peace is spreading! Praise God!"

People clapped and cheered again. A low chant began in the

back of the room, building until the sound was deafening. *"Effie! Effie! Effie!"*

Dora's narrowed eyes and focused expression told me the preacher had all her attention, but she gripped my hand tight enough my fingers ached. She clung to Randy as well, fighting not to be swept away on a tide of emotion. The rising power in the room battered at me. I couldn't imagine how bruised Isadora felt.

Movement at the back of the stage drew my attention from the preacher. Maximillian had moved forward, coming more into the light. Behind him, the hazy forms of dozens of ghosts took on more shape and substance, moving with him. All the spirits following the hunter were children.

At the very front of the throng of sad-eyed young haunts stood the little girl spirit. She watched me intently. I'd no doubt that in the midst of the noise and the commotion, the cheers and shouts, she'd made sure I'd see her and pay attention.

One by one, the small ghosts transformed to streams of silver gray mist that darted toward the little girl spirit. She absorbed each phantom child into herself, outwardly appearing unchanged.

Bright blue eyes stared into mine, leaving behind a kind of truth that left me wanting to retch. All the child ghosts following Gabe home, gathered on street corners for me to see and watching outside the police station; Maximillian had marked all of them as prey, waiting his chance to take them unobserved. They'd all died at his hand.

Dora's words came back to me. Not all monsters confined their hunting to adults.

I still didn't know whether this innocent-looking little girl was a demon or a benevolent guardian, not for certain. Nor could I say what power brought this spirit into being, but now I knew her purpose. She hid the spirits of his victims from Maximillian and kept him from adding to Effie Fontaine's power. Not all his victims had escaped or found shelter with her. Her hatred of Maximillian and what he'd done sat in her eyes. She knew, as I did, that their souls were lost forever.

She looked tiny, frail, but she had the strength to resist all my efforts to banish her from my life. All ghosts were strong in the way they clung to the world of the living, refusing to move on until they'd fulfilled their purpose. Now that I knew her secret, I prayed she'd leave Gabe alone.

Music swelled again and the preacher onstage stepped to one side, looking expectantly toward the opening in the curtains. Light glimmered behind the small ghost, a hole in the shadows filling the back of the stage. The little girl spirit faded into the summer day I'd glimpsed before, taking her charges with her. Fleeing before the looming darkness preceding Effie Fontaine swallowed them all.

Miss Fontaine was smaller in stature than I'd imagined, compact and square shouldered under the scarlet robe billowing around her ankles. Dark curls framing her face were held back by a crown of flowers perching on top of her long, loose hair. She smiled and waved to the crowd, reminding me more of photos I'd seen of cinema stars greeting admirers outside the theater. People greeted her as such, getting to their feet and cheering wildly.

The people screaming her name couldn't see the darkness that rose around her, a murky twin taller and wider than the small woman standing on the edge of the stage. They'd have fled otherwise, or crawled under their seats to cower, heeding the animal instinct to avoid predators. I did see, but I couldn't run.

A sweet, rotten fruit smell filled the church hall, distracting me from Miss Fontaine's looming doppelgänger. The aroma was inescapable in the overheated room and teetered on the edge of being nauseating.

I didn't have to search far for the source. Curls of pale smoke rose up from incense burners a group of men placed against the foot of the stage, along the walls, and on tables near the door. Their clothing was much too rough to be a part of Miss Fontaine's inner circle. Day laborers no doubt, like the men Gabe told me about.

Dora leaned close to speak in my ear, her nose crinkled in distaste and pain lines deep around her eyes. She was panting, worrying me even more. "I've seen enough, we're leaving. I'm certain there's something more to this stench than merely bad-smelling incense. I'd rather not tempt fate. We'll make an exit as soon as she gets fully under way. Hopefully we can slip out without attracting too much attention. Try to hang on until then, Dee."

"Don't worry about me." The music had gotten louder again, making it impossible for her to hear unless I shouted in her ear. I squeezed her hand, hoping she'd understand.

Randy gripped Dora's other hand tight, but his attention was divided between hovering over her and keeping track of the people around us, watching everything at once the way Gabe and Jack did. He craned his neck, straining to see something at the other end of the room and sat back again, scowling. With Dora between us, I couldn't ask what he'd seen.

Effie Fontaine words echoed through the hall. The murmur of excited whispers, the sound of people shifting in their seats, and the small, random noises any group of people make faded away. All I heard was her voice.

"Bless you, brothers and sisters. Bless you all!" She spread her arms wide, a gesture encompassing the entire audience. "You help us do God's work when you spread the message of peace and bring others to hear me speak. Every new face I see tonight is a fresh chance to sway another heart, another soul to our side. I couldn't do this without you. Bless you all!"

The sight of Miss Fontaine smiling and the monstrous shadow mimicking her movements was horrible, trapping me in a waking nightmare. A second voice parroted her words if I shut my eyes to listen, and that was far, far worse. That other voice was deeper, larger, and held the ghost of a growl and the scrape of stone on stone.

I'd only half believed when Dora spoke of demons and other evils that walked the world, thinking them products of another age, another time. She'd explained that such creatures always found willing vessels among humanity, people whose hunger for power blinded them, or those weak willed enough to believe the promises made without counting the cost. That anyone was willing to damn themselves that way was nearly impossible for me to grasp.

But I couldn't deny what I saw while watching Effie Fontaine, or ignore the tremors snaking up my spine. Every word Isadora had said was true.

Cheers and applause punctuated Miss Fontaine's speech as she outlined why God's plan was for America to stay out of the European war. The power in the room rose higher with each shout, each chant of "Effie, Effie." A few people in different sections of the church hall appeared to faint. Miss Fontaine's men rushed to take them away, leading those overcome by the moment through side doors that likely led to choir rooms, or Sunday school classrooms. My stomach clenched, afraid these unfortunate people had been marked by Maximillian and knowing they might never emerge again.

Dora's eyes were closed tight, shutting out the sight of Fontaine looming over us and the rapt devotion on the faces all around. Neither Randy nor I had proved useful in cushioning the double blow of power and emotion pummeling her. If the decision to leave were mine, we'd have already gone, and I'd begun to regret promising to wait on Dora's signal. The longer we sat in Fontaine's shadow, the more I worried.

Effie Fontaine's voice grew louder, more passionate, and that growling undertone echoed behind each word. "The way to lasting peace is not through more war! War is not God's plan. I beg you, brothers and sisters, don't listen to the lies of those who claim war is the answer." She pointed at people in the audience, seemingly at random. "If they come to you, cast them out! Cast them out!"

I didn't see Miss Fontaine so much as look in our direction, but Dora shuddered violently, her breathing ragged and strained. Her eyes flew open wide, full of panic. Randy looked at me and I saw he'd come to the same decision. We couldn't wait. We had to get Dora away or risk losing her.

One of the double doors into the foyer at the back opened for an elderly man and woman, and closed behind them again. No one made a fuss about them leaving, raising my hopes we wouldn't be noticed in the confusion. And if Miss Fontaine's people did try to make trouble, Gabe and Jack and the men from the squad were just outside. All we had to do was get to the front walkway.

I leaned across Dora and shouted at Randy. "Help me get her on her feet! Don't stop for anyone!"

We half dragged her out of the row of seats and into the center aisle. Her chest was heaving and the tremors more frequent, all of which kept Dora from walking on her own. Looking into her face, I was certain she'd swooned. I got her arm over my shoulders and Randy took most of her weight, but she was so limp, so helpless, that moving toward the door was a struggle. That struggle was made more difficult by people reaching out to grab at our arms, our clothing, and pleading with us to stay, to embrace Effie's mission of peace. I'd begun to feel woozy as well. The thought of fainting and not being able to escape this mob terrified me.

I'd read accounts of crowds seized with a kind of madness that spread from person to person, sparked by the fervor of the moment. Being the focus of that madness was terrifying, made more so because I was sure this desire to keep us in the church hadn't arisen naturally. Crazed mobs were a superior delaying tactic, designed to keep us from leaving quickly.

Effie Fontaine had known we were coming all along. She was toying with us. Toying with Dora.

"To hell with it, Delia, I'm going to carry her. We'll never get out of here otherwise." Randy fended off a man grabbing for his coat and swept Dora up into his arms. "She can yell at me tomorrow if she chooses. Stay in front of me and in the center of the aisle. Let's go."

I'd half expected the door into the foyer to be locked, or for people to block the way, but neither of those things happened. The door opened easily and I held it so Randy could bring Dora through.

Three men stood between us and the door to the outside. Two of them were big, brutish-looking men, but they were just men. The third man was the one who made me wary. He carried the same tainted shadow double as Maximillian and Effie Fontaine.

This man was older and not overly tall, with thinning brown hair and a small mustache. My mother might have thought him dapper in his neat gray suit. I thought him dangerous.

"My name is Jonas Wolf. I work closely with Miss Fontaine." He stepped forward, concern on his face, but not in his eyes. His eyes held victory and a look I could only call hunger. "Your friend is ill. Bring her back inside and let us take care of her."

My eyes didn't want to focus, but I put myself between Jonas Wolf and Dora, determined to bluff my way through if nothing else. Randy pulled her closer, acting on the same instinct to protect her. Of the three of us, Isadora was the one most at risk.

We couldn't let this man touch her or take her anywhere. I clung to that thought in the fog filling my head. "There's no need to concern yourself on our behalf. We're perfectly capable of looking after our friend. She'll be fine once she gets some air and has a chance to rest. Now, if you and your men would just move aside—"

He smiled and the darkness around him rose, deepened, and seemed to reach for me. Fear prickled my skin, but I didn't back away. Jonas's voice was reassuring, a father trying to calm a panicked child. "Be reasonable and think of your friend's well-being. A long car ride will only make things worse. Come inside."

"She told you no, mister. Maybe you should listen. Tell your goons to get out of the way." Randy's voice was hard, angry, and his expression said he'd broach no arguments. Yet underneath, I knew he was just as frightened as I was, maybe more so.

The little girl ghost shimmered into view in the space between Jonas and me. She stared at Jonas for an instant, her face sad and wistful, and real sorrow filled her eyes. Whoever she was, I was certain she'd known him in life and he'd betrayed her somehow, but she wasn't asking me to right past wrongs. She only wanted me to understand all that had been stolen from her.

I was more confused than ever about this spirit and uncertain

what she wanted from me. The hostility she'd shown from the beginning was gone, replaced by a wistfulness that brought tears to my
eyes. I didn't dare trust that feeling.

"You're making a mistake, young man. Your friend will be much
better off if she rests before leaving." Jonas's expression remained
concerned and friendly, but he'd concentrated all his attention and
efforts to persuade toward Randy. His eyes widened, and I knew he
saw something other than a tall, angry young man defending Isadora. For an instant, something cold, predatory, flashed across his
face and vanished again. Randy was a prize in Jonas's eyes, a person
to be exploited to best advantage.

Whether Randy survived or not once Jonas finished with him
didn't matter. This distinguished, dapper-looking man was a truly
repulsive creature at heart. That was the truth about Jonas Wolf, a
truth people passing him on the street would never know.

The little girl spirit moved closer, her china doll clutched tight in
one arm and bright blue eyes staring into mine. I remembered Gabe
telling me about the young reporter from the *Call*, Samuel Butler,
who'd tracked Effie Fontaine from small town to big city over the
last two years. Her people never came after him, because Sam Butler
saw the lies and the darkness behind the public face, and knew her
for a murderer. Even knowing all that, he was never afraid for himself.

Effie Fontaine never hurt Sam Butler, because she couldn't. He
wouldn't give her that power.

The same lies and rot squirmed below the surface of Jonas's skin.
He couldn't hurt me unless I let him, and I wasn't about to let that
happen.

Fear fell away and with it, some of the feel of being wrapped in
cotton wool. Anger took its place, clearing my head. I could think
again.

"We're not going anywhere with you, Mr. Wolf. I wouldn't ad-
vise trying to stop the three of us from leaving either, or I'll be forced
to make a scene. The police are waiting just outside, including my

husband, Captain Ryan. He's certain to hear if I make a fuss and begin to yell." I didn't know the proper cantrips or charms to banish creatures like Jonas Wolf, but I didn't need to. Command and will filled my voice, and all the stubborn determination to protect Dora that I could muster. I trusted the right words would come. "I'm not afraid of you. Get out of our way."

The smoky murk around Jonas swelled, rising toward the ceiling and dimming the light. Isadora groaned and shook harder. Randy couldn't see or feel the change in Jonas, but he knew something was wrong. He hugged Dora tighter, watching warily.

"I'm still not frightened." I stood my ground, matching Jonas Wolf stare for stare and pretending to nonchalance. Letting even a fraction of my concern for Dora show would let him claim victory. That would call disaster down on all our heads. "I'd banish you to hell for your crimes if I could."

"You wouldn't be the first to try, Mrs. Ryan." Jonas smiled and motioned his men away from the door. He stepped to one side as well, smug and openly amused. "I'm sure we'll meet again."

I waited until Randy pushed through the outside door with Isadora to turn my back on Jonas and follow. Marshall Henderson ran toward us from a doorway across the street, a promise of help that should have filled me with enormous relief. Instead, swarms of pinpricks crawled over my skin as I fled the warm church for the cold, moonless night, a warning that stole all thoughts of safety.

Victory had gleamed in Jonas Wolf's eyes. We'd escaped far too easily.

CHAPTER 22

Gabe

Light shone from the church windows, casting pale streaks across the winter-brown lawn and out to the sidewalk. Leaning forward over the steering wheel put a crimp in Gabe's neck, but didn't change the view or allow him to see what was happening inside. He sat back again, trying to relax his shoulders and struggling against the push he felt to barge through the church hall doors.

He'd promised Dora time to discover what she could about Effie Fontaine. Now impatience gnawed at him, an almost unbearable urgency that spread from the center of his chest, down his arms, and made his fingers tingle. He couldn't shake the conviction that time was running out. Gabe prayed he wouldn't live to regret keeping his promise.

Jack reached into the bakery bag on the seat between them, white paper crackling as he pulled out another cookie. His partner had eaten most of the cookies Annie sent while they waited. Tension rarely killed Jack's appetite or dried his mouth so that swallowing more than a bite was torture.

"Are you sure you don't want more of these?" Jack offered a sugar-dusted piece of shortbread. "Annie will be disappointed when I tell her you only had one."

"Then don't tell her. We'll keep that a secret between the two of us." The front door of the church hall opened, causing both Gabe and Jack to lean forward, straining to see who came out. An elderly man led his wife away, arm wrapped tight around her shoulders. Gabe sat back again, more restless than before. "Just make sure you brush the sugar off your jacket before you go inside. Annie will wonder what you've been up to otherwise."

"She always wonders." Jack rolled down the top of the cookie bag and twisted around to set it on the rear seat. "Robert Lindsey telephoned the house today. Adele came through the birth just fine. She asked her father to let Sadie know she'd had a little girl. Sadie's going to call round and bring a gift once Adele's had a chance to rest."

"That's good news. Really good news. Lindsey must be relieved." Good news of any kind had been scarce of late. He rubbed the fingers on his right hand, trying to ease the cramped ache that had begun to settle in his joints. "I'm glad you told me."

"I have more good news." Jack glanced at Gabe, an unreadable expression on his face, and went back to watching the church. "Sadie's pregnant again. The doctor says the baby will be here by midsummer."

Gabe smothered a pang of envy. He grinned and offered Jack his hand. "Congratulations, Lieutenant Fitzgerald. You and Sadie must be over the moon."

"It's sooner than we'd thought, but both of us want a big family. Neither one of us wanted Stella to grow up an only child. And maybe we'll have a boy this time." Jack shrugged, his smile a little embarrassed. "Not that it matters if we have another daughter, but I'd like to try to do a better job raising a son than my pop did."

"You will, Jack." Gabe didn't know what else to say, so he let it drop. Patrick Fitzgerald had been a brilliant businessman, but he'd also been a liar and a drunkard, and more concerned with his social position than with his son. Jack's childhood had been rocky at best and he grew up believing that everything his father told him was a lie.

He hadn't been far wrong. Pat Fitzgerald went to his grave without telling his son that his mother had vanished one night when Jack was a baby. She'd been murdered, something Jack might never have known if not for another case they'd worked.

Gabe had been damned lucky growing up to have Matt Ryan as a father. If he ever forgot that, something always happened to remind him.

"Sadie's a little worried about telling Delia. She doesn't know how Dee will take the news." A tall, thin man dressed in a heavy coat and with his hat pulled low over his face crossed the street. The stranger glanced over his shoulder at the church and walked faster. Jack and Gabe both sat up straighter, watching. "Dora talked to Sadie after Delia lost the baby. She thought Sadie should know there might not be another."

The stranger was getting closer and clearly headed for their car. Gabe cleared his throat, attention split and not wanting to remember his conversation with Isadora. "Stop worrying, Delia loves Sadie. She'll be happy for the two of you. And Dora's only guessing about why Dee lost the baby. Hell, she admitted as much to both Delia and me. She can't know for certain that we'll never have a child."

Gabe spent a lot of time trying to deny there was any truth in Dora's warning. If he managed to fool himself, maybe fate would be fooled as well. Of all the difficult things the ability to see ghosts and haunts, phantoms and spirits demanded of his wife, stealing her ability to be a mother struck him as exceedingly cruel.

Delia wanted a houseful of children as much as Sadie. So did he.

The tall man reached the car and tipped his hat back, looking directly at Gabe and smiling. "Christ Almighty, Jack, it's Butler."

Sam Butler opened the rear door and clambered into the backseat. He ended up with his knees almost under his chin at first, but Sam was used to fitting his long, lanky frame into tight spaces. It took only a few seconds for him to sort himself out.

"What are you doing here, Sam?" Two more people came out of the church entrance, both younger men this time. They staggered as they went down the walk, pausing to lean against the sign announcing Sunday's sermon before going on. Gabe frowned. Both men lurched down the sidewalk as if they'd spent the entire night in a tavern. Something was very wrong. "I hope you have a damn good reason, other than hunting for a story."

"If I just wanted a story, I'd write one." Sam rested an arm along the back of the front seat. He watched the front of the church as intently as Gabe and Jack. "I got to thinking about Bill Woodman and how angry he was with Jonas Wolf. He never said, but I figured that he had to know why Wolf was in the German embassy. So I played a hunch and went looking for Mr. Woodman tonight. He was in the same tavern as before. Once he found out I was buying the whiskey, Woodman didn't have any problem talking."

Jack half turned to look at Sam, amused admiration in his voice. "I take it Woodman knew what Wolf was up to or you wouldn't be here."

"He knew, all right. Wolf's trying to push through all the final papers he needs in order to take his family back to Germany. He and Fontaine have a six-year-old daughter who lives back in New York." Butler looked between Gabe and Jack, frowning. "The little girl's medical condition was part of the paperwork Woodman filed. She nearly died of infantile paralysis two years ago, and she's still in a bad way. That's why Fontaine goes back there so often, to see her daughter. Two years I've been following her, Gabe. I never heard a whisper about a daughter."

"I'm not surprised." Gabe rubbed the sore muscles in the back of his neck, trying to loosen knots that never went away. Having a child, one she cared for, was a weakness Effie Fontaine couldn't afford to admit. "My detective friend in New York questioned Fontaine's uncle. Theo's telegram said the uncle admitted Fontaine visited him often, but the old man never said a word about a sick child. She wanted her daughter kept a secret."

"Smart decision." Sam studied the floor at his feet for a few seconds before looking back at Gabe. He didn't try to hide his anger.

"There's enough folk who've lost family that someone was bound to go after her little girl. Lots of people still believe in an eye for an eye."

"But not you." He looked Sam straight in the eye, searching for hints of the kind of man Sam Butler was. "You don't believe."

"No, Gabe, I don't." Sam didn't flinch. "I can't say I didn't feel that way when I started after her, but that didn't last. The only person I want to see punished is Effie Fontaine."

"I needed to hear you say it." Thinking of all the people—all the children—who had died at Fontaine's hands over the last two years made him ill. Gabe swallowed the burning in the back of his throat. "How soon does Wolf plan to leave the country?"

"The ship they're sailing on leaves New York in two weeks. That's why Wolf pushed so hard. Their little girl doesn't have a German passport or other papers that will let him take her into the country." Sam gestured toward the church. "Tomorrow night is Fontaine's last lecture. They plan on taking a train back to New York the next morning."

They didn't have much time. Gabe ran down the list of all the evidence they'd found, all the connections between victims and Effie Fontaine he could prove. All the evidence they had was solid in his eyes, but Judge Alger hadn't thought Gabe's case was compelling enough. He could only hope that Isadora would discover some final piece of the puzzle that the judge couldn't dismiss or ignore.

He wasn't letting Effie Fontaine leave town a free woman. Not without a fight. If circumstances forced his hand, he'd arrest her and all her entourage, and worry about finding a way to make the charges stick later.

A man and a woman came out of the church and hurried across the dark lawn at an angle, heading for the line of parked cars down the block. Jack recognized them first and groped for the car door handle. "Gabe—that's Delia and Randy Dodd. Something's happened to Dora."

He was out of the car and running before Jack and Sam got their doors open. Marshall Henderson saw what was happening and ran across the street from his hiding place, weapon drawn. *Thank God, thank God,* ran through Gabe's head, a chant that kept time with the pounding of his feet. All he could think of was that Delia was safe and Randy wasn't struggling to carry her toward the car.

A guilty thought, one that made his heart thud painfully. Dora lay limp against Randy's chest, quiet and so still, he wasn't sure they hadn't lost her. Relief at seeing her fingers move was nearly as painful. Gabe ran faster, grateful he didn't have Isadora's death on his conscience.

Delia rushed into his arms, shaking and gasping in a way that came awfully close to sobs. He wanted to turn around and take her home, far from Effie Fontaine and the dangers Fontaine's followers posed. But he was a cop, and cops weren't allowed to be that selfish. He'd often thought that Delia accepted the price his job demanded better than he did.

Jack and Sam caught up with him. They took up places near Henderson, keeping watch. Gabe allowed himself one brief moment to hold his wife tight before stepping back and holding her at arm's length. "What happened, Dee? Can you tell me?"

"I'm . . . I'm not certain. My head feels all turned around, and thinking makes me queasy." She shut her eyes, slumping against this chest. "It's all muddled."

Gabe brushed hair back from her face and patted her cheeks. "I need you to tell me what happened to Dora. Talk to me, Delia. Tell me what they did to her."

Her eyes flew open and she pushed away from him, staring at Dora. Horror and guilt flashed across her face, replaced by a confused expression that made his stomach lurch. He'd seen the same look on Archie Baldwin's face the day he wandered into the police station. But Delia was stronger than Baldwin had ever been. He needed to remember that.

"Oh, God, I'm trying, I'm trying. I don't remember what they did to her. I know the hall was full of spirits and . . . and people fainted. Dora said there was something hidden in the smoke from the incense—" She frowned, forehead screwed up in concentration and thinking hard. Delia's eyes went wide. She'd remembered. "Miss Fontaine's audience kept us from leaving. The smoke kept getting thicker and Dora couldn't walk any farther. Jonas Wolf was waiting for us in the foyer. He knew, Gabe. He tried to force us to leave Dora with him, but I refused. I had to tell him you were outside before he'd let us go."

"She's right, Captain. Whatever was in that smoke made Dora ill. She was hanging on until then. Now she won't wake up." Randy cradled Dora closer, his struggle to hide terror sitting in his eyes. "If you ask me, the whole night was a setup, a trap. Luring Dora here was the reason Maximillian gave her those tickets. He knew who she was from the start."

They never found Dora's driver after he'd spoken to Maximillian. He couldn't dismiss that connection or Nathan's disappearance as coincidence. Part of him wondered if Nathan had driven the car that killed Sal and his wife.

The cold itch between his shoulder blades made Gabe glance toward the front of the church. He couldn't be sure he saw the door swing closed a final few inches, but he couldn't swear he hadn't. "I'm not saying you're wrong, Dodd. Maybe you're dead right. But we need reasonable cause to raid Fontaine's lecture. Otherwise, a lawyer will have her out again within the hour."

Dodd scowled. "I can give you reasonable cause, Captain. I saw Eli Marsh in there. He was one of the men setting out incense when the lecture started. I saw him again just before we left. Marsh is working for Fontaine."

He'd heard stories from his father about bad cops, men who'd tossed away the trust of the other officers they'd worked with for money. More was at work here than just greed, even if he couldn't say for sure what. Somehow, that made Marsh's betrayal worse.

But Eli Marsh was already under suspicion for Archie Baldwin's murder. Finding him working for Fontaine was another link, another piece of evidence to take to the judge. That gave Gabe and Jack a reason to go inside. A reason that would hold up in court.

Jack paced a few steps away and turned back, fists clenched at his side. "That sneaky low-life bastard. Are you positive Marsh is the man you saw?"

"I'm sure. That red hair of his stands out. No offense, Lieutenant."

"None taken." Jack looked to Gabe, knowing the answer he'd get, but seeking permission to give the orders anyway. "Mercy Hospital is only a few blocks away. Take Dora there and insist on seeing Dr. Jodes. Show your badge, yell, and use my name if you have to, but make sure Scott Jodes is the only one who takes care of Dora. He knows her and understands she's different. Do you need Henderson or Polk to drive?"

"I can drive, Lieutenant." Sam Butler stepped forward. He shrugged at Gabe's surprised expression. "If I drive, you won't be short an officer. You'll need every man you have here, Gabe. Even then, you won't have enough. I'll get my story once Effie Fontaine's behind bars."

"Then go." Gabe felt time slipping past and with it, his chance to catch Fontaine. He pulled Delia close to say good-bye, reluctant to let her out of his sight again. "Make sure the doctor takes a good look at you too."

"I will." Delia held on tight when he tried to move away, still trembling. "Gabe, they took a lot of people into those back rooms. You have to find them. She says to hurry, it's important."

"Who says? I don't know what you're talking about." He turned her so that the streetlamp shone full on her face, strangely unwilling to dismiss what she'd said as an aftereffect or the result of shock. Delia's eyes were unfocused and slightly glazed, watching things he couldn't see.

Ghosts.

"They're doing this for her, to keep her here. She never wanted them to hurt people, but they won't listen. They won't stop. She says she can't hide the others much longer, they're too strong. They get angry and make her do bad things." Delia shuddered and looked at Gabe, eyes clear again. "She doesn't want more people to die for her. She says you have to make them stop."

Cold knifed through his middle. Impossible things intruded into their lives every day, demanding he pay attention. In the beginning, he'd fought against accepting any of what he heard or saw as real. He was a detective, grounded in what he could prove and touch. Spirits and phantoms, or messages from beyond had no place in his world.

How easily he'd come to believe the impossible surprised him.

He cupped Delia's face in his hands. "I'll stop them. Tell her I promise."

Sam took Delia's arm, walking her to the long black touring car at the curb. Gabe had thought about asking her if she knew who this little girl spirit was, but decided against saying anything. He knew, or at least he thought he did.

Knowing would likely give him fresh nightmares.

Gabe waited until everyone was safely inside the car and Sam had driven away to look back at the church. Only a few minutes had passed since Randy and Delia ran out the front doors. Light still shone from the windows, the faint sound of an organ playing hymns drifting toward the street. Above the entrance, a banner proclaimed that a lecture on pacifism would be given that night. A breeze rippled the painted canvas.

People passing by wouldn't see anything out of the ordinary. He envied their innocence.

Henderson had fetched Polk and Finlay from their assigned post down the block. With the two patrolmen, there were five of them to take on Effie Fontaine and her followers. Gabe drew his weapon and waved his men toward the front doors.

No one turned to see what was happening when they burst into the church hall. An older woman continued to play hymns on the organ, filling the room with sounds that echoed off the high ceilings. People in the audience ignored the policemen completely, sitting glassy eyed in their seats and staring at the empty stage. Smoke still rose in lazy curls from brass pots at the foot of the stage and along the walls, filling the room with a bluish haze.

Effie Fontaine and her people were gone.

Jack pressed a handkerchief over his face before kicking over one of the smoldering brass pots. "Gabe?"

"I smell it. Opium." He covered his face as well, slowly surveying the room and counting empty seats. They'd taken at least twenty to twenty-five people away. There was no sign of the choir either. "Mother of God, she addicted them. No wonder people couldn't wait to come back night after night. Henderson, Polk, get those doors open to the outside and start leading people out. I want this room empty as soon as possible. Finlay, get the windows. Break them if you have to, but get some air in here."

He and Jack cautiously searched the Sunday school and meeting rooms attached to the main hall, pistols drawn. All in all, they found sixteen people slumped over tables, flopped in corners, or stretched out on the floor. The choir filled the wings on each side of the stage. His heart hammered each time he felt for a pulse and found one.

In the big assembly room behind the stage, they found two more. The young woman and man were dressed in choir robes and sprawled on the floor, puppets with cut strings. Open blue eyes stared at the shadowed ceiling, their skin already taking on the waxy sheen of death. He guessed the couple couldn't be more than nineteen or twenty.

Jack checked each of them for a pulse anyway. He looked at Gabe, anger smoldering in his eyes.. "Their skin isn't cold yet. Looks like Fontaine's people killed them on the way out. Damned if I can tell how."

"That's the coroner's job." He thought of Sal and brushed the touch of grief away. "They didn't leave everyone behind. Fontaine took people with her. We need to find them."

"Easier said than done, Captain Ryan. We've checked every hotel and rooming house in the city limits looking for her. I even sent two men to Sausalito on the ferry to check a few of the inns." Jack shoved his cap to the back of his head and wiped beads of sweat off his forehead. "No luck. The only thing that makes sense is that Miss Fontaine is tucked up in a private residence. Finding her will be a pretty trick."

"We'll find her." He stared at the young couple, memorizing their faces the way he'd memorized Sung Lan's. "There should be a phone in the church office. Call Rockwell and have him station men at all the train stations. I don't think she's arrogant enough to just stroll into the depot on schedule, but I won't take that chance. My guess is she'll look for another way to leave town. The longer we can keep her bottled up in San Francisco, the better. Time is on our side. She still has to make it to New York before that ship sails."

Jack cocked his head to the side, thinking. "From what the papers say, if she misses this ship, there might not be another. You're hoping she makes a mistake."

"Damn right. We might be able to push her toward making more than one if things go our way. Fontaine made a big splash in society. I'm hoping she goes looking for help from followers who owe her favors. I plan to make it hard for her to cash them in. And if she tries, someone will get nervous and tell us where to look for her."

Gabe took a last look around and walked away. Jack followed him back out onto the stage and down the steps onto the main floor of the hall. The seats were empty, the air clearer. Broken glass littered the floor where Finlay had smashed the windows, but he doubted the church board would put up a fuss. Renting the hall to a murderer would loom large over everything.

Jack went in search of a phone while Gabe watched the huddled groups of people shivering on the church lawn. The cold would help to clear their heads, but the more devoted followers who had come to see Fontaine night after night had a rough time ahead.

His bad cop, Eli Marsh, wasn't amongst the crowd, but that didn't surprise him. Marsh would have gone with Fontaine and her men, helping lead away the twenty or more people taken from the church hall. Eli Marsh fully expected Fontaine to keep her promises and be rewarded for his loyalty.

Marsh would be dead before morning. So would Luther and Walsh, loose ends Fontaine and Maximillian wouldn't leave dangling. The only question was whether the three rogue cops' bodies would ever be found.

Henderson had found two beat patrolmen on the next block and pressed them into service. With Polk and Finlay, they were leading the last of the choir out of the church. More officers were on the way from the local station house as well, summoned from a corner call box.

Gabe felt better about his plan to abandon them all. Selfish as it felt, he needed to go to the hospital and check on Delia and Isadora. He needed to know both of them were all right.

And he needed to have a long talk with Samuel Clemens Butler. Gabe had promised Sam a story. Most of that story would be true, but once he'd explained, he didn't think Sam would object to taking a few liberties with the truth.

And if a little yellow journalism brought Effie Ladia Fontaine to justice, so much the better. Gabe had other promises he intended to keep.

CHAPTER 23

Delia

We brought Dora to our house from the hospital the next morning. Dr. Jodes had watched her carefully all night and done all he could, but nothing roused her.

Scott Jodes was tall and broad shouldered, but his long-fingered hands struck me as delicate. The hands of a painter or a pianist, not a doctor. Gray frosted his temples, but his face looked years too young for such signs of age. Nothing about his appearance fit properly, but he was kind and gentle, and I knew right off why Jack had insisted Dr. Jodes care for Dora.

"I'll call round to check on her tomorrow night. If she wasn't accepting sips of water and broth without choking, I'd keep her here." He scribbled notes on her chart and handed it to a nurse. "Give her a little every few hours. With luck, she'll come around before not eating becomes a problem."

I cleared my throat and tried to smile. "I take it that whiskey is forbidden."

"Expressly forbidden. Doing without might convince her to come around." He glanced at me, obviously amused, and I liked him even more. Dr. Jodes brushed a strand of hair off her face before stepping back to let the orderlies lift her onto a stretcher. "I always imagined Briar Rose looked just like this. I hope the curse lifts soon and Dora wakes up."

Gabe put an arm around my shoulders and frowned. "Is that what you think is wrong, a curse?"

"Is that my official medical opinion? No, Captain Ryan, it's not." Dr. Jodes shrugged. "Unofficially, a curse makes as much sense as anything. I've known Dora a long time. Given who she is and what she does—I'm not ready to rule anything out."

The hospital wasn't far away, and the drive home not long. Neither Gabe nor I felt like talking. Knowing Dora was in that ambulance, quiet and seemingly unaware of all that went on around her, was an empty feeling. I thought hard about what Scott Jodes said about curses.

Randy Dodd was on our doorstep when we pulled up behind the ambulance. He looked haggard and worn, still wearing the expensive suit he'd dressed in to attend the lecture. I was certain he hadn't slept at all.

Officer Perry left his post at the end of our walk and came to Gabe's side of the car. He tipped his hat and smiled. "Everything's quiet, Captain. No sign of anything out of the ordinary. Taylor's out here with me, Baxter and Mitchell are around the back. Sergeant Rockwell has four men watching the lieutenant's house too."

Gabe gestured toward the porch. "How long has Dodd been here?"

"All night, near as I can tell. He was here when I came on at six." Perry glanced at Randy, his expression unsure. "Should I send him on his way?"

Gabe gestured toward the ambulance. "Help the orderlies get Miss Bobet inside. I'll take care of it."

I touched Gabe's arm before he got out of the car. "Let Randy stay. His being here might do Dora a world of good. Remember what she said about him bleeding away negative spiritual energy? That might be exactly what she needs to fight this off."

"You're serious." Gabe stared at Randy, shoulders tight and gripping the steering wheel hard enough, his fingers were white. "You think Jodes was right about Dora being under a curse."

"I can't say for certain. But I keep thinking about Archie and what Miss Fontaine did to him. She's to blame for Dora's condition, that I am sure of, but I'm not experienced enough to know how she managed. And I've not the first idea how to fix it." I put my hand over his and managed a smile, wan and small, but a smile nonetheless. "Both of us are swimming in deep waters, Gabe Ryan. I'll take all the help I can find."

Some of the tension went out of his shoulders. Gabe wrapped his fingers around mine. "All right, he can stay. I just hope Dodd doesn't make himself sick. He looks exhausted."

"So do you. But sitting at Dora's bedside won't do Randy any harm. He'll be sitting in one spot and forced to rest. He's more apt to fret if he's not with her." I squeezed his fingers. "I should get inside. I want to get Dora settled. Will you be late?"

"I hope not, but I can't promise." Gabe kissed my cheek. "Jack and Sam Butler are waiting in my office. Don't worry about supper. I'll make something when I come in."

He'd come home as always, I knew that, but saying good-bye was hard. I stood at the curb, waving until his car was out of sight. Turning to follow the stretcher carrying Dora into the house was even more difficult. How much our slow progress toward the front door resembled a funeral procession struck me hard.

Mai came out of hiding once the ambulance attendants left. She sat on the chest of drawers, tail flicking, and watched while I tucked pillows under Dora's head and made sure she was well covered. Randy stood at the end of the bed, clutching the scrolled-iron footboard, his expression bewildered and lost. "What can I do to help? There must be something."

"There is." I pointed to a small, upholstered armchair in the corner. "Help me move this."

Together we dragged the chair to the side of the bed and positioned it next to Dora. I pointed at the comfortably padded seat. "Sit down, Officer Dodd. Hold Dora's hand and don't move until I come back. That will be a huge help."

Anger glinted in Randy's eyes and he remained standing. He was a true match for Dora and her stubbornness. "I held her hand all the way to the hospital. Damn lot of help that was. If I'm in the way, say so."

Mai leapt from the top of the chest of drawers and landed on the coverlet. She made her way from the foot of the bed to Isadora's side, curling up so that her chin rested on Dora's chest. The small gray cat stared at Randy. I don't think I imagined the reproach in her eyes.

"You're not in the way, I promise. I need you here." I sighed and sat on the side of the bed. "Call it a hunch if you like, but I think Dora might have slipped away if you hadn't been there last night. None of us were prepared for this, Randy, least of all Dora. I need your help keeping her anchored here until I find a way to bring her back."

"You really think I can help." Weariness weighed down each word. "You're not just saying that."

I nodded. Indecision warred briefly with his pride, but good sense won in the end. Randy sat on the chair and took Dora's hand, sheepish and flushed, but holding tight. "I still don't know what good this will do."

"Maybe none at all. But if nothing else, Dora will know she's not alone. She needs to know we're here." Tears burned the back of my eyes. I stood, brushing down my skirts and not daring to look at Randy for fear I'd cry. "First I'm going to the kitchen to make some broth. The doctor said to feed her some every so often to keep her strength up. Then I'm going to write a note to Mr. Sung in Chinatown asking for help. Gabe won't like me contacting him, but I've no one else to turn to."

"You know more about this than the captain does. Do what you think is right, Delia." Randy leaned back in the chair, eyes half closed. "Dora trusts you. So do I."

She did trust me. Now I needed to be worthy of that trust and find a way to bring her back.

Heating broth didn't take long. Putting cheese, apple, and slices of yesterday's bread on the tray took a minute more, but I'd have wagered Randy hadn't eaten since supper last night.

I carried the tray into the guest room to find Randy fast asleep. He'd pulled the chair even closer to the bed and he'd laced his fingers through Dora's, holding tight even in sleep. Mai had moved as well, lying half across Dora's chest so that her head rested near Isadora's heart. The cat opened one eye to peer at me and purred loudly, a signal that all was as well as could be, at least for now.

Randy loved Isadora, quietly and deeply, and knowing all the obstacles that stood between them. Dora's relationship with Daniel was the greatest obstacle of all. But given a chance, Randy would bring all those hidden depths of his to bear and make a life with her. Love was a kind of power in and of itself, one that would help give Dora strength to recover. I found a great deal of real hope in that.

Sung Wing represented a different kind of hope, the hope of Dora waking again and going on as before, hale and hearty. He knew as much about the darker aspects of the spirit world as Dora and much, much more about how to counter those aspects than I did. I wouldn't consider the idea that he'd ignore my message or say no.

I couldn't. I had to believe.

Gabe

Raised, angry voices carried down the corridor from Gabe's office. He recognized Robert Lindsey's booming voice trying to drown out Jack's shouted replies, but his partner was holding his own. Jack wouldn't give an inch unless forced to it. If anything, years of fighting with Sadie probably gave him an advantage.

Gabe shoved his hands deep into his coat pockets, hiding clenched fists and white knuckles. Enough obstacles stood in the way of finding the place where Effie Fontaine had gone to ground. Interference from the police commissioner was the last thing he wanted to deal with.

He shoved the office door all the way open and stood framed in the doorway, his no-nonsense command expression firmly in place. Gabe reserved his coolest stare for Lindsey, giving Sam and Jack no more than a passing glance. The scene was just as he'd pictured it. Commissioner Lindsey stood toe to toe with Jack, attempting to roll right over him. One of the morning papers pulled from the pile in the center of the desk was crumpled in Lindsey's fist. That explained the yelling.

"Good morning, Commissioner." Gabe nodded to Lindsey and hung his overcoat and hat on the coatrack behind the door. He turned, arms folded over his chest. "What can I do for you?"

Sam Butler leaned casually against the file cabinet, bouncing Jack's baseball in one hand. He cleared his throat, drawing Gabe's attention. "The commissioner takes exception to the article I wrote for the *Call*. He's not too fond of the *Examiner* or the front page of any of the morning papers, for that matter. I suggested he might want to avoid the afternoon and evening editions too."

Lindsey shook the paper in Gabe's face. "This is slander, Ryan. I want these papers off the street right now! You said Adele was in danger from these people. This . . . this says Bradley embezzled money and Effie Fontaine blackmailed him. Do you know what you've done?" He tossed the paper against the wall, face scarlet with rage. "If Adele sees this, it will kill her."

Jack raked fingers through his hair. The frustration on his partner's face might have been funny if the situation weren't so serious. "Robert, stop yelling and listen. Adele knew about the article last night. Gabe and I told her all about what Sam wrote before we gave him the go-ahead to print it. It's a hoax we cooked up to flush Effie

Fontaine from hiding. Read the damn thing again. Nothing in that article says Bradley stole money."

Commissioner Lindsey gaped, his face growing redder and the cords in his neck bulging. Gabe dragged a visitor's chair over and steered Lindsey into it. "Have a seat, Commissioner. Take a minute to calm down."

He moved past Lindsey to pull a copy of the *Call* off the stack. Effie Fontaine's picture looked back at him from under a banner headline reading, PACIFIST USES CAUSE FOR FRAUD!! The accompanying article was full of names from San Francisco high society who'd been fixtures at Fontaine's lectures. Alleged blackmail, extortion, unpaid loans, and fraudulent business deals were mentioned all through the piece. Henderson's nickel-weekly stories had fewer crimes committed.

It was all very vague, a masterwork of implication unsupported by facts or solid connections. Anyone reading Sam's story would come away thinking that Effie Fontaine had stolen from half the population of Nob Hill, and swindled the other half. Bradley Wells's name was never linked to Fontaine. That Lindsey had read the story that way gave Gabe hope his plan would work.

Gabe finished reading and dropped the paper back on the stack. "I'm impressed, Butler. I wasn't sure you could pull it off."

Sam shrugged. "Writing was the easy part. Getting the other papers to go along was what took some work. My editor helped by calling in some favors."

Lindsey looked up from the paper in his lap, more than a little crestfallen and the belligerence bled away. "Very clever, Ryan, but what's the point? Everything you've told me points to Effie Fontaine murdering people. Why not put that on the front page?"

"Because having their money stolen makes people mad. They don't want to look like fools, especially the kind of people Fontaine has been hobnobbing with. I want her believers to turn against her." He sat in his desk chair, leafing through the morning papers and noting the small differences in headlines, or the size of the photo-graph. "Someone knows where she's hiding. I want that person to turn her in, not stay quiet because they're afraid she'll come after them or that they'll be arrested as an accessory to murder."

"And if no one comes forward?"

Gabe slumped back in his chair and traded looks with Jack. "I'll hold a press conference tomorrow afternoon and connect her to some of the murders and disappearances. The idea is to keep the pressure on and give her no place to hide. She'll make a mistake if she feels cornered."

Sam frowned. "Or she'll claw her way out and not care who gets hurt. Don't underestimate her, Gabe."

He thought of Sal and Dora, of Sung Lan and Archie Baldwin, Thad Harper and unnamed young women washing up under half-built piers.

Underestimating Effie Fontaine would be difficult.

CHAPTER 24

Delia

Owen Perry found me in the kitchen around four that afternoon. He knocked on the doorjamb, warning me before walking in. "Pardon me, Mrs. Ryan. There's an old Chinese gentleman at the door. He insists you sent for him."

I managed not to drop the teacup I was washing, but it was a near thing. Hope Mr. Sung would come to my aid had faded with the waning sunshine. "That's Mr. Sung and I did send for him. Is he alone?"

Owen's expression was distinctly unhappy. "He's got three men with him. One of them looks harmless enough, but the two youngest are a rough-looking pair of hooligans. I'm not sure Captain Ryan would want them inside the house."

Captain Ryan likely wouldn't want any of them in the house, including Sung Wing, but I'd already crossed that boundary. "It will be fine, Owen, I did invite him. Put the two young men in the parlor. Bring the other man back here with Mr. Sung, please."

He frowned and muttered as he left, but did as I asked. I had tea brewing and cookies set out on a plate by the time Owen Perry led my two visitors to the kitchen. Mr. Sung paused at the threshold, a small smile on his face as he studied the entrance. He wore his brown suit and held a bowler hat in one hand. "Mrs. Ryan, may we enter?"

He saw my wards, I was sure of it, and didn't want to test them. I smiled and gave hurried permission, nervous and desperately needing this to go well. "Come in, please, both of you. Would you like some tea before seeing Isadora?"

The younger man accompanying Sung Wing was grave and dignified, and moved as if the weight of his responsibilities was almost too heavy to bear. His hair was beginning to gray, but I didn't think he was too much older than forty. He carried a black lacquered box by the brass handles attached to two sides, carefully setting it in the middle of my kitchen table.

"Tea would be lovely, but I'm not sure Miss Bobet can wait. Let me introduce my nephew, Sung Zao, Mrs. Ryan." Mr. Sung placed his hat on the seat of a chair, but didn't sit. Zao nodded, the barest hint of a smile lightening his expression, and remained standing as well. "Zao is my brother's son and learned to mix medicines from his father. Forgive me for presuming to bring him along without asking first. I didn't know if we might have need of his skills in attempting to cure Miss Bobet."

"Cure" was such a lovely word. I savored that for an instant, resolutely ignoring that Mr. Sung had also said they'd attempt to help Isadora. He hadn't said he could guarantee their efforts would be successful.

"I'm very grateful you came. And of course your nephew is welcome." I untied my apron and laid it aside, hiding how nerves and the thought of Dora never waking made my hands tremble. Feeling helpless in the face of her condition was torture. "I have to admit I'm over my head, Mr. Sung. I don't have the first idea of where to start."

He followed me down the hall toward the guest room, Zao trailing a few steps behind us both. "Wu Mai taught me that admitting what we don't know was the first step toward finding answers. I've heard only street whispers about the woman who gave the lecture. Tell me what happened and what you know about Effie Fontaine."

Dora had once said that the less Sung Wing knew about Effie

Fontaine, the better, but circumstances had changed. I put her warning aside and told him all I knew, pausing in the middle of the hallway to finish the tale. He listened quietly, frowning at times or asking a question to make sure he'd understood, but for the most part he let me tell the story uninterrupted.

Zao's scowl never lightened from the first mention of the shadows surrounding Maximillian through my telling about the souls sheltered by the little girl spirit. Once I'd finished speaking, he said something to his uncle in Chinese. I didn't understand the words, but the harshness of his tone was unmistakable.

"English, Zao." Mr. Sung frowned. "Show Mrs. Ryan the respect she's shown us. She is Miss Bobet's apprentice as I was apprentice to Wu Mai and Sung Lan was apprentice to me. There shouldn't be secrets between us. Tell her."

Zao stared at his uncle, his expression blank, before bowing his head. "Your pardon, Mrs. Ryan. I told my uncle this is a fool's errand. The man you describe, Maximillian, is a shadow demon and a spirit hunter. No medicines I could mix will cure his touch."

"But he never touched Dora last night." I looked between the two men, stubbornly refusing to believe the churning in my stomach or that Zao's words held any truth. "None of Miss Fontaine's people touched her, only Randy and I. Something in the smoke made her ill."

"Opium is very powerful and opens spirit pathways best left closed, especially for someone as sensitive as Miss Bobet. The chance of someone practicing black arts using opium alone is very small. It may very well be as you say, but we must consider other outcomes." Mr. Sung took my arm. "Is this the room?"

Randy looked up quickly as the three of us entered the room. He had a book balanced on one knee, but still held tight to Dora's hand. I'd taken to forcing Randy away from the bedside every few hours, to eat and splash water on his face. Making himself ill wouldn't do Dora any good.

The cat was coiled tight against Dora on the opposite side of the bed. Mai opened one eye to peer at Sung Wing and promptly went to sleep again. Mr. Sung stood on that side, stroking Mai's head.

"This is Officer Randolph Dodd. Randy, this is Mr. Sung Wing and his nephew, Sung Zao." I fussed with straightening the bed-clothes and shifting Dora's pillows, giving myself something to do other than wring my hands. "Mr. Sung might be able to help."

Randy struggled to stand and not let go of Dora's hand. Mr. Sung waved him back into his chair. "Please, Officer Dodd, sit. Miss Bobet rests easier with you near."

I'd no doubt that someone as accomplished as Mr. Sung had easily discerned how Randy channeled harmful energy away from Dora. Sung Wing wore the same faraway expression I'd grown ac-customed to seeing on Dora's face these past two years. He looked beyond the here and now and the surface world, searching for the secret that would explain why Dora wouldn't wake.

He glanced at me, his frown angry and sad at the same time. "Miss Fontaine's man may not have put his hand on Isadora, but he marked her as prey just the same. Her will is very strong or she'd have already fallen to Maximillian."

Confusion filled Randy's eyes for an instant. "Hang on a min-ute. Maximillian's not here, and he wasn't anywhere near Dora last night. Are you saying he's responsible for her not waking up?"

Mr. Sung whispered something in Chinese, the words soft and sounding not unlike a prayer. He touched Dora's cheek. A blessing. "Miss Bobet's spirit runs and hides from the hunter nipping at her heels. Her body is here. She fights her battle elsewhere." He straight-ened up, tugging down the front of his suit coat. "Stay with her, Of-ficer Dodd. Help her fight."

Without a word, Sung Wing left the room. Zao and I followed him to the kitchen, both of us hurrying to keep up. He'd already taken a seat at the kitchen table and begun rummaging through Zao's case of medicines when we reached the kitchen. I sat opposite him, a platter of cookies and a pot of cold tea between us. Sung Wing looked at me over the glittering vials and pile of muslin bags.

"Forgive me, Mrs. Ryan. I didn't take the threat of Effie Fontaine and her hunters seriously enough. That was a grave mistake on my part, one I won't make again. I should have listened to my brother, Liang. Keeping her hunters away from my people wasn't enough. I should have done more." He continued sorting through the box, his expression grim. "Undoing my mistake will take time and preparation. But first we must do what we can to strengthen Miss Bobet in her fight against this creature. Then I can begin."

My hopes plummeted. "I'd thought—You're saying you can't wake her."

"The cure for what's wrong with Miss Bobet doesn't lie with me. I have many skills, but I'm not in the business of working miracles." He held out two small bags, sympathy and compassion in his eyes. "There are things I can do, but they are things of this world, not magic. Keep the young officer with her and add these herbs to her tea. Both will make her stronger. You'll know if I succeed."

I took the packets of herbs from him, not knowing what they were, caring only that they'd help Dora. Sung Wing and Sung Zao repacked the box, preparing to leave. I couldn't just let him walk out. "Mr. Sung, I have to ask. If what you try doesn't work, how long will Dora stay this way?"

"You're asking what will happen if I fail her." He studied the lid of the box for an eternity, considering. "You deserve the truth. Isadora will sleep until she wins or loses the battle for her spirit, or until her body gives out. She's a strong woman. I can't say how long she will survive."

I nodded, numb and unable to comprehend the possibility of her dying. Dora was young and vibrant. People like her didn't die. She couldn't.

Mr. Sung's hand on my shoulder startled me. "Don't mourn her yet. This Maximillian and Miss Fontaine have harmed far too many innocents. I don't intend to fail."

Zao picked up the big wooden box and followed his uncle out of the house. I sat there long after they'd gone, watching the pale blue winter sky darken into an indigo twilight, thinking hard about hope and belief.

Gabe

The battered old clock over the door chimed six, startling Gabe. Darkness came early in January, and he'd turned on the desk lamp long before and lost track of time. He'd spent the entire afternoon reading over all the autopsy reports recovered from Sal's home. Searching the home of victims for clues about why they'd been killed was standard. In Sal's case, what he and Jack uncovered confirmed what they already knew.

Gabe slumped back in his chair, easing the ache in his shoulders, and attempted to wipe the tiredness from his eyes. The deputy coroner had made duplicate files for all the cases they suspected involved Effie Fontaine, keeping the second set in his study at home. Sal must have had a reason to suspect that filing the autopsy reports in the morgue alone might turn out to be a problem. Whatever Sal Rosen's suspicions or the reasons behind them, he'd been right. All the case reports Sal had filed over the last two months had disappeared from the coroner's file room.

How daring Effie Fontaine was in covering her tracks and how far her reach in his city extended were frightening.

Jack nudged the office door open with his shoulder, two brimming mugs of coffee in his hands. Gabe had overridden Jack's protests and sent his partner home to have dinner with his wife and baby. "Sergeant Riley had just made a fresh pot of coffee when I came in. I pulled rank on Baker and that new kid, Quinn, to get the first two cups. Sadie said to say hello and told me to thank you. We had that talk like you said. It's killing her that she can't help take care of Dora, but she understands it's too risky."

"I worry enough about Dee and Isadora being in the same house. And thank you, I need coffee." He sipped from the mug, not really tasting the liberal portion of cream or the two cubes of sugar. "I've read the Baldwin autopsy twice. Sal comes right out and says he doesn't believe Archie Baldwin killed himself. He found marks on Archie's arm that were consistent with recent hypodermic injections."

Jack scowled, but the tone of his question was cautious and careful. "How recent?"

"Within an hour or two of death. The punctures hadn't healed at all." He flipped the file around so Jack could read. "Archie had been in that cell for days. Sal's conclusion was that Baldwin was probably drugged so his killers could make his murder look like a suicide."

"Son of a bitch." Jack flipped through a few more pages and shoved the folder away. "We know Marsh was in that cell."

"And thanks to Dodd, we know Marsh was working for Effie Fontaine. I've already sent a message to Judge Alger." Gabe stacked the folders neatly, grateful that Sal had been the overly cautious type and angry all over again that his friend was dead. "This is the proof he wanted. Alger will have to issue a warrant now."

A loud rap on the door was all the warning they had before Sam Butler stuck his head inside the office. The victorious smile on Butler's face made Gabe's heart race. "Captain Ryan, I'd like to introduce you to someone."

Sam opened the door wider and ushered in an obviously nervous young woman. She wore a plain blue coat, a matching hat with two white ostrich plumes, and black skirts. Working-class clothing, clean and practical. He'd expected any response to their attempt to flush out Fontaine to come from a member of high society, but Gabe had faith in Sam Butler. The reporter wouldn't bring this woman to his office without a reason.

Springing the trap on Effie Fontaine was the best reason Gabe could think of.

"Captain, this is Miss Rosie Taft. Miss Taft works as a housemaid in Bernal Heights and her employer, Mrs. Cummings, owns several houses in the city. Miss Taft came to see me this afternoon about an article the *Call* ran this morning." Sam stayed close to Rosie Taft, hovering and likely keeping her from bolting. "I thought you'd be interested in hearing what Miss Taft has to say."

"Come in, Miss Taft. Please, have a seat. How can I help you?" Gabe smiled and tried to look calm and welcoming, hiding how his heart pounded. He pulled over one of the visitor's chairs before taking his own seat behind the desk. Looming over her would only add to her nerves. Jack stepped back as well, placing himself off to the side and out of Rosie Taft's line of sight.

Rosie perched on the edge of the chair, her fingers wrapped tight around the top of her handbag. "It's not me that needs help, Captain. Mrs. Cummings is the one I'm worried about. She's getting on in years and she's got no one to watch out for her. I knew I had to tell someone. I go twice a week to tidy up the house Mrs. Cummings owns at 29 Prospect Avenue." She opened her handbag and pulled out a folded sheet of newsprint. Rosie held it out to Gabe. "The woman in this picture has been staying in the Prospect house. I'd feel terrible if she did something sinful to Mrs. Cummings and I didn't tell the police what I knew."

The sheet of newsprint was the front page of the *Call*, complete with Sam's article and Effie Fontaine's picture. Gabe passed it over to Jack and clamped down hard on his emotions. "You did the right thing, Miss Taft. When was the last time you saw Miss Fontaine?"

"Just a few hours ago. Today was my day to clean over there." She glanced at Sam, who smiled and nodded encouragement. "I went in through the kitchen as always, but I knew right away something wasn't right. There were broken dishes all over the floor and I could hear shouting in the parlor. My mama taught me eavesdropping is wrong. But I went down that hall quiet as I could to see what was going on. Starting in sweeping up the mess in the kitchen didn't feel right, you know?"

Gabe traded looks with Jack. "I do know, Miss Taft, and I don't blame you in the slightest. Coming in to work and finding things in an uproar must have been frightening. Was Miss Fontaine in the parlor?"

"I was told to call her Mrs. Wolf, but she's the same woman in the paper." Rosie hugged her handbag to her chest. "She was in a terrible state, crying and huddled up on the settee while that husband of hers kept yelling. Mr. Wolf wasn't speaking English, but his face was all red, and whatever he said made her cry harder. I decided right then and there I wasn't staying around. I tiptoed back to the kitchen and left."

Jack came around to stand next to Rosie. A small muscle in his jaw twitched, the only sign of emotion he let slip. "You did the right thing. Did you see anyone else with Mr. and Mrs. Wolf?"

She glanced at Jack and back to Gabe. "The tall blond man that stays in the small bedroom wasn't in the parlor. He might have been upstairs, but I wasn't going to look for him."

Gabe stared at his desk blotter, calculating how long a trip to Bernal Heights might take once Judge Alger drew up a warrant. Trying to decide how many men and weapons to gather. He wouldn't send his men after Effie Fontaine and Jonas Wolf unarmed.

And Maximillian's absence from the house bothered him a great deal. His imagination was far too ready to provide bleak explanations of where Maximillian was or what he might be doing. Sending more men to guard both his and Jack's houses would help ease the knot forming between his shoulders.

Rosie's hesitant question brought him back to the here and now. "Is it all right if I go home now, Captain?"

"Do you live with family or a roommate, Miss Taft?" She shook her head. Gabe didn't want to frighten her, but he'd never forgive himself if something happened to Rosie Taft. He scribbled out the address for Mrs. Allen's rooming house and passed it to Sam. "I don't think you're in any real danger, but I think it might be best if you stay with a friend of mine tonight. Sam will take you there. Katie Allen is a wonderful person and she'll take good care of you."

Rosie Taft looked at Gabe and Jack in turn, and then Sam,

taking in their grim expressions. He knew she wasn't fooled, but she kept up the façade and pretended not to be frightened. "All right, if you think that's best. I'll stay with her for the night."

Jack turned to him once the door had shut behind Sam. "We've got her. Your plan worked."

"We don't have her yet." Gabe locked up his desk. "I'm going to call Judge Alger from the chief's office and tell him we need that warrant right now. You gather the squad from the list we made. Make sure all of them are armed. Don't tell anyone where we're going until I give the word to leave."

"How long are we going to wait for that warrant?"

"Not long." He yanked open the door and waited for Jack to hurry out. "I'll give Alger an hour. If it's not here by then, we go anyway."

The house on Prospect Avenue was large, a two-story with a peaked roof that housed an attic. Gabe saw right off why she'd chosen this location. Neighbors were two or three empty lots away on either side, leaving Effie Fontaine's hideout isolated from the rest of the neighborhood. A box hedge ran along one side of the yard, but approaching the house either from the front or back left his men in full view.

Clouds covered the waning moon, rendering the night exceptionally dark and his officers' deep blue uniforms more difficult to see. That might be the one advantage he and Jack had. Gabe prayed the clouds would stay in place. Hoping they'd thicken was pushing his luck too far.

Ten men he knew he could trust guarded Delia and Sadie. He glanced to either side. Counting Jack, he had eleven men with him. Eleven good men would have to do.

"Are you ready, Lieutenant Fitzgerald?"

Jack slipped the last cartridge into his pistol and snapped it shut. "Lead the way, Captain Ryan. I'll watch your back."

Gabe gave the signal. As a group, they burst out of the shadows and dashed across the road, pausing to gather together again under the shelter of a clump of trees. The same dim light shone downstairs and from one curtained window on the second story. As far as he could tell, they hadn't been spotted.

He waved three men toward the back of the house. Baker, Finlay, and Polk took off at a run, using the box hedge to help shield them from view. Gabe slowly counted to a hundred, giving them time, before leading the rest of the group up the porch.

Daniels and Perry positioned themselves to kick in the front door, but the cold itch on the back of his neck made Gabe wave them away. He cast about for a way to bash down the door without any of his men standing dead center. The answer was a cast-iron bench sitting under a window. Two swings with the bench slung between Perry and Daniels, and the door ripped off the hinges.

Jonas Wolf stood a few steps up from the bottom of the staircase, holding a pistol in each hand. He didn't hesitate to open fire.

One of the men behind Gabe screamed and went down. He heard another body fall, but didn't stop to turn and see who'd been hit. Wolf's form grew larger and wavered like smoke spreading on the wind, making it almost impossible to aim. Jack and Gabe stood on either side of the door, firing, yet none of their bullets appeared to find their mark. He realized with a start that Wolf was picking off the men behind them, completely ignoring him and Jack. Cold sweat trickled down his neck, and he remembered what Dora had said about Wolf and Maximillian not being completely human.

Finlay and Polk came running down the hallway from the back of the house, wailing like banshees from his grandmother's stories and startling Wolf. Their distraction worked. For an instant, the wavering shadow form vanished, leaving Jonas Wolf solid and no more than a man. Gabe took aim at the center of Wolf's chest, firing his last two bullets in rapid succession. Jack did the same.

Blood spread in dark, weeping patches across the front of Wolf's expensive serge suit. He dropped the pistol in his right hand, touching the blood and staring at the stains on his fingers. Jonas looked at Gabe and smiled before tumbling down the stairs.

Jack reloaded his pistol before they approached Wolf's body. His partner kept the barrel pointed at Jonas while Gabe rolled him over, feeling for a pulse.

Gabe stood, rubbing his fingers on his coat to wipe away the oily feel of Wolf's cooling skin. He glanced at Jack. "He's dead, but keep that pistol out. We still don't know where Fontaine and Maximillian are."

"Captain." Perry stood behind him. Blood trickled down the side of the dark-haired officer's face from a gash over his eye. "Durst and Monroe are dead. Taylor got hit in the leg, but he's going to make it. Baxter thinks the bullet went clear through and missed the bone. The bleeding's almost stopped."

He was the officer in charge, responsible for the men under his command. Men under him had died before, but the guilt, the sense that he could have done something to prevent their loss never went away. Neither did the grief he couldn't show to anyone but Dee or Jack.

Gabe cleared his throat. "Get one of the cars. Help Baxter get Taylor to a hospital. Durst and Monroe will have to wait until we're finished here." He turned to Jack. "Let's find Fontaine."

Effie Fontaine wasn't hard to find. She sat on the chesterfield in the parlor, dressed in a stylish traveling coat and veiled hat, a packed valise at her feet. She held a small silver frame and stared at a photograph of a little girl. Her gaze never wavered from the photograph.

He wasn't certain she knew they'd come in. Gabe cleared his throat. "You have to come with us now, Mrs. Wolf. It's over."

"Don't patronize me, Captain Ryan. I've known you were coming since your men parked their cars down the block." She looked up at him, her bright green eyes full of disdain. "You know murder charges won't stick. I'm a German citizen. My daughter and I will be on a ship bound for Berlin before the month is out."

"You could be right about not being able to try you for murder, Mrs. Wolf. But I wouldn't hold out much hope of going to Berlin or seeing your daughter again." Gabe put a hand under her arm and forced her to stand. "Espionage and treason are charges I can make stick. Even if the courts are lenient and you don't hang, you'll spend the rest of your life in prison. Justice will be served either way."

"You're bluffing." Gabe didn't answer, matching Effie Fontaine stare for stare. Her arrogant façade cracked, and hints of panic appeared in her eyes. "You can't do this. Maximillian promised us they'd make her well again. I have to get Ella to Berlin or all this will have been for nothing."

"It was always for nothing, Mrs. Wolf. Always." Gabe took the frame holding Ella's photograph, stepping back so that Jack could snap handcuffs around Effie Fontaine's wrists. "Take her to the car, Lieutenant. I'll be out once I'm sure the house is clear."

He trailed behind them to the entryway. One of his men had pulled the heavy damask drapes off the windows to cover Monroe and Durst. They'd left Jonas Wolf as he was until the coroner's van arrived. Effie stumbled as Jack led her past her husband, but didn't make any attempt to go to the body.

A search confirmed Maximillian wasn't in the house, but he'd guessed that from the start. Gabe stayed in the entry, taking reports from his men and supervising the removal of the bodies. Before he went home, Gabe would visit Durst's and Monroe's families and break the news. The thought made him slightly ill, but he wouldn't pass that duty off on anyone else.

The last stretcher and the last of his men went out the front door. He righted an overturned chair and sat, needing a moment of quiet. Gabe stared at Ella's photograph, memorizing her face as he'd memorized Sung Lan's and the young couple from the choir. He touched the smiling face in the photo. "I kept my promise, Ella. I'm sorry."

"Gabe?" Jack stood in the doorway, watching. "Are you all right?"

"I'm fine." He stood, slipping Ella's photograph into his coat pocket. "Let's go. We still have a long night ahead."

Notifying Durst's and Monroe's families was as difficult as Gabe imagined. He and Jack did their best to be kind, but there wasn't a good way to deliver this kind of news.

They got back to the station after eleven. Questioning Effie Fontaine was exhausting in a different way. She folded in on herself more and more as the night wore on, all the arrogance and confidence she'd displayed bleeding away. Whatever power she'd gained had vanished with the death of her husband and Maximillian's disappearance. By the time Finlay took her back to her cell, Gabe had to concede that she didn't know where Roth had gone.

He wouldn't let his guard down, not yet. Not until Maximillian Roth was in a cell or in the morgue.

By the time the patrol car dropped Gabe in front of his house, the sky was beginning to lighten toward dawn. Marshall Henderson was waiting for him on the front walkway, still watching the street and the shadows.

"Everything's quiet, Captain." Marshall gestured toward the house. "Delia made supper for all of us and went to bed early. Nothing's happened since."

Gabe rubbed his eyes. "Any change in Dora?"

"No, sir." New lines in his face made Marshall look older than twenty-three. "She's just the same."

He clapped Henderson on the shoulder and went on into the house, moving quietly as he could. Gabe found his wife curled up on the sofa in the sitting room, fully dressed and sound asleep. The blanket covering Delia had partly slipped to the floor, so he pulled it over her again. She stirred and half sat up, bleary eyed. "Gabe? What time is it?"

"Late. Somewhere around four." He took off his suit coat before wedging himself into the corner of the sofa. Gabe pulled Delia up next to him so that her head rested on his shoulder and arranged the blanket so they'd both be warm. "We arrested Effie Fontaine. Jonas Wolf is dead, but he wounded Taylor first and killed two of my men. That's one reason I'm so late. I had to tell their families."

"Oh God . . . I'm so, so sorry, Gabe." She brushed a hand over her eyes. "What about Maximillian?"

"We haven't found Roth yet. I've got men looking all over the city." He yawned and settled deeper into the corner, eyes closed and barely awake. "We'll find him."

"Gabe." Something in the way she said his name jerked him back from the edge of sleep. "Your men aren't the only ones searching. Sung Wing is looking for Maximillian too."

He didn't comment as Delia told him about Sung Wing's visit and what the tong leader had said about Dora fighting Maximillian for her spirit. Gabe accepted this impossible thing as truth, just as he'd accepted all the others. He flinched hard over the possibility of Isadora losing that battle.

"Asking Mr. Sung for help was the only thing I knew to do. I don't know enough on my own to help her." Delia's voice was thick, choked. "And I couldn't let her go without a fight. I had to try."

"Don't give up hope, Dee." He brushed a tear off her face. "We'll find him."

He lay awake long after Delia fell asleep, thinking. Maximillian Roth was the one being hunted this time, sought by men with very different ideas of justice. Gabe wasn't sure what he'd do if Sung Wing got there first.

That thought kept looping through his head, tangling with memories of Sal, Ella's face, and seaweed snagged in a dead woman's hair.

CHAPTER 25

Delia

The phone rang not long after nine, waking us. Henderson was already in the parlor and answered, saving Gabe and me from staggering into the other room half-awake.

Gabe yawned and sat up before kissing my cheek. "My grandmother used to say that good news waits until late in the day. Phone calls this early must be warning of disaster."

"That's a cheery thought, Gabe Ryan." I brushed hair back from my face, already thinking about making Dora's herb-infused tea and feeding all the men guarding our house. "We've had quite enough calamity. Let's not tempt more to arrive."

Marshall appeared in the doorway. "Captain? Lieutenant Fitzgerald is on the line. He says it's important."

Gabe rubbed a hand over his face and went to answer the phone. He was back, grim faced and weary, before I'd finished folding the blanket and moving the throw pillows back in place. "Delia . . . I have to leave. A report came into the station that Maximillian Roth is dead."

"Oh." I hugged the needlepoint pillow in my arms, heart pounding equally with hope this meant Dora would wake, and dread that his death would make no difference. "How did he die?"

"I don't have many details yet. A groundskeeper at the Conservatory of Flowers found two bodies in the orchid exhibit. From the description, there's a chance one of them is the chauffeur who stole Daniel's car, Nathan. The officers on the scene identified the other man as Maximillian Roth. I'm leaving the guards in place until I'm sure it's really him." A strange expression passed across Gabe's face, as if he'd remembered something. He gathered up his suit coat, pausing to take a small picture frame from the pocket. Gabe studied the photograph briefly and held it out to me. "Take care of this for me. It's a picture of Ella Wolf, Effie Fontaine's daughter. I think this is the little girl you keep seeing. It's a long story, but Ella's dying. Funny, but I didn't realize until now how much she reminds me of Penelope."

He kissed me good-bye and left in his sleep-rumpled shirt. I sat on the sofa, studying the face of the happy little girl in the photograph, a face full of life and promise. Gabe was right. Brushing the edge of death and the spirit realm had changed her, made her features appear older and harder than a young child's, but Ella was the little girl I'd seen so often. I suspected she was the little girl in Gabe's dreams as well.

Someone bound her to this world, an unnatural tie she couldn't break. I understood more of her anger now.

I finished tidying the parlor and went to the kitchen to make breakfast, trying not to think that Maximillian's death might be the key that let Ella rest and unlocked the remainder of Dora's life. And I so desperately wanted Isadora to live, to continue being my friend and teacher. That one life resuming might depend on another ending struck me as an unfair bargain.

Randy yawned and wiped a hand across his face as I entered the guest room with Dora's tea. The cat opened one eye, but Mai never stirred from her place. "Did I hear Captain Ryan go out?"

"Jack called. They found two bodies in Golden Gate Park." I shooed him out of the chair and tucked a napkin under Dora's chin. Nothing had changed, but I refused to stop hoping. "There's a chance that one of the dead men is Maximillian Roth. The other might be the missing driver, Nathan. Gabe's meeting Jack at the park to make certain."

Randy raked fingers through his hair, staring at Dora's still face. "If Roth is dead, why isn't she awake?"

"I can't say. She may need time to find her way back. Go wash up. I left your breakfast on the back of the stove." The same unanswered question swirled through my head. I truly didn't know the answer. This was unmapped territory, a place I'd never thought to find myself.

"It's safe to come back now, Dora. Maximillian is dead. Gabe's gone to make certain, but I know it's true. I can sense it." Dora swallowed each teaspoon of tea, but she'd done that from the start. "Randy's going to worry himself to a shadow if you don't open your eyes soon."

Mai lifted her head, eyes wide and staring toward the foot of the bed. The little girl spirit—Ella—shimmered into view, her china doll clutched tight. Ella appeared faded, her ties to the world weaker.

She was dying.

The flock of child ghosts I'd seen in the church hall shimmered into view, surrounding Ella. One by one they became wisps of pearly mist, twining around each other as they rose toward the ceiling and winked out of view. I heard laughter and scraps of song, but the sound held only joy. They were free.

I'd no doubt Ella was a true ghost now, growing more transparent and tattered as I watched. The door into the bright summer day I'd seen before opened behind her. She smiled happily and skipped through, singing in a high, clear voice:

Hush-a-bye dolly on the treetop,
When the wind blows, her cradle will rock,
Father's a nobleman, mother's a queen,
And Ella's a lady who wears a gold ring

Sunshine and birdsong faded, taking Ella with them. I brushed away tears and muttered a charm, sending all the lost children on their way to find rest and peace.

Mai meowed and jumped off the bed, sauntering out of the guest room with her tail held high. The cat had refused to budge from Isadora's side until now, a small fierce guardian protecting her from any spirit creatures that crept near. I'd been grateful. Mai sensed things I couldn't, and several times I'd entered the room to find her crouched over Dora, growling. All the spirits were truly gone from the house if the cat left Isadora unguarded.

I turned back to Dora. She batted the spoon away.

"Dear God, Dee, are you trying to poison me? I don't know what's in that tea, but it tastes utterly vile." She coughed and made faces, wiping a hand over her mouth. "The least you could have done was mix in a little whiskey to make it palatable."

"Dr. Jodes said whiskey was strictly forbidden until you woke." I set the tea aside, trying to dig up more wit and not let on how tight my throat had grown, or how badly I wanted to cry. "He suggested denial might even bring you round sooner."

Dora tried to sit up, but couldn't manage. She sank back on the pillows, shaking and pale. "How long have I been here?"

"Three days. Four if you count the night in the hospital. Randy and I took turns sitting with you. We're both quite fond of you and didn't want you waking up alone." I rearranged the pillows behind her, ignoring her annoyed frown and token protests. "The truth is, both of us were afraid you'd slip away without ever opening your eyes."

"Really, Dee." Dora quirked an eyebrow, her smile full of false bravado and a little afraid. "Aren't you being a tad overdramatic?"

"Not in the slightest." I sat on the bed and put my arms around her, hugging her tight and not caring if she disapproved. "You scared the life out of me, Isadora Bobet. Don't ever do that again."

"I won't, not of my own accord. That's a promise." She sighed and hugged me back. "I've never been so frightened, Dee, but I've never grappled with a demon before now. Maximillian weakened at the last moment or you might have lost me. I've no idea why I suddenly had the upper hand. Now, tell me what I missed."

I suspected Mr. Sung was at least partly responsible for Dora's victory, but I left that part out while recounting events. By the time I'd finished, Randy was back, his heart in his eyes. "Dora . . . you're awake."

She smiled flirtatiously, doing her best to hide weariness and fear; pretending nothing had changed. "Why, Randolph Dodd, I'm disappointed. You sound surprised."

"No, Dora, not surprised." Randy sat in the same chair he'd spent the last three days in and took her hand. "Relieved. More relieved than I can say."

I left them alone and went to call Sadie.

April 1917 began with cold rains, but had redeemed itself by the eighth with clear skies and warm breezes. Sadie took full advantage of the change in weather, throwing an impromptu garden party for Stella's first birthday. I agreed that an outdoor party was one of her better ideas. Winter had been dreary and frightening, a season I'd just as soon forget. Sunshine and warmth would go a long way toward that.

Wanting to forget didn't mean I should. Some lessons were too hard and painful to be learned again. And far too many reminders remained.

Effie Fontaine was still in a cell in Gabe's station, a broken woman awaiting trial for murder. Her following in San Francisco society had melted away as her crimes came to light. Other cities and towns squabbled with the mayor and chief of police over the right to punish her, each far-flung community wanting justice for the lives she'd stolen. Gabe and Jack fought just as stubbornly to keep Miss Fontaine in San Francisco. Her trial was scheduled to start in a few weeks.

The dead men found in the conservatory had been identified as Maximillian Roth and the missing chauffeur, Nathan. Being relieved to discover another person dead was an odd feeling, one I didn't much like. Gabe knew, as I did, that Mr. Sung had a hand in their deaths. He opened a murder investigation, but the case file was a formality, the trail cold and untraceable before Gabe started.

On Isadora's advice, Maximillian's and Nathan's bodies were cremated, and Randy borrowed a small sailboat to scatter their ashes over the bay. We all slept better once that was done.

Knowing Maximillian was never coming back, his ashes spread thin on the outgoing tide, had another unforeseen effect. My fear of spending time with Sadie and the baby vanished. We'd taken up where we left off, the best of friends.

Watching her now, I was doubly glad. Sadie was the perfect hostess as always, attentive to all her guests and dressed in the latest style. No dress, no matter how fashionable, could disguise how large her belly had grown, but Sadie didn't care. She brimmed with good health, radiant and smiling. If she doubted for an instant that she looked beautiful, all she need do was look in Jack's eyes.

Adele Wells and Marshall's fiancée Adeline sat at a small table near the house with Sadie, trading gossip. I'd volunteered to look after Stella, leaving Annie free to overload the table with food and enjoy the party with the rest of us. Watching the baby toddle after the ball I rolled across the grass and her delighted laugh each time she caught it made me smile.

I scooped Stella up and hugged her, envious of her innocence. There was little enough laughter in the world.

Jack and Gabe stood under a plum tree in the corner of the yard, discussing President Wilson's declaration of war with Marshall, Robert Lindsey, and Sam Butler. A draft of young, able-bodied men had been proposed to swell the army's ranks. While Gabe's and Jack's ages and jobs made them exempt from conscription, Marshall and Sam could well be called to war. Grim faces were the order of the day in their corner. I couldn't fault them for that.

"Dee, honey." Annie stood framed in the back door, twisting her apron with both hands. "Give Stella to her daddy, please. I need your help inside for a minute or two."

Gabe glanced between me and Annie, and crossed the yard. He wrinkled his nose at Stella, mugging outrageously to make her laugh. "I'll take Stella. Jack monopolizes my goddaughter too much as it is."

Jack raised his glass and grinned. "I'll be happy to let you have the midnight shift, Gabe."

Annie went back inside before I'd handed the baby to Gabe. I hurried after her, a cold that had little to do with an early spring breeze creeping across my shoulders.

I found her in the kitchen with Randy Dodd. He looked haggard and sleepless, the circles under his eyes dark as overripe blackberries. Dora and Randy had planned to come to the party together, but I hadn't given a thought to them being late. Their friendship deepened more each day, but even Randy couldn't make Dora punctual. "Randy, what's wrong? Where's Dora?"

"She asked me to bring Stella's birthday gift. Dora didn't want to spoil Sadie's party, but she wanted you to know why we can't be here." He held out an elaborately wrapped package. "A letter from Daniel's sister arrived by courier last night. Daniel's dead."

"Dead?" I took the package, the cold that had brushed my shoulders growing to fill my chest and numb my fingers. Annie put her arm around me. "How?"

"A Portuguese coronel was conscripting men to fight in France. Daniel had finally arranged passage for his family to England and on to New York. The coronel caught them just as they were boarding." Randy raked fingers through his hair. "Daniel refused to get off the ship. The coronel shot him. His sister wrote to Dora once they reached New York."

I leaned against Annie, too stunned to cry. "Oh God . . . Daniel. Dora must be shattered."

"I'm grateful I was there when the message arrived. She . . ."

Dora cried all night. She asked that you not tell Sadie. Not yet." Randy buttoned his jacket and smoothed down the front. "I need to get back. Dora was laying Daniel's ghost to rest, and she shouldn't be alone. Give Sadie my apologies. I'll see myself out."

Annie and I held each other a few minutes longer, listening to the sounds of laughter and cheerful voices drifting in from the yard. Adele's baby fussed fretfully, but quickly hushed again. I could picture Adele cradling her little girl close, soothing her child back to sleep.

This war cast its shadow across all of us. Sadie's and Adele's children would grow up in a world far different from the one we'd known, transformed in ways I couldn't begin to imagine. No one knew what changes the war would bring, only that change was inevitable.

I hugged Annie and stepped away, pulling myself together. Some things would remain the same, no matter how dark war's shadow grew. Love and friendship would endure, unchanged, as would the need to keep our children close and watch them grow. We'd still protect those we loved and nurture hopes for the future.

If I ever needed proof of hope, I'd only to look toward Stella's smile and the longing in Gabe's eyes as he held her.

Not in the hands of boys, but in their eyes
Shall shine the holy glimmers of goodbyes.
The pallor of girls' brows shall be their pall;
Their flowers the tenderness of patient minds,
And each slow dusk a drawing-down of blinds.
— Wilfred Owen, "Anthem for Doomed Youth"